Stealing Harper

Also by Molly McAdams

From Ashes
Taking Chances

Stealing
Harper

MOLLY McADAMS

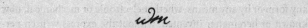

WILLIAM MORROW
An Imprint of HarperCollinsPublishers

Excerpt from *Forgiving Lies* copyright © 2013 by Molly Jester.
Excerpt from *Taking Chances* copyright © 2012 by Molly Jester.
Excerpt from *From Ashes* copyright © 2012 by Molly Jester.

EPub Edition JUNE 2013 ISBN: 9780062292117

Print Edition ISBN: 978-0-06-229212-4

10 9 8 7

For my Book Broads. Without all of you, Chase's story would have never been heard. Love you girls!

Stealing Harper

Chapter One

"THAT IT?" I asked one of my housemates, Derek, as we passed each other in the hall.

"Yeah, this is the last box. I'm ready for Brandon to be here and all, but, Jesus, I'm glad he won't be here 'til next weekend 'cause if we move one more person into the house today, I'm gonna die."

I laughed and stretched out my arms before lifting the bottom of my shirt to wipe the sweat off my face and neck. "That's what you get for being the first person back here."

"Yeah, yeah. Whatever."

Drew rounded the corner, holding a flattened inflatable doll. "My car's empty; did you guys get everything already?"

"No thanks to you." My eyes went flat as I watched him start blowing up the doll, "Where the hell did you go?"

He held up the doll before going back to blowing air into her.

"Nice. I'm glad that's your priority."

"At least he's come to terms with the fact that a doll's the only way he's gonna get some," Brad, another housemate, said as he smacked Drew's head and pushed through us.

"Then Drew"—I looked down to the thick, leather-banded watch on my wrist—"you can go pick up *and* pay for the kegs tonight."

"But—" he began.

"Might want to go soon; people will be here in a couple hours."

"Bastards," Drew mumbled under his breath, as we all left to go to separate parts of the house.

"Quit bitching. You're the last one to move back in, and you didn't even move your own shit in." Even after nine hours of moving the guys in, I couldn't help but smile as I went to take a shower. First and last parties of the year were always the best; and the first always meant a lot of women and plenty to come.

"God," I groaned, and couldn't help it when my hand formed a fist in her hair, urging her to continue—I was so close. She moaned around me, and my eyes shut as I lost it. From the way she jerked, I knew she hadn't been expecting it. I probably should have warned her, but that was the last thing I'd been thinking about just then.

As soon as she was done, I let her pull away and, as

I put myself back in my pants, I looked around to see if anyone had come to this side of the house.

"Thanks, Chase."

I froze momentarily, then huffed a short laugh and glanced at her as she stood back up. *She's thanking me?* Usually, I had to do something for them first before they started thanking me, but I wasn't one to judge. "Uh, yeah. Ready to go back in?"

She nodded enthusiastically and reached for my hand, so I quickly draped my arm around her shoulder and led us through the backyard and into my house. "Oh, Chase, can we dance? I love this song! Pretty please?"

Pretty please? What are we, five? I tried not to groan and forced a smile on my face. We walked toward the center of the mass of people dancing in my living room, and my hands went to whateverhernamewas's hips as she ground her butt into me. Her back arched, and I had an even better view of her already exposed chest.

"I'm so glad we can start this before school starts; I was dying to date you all last year," she whispered, and I ground my teeth.

Date? Oh hell no. I tried to remove my hands from her hips at the same time she pushed them tighter to her body, and someone knocked into us. My already narrowed eyes looked up to see wide, terrified, gray eyes turn toward me. I literally felt my heart skip a few painful beats before my pulse started racing.

Her cloudy eyes looked at the delusional blonde I was pressed up against, then flashed back up to mine. They got wider, and her head slightly shook back and forth like she was on the verge of panicking from what she was seeing as she stumbled over herself trying to back away.

Wrong thing to do, sweetheart. I always did love a challenge.

I finally detached myself and made quick work of getting away from the tightly packed bodies and headed in the same direction she'd just taken off.

"Chase!"

I looked up to see Zach sprinkling salt on a redhead's chest on the island in the kitchen. "Body shots?"

Zach shook his head to the side and put a shot glass in the girl's mouth, then filled it with vodka. "No, but do you want the honors?"

The redhead curled her index finger toward herself, and when I got close, ran her fake nails across my lower stomach. I licked her chest, curled my lips around the shot glass in her mouth, and lifted it out, letting the liquor slide down my throat. Zach poured the next shot as I sucked on the spot on her neck where Zach had rubbed lime juice before making my way to lick her chest again and take the second shot. I resumed biting and sucking on her neck as I sprinkled more salt on her, then repeated the process for the third.

I'd almost forgotten why I'd been coming to the kitchen in the first place, but an annoying feeling like being watched finally broke through, and my eyes shot up to find wide gray eyes locked on mine again. Drew was talking to her, but she was focused on me. Her eyes looked like they were about to bulge out of her head, and her mouth was slightly open. She looked disgusted.

I licked the redhead's chest and winked at this timid-looking girl before taking the fourth shot. *I am going to tear you apart, little girl.*

I wiped my mouth and bent low to the redhead's ear, "Thank you, beautiful." I let my teeth graze her ear and smirked when she shivered.

Straightening quickly, I looked ahead, only to find the timid girl gone and Drew looking in the direction of one of the halls. I immediately took off in that direction and ran into Bree.

"Hey, bro! Awesome first party!"

I hugged her tight and kept looking for that girl. Why did she have to be so damn short? I was never going to find her in this now.

"Who're you looking for?" Bree asked, and when I looked down at her, saw she was looking around, too, but in the opposite direction.

"A girl, who are you looking for?"

"My roommate, she ran off."

"Ah shit, Bree, I forgot to ask. How is your room-mate?"

She waved a dismissive hand. "She's awesome, a little sheltered, but I can already tell I'm going to really like her. Now I just have to find her. Can we have your room tonight?"

"Of course, find me whenever you get tired, room—"

"I know, Chase, room's locked. Like always. I'll find you later, I gotta go find Harper."

Harper ... what the hell kind of name is Harper? Sheltered girl named Harper, I already felt bad for my sister. I laughed softly as I continued to walk toward the hallway; after looking up and down it and not finding her, I went back out toward the kitchen to look for her there.

"Hey there, handsome."

My brow scrunched as I turned to look at who had just whispered in my ear but relaxed when I saw her. "Natalie. How was your summer?"

She wrapped her arms around my shoulders and leaned close. "It was fine, spent most of it with my boyfriend."

I nodded and kissed right below her ear. "And how is he?"

"Not here."

"Shame."

Her body pressed even closer to mine. "Isn't it? I was thinking since I'm just *so* upset about that, you should help me enjoy tonight."

My fingers trailed under her shirt and against her hot skin, "Bathroom?"

"Where else?" She laughed low and took my other hand as we turned to go one of the bathrooms on the hall I'd just been.

We'd turned the last corner when a little blur smashed into me and began falling backward from the impact. My arms had automatically gone out to steady her, and I instantly recognized the auburn hair moments before the gray eyes met mine.

"I'm so sorry, I—" Her mouth snapped shut, and her gorgeous eyes narrowed.

I couldn't help but smile at her; she looked like a fierce

little kitten the way she was glowering at me. Her eyes lost their anger, and her cheeks reddened slightly as her eyes locked on my lips. I doubt she realized she had pulled her bottom lip into her mouth and was currently biting on that perfectly full, soft-looking lip. I tilted my head to the side and smirked at her; I knew that look. Hell yeah. This was gonna be fun. *Oh, sweetheart I am going to break your heart.* "Now who are you?"

She blinked rapidly, and a determined look came over her face as she tried to get out of my grasp. No way in hell was I letting her leave yet.

"What, you're too good to tell me?"

Her expression deadpanned, and her eyes shifted to my left, then down to my waist. Shit, I'd forgotten about Natalie. One of her eyebrows arched, and she looked at me like I disgusted her. "Apparently."

Excuse me? Who the hell does this girl think she is? She's going to look at me and talk to me like that at my party in my house? She was looking at me like she was royalty, and I was some peasant in her way. I let go of her and crossed my arms over my chest, but for the life of me, I couldn't tell if I was more pissed off or intrigued. I'd had a girl thank me for letting her blow me earlier, and this girl wouldn't even give me her name? "Excuse me, Princess?"

Those eyes turned into damn thunderclouds as she roughly shouldered her way past me. "You're right, *excuse me.*"

I stood there stunned for what had to be a full minute before Natalie was able to pull me toward the bathroom again. *What the hell just happened?* I looked behind me, like the freakin' princess would still be standing there, and shook my head slightly as we hit the bathroom and locked it behind us.

"On or over?" she asked, and was already reaching for the button on her shorts.

That's what I liked about Natalie. No bullshit with her. Just sex. She had a guy back home, and I didn't want a relationship. "Over." I pulled a condom out of my wallet and shed my pants and boxer briefs before rolling it on. Natalie was already bent over the countertop, and I didn't waste any time.

We both groaned when I slammed into her; I kept one hand on her hip, the other went to her shoulder. I looked at the long blond hair falling across her back and onto the countertop, and my eyes shut as images of auburn hair filled my head. *What is it about that girl?* I'd seen her for all of three minutes, and already she was consuming my mind this way? Why? She was disgusted with me . . . that was more than apparent. That had to be it. I was used to *this,* used to tonight. The blonde earlier, the redhead in the kitchen, and now Natalie. I wasn't used to insignificant girls not wanting me. And she had no idea how bad that was for her. It just made the challenge that much better. I would get her. And I would enjoy breaking her heart. I almost smiled to myself, but then flashes of her wide, innocent, gray eyes and her perfectly white teeth digging into her lips assaulted me. I thought about biting that lip, and my thrusts quickened; thought about her underneath me and in my arms, and I gripped Natalie tightly as I came harder than I ever had before.

"Hell, Chase," she said roughly, her breathing ragged.

"I'm sorry." I took a deep breath in and released her before sliding out.

"Why are you apologizing—that was—just holy crap."

I wanted to ask what else she expected. But I hadn't even lasted four minutes and had been so lost in a gray-eyed princess that I don't even remember it. "Get dressed, Natalie."

After pulling on my own clothes and waiting for her to situate herself, I unlocked the door and led us back into the hall. Without another word, I let go of her and went toward my room in another part of the house. Once I was locked in, I groaned into my hands. What the hell just happened? Why had I pictured her in that way? Sex only, making love never. Those images had definitely been me making love to her, and how was I already getting hard again thinking about this? And about her, especially? That's it, it's official . . . there's something wrong with my dick. She's a challenge, yeah, but that's all.

Shutting my eyes tightly, I tried to think about anything other than her and those fucking mesmerizing eyes, but nothing was helping. With a frustrated groan, I shot off the bed and dug around my desk until I found my latest sketchpad. I focused on some pieces I was working on for myself, as well as my buddy Brian at the shop, and tried to push that girl out of my mind. And no, the fact that I hid the word "princess" within the design I wanted to complete my right sleeve had nothing to do with her or the fact that I couldn't stop thinking about her. At all. *Fuck.* I slammed my sketchpad shut and shoved it into my desk.

I stretched my arms and back before leaving my room and locking the door behind me. I'd almost gotten to the end of the hallway when I heard Drew's loud slur.

"YYYEEEAAAH, Bree and fresh meat are sleeping over tonight!"

I figured "fresh meat" was Bree's new roommate and felt bad for once again forgetting to meet her. I needed to make sure my sister wasn't going to be rooming with some crazy person. When I got into the living room, Bree was over taking shots with Drew and Zach, and there, standing near the doors to the backyard, was my gray-eyed princess. This better be a fucking mistake.

Plastering a smile on my face, I couldn't help but embrace the images that were now burned into my mind, "Well, well. If it isn't the princess."

She froze when she heard me, and as she turned to look at me, her eyes narrowed, and the fakest smile I've ever seen crossed her face. "I almost didn't recognize you without a tramp attached."

Seriously, who the hell does she think she is? I leaned close and whispered harshly in her ear, "Would you like to change that? I'm not up to my limit tonight yet."

The princess leaned away, and her eyes went wide, "Oh, I'm sorry, but I don't have any STDs, I'm not your type."

Bree started choking, and I knew I should make sure

she was okay, but my jaw had dropped, and I couldn't stop staring at his frustrating girl. "Chase, you better stay away from my roommate. I told the guys she's off-limits."

I cringed at Bree's words. Not a mistake. This really was her roommate.

"You know him?" the princess asked, hardly trying to contain her revulsion.

"Well, I'd like to think so, he *is* my brother."

The most beautiful blush I've ever seen instantly spread across her cheeks, and for a second I forgot why I didn't want to be completely taken with this girl.

"Wait. Harper, is this the guy you said was a jerk?"

Harper. That's right, her name is Harper. I don't know why I didn't like it earlier; I couldn't think of anything more perfect for her. It fit her, and I wanted to say it myself, but then I remembered why she was pissing me off and decided to stick with what seemed to piss her off more. Her eyes flew to the ground, and my lips quirked up into a smile.

"You said I'm a jerk?" I laughed and walked over to my sister. "She's the one that just practically called me a dirty man-whore."

"Don't be rude to my friends, Chase!" Bree punched my arm, and I tried not to roll my eyes at how pathetic her punches were.

Princess turned quickly and went outside, and I tried not to let it show that I watched her leave. "Great roommate, Bree," I scoffed, and grabbed a bottle of water out of the fridge.

"She is, but she said you weren't nice! So be nice. I told you, she's pretty sheltered."

I turned my back to Zach and Drew and leaned onto the island close to Bree. "Sheltered how?"

"She grew up with only her dad, and she said he's been in the army or navy or whatever for her whole life." Bree took two more shots, and I shook my head at her; at least she was staying here. "And get this! She's never worn makeup *or* been to a mall!"

My face fell in mock horror. "Never been to a mall? Oh no."

"Go be nice to her, you big jerk!"

I kissed Bree's forehead and made my way outside. It was dark, but it didn't take long to find her. Her face was in her hands, elbows on her knees. *Is she crying?* I usually hated when women cried, but I had to force myself not to rush up to her to make sure she was okay. *God, get a grip.* I sank into the seat next to her and waited until she peeked up at me. Not crying. Thank God.

"You hiding?"

"Is it that obvious?"

I looked at the empty backyard. "A little." I took a deep breath in and got more comfortable. "Tell me, what's a princess like you doing at my party?"

"I'm not sure what you mean," she ground out, "but I was invited."

I couldn't care less if she was invited or not. I just didn't want her around me. I didn't want her in my house, and I didn't want to be getting hard again thinking about her in my bed. Challenge or not, she was already getting under my damn skin too much for me to think clearly. She needed to go. I curled my lip and looked at her with the disgust she'd been serving me with all night. "You don't have to be invited to come to the party, but in case you didn't notice, you don't exactly fit in here, *Princess*."

She looked shocked and hurt. Good. Maybe now she'd stay the hell away.

"If the way we are disgusts you so much, feel free to stay at school next time." I stood, and hated that I couldn't help but look at her once more before walking away.

"Chase."

My eyes shut, and I took a deep breath in. Would it have been weird to ask her to say my name again?

"I'm really sorry, I was out of line."

Wait—she was apologizing? I turned and looked at her, confused. Oh God, it was a bad idea to turn around. If her sweet-as-hell voice hadn't been bad enough, the way her eyes had gone back to completely wide and innocent was about to do me in.

"I was raised not to back down to people, but what I said was too much. So, I'm sorry. I don't know you, I shouldn't judge you."

I huffed, and the corners of my mouth twitched. Snarky and sweet. Bad combination. Sexy combo—so damn sexy. But bad. I shook my head, and my brow rose when I realized I wanted to get to know this girl. Now *that* was a bad idea. I turned and took the long way around the house, giving my hard-on time to go down.

"... you kiss anyone tonight?" Bree's voice reached me as I stepped through the front door, and I closed it quietly when I heard Princess murmur, "No."

"I can help with that!" My hands formed into fists over Zach's words, and I growled. *Over my dead body.*

"No, no, no. I told you guys, she's off-limits!"

Thatta girl, Bree. I took the last few steps toward the living room when Zach spoke again.

"Come on, Bree, what's your deal?"

"'Cause she's *pure.* Completely. Pure."

I froze. *What the hell, Bree?* Shit, from the way Harper's cheeks went fire-engine red, Bree wasn't lying. She *was* pure. I looked at Harper's mortified expression, and the urge to take her in my arms and take her away from this overwhelmed me. I didn't know where the protectiveness for her came from, but somehow I knew I'd do anything for this innocent girl, and I'd kill anyone who tried to take that innocence from her.

Bree's index finger went to tap Harper's lips, and Harper grabbed her wrist, pulling it back "Breanna!"

"Shh!" Bree covered her own lips with her index finger this time. "Harper, don't tell them!"

Harper looked up, and her jaw clenched as she took in Brad, Drew, Derek, and Zach bursting out laughing. I wanted to punch every single one of them.

Derek was wiping tears from his eyes. "Oh my God! Princess, is she serious?"

I growled again. That was my name for her.

She swallowed roughly and disentangled herself from Bree before heading straight toward me. My heart started pounding until I realized she hadn't seen me yet, and I was standing in the way of the front door.

Jolting back slightly when she realized I was in her way, her eyes looked everywhere but at me. "Please. Move."

And let her leave? Hell no. I grabbed her shoulders and turned her around at the same time I started walking us toward my room.

"Don't touch me!"

"Just trust me," I growled, and walked her through the living room, where everyone was still laughing.

"Looks like Chase is gonna take care of that problem for you, Princess!" Brad yelled, and I've never wanted to punch my friend more than I did then. I paused and cursed, but knew I'd rather take care of her right then than let all of them know how much they were pissing me off.

I unlocked my door and pushed her in; as soon as the light was on, she gasped and started bucking against me. I held her by pushing her elbows into her side so her jerking arms couldn't hit me.

"No! Get off me!"

"Not until you stop trying to hit me!"

Instantly, Harper stopped moving, but her body was practically vibrating with tension. I waited almost a minute before releasing her and feigning indifference.

"Calm down, Princess, I'm not going to do anything to you."

"I really wish you would stop calling me that."

I rolled my eyes. Why else did she think I still called

her that? I opened up one of my drawers and pulled out a pair of mesh workout shorts before throwing them at her and walking toward my door. "Put those on, I'll be back."

"Why?"

"Did you want to sleep in that skirt?" I raked my teeth over my bottom lip as I thought about her sleeping in nothing at all. "I swear I wouldn't mind it, but I figured you'd be uncomfortable, though."

"Breanna said I would be in a room with her tonight, and if that's not happening, I'd rather just go back to the dorm."

"I can assure you she'll be sleeping in the bathroom. I'll give you a minute to change; I'll be right back."

"I am not sleeping with you in here."

"Look, you're seriously hot; that alone is going to have them chasing after you. But top that off with the few words you've even said that shows me just how snarky and sweet as hell you are, that is one hell of a tempting combination. Trust me when I say they're going to want to change what they just found out about you. So if you don't mind, I'd rather make sure that doesn't happen." I'd already vowed to make it my mission in life to make sure that didn't happen.

I slammed the door with more force than necessary and stalked out to the living room, "What the hell is wrong with all of you?"

"She putting up much of a fight, Chase?" Drew sneered, and put more bottles of liquor away.

My hands balled into fists again, "You're all assholes, and you just embarrassed the shit out of her." I turned to look at Bree, who looked like she was five minutes from passing out. "You're on your own tonight, sis. Or ask one of the other guys to take care of you."

"Chase," Brad said with a confused look, "seriously? She's your sister, that"—he jerked his head toward one of the hallways—"is just some chick that ain't gonna put out for you."

Don't punch him. Don't freaking punch him. "She's your problem tonight," I said through clenched teeth and went back to my room.

"That was rude, she's your sister. She should be in here, too."

Harper, too? Did no one else realize how much of a bitch Bree just was? "Are you serious? You're gonna defend her after she just spilled that?"

"She's drunk. I'm sure she didn't realize it."

"That's not an excuse." I almost groaned; there she goes being sweet as sin again. "Come on, Harper, get in."

I watched her crawl onto my bed, and my heart started hammering. Bree slept alone in my room when we had parties, but other than that, no girl had ever been in any of my bedrooms, and definitely not in my bed. And I was about to get in it with her. I could easily go crash on the couch or Brad's floor, but the thought of waking up next to Harper was too tempting. When she was under the covers, I switched off the lights and crawled in beside her; she immediately flew up into a sitting position.

"What are you *doing*?" she hissed.

"What do you mean?"

"You can't get in here with me!"

So innocent. I laughed softly, but inside I was terrified she would actually ask me to leave, "It's my bed, I'm sure I can do what I want."

Without another word, her half of the covers were flipped onto me, and the weight left her side of the bed. *Her side? No . . . the side she was on. She doesn't have a side. This is just for tonight, right?*

"Get back in the bed, Princess."

She scoffed, and I sighed. Snarky, sweet, and stubborn as shit. God, I wanted her. I rolled off the bed and picked her up off the ground.

"Oh my word! Put me down!"

With pleasure, Princess. I dropped her onto the bed and crawled over her body, trying to stifle my groan when I felt her body press against mine.

"Chase! No!"

"Calm down, I'll stay on my side. We can even put a pillow between us if it'll make you feel better." I was serious. With the hard-on I was sporting again, I needed a brick wall between us.

She scooted as far from me as the bed would allow, and I forced myself not to pull her back to me. "I swear, if you touch me, I'll go Lorena Bobbitt on you."

Lorena Bobbitt? Why does that sound—oh my God, the lady that chopped off her husband's dick? I busted out laughing and put my pillow over my face. "Oh my God! Princess! You're my new favorite!" That's it, that comment right there, and it was sealed. I would do anything to have this beautiful gray-eyed princess lying next to me, as mine.

"That wasn't a joke."

I moved closer and let the tips of my fingers trail up her slender arm. Could she hear how hard my heart started pounding at just being able to touch her? "One of these days, you'll be begging for me to touch you."

"I'm serious, Chase. I'm not like all those girls I saw you with tonight."

"That's an understatement." God, I wish she hadn't seen any of that, and she didn't even know the half of it. "Get some sleep, Princess, I'll see you in the morning."

Chapter Two

I VAGUELY REGISTERED a subtle vanilla scent and a small, warm body curled up in mine. That was seconds before I felt it shoot out from under my arms, and I swear I stopped breathing. *Did I forget to lock my door? Did I get that wasted last night that I let a girl in here?*

"Son of a bitch, what the fuck are you—" *Oh good God. Harper. Was she this beautiful last night?* "Jesus, Princess! You almost gave me a heart attack. I thought I had a girl in here." I fell back onto my pillow and ran my hands over my face. I wish I had remembered I'd had her in here; I would've made sure she stayed in my arms.

"Chase?"

"Hmm?"

"Sorry you didn't seem to notice, but I *am* a girl."

Thank God for that, or I'd have had to question my manhood. "I noticed last night, trust me." She just kept staring at me with those wide eyes, clearly confused.

Damn she was cute. "I meant, I thought I let a girl stay the night with me."

"Uh . . . ?"

"Someone I'd been with, Princess. I thought I banged a girl and let her stay here."

"Oh." Her face twisted, and a hint of that disgust from last night was there again.

"Sorry. Is that too much for your PG ears?"

"No, I just don't understand why that would be a bad thing."

Of course you don't because you're innocent . . . and perfect. I sighed; she was perfect. Which meant I didn't have a chance in hell with her. Princesses need a Prince Charming, not a nightmare of a guy. "Girls I screw around with aren't allowed to come in my room, let alone stay the night. This is the only place that is mine, and I'm not about to share it with them."

"So you sleep with women, then make them leave?"

Good girl, keep looking at me like you can't stand to be near me. You need to run far away, so I can't catch you. Because if I get you, I'm keeping you, and you deserve so much better. "No, I *screw* women . . . and then make them leave."

She recoiled and shook her head at me as she turned toward the door. "You're a pig."

I laughed softly. Yeah . . . and for the first time in my life, hearing that come from a girl actually bothered me.

As soon as she shut the door, my smirk disappeared, and I continued to stare at where she'd just been. *Whatever the fuck this is, it isn't normal.* I didn't fall for girls like this . . . ever. Especially after only one innocent look and a bitchy comment. So why was she doing this to me? Why was I wanting to pull her close but having the ridiculous urge to push her as far from me as possible. And it wasn't for me—not at all—I wanted to keep her away from me for *her*. *God, why am I still thinking about her at all?*

I got out of bed and walked into the bathroom, hating that I loved hearing her voice as I crossed the hall. *She's just a girl, man, just a girl. And she's not for you.* I ground my teeth as I walked back into my room, resolving that I needed to continue disgusting her—which obviously I was already a pro at—and she'd run away screaming soon enough. I threw the door open roughly, and, to be honest, I'm not sure if I held back my groan or not. She was bent over in a pair of neon blue underwear, and I decided right then that was my new favorite color. Harper jerked up quickly, pulling the little skirt with her. Didn't help. I'd already seen her without it. But my lips still fell into a slight frown.

"It's really a shame you don't let anyone see that sexy little body." And by anyone, I meant me . . . again.

By the time she turned, her face was so red it looked like she'd just run a marathon. God this girl blushed a lot . . . but I freakin' loved it. Her already wide eyes got even wider, just like they had when Bree had said spilled about her virginity. Shit, I'd embarrassed her—my stomach clenched, but I shook it off, knowing I had to keep going. "Calm down, you don't have anything I haven't seen before. Not saying I wouldn't want to see yours."

Her face was still red, but her eyes narrowed into tiny slits. Vicious Princess was still cute. "Bite me."

"Is that an invitation?" *Please God, let it be one.*

"Not even close." She was headed for the door and without my even thinking about it, my arm shot out and wrapped around her waist, pulling her into me.

Her body stiffened, and I couldn't help but lean my head toward hers, skimming my nose along her jaw and subtly breathing in her sweet scent. "One of these days, Princess, I promise you." Did she not see what she was doing to me? My body was practically humming, having her pressed up against me, and my breathing got rougher. I silently pleaded with her to run as I tightened my arm on her waist. *Mine.*

"I would never be desperate enough to want you."

I might have believed that if her voice hadn't gone all breathy on me, my lips stretched into a grin—oh yeah . . . she'll be mine. "We'll see."

"ARE BREE AND Princess coming tonight?"

My hands curled into fists for the freaking fifth time today as I turned to look at Zach. "Probably, and stop calling her that."

"Who's Princess?"

The guys in the kitchen all broke out into cheers as I turned back around, a wide smile crossing both Brandon's face and mine. "Glad you're finally here, bro!"

"Tell me about it; that's a long fucking drive." He dropped a bag on the ground and stepped forward to man-hug Derek and me and shake the rest of the guys' hands. I made sure he remembered Zach and Drew; just because they knew Brandon from his fights didn't mean he knew them.

"I bet. All your stuff in your Jeep?"

He nodded. "It can wait. I just want to relax for a bit. So what's going on? Obviously, I'm the last one here."

"Missed a hell of a party last week, man," Derek said as he took a seat on the island. "But there's another one tonight."

Brandon yawned and rubbed his hands down his face. "Is that what you were talking about when I came in? With Bree and Princess? Bree's your sister, right?" He looked at me, and I nodded, "Then who is Princess?"

"Good God, Brandon, you have *got* to see this chick," Zach began, and my hands instantly went back into fists.

"She hot?" Brandon asked

A mix of "Hell yeah," "You have no idea," and "Wait 'til you see her" came from the kitchen. I clenched my jaw.

When I didn't say anything, Brandon looked at me curiously. "Is she not?"

I shrugged. "She's just another girl."

"Chase is just pissy because she didn't put out for him," Drew said.

Brandon raised an eyebrow at me and burst out laughing, "That had to be a first."

"You're all acting like I even tried to hit that."

"Chase—man—you had her in your bed!" Brad said

between laughs. "Another freakin' first! You can't act like you didn't try to bang her."

"Exactly, I had her in my bed, which shows you I didn't want to touch her. If I want a girl, I'll take her anywhere else but there."

"Shit, a girl that didn't fall all over herself to get to Chase, and she's hot?" Brandon asked, and barked out a short laugh. "I've got to see this! Will she be here tonight? You said her name's Princess?"

"Chase calls her Princess."

Damn right, Zach. Remember that.

Brandon looked even more confused, "Well, what's her name?"

All the guys shrugged. "Princess."

"Well, it's not looking good for you, brother. You had her in your bed, you didn't sleep with her, *and* you gave her a nickname?"

"Because she was acting like an entitled prissy bitch, it fit."

Everyone, including Brandon, started laughing. As soon as he could catch his breath, he shook his head sadly at me. "Never thought I'd see the day Chase Grayson was brought to his knees by a girl."

"Whatever." I sighed and walked outside to start moving his stuff in.

A girl bring me to my knees? Hell. No. Never, and I'd prove it. Whether my gray-eyed princess — no . . . not mine. I didn't want her, I must have just been losing my mind last weekend—whether Harper was here tonight or

not, I'd prove to her and myself that she didn't have any
type of hold on me.

"MA—DAD? I'M HERE." I breathed in the heavy scent of
bacon, and my stomach growled. God, I loved Sundays.
Walking into the kitchen, I kissed Mom on the cheek and
snatched a few pieces from the growing pile on the plate
near Dad and clapped him on the back as I went to sit on
the counter.

"Hi, honey!"

I nodded and spoke around the food. "What's goin' on?"

"Oh, you know, just chilling."

"Mom"—I laughed—"you just gotta stop trying."

"One of these times I'll get it, and you'll be so im-
pressed, I'll be cool enough to hang out with you."

I snorted. "I'm here, aren't I? Bree here?" Speaking of
my sister . . . would she bring the princess?

"Not yet, she was doing something with her roommate first, then she was coming over."

Nope. Damn it. "Have you met her yet?"

"Harper? Oh, she's a doll; she slept over last weekend!
You'd like her, Chase," Mom said with a weird smile.
"She's really cute."

Yeah she is.

Mom gasped. "So you've met her!"

Shit, had I said that out loud?

"Tell me what you think!"

"She's cute." I shrugged. "But I've only seen her once;
they didn't come to the party on Friday."

"That's it? She's cute? I may or may not have heard she slept in your room with you the night of the first party."

"Robert! How did you know this and I didn't! You're supposed to tell me everything, especially something like that."

Dad laughed and pulled some more bacon off the skillet, "I said may or may not have."

"Oh, you are so in the guest room tonight, mister!"

My brows were pulled together listening to them, and how did Dad hear about that?

"Well, are you going to explain yourself, Chase? Or am I going to make sure you don't get any more bacon? Because that is a sweet girl, and if you hurt her—"

No more bacon? That's just not right. "It wasn't like that, Mom, I was just making sure she was safe."

Mom's brows shot up under her bangs, and her lips pursed.

"Bree *may* have told all the guys at my place that she's basically never done anything with a guy, and I mean anything. Everyone started making fun of her, and she looked so damn embarrassed. And with those guys— hell, maybe even Brad—I know they would try to change that, and I wasn't about to let anyone touch her; so that was my way of keeping her safe."

"You kept the virgin safe . . . by putting her in your bed with you," Dad deadpanned, then nodded. "Actually, that makes sense."

"No it does not! Chase—"

"Mom, I swear I didn't touch her!" Well not entirely true, and it's not like I didn't want to do a lot more touching than I did. "I just needed to make sure no one else got their hands on her either. Jesus, it's not like she would have let me even if I tried." I snorted and shook my head once, "First, she got mad that I got in bed with her, so she got on the floor—"

"You did *not* make her sleep on the floor!"

"Ma, really? No. I picked her ass right back up and dropped her on the bed." Dad laughed, and Mom swatted him on the back. "Then get this, cutest damn thing I've ever heard, she more or less tells me that if I touch her, she is going to chop my dick off."

Dad winced; Mom crossed her arms over her chest and nodded. "Good girl."

I laughed. "Cracked me up. She can be feisty as shit, but God she's sweet. She just—she's . . . I don't know." Her wide gray eyes were flashing through my mind, and I hoped my sister would bring her. I exhaled deeply and blinked away the images, finally noticing that Mom and Dad had both turned toward me. My dad was grinning mischievously, and Mom was tearing up. *Fucking hell . . . can't I go more than a few minutes without talking about her like an idiot?* "What?"

Mom bounced up and down on her toes. "Oh, honey!"

I shook my head and hopped off the counter to grab more bacon. "She's just a girl, Mom."

Chapter Three

THERE SHE IS, my gray-eyed princess. I watched her walk into the cafeteria, and stopped sucking on Natalie's neck. "Gotta go, see you."

"Bye, handsome."

I jogged over to the cafeteria doors and tried to follow at a safe distance from her. I could only see her back, but that was more than enough. She was wearing these tiny black shorts that perfectly hugged her butt and gave me the best view of her legs. Those shorts may not pass her PG rating, but I certainly approved. Before seeing her bent over in my room, and like she was just then, I would have sworn short girls didn't have killer legs. God, I was so wrong.

I was so focused on her and the way my heart had gone into overdrive since she first walked into my line of sight that I ran into the corner of a wall and a scared-looking freshman coed. I steadied the girl, mentioned what I'm sure was some form of an apology, and looked around quickly, only to find my princess gone. Taking in a deep breath, I popped my neck on both sides and grabbed a bowl of pasta. I needed to calm down. She was driving me crazy, and she hadn't even looked at me yet.

Get a freakin' grip, she's just a girl, a girl that you don't even want—a girl who pisses you off more than anything. I heard Zach's and Drew's loud voices, and my head snapped up. A small smile crossed my face as I watched her sit down next to Bree. I couldn't even be annoyed with them for calling her Princess again; she'd been hiding from me for almost two weeks, and now here she was, in all her snarky and sweet glory.

Her shoulders hunched slightly, and I wondered if the guys were embarrassing her again, but I didn't give myself time to think about it too long. I set my bowl down next to her salad and planted my hands on either side of her plate. I leaned close, letting my chest press against her back, and I almost groaned when I smelled her soft, vanilla scent again. *Not just a girl. Not even close.*

"Have you been hiding from me, PG?" I whispered in her ear, and she shivered against me, her arms instantly covered in goose bumps. I had to force out a soft laugh, so she wouldn't hear my next groan.

"Why?" Her voice was breathy, and I swear my jeans got tighter. "You miss me?"

God, yes. "Of course. You're my favorite, remember?" As I let my nose run across her neck and breathed her in more, a soft sound of pleasure sounded in her throat, and

I couldn't help but smile; but that quickly turned into a frown when she leaned away from me.

"Sad to say you're not mine."

Little liar. "You sure about that?" I tapped on her arm, which was still covered in goose bumps, and her body stiffened.

"Chase! Stop bugging her and go sit down."

I almost growled at my sister. Could she not see I was busy driving my princess crazy? Straightening up, I grabbed my pasta and walked down a few seats to sit across from Brandon. I slapped his hand as I sat, and my eyes narrowed when I realized his kept drifting over to Princess. *Oh, hell no.* Derek and Brad had girlfriends, so while I would still keep her from them, I knew I really didn't have to worry about them. And, let's face it, no one had to worry about Drew; he made sure no girl would ever want him. Zach—eh, that was up for debate, but Brandon? He had more girls throwing themselves at him than I did, and with his personality . . . there's no way in hell I could let Harper near him. He smirked, and I had to force myself not to look over at what I'm almost positive would be Princess staring back at him. My entire body tensed, and I was working my jaw when he looked back over to me.

"Stay away, brother—I'm not joking."

He raised an eyebrow at me. "So she has brought you to your knees." His eyes darted back to her, and I watched them darken; my hands curled into fists under the table.

I took a calming breath and snorted. "Hardly. She's

my little sister's roommate, I need to make sure they're both safe."

"And you're saying I wouldn't do that?" His smile widened, and we both knew he had me on that one. Brandon might have girls falling all over themselves, but he doesn't do anything about it. He's a relationship kind of guy, the kind of guy Harper needs. *But even Brandon isn't good enough for her. I love the guy, he's like a brother to me and vice versa, but no one would ever be good enough for Harper.*

"Fuck you."

Brandon laughed loudly and leaned back to stretch his arms before resting his forearms on the table again and turning his head to look to my left. I wanted to grab Princess and run her out of the cafeteria and away from him. This was a disaster for me waiting to happen. Swear to God, I thought, if he smirked and flashed that dimple at her one more time, I was going to punch it off his face. I could hear her talking to Bree, but I couldn't look at her, I couldn't stop watching as Brandon tried and failed to keep his eyes off her.

"So, Princess"—Drew's voice was able to interrupt my glaring and Brandon's staring—"how come we haven't seen you lately? It's been like two weeks, and I feel so unloved."

"Oh I'm sorry. Did your girlfriend deflate already?"

Even I couldn't help but laugh at that. God, she was cute. And yeah, I definitely didn't need to worry about Drew. I looked back at Brandon, staring at her, and kicked his leg under the table. He jumped slightly and turned to glare at me. "Tell me right now, do you have something with her? Yes or no."

Yes I do, she's mine. "I told you, Harper's just another girl. She means nothing to me." I stabbed my fork into my pasta and looked up in time to see Brandon's eyes cloud over as he mouthed her name and looked at her again.

His eyes shot back to mine, and he leaned closer. "Then Harper's fair game, bro. You know I won't hurt her."

One of our friends, David, started asking him something from next to me, but I couldn't focus on him. All I could think about is if Brandon wanted her, I had no doubt he would have her. And I couldn't let that happen. Without realizing why, I turned to look at her and found her confused eyes looking at me. For once, she wasn't looking at me like I disgusted her, and having her look at me at all had my entire body relaxing for the first time since I sat down. I would do anything to keep that girl safe, and I had no idea why, but deep down I still knew the first part of keeping her safe was keeping her from looking at me like she was at that moment. I nodded at her and finally started eating.

Zach asked the girls if they were coming to the party that night, and I couldn't help but laugh when Princess started grumbling about it and looking terrified. Looks like I'd have to keep her safe again, and this time I wasn't letting her jump out of my arms first thing in the morning. *I may need to keep her from wanting me, but that doesn't mean I couldn't enjoy her while I did it.*

"Looking forward to sharing my bed with you again, PG."

Brandon abruptly stopped talking to David and narrowed his eyes at me. I just raised an eyebrow at him and waited to see what he'd do.

"Thanks, but I'd rather share a bed with Drew's blow-up doll."

Ooo, my snarky and sweet-as-sin girl. You just had to go and remind me why I want you so bad. I turned to look at her and silently cursed her for driving me fucking crazy. I never thought about a girl this much anyway, but to make me feel like I'm going insane because I can't make up my mind with how much I wanted her and how bad I want to keep her safe and from me was literally making me feel like I was crazy. How could one little girl cause this much turmoil?

Kristen sat down on my lap and her lips were instantly on my neck and jaw. My fingers dug into her hips, but I couldn't force my eyes from Harper. Her narrowed eyes had widened as soon as Kristen sat down, and I watched as pain flashed across her face for a split second. Shit, I didn't want to see that; I didn't want to know this bothered her in any way other than disgusting her. There went my Dr. Jekyll and Mr. Hyde personality again. Half of me wanted to push Kristen off and grab Harper, pulling her into my arms instead; the other was telling me to keep going, to make her think she meant nothing to me.

"I'd be happy to share that bed with you, Chase," Kristen said like a freaking toddler seconds before her mouth was on mine.

My princess looked like someone had hit her, and I watched as she tore her eyes from mine and looked across from me. I shut my eyes, so I wouldn't have to watch her look to Brandon after I'd just crushed her. He was right, he wouldn't hurt her. I didn't want him to have her, but he would never do what I was doing to her at that moment.

My fingers flexed against Kristen's hips when I heard Harper's soft voice; I had done that, taken the sass from her and brought her right back to the shy, unsure Harper. "Um, I'll uh—see you all tonight then, I guess. Bye, everyone."

"Harper," Brandon called, and it felt like someone had just punched me in the chest. I needed this to happen, them meeting, but God I didn't want it to.

I held Kristen's head away and turned in time to see Harper's eyes grow wide and her cheeks get slightly pink as she watched Brandon walk up to her. He held out his hand to her and said something, but they were already too far away for me to hear them. She smiled brightly at him, and again it felt like someone was punching me. I don't think I'd ever *really* seen her smile until just then. And it wasn't even directed at me. Brandon couldn't keep his eyes off her as they walked to the doors and outside. I really couldn't let this happen, I decided.

"Up . . . get up, Kristen. Up." I more or less pushed her off me and took the few steps toward Bree, who was talking to Zach about that night's party. "You girls planning on staying all weekend or coming and going for the parties."

She looked up at me like I was dumb. "Uh, staying. And we get your room."

"Always. Go pack for the weekend, we're leaving within half an hour, I'll go get Princess."

"Don't be mean to her, Chase!"

I shook my head as I quickly walked toward the door. I couldn't decide how I was going to be toward her yet. I just needed her away from Brandon. As soon as I was out the door, I saw them, and I couldn't stop the growl that climbed out of my chest. They were standing close and just staring at each other. *Stopping this. Now.*

Grabbing her arm, I didn't stop walking, I just took her with me, "Come on PG, let's go."

"Chase! Stop!" She pulled her arm free and looked up at me like she wanted to go off on me. Such a fierce little princess. "What is your problem?"

"I'm taking you and Bree to the house, and you need to pack for the weekend, so let's go."

Harper dodged my hand when I went to grab her again and looked at me, clearly confused, "The weekend, what?"

"You're staying with me; go pack."

"Fine, hold on."

"Harper."

"Go away, Chase, I'll meet you in the room in a minute. Go find Bree."

Yeah, not a chance. I stepped up right behind her and kept my gaze on Brandon. He was looking at her like she was the damn world, and I wanted to put a football field between them.

"Sorry, apparently I have to go. I'll see you tonight?"

Brandon smiled, and his hand trailed down her arm; I almost yanked her away from him and into me. "See you then." I met his glare when his eyes flashed up to mine.

I just raised an eyebrow, and he nodded before turning away.

Princess kept up her fierce-kitten act the entire way back to the dorm room she shared with Bree, who was already packing, and even as she packed, didn't let up as she approached me where I was standing in the doorway.

She held another fake smile on her face, the only ones I seemed to get, and held up her duffel bag as she spoke in a sugar-sweet voice, "Why don't you be a dear and carry this for me."

My lips twitched, God did she not realize how damn cute she was? She tried to get past me, and I curled my arm around her waist, pulling her close to whisper in her ear, "Anything for you, sweetheart."

Her body swayed toward mine, and I heard her breath catch as her hands relaxed against my chest. My heart started pounding, and I didn't doubt she could feel it, if not hear it. Her large eyes looked up into mine, and suddenly they hardened at the same time she pushed against my chest until I let go. "God, you piss me off."

"Whoa, whoa. Did you just say 'piss'? I'm not sure if that's PG approved."

She gave her best glare and stormed down the hallway and toward the parking lot. By the time Bree and I got out there, she was sitting on the curb texting someone on her phone, but her seriously-pissed-off look hadn't left her face yet. *Oh well, I like her like this.*

Once we were back at my place, she refused to look at or talk to me even though we were the only two in the living room, and she finally gave up by flopping onto one of the couches. I watched her bare legs sway back and forth as she watched—the news? *Who the hell watches the news? Especially an eighteen-year-old girl!* I shook my head and smiled to myself as my eyes found her legs again. Before I could stop myself, I was crossing the room, picking up her feet, and sitting on the couch. I laid her legs back onto my lap and had to force my hands not to run up and down them. Princess had stiffened momentarily, but she didn't move her legs, and her body slowly relaxed back into the couch. I had to bite down on my cheeks, so I wouldn't smile.

I looked slowly up her body and over to her red cheeks, her teeth worrying her bottom lip. I zeroed in on one of the new piercings I'd been catching a glimpse of all afternoon and suddenly wished I hadn't put her legs in my lap. I'd have to thank Bree for her hand in that Monroe piercing, but I couldn't see this girl letting someone talk her into something like this. "So I see my sister is already influencing you poorly."

"Do I even want to know what you're talking about?"

"This." I touched just above her lip and had to bite back another freakin' groan when she shivered against me.

"What, you don't like it?"

"I never said that, it's hot as hell." That was an understatement. "But I'm disappointed you'd let her start talking you into stuff already. Figured you weren't one to give in to people like that."

She roughly withdrew her legs from my lap, and I'd turned to ask what her problem was when I saw her expression, and the question died on my lips. "Not that it's your business, but I was the one who wanted them and brought it up. I didn't know at that time that she would want to get them, too, and I certainly wouldn't let someone talk me into something like that. Glad to know you think so highly of me." Without another word, she hopped off the couch and went down one of the halls toward my room.

What the hell? Why does she do things like that? Like with Kristen earlier, why does she have to look like I'm hurting her rather than just pissing her off even more. I thought I needed her to stay away; I'd already come to terms with the fact that I couldn't stay away from her even if I tried, so I needed her to leave. When she looked at me like I was hurting her, it just proved that everything she was showing me was just that—a show; and it was killing me.

I stood up to go after her when my phone rang. Brandon. I sighed and answered as I walked outside. "Yeah?"

"All right, I'm not going to ask you again after this, you're like a brother to me so I need to know. Is there something going on with you and Harper?"

"I'm getting seriously tired of this shit. No. She's just a girl."

He laughed hard once. "Then why did you keep looking at me like you wanted a round with me?"

"I wasn't," I said through gritted teeth.

"Fine, then is she there?"

"What?"

"There you go again, brother." He sighed, and I heard

his Jeep start up. "I want to talk to Harper; can you give her your phone?"

I kept my mouth shut and ground my teeth together as I opened the sliding glass door, only to find her on the couch again. I held the phone out as I neared her, and she jumped slightly when I said, "It's for you."

She looked at me with confusion, and mixed in there was some of the same hurt from earlier, "He-hello?" Her eyes widened, and she glanced at the screen of the phone before bringing it back to her ear, a smile crossing her face as she relaxed into the couch. "I don't mind, what's up?" That gorgeous smile of hers got even wider before she could bite down on her lip to try to contain it. "I'd like that. Did you want me to meet you somewhere . . . ?" She sat up quickly before talking again. "See you." She practically threw my phone back at me before taking off down the hall and pounding on what could only be my door.

"Brandon's coming to pick me up for coffee!" was the last thing I heard before stalking out of the house and to my truck.

A COUPLE HOURS later, I had just finished setting everything up for the party when Harper came walking back into the house. Her eyes were clouded over, and she was smiling to herself as she walked right past me and toward my room. *Seriously?* I took in a deep breath and grabbed my phone out of my pocket. He answered on the first ring.

"I got her back safe, Chase."

"I saw that."

"All right, then what's up? I have one more class tonight, then I'll be back at the house."

I crept toward my hall, but I could hear Harper talking excitedly to my sister, so I figured I was safe for a while. "You'll stay away from her, Brandon, you got me?"

"Seriously, man, this is getting old! What is your deal? You know me, and you know I wouldn't do anything to hurt her."

"I know you're not an asshole to your girlfriends, but that doesn't mean anything. She needs someone to protect *everything* about her, and I know you, so I know you can't be that guy."

"What the hell? Protect everything—what are you even—I will!"

He may be a relationship guy, but I knew for sure he wasn't a virgin, and I needed to make sure Princess stayed that way. So no, he wouldn't protect everything about her because I doubt she'd tell him. "You don't know her; this shouldn't be too much of a hardship for you. Stay away from her."

"And you do? Look I'm sure—God I *know* this sounds crazy, but I'm not going to be able to stay away from her. I've never met a girl like her, so just get the fuck over it."

I froze. "Last time, and let me make myself clear, bro, she's taken. She's been in my bed once, and she'll be in my bed again this weekend. Got it? Do. Not. Come. Near. Her."

Brandon stayed silent for a few seconds before his flat voice came through. "Taken? You're really starting to piss me off, man. I'm not gonna deal with this shit from you. There's something about her; I'm not backing off until she tells me to."

Before I could say anything else, he hung up, and I gripped my phone tightly as Harper's laugh reached me from the other end of the hall.

Chapter Four

I HEARD SOMEONE saying my name and lifted my head slowly from Natalie's neck. Normally, I didn't spend so much time with one person, and this was the fifth time in two weeks I'd spent time with her. But we still had our agreement. She still had a boyfriend, and she knew there were too many girls wanting to see if they could tie me down since school had just started. It was just easier when the girl already knew all the rules.

"*What?*" Harper's voice broke into my already too-tipsy mind, and my eyes easily found and narrowed in on her and Brandon. I'd told him to back off.

He leaned slightly toward her and spoke softly. She looked shocked, and her eyes flashed to mine and briefly reduced to slits. I winked and saw her cheeks redden as Natalie looked over her shoulder at my princess before claiming my mouth with her own. She bit down softly on my bottom lip, and I leaned farther into her.

"So that's her, huh?"

Just as I started to ask, *who?* her tongue met mine, and she wrapped her arms around my neck. Harper laughed, and my fingers dug into Natalie's hips. What the hell was he saying that was so damn funny? I started to pull away, but Natalie kept me close, only removing her lips enough to whisper against mine.

"She's driving you crazy, Chase; might as well give her some of her own medicine."

I leaned away and looked at her like she was insane. *Is she a damn mind reader?* "Natalie, what the hell are you talking about?"

She batted her blue eyes like there was something in them and spoke in a sugar-sweet voice, making her sound like Kristen had that afternoon. "Little miss thing over there with your boy. You've been acting all kinds of weird these last two weeks, and it's starting to make sense."

"You don't know what you're talking about."

"Chase"—Drew nudged me, and I let go of Natalie with a shake of my head to start looking for my gray-eyed princess again—"table's set up, you ready for beer pong?"

"Yeah sure—" I instantly took off toward the living room and saw Harper and Brandon sitting on one of the couches. They were close, too damn close. They both started leaning in toward each other, and I was glad she'd sat on this side of the couch. I leaned over the arm, grabbed her around the waist, and hauled her away from him and over my shoulder. "LET'S GET THIS BEER PONG TOURNAMENT STARTED!"

"CHASE! Put me down!"

"No way! The princess needs her throne!" And besides, I was enjoying having her ass directly next to my face and my hands high up on her thighs.

I swear she growled, and I couldn't help but laugh, especially when her tiny fists started pounding on my back and her whole body wiggled as she tried to get down. I couldn't resist anymore, it was right there and shaking; I smacked her butt, and she froze for all of two seconds before pounding both fists at the same time, all the while yelling, "If you don't put me down, I will make good on my previous threat!"

Brandon walked into my line of sight and crossed his arms over his chest as he watched us, and my laughter died as I set Harper down. I hated seeing that possessive and concerned look in his eye when he looked at her. I hated that he was looking at her at all. I pulled her away from everyone in the kitchen and waited until we were in the entryway before turning around and pulling her close to me. "I don't want you with him."

"What is your deal with him? Is there something he did that you'd like to share?"

He looked at you! "He's not good enough for you."

"How do you know what is and isn't good for me? You don't even know me!"

All of a sudden, Brandon's hands were on her shoulders, and I realized I'd been holding her against me. I dropped her arm and took a step away as my eyes burned holes in his hands, which were by then going up and down her arms.

"I thought I told you to back off, man?"

"I don't really think that's up to you."

No, but God I wish it were. I glanced up at Harper's innocent face as I fought with myself over what I wanted and what I knew she needed. "You hurt her, I swear to God, I'll break your neck."

I stalked past them and into the kitchen, grabbing a new bottle of Patron and walking over to one of the many hallways off the main room. I didn't bother with a glass; there wasn't much of a need at this point. That girl in the entryway with one of my best friends was driving me absolutely insane, and I hated it.

"You don't know what I'm talking about, huh?"

Glaring up at Natalie, I kept my eyes on her as I took another swig out of the short bottle. I closed my eyes and enjoyed the heat as it made its way through my chest. "Shut up, Natalie."

"I'm just saying—"

"I don't want to hear it!"

People started cheering in the kitchen, and I rolled my eyes as I took another large gulp before wiping my mouth on my forearm.

"Do you want me to help you relax?" she asked huskily, and began pulling at the buttons on the top of her shirt.

I let my eyes fall over Natalie's tall, slender frame. "Later," I said as I made my way back to the kitchen to make sure they weren't letting my princess play. Of course they were, and Brandon was playing against her. *How is this protecting her?* I watched her laugh outrageously with everyone and flirt way more than was necessary with

Brandon. Who taught her to look up from under those insanely long eyelashes? And who gave her those shorts? I would kill Bree for taking her to the mall if this is what came from it. No one else needed to be looking at her. I thought about Natalie's barely there skirt and thanked God that at least she wasn't wearing one of those.

I took another long gulp of the liquor and almost choked on it as Brandon walked right up to *my* princess and kissed her, picked her up, and took her into the living room. What the hell was this and where was the pure-as-snow Harper? Her legs had instantly wrapped around his waist, and when he sat them down, she arched her body into his. I pushed off the counter too quickly and had to grab onto the pantry door to steady myself as the alcohol really started to catch up with me.

"Easy there, tiger." Natalie wrapped an arm around my waist and started pulling me toward the living room. "I saw them, too. You ready to relax now?"

With Natalie? For once, no. I wasn't. But with the way Harper was acting, I sure as hell was going to act like it. *Two can play this game, Princess.* I let my arm fall around her shoulders and nodded once. "Let's go."

"Calm down," Natalie whispered, and grabbed at my hand.

My hand had curled into a fist as I watched Brandon kiss down Harper's neck. I knew this would happen. He had no idea because she was acting like a fucking slut, and all too soon one of the best traits about Harper would be gone. Time to throw on Brandon's emergency brake. If it weren't for the fact that I was sure she was about to hate me, I wouldn't have been able to stop smiling. "So much for the PG rating."

Princess's eyes snapped open and widened as she took in her surroundings and scrambled off Brandon's lap. Good.

Brandon shot a quick glare at me, and I could actually see my words click in his brain, and he looked at Harper, confused. "Wait, 'PG' is a rating they gave you?"

That's right, brother. My rating for my girl. "What, she didn't tell you? Princess over here was as virgin as someone could possibly get until she met you. Now she's just simply a virgin, I guess we can raise it to PG-13 until later. I'm sure she's ready to get rid of it altogether. Maybe you'll have better luck than I did." I ground my teeth and tried not to finish with, *But I'll kill you if you touch her more than you have.*

Natalie laughed softly and shook her head but otherwise kept quiet until we were outside. "Oh my God. I seriously can't believe this right now."

I withdrew from her and couldn't help but look back into the living room in time to see Brandon facing the sliding glass doors and Bree talking animatedly to him. He looked pissed. I didn't blame him, but I didn't care either.

"Chase Grayson is whipped."

"Not whipped, Natalie."

"So I'm guessing you don't want to *relax* the way I had in mind?"

Bree took off for the hallway that led to my room. Had Harper gone in there? Brandon looked up and met my stare, and he looked ready to murder someone. I smirked, and his head snapped in the direction of my hall seconds before he took off for it. *Shit, she must be in there. Oh God, did I make her cry?* I took two steps toward the door before Natalie caught my arm.

"That's probably not the best idea right now."

"I have to—"

"No, what you need to do is calm the eff down before you make that situation worse. Don't get me wrong"—she laughed and dug around in her purse before pulling out a metal container—"that was priceless to watch; especially since it involved you. But I've seen your boy fight, and he looked *pissed,* so you might want to stay away."

I looked up in time to see Brandon stalk off in the direction of his room, and Bree came our way with a look on her face that would make me proud if it weren't directed at me.

She flung the door open and held her hand out as she continued to punch me in her mind. "Key, asshole. Now."

Ouch. Guess I deserved that one. I dug it out of my pocket and dropped it in her hand, "Love you, too, sis."

"Go to hell, Chase." She huffed and slammed the door shut. I really wanted to go in her place.

"Huh, sweet girl," Natalie said from behind me.

I heard the click of a lighter and turned to watch Natalie light up a joint. "Seriously, Natalie? Put that shit away. No drugs in or around my house." Legalized or not. Too much changed and could go wrong if you put that into the mix. The couches inside the house were already tilting up as it was from the liquor; I really didn't need any secondhand benefits from her right now. System of a Down started playing, and I reached for my phone. "It's the shop, I gotta take this."

"God, you got boring over the summer."

"Then feel free to leave. You already figured out why I needed to keep you around these past couple weeks, and obviously I'm done with you now, so go." I watched her walk away and had to really focus on the screen, so I would hit the green button instead of the red. "Yeah?"

"Hey, man, sorry; I know you have the night off, but we're slammed, and some people are requesting you. Can you come in?"

Bree came back out and went straight to whoever this guy she brought for the night was. Where was Harper? "Uh, no, Brian. Sorry, but I can't swing it tonight."

"There's a couple really hot chicks asking for you."

"That's great, man, but I can already barely stay standing as it is, there's no way in hell I could drive or hold up my gun long enough to ink anyone—not to mention make it what they want."

He laughed loudly away from the phone and brought it back. "God, I miss college. All right, man, see you tomorrow. Do everything I wouldn't do; I need to live through you since I'm tied down."

"Nice. I'm telling Marissa that next time I see her."

"Do, and I'll deny it."

I looked back through the glass doors and realized Harper still wasn't there. *Had I upset her that bad?* I looked again, and Brandon wasn't there either. I swore to God that if they were in *my* bed together, I wasn't threatening anymore, I was doing. "Yeah, yeah; look, man, I gotta go. See you tomorrow."

"Later."

I was through the door and storming down the hall before I could hit the END button. Thank God she hadn't locked the door because I slammed right into it as I threw it open. I almost sighed in relief when I wasn't met with yells to get out from Brandon, but wanted to curse myself for making her want to be alone like this.

"Can't you just leave me alone?"

That was almost laughable. *No.* "Once again, Princess, you're in my room."

"Fine, then *I'll* go." She got off the bed and tried to walk around me, but I held her in front of me. "Chase, let me go!"

"Not until you talk to me."

"We have nothing to talk about!"

We have *everything* to talk about. "I'm sorry I hurt you, but I was just so damn mad!"

"Do you know how immature you sound right now? You decided to hurt me because *you* were mad? What did I ever do to you, Chase? And why do I always end up with your hands on me? Let. Me. Go."

Maybe because I want to touch you, and you're always running away? "Because you won't stop and talk to me for five minutes!"

"Then you should understand that I don't *want* to talk to you. Answer me! What did I do to make you mad?"

She thought *she* was making me mad? SHE WAS! But she wasn't. Hell, I was confusing myself! I was making me mad, Brandon was making me mad even though he'd asked me too many times if there was anything going on between me and Harper. I didn't want them together, I wanted her for myself, but I couldn't be with her. Wait, what? *Why the hell did I drink so much tonight? The way I feel for this girl is confusing enough on a normal, sober day; but tonight I feel like I need someone to put me in a straightjacket and a padded room.* "Nothing! You did nothing; I'm not mad at you!"

"Seriously, you're hurting me! Get off me and leave me alone!"

Hurting her? How am I hurting her? I'm trying to protect her!

"What the hell, Chase!"

Oh my God, what now? I turned and had barely made out Brandon, Bree, Brad, and Derek all in the doorway before Brandon's fist was flying toward me. *Aw hell, this is going to hurt like a bitch.*

WHY IS IT so bright? Did I leave the light on in my room? I groaned and rolled over as I smashed my face into my pillow. *What the hell?* My eyes snapped open to see green underneath me, and I leaned up quickly to see grass. Who the hell put me outside? With another groan, my arms gave out, and I face-planted into the wet grass. "Ow." Turning my head to the side, I rubbed at my jaw, and last night came rushing back to me just as I heard someone yell my name from inside the house.

Pushing off the grass, I stumbled to get myself upright, then stayed still for a moment to make sure I was steady. *God, I still feel drunk.*

"Chase, open the damn door!"

And that would be Brandon. I looked toward the house, and sighed. "Gladly," I mumbled and sauntered over to the sliding glass doors. Ugh, someone needed to tell the sun to go away for a few more hours. I rubbed at my burning eyes and opened the door to see Brandon pounding on my bedroom door, "What's with all the yelling?"

"You son of a bitch!" Brandon yelled, and started stomping toward me.

Seriously? This bastard must not have had anything to drink last night; it's way too early for fighting.

"Brandon!" Harper hissed, and stepped in front of me.

That woke me up. *Hell. No.* I grabbed her around the waist and pulled her back before situating myself in front of her. I didn't know what was happening that morning, but whatever it was obviously involved the three of us. And while I knew Brandon wouldn't hit a girl, I wasn't letting Harper get anywhere near a fight, let alone in the middle of one. I prepared myself for when Brandon hit me, and the damn girl moved back between us.

"No. Brandon, just stop!" she said, exasperated, and I reached out to grab her and pull her into me; but she put a hand on my chest.

"Harper," he snarled, "please move."

"No."

Oh my stubborn princess. I got ready to pull her into me again when she moved away and went to Brandon, placing both hands on him. That hurt worse than face-planting on my already sore jaw.

"You have got to be kidding me! He—"

She cut him off, but I wish she hadn't since I really wanted to know what I'd done this time.

"Will someone tell us what's going on?" Brad asked from somewhere on my side.

I almost said I wanted to know the same thing when Harper pulled Brandon's head down toward hers and kissed him. *Screw being partly still drunk and partly hungover. I'm ready for this fight.*

Brandon's gaze glanced up to meet mine quickly before looking back at *my* princess and exhaling loudly. He whispered something to her and picked her up, walking her out of the living room and toward the hall that led to his room. She wasn't a child! She could walk just fine.

"Chase, what did you do to her now?" Bree asked accusingly.

I didn't respond because not only did I not know, but I was still itching to have my fight with Brandon, and anyone who got in my way wasn't going to enjoy being around me until then. I walked up to Brandon's room and heard low murmurs as I knocked and opened the door. Brandon was sitting on the bed but shot up off it when he saw me, and for a split second, I got excited that we were going to get our round. But then my gray-eyed princess put her hand on his chest, and the bastard stopped walking.

"Well, you just woke everyone in the house. Care to clue me in?"

On the one hand, Brandon looked ready to kill me; on the other, he looked like he wanted to take Harper away from me. I knew exactly how he felt.

Harper sighed and broke the silence, "Chase, how drunk were you last night?"

Enough to still be slightly drunk now. "Not drunk enough to forget why my jaw hurts."

"Well, you deserved that one, you were being rude."

Apparently that's all I knew how to be around her! My arms flew out to the side in exasperation. "I was just talking to you!"

Brandon pulled my princess toward his body. Before I could curl my lip at him, he lifted up the sleeves of what had to be his shirt on Harper, and asked harshly, "*This is just talking to her?*"

What is just talk—oh holy shit. It felt like someone had punched me in the stomach. *No, no. No way I did that, I wouldn't do that to any girl but never to Harper. When would I have even done something like that to her?* Parts of last night flashed through my mind again. *Seriously, you're hurting me. Oh my God. No.* I shook my head and looked up at her understanding face. Why did she have to look at me like that? If any time was a good time for her to look at me like she hated me, this was it!

"Oh God, Harper. I di—I." *What the hell is wrong with me?* "Harper, I'm so sorry. I had no idea, I swear I didn't mean to hurt you." God, I would never have hurt her, not like that. I would have tried to keep her from me, but I wouldn't have done this!

I stepped closer to her and ignored the warning growl

Brandon sent my way as I placed my fingers on the large bruise on her arm. I'd done that, I'd hurt this perfect, innocent, frustrating-as-hell girl.

"Harper"—my voice gave out, and I had to clear it a couple times before I could talk again—"can I please talk to you alone?"

I couldn't even care when Brandon kissed her and spoke softly to her. All I could see were the bruises on Harper's arms. He kissed her, and though a part of me felt like it died again, I couldn't find it in me to do anything about it. As soon as he left, and I heard the front door shut, I exhaled roughly and couldn't keep quiet anymore. "Are you okay? God, that's a stupid question, of course you're not."

"No, I am. I'm fine."

"How can you even say that?"

"Because I am. They don't hurt, and I didn't even know they were there until Brandon saw them."

So stubborn and frustrating! *Yell at me, please! Tell me you hate me and never want to see me again, anything; just don't act like this is nothing.* "I just—I never meant to hurt you, I swear."

Her hands found their way around my neck, and she pulled down until my forehead was resting against hers. I was so shocked by what she was doing, I couldn't even try to push her away like I knew I should. I took in a shaky breath. *God, what is it about this girl?* "I know you didn't, Chase. It really is okay; you were drunk, and I was being stubborn."

There she went again! "Don't do that. Don't act like it's okay when it's not. You do this with everyone. And please don't make excuses for me. Yes, I was drunk, and I don't always realize what I'm doing after I've been drinking, but that's no excuse, Princess."

Her soft laugh and the way she gently squeezed my neck tugged at my heart. "Well, maybe you shouldn't drink then."

"Maybe I shouldn't." *If I had it my way, Harper and I wouldn't be standing in this room right now, we wouldn't be pressed against each other. I would just be her room-mate's brother who pisses her off.* But when it came to this girl, I was no longer in control of anything. She consumed me in every way possible. My brain was telling me to run from her, to keep her safe, to keep her from someone like me, but she had my heart completely, and that was winning out. I wanted her, I wanted her to want me and only me. Not Brandon even though I *knew* he was the better choice for her. But that just didn't matter to me at that moment; all I cared about was the fact that one of my best friends was winning over the only girl that would ever mean anything to me. "Why him, Harper?"

"What do you mean?"

"Why Brandon? You'd never been kissed, why'd you choose him to change that?"

"Why not Brandon?"

I snorted. *Because I'm right freakin' here wanting nothing more than to love you forever.*

"Why does that bother you so much, Chase?"

"Because you deserve someone who realizes how amazing you are. You shouldn't have just let the first guy who gave you the time of day kiss you."

"You're acting like I gave him everything, and all we've done is kiss! And who are you to judge who I do and do not kiss?"

She'd removed herself from my arms and went to sit on the bed; that was too far for me. I just followed her and put my hands on each side of her as I rested my forehead against hers again. "Please don't. Don't give him everything. He doesn't deserve you, Harper."

"And who does, Chase . . . you?"

God, why did she have to talk all soft and breathy like that? Why did her chest have to rise and fall so quickly; I knew I just had to say the word, and I could make her mine. *Say it. Say it, you stupid bastard!* I squeezed my eyes shut and let my head fall from hers. "No. I don't deserve you either. You need someone who will cherish you, protect you, and take care of you. Someone that realizes they'd never be able to find another you in the world, no matter how hard they looked." I looked back into her soft gray eyes and continued to fight with myself on taking what I needed and giving her what *she* needed. Without thinking about it, I leaned in close until I could feel her breath against my lips; I would have given anything to kiss her. Just as I started to close the already minimal space between us, her voice stopped me and snapped me back to my reality.

"Chase . . ."

"That first night, I *did* realize I would never meet another girl like you. But you deserve someone who has waited for you as long as you have waited for them. And no matter how much I wish I could be that guy, I can't, Harper." I leaned back, and she collapsed onto the bed with a hard sigh. I couldn't stop myself then, and I leaned over her and kissed her soft throat. That was all I could allow myself. "You're amazing, Harper. There will never be anyone good enough for you."

I started to stand up again when her hands were in my hair and holding my head just inches from hers. Her breathing was heavy, and I knew mine matched it. I waited to see what she would do, but as I waited, her eyes told me everything her lips weren't. Her indecision, her worry. Good girl. Smart girl. She'd kiss Brandon without a second thought but couldn't bring herself to kiss me without already feeling the fear of what a guy like me would do to her. Though she was making the better decision for her, it didn't crush me any less; and I knew if she rejected me, it would kill me. So I stopped it before she could. I let my nose trail up the inside of her forearm as I took in her subtle vanilla scent and kissed her wrist before removing her hands and walking out the door. I rubbed at the ache in my chest and shook my head as I went to crash on Brad's floor for a couple hours before work. That guy Bree had brought with her last night had been standing with her when I walked in, which meant I'd have to buy new sheets a-freakin'-gain before I could sleep on my bed. If I didn't bring girls in my room, she had to stop bringing guys.

"CHASE"—MY BODY ROCKED to the side once, and I groaned as it flopped back down—"get up. Your phone's going off."

"Breanna. Go. Away."

A tiny foot jammed into my ribs, and I grunted hard. *Bitch.* "Fine, miss work, but don't act like I didn't try to help you out."

Aw hell. I rolled over and yawned as she dropped my phone on my stomach. "I'm up. How'd you have my phone?"

"Fell out of your pocket when Brandon punched you in your room. I turned the alarm off, but you better get up."

"Okay, Mom." I snickered as I stood and hugged her loosely. "Gonna take a shower before I head out. If anything happens to you or Harper tonight, you call me, and I'll come back."

"Pft. I can handle myself, and Harper's got a date tonight."

My body went rigid.

"Oh, and Harper's just about to get in your shower to get ready for it, so use Brad's," she called over her shoulder as she left Brad's room.

She was going on a date with him? Not like I expected anything else—okay, that's a lie, yes I did. I still half expected her to realize she felt the same way for me that I felt for her and leave Brandon to find someone else. Anyone else. I hurried through my shower, got dressed, and paced the floor of my room for all of two minutes before

I couldn't wait any longer. I found the key sitting on my desk and went to my bathroom. The shower was still running, and I swear, my pants got smaller. I went over to sit on top of the toilet seat as her shaky voice filled the small bathroom.

"Uh . . . Bree?"

"Nope, just me."

"Chase! What the heck are you doing in here?"

Um, good question. What am I doing in here? Right now, all I can think about is the water running all over her naked body. I groaned and ran my hands over my face. "Calm down, Princess, I won't peek." I don't know if I was trying to reassure her or force myself to stay sitting.

"I could've sworn I locked that door."

"You do realize how easy it is to unlock *my* bathroom door when I have the key, right?"

"Can you please leave so I can get out of here?"

As soon as the water turned off, I grabbed a towel and shoved it through the side of the curtain, forcing myself not to look in that direction. "Answer one thing first, and I'll leave." She didn't say anything, so I took that as confirmation she would answer. "Are you going out with him tonight?"

"Yes, Chase, I am."

"Is that what you want to do, or are you trying to get back at me for telling you not to?"

"I thought I only had to answer one question?"

Snarky brat! God, she drove me crazy. "Harper."

"Ugh, no, I'm not doing it to get back at you. Yes, I really want to go out with Brandon tonight. And if he asks me out again after tonight, I'm telling you right now I will say yes. I don't see why I shouldn't go out with him, and since you clearly don't want me, I don't think you're allowed to have a say in the matter."

Whoa, what? How the hell did she get anything *I'd said as not wanting her?* I grabbed the side of the curtain and hoped for her sake she'd put the damn towel on as I slid the curtain across the bar. "I didn't say I don't want you. I said I don't deserve you."

"That's practically the same thing. We both know how you are, Chase. You screw every female you come in contact with. I don't want to be just another girl to someone, and when it comes to Brandon, I won't be. If you can convince me right now that I have a reason to not be with him, then start talking. Otherwise, you and your confusing words need to stop."

She really thought she was just another girl to me? Sure, I told everyone that, but she had to know that wasn't true. And it's not like I'd told *her* that—I told her the opposite! I'd never felt anything like this for anyone, and she thought she was just another girl for me? I thought about all the girls she'd seen me with since meeting her and wanted to curse myself for ever trying to push her away; I'd done this to myself. Until I showed her differently, she'd always think she didn't matter to me. And other than wanting her to be with me, I didn't have a legitimate thing to say against Brandon. He was the best guy I knew, the only guy I'd trust her with. "As long as he is what you want, I'll stop bothering you."

I thought about the way he'd come after me that morning because I'd bruised her. Yeah, he was in just as deep as I was. I let my fingers trail across the biggest bruise on her arm and wanted to kill myself. I leaned over the tub and kissed that bruise, moved up to kiss the smaller one on her shoulder, then across to kiss the identical one on her right shoulder. If only that could make them go away. "I'm so sorry, Harper," I whispered, just before kissing the corner of her mouth. She'd never know how sorry I was for everything that I'd done to her in just two weeks of knowing her. "Get my number from Bree. I have to go in to work tonight, but if anything happens, call me, and I'll be there."

Before I could do anything else, like take her in my arms and never let her leave, I made myself turn and walk out of the room. I was already running late getting to the shop—not like anyone would care—but I needed to get there and clear my mind of my princess. I snorted as I cranked the engine of my truck. Yeah, like that was possible.

"HEY, MY MAN! Wasn't sure if we'd be expecting you or not after our convo last night!"

I laughed and slapped Brian on the back as I went to my station. "Yeah, well, you got me tonight, so stop your bitching."

"I'm so serious, bro, you missed some crazy hotties last night, and all they wanted was a piece of Chase."

"Yeah—about that. I'm pretty sure I'm done with other women."

His back straightened, and he spun around in his chair to face me, "Uh, 'scuse me?"

"You ever have a problem with someone else wanting your wife? Not just wanting her, because, Marissa's hot, and we all know that. But I mean someone *really* wanting her, and her wanting him? Before you guys got married or anything like that?"

"Swear, bro, you should have started with that, because I thought you were going to start batting for the other team."

I narrowed my eyes at him and went back to setting up my station.

"All right, fine, uh, not really. I mean guys have gone after her, chicks, too, but it's always been me and Marissa . . . err, well, except for that one time."

"Yeah"—I huffed out a laugh and repeated his words—"except for that one time. But that was you, Bri, not her."

"Whatever. You know I'm making up for that shit. Why'd you ask anyway?"

Sighing loudly, I put a couple sketchpads back down and looked over to see the lobby empty, "There's this girl—"

"*Oh, no way!* Chase Grayson is whipped!"

"Do you want to hear this or not?"

He nodded as he chuckled and grabbed his phone. "I gotta tell Riss. Keep talking."

"Bastard," I whispered, and shook my head as I dragged my chair closer to his station. "I don't know what it is about her; I can't stop thinking about her, and I'm telling you I don't even care about other girls anymore. At first, I just wanted a go at her because she was a challenge, but that didn't even last two hours before all I could think about was protecting her and keeping her with me."

"Oh, shit, you love her."

I looked up at Brian and flinched back, "No way. I mean, she's different. So different. You know I don't get like this over women. And there are things about her that drive me crazy in the best ways possible, yeah, but I don't love her."

"Yeah, you do. I can see it all over your face when you talk about her. Man, you're not whipped, you are straight up in love with this chick."

Love her? Hell no. I just met her. There are things she does that I love, but I don't love her. "Nah, Brian you're taking this too far."

"Whatever, I'm not gonna argue with you. So what's the problem, then? You asked if guys went after Marissa. Someone going after your girl?"

"Well, she's not *my* girl. She's too good for me, she deserves someone that's the exact opposite of me. So, I've been trying to make her realize that, too. But now, too late, I'm realizing I don't want her anywhere except with me. And now she and Brandon are dating, I guess. You remember Brandon?"

"Oh man"—he nodded—"that dude's like your brother."

"I know. This is ridiculous, I don't know what to do. Brandon's the best guy for her, I know that, but I want her. And I'm constantly pushing her away and pulling her toward me; I'm pretty sure I'm giving us both whiplash."

"Look, Brandon's great and all, but you're being too hard on yourself. I wouldn't agree with you that he's the best guy for her. I think any guy that loves her the way you do is the best guy for her." I started to tell him I wasn't in love with her, but he cut me off. "You are, and you'll realize it one day."

"Whatever, so what would you do if you were me? I *know* I should let her be with him, but I don't know if I can."

"I'm just going to compare her to Riss because that's exactly how I think of her, so if someone was trying to take my girl from me—even if she weren't my girl yet— I'd fight for her. No way I'd let Marissa slip away, and you shouldn't let this chick slip away. What's her name?"

"Harper. Princess. Whatever fits at the moment." Brian raised an eyebrow at me, and I shrugged. "When I first met her, the title fit. Now it just pisses her off, but it still kinda fits her."

"That's weird. I'll stick with Harper."

I laughed. "Shut up, man. You'd like her. She's hot, God she's so damn sexy, and she has *no* idea. She's everything I never wanted in a girl and everything I want from her. She's snarky and at the same time sweet as hell; she's probably shorter than Bree, and she's fierce, but she looks like a pissed-off little kitten when she is." Brian's chuckles cut me off, and I blinked up to look at him. "What?"

"*Chase Grayson is whipped and in love!*" he shouted loud enough to be heard throughout the tattoo parlor, and I glared at him. "Oh, man. Screw texting Riss about this. I gotta call her and tell her; you know she's gonna give you hell. And she's gonna want to meet her, so I know you and Brandon got some bro-mance going on, but don't let her go, man."

I thought about my princess, I'd already screwed things up bad enough, but I was done with it. I was done with everything else but her. She didn't want me to drink? Then I wouldn't. All that happened when I did was mistakes with other girls, and no other girl mattered. Not anymore. I didn't know how to go about fixing what I'd already fucked up, but I'd change everything from here on out, I needed her. "I won't."

Chapter Five

I DIDN'T SEE Harper again until Monday, and I was starting to wonder if Brian was right. At the risk of sounding supercheesy and sappy, my chest literally swelled, and my heart took off as I watched her walk across the courtyard with my sister. She looked perfect. Everything about her. I didn't need to be here 'til later, but I knew she was here and had hoped to catch a glimpse of her. I don't know what I was going to say to her, but I needed to talk to her. As soon as I stepped away from Drew and Zach, my steps faltered as Brandon walked up and swung her up into his arms to kiss her. My hands fisted, and I had to turn away, so I wouldn't watch them. I needed to fight for her smart; running up to them and punching him would definitely not win me any points.

"Zach, give me some paper and a pen."

"What? Why?"

"Just give me some, fast."

I ground my jaw as I forced myself not to look back over at them. I could hear Brandon talking, so I knew they were still there, I just really didn't want to see her in his arms again. As soon as Zach tore out a sheet of paper, I ripped the bottom off and scrawled a note on it before handing his pen back.

"Take care of my girl, Bree," I heard Brandon call from behind me, and I swear I growled.

Motherfucker. My girl.

"Chase, you all right?" Zach asked, and he was looking at me like I was crazy. I felt like it.

"Yep. Catch you guys later." I turned and had to look for a second before finding Bree and Harper walking away. I caught up to them quickly and realized I still didn't have a reason to talk to them. At the last second, I threw an arm around Bree's shoulder, and asked. "What's up, sis?"

"Uh, nothing. I thought you didn't have classes 'til later?"

"Had some things I had to take care of earlier, didn't feel like going home." I had placed myself between her and my princess, so it wasn't hard for me to press the paper telling Harper she looked beautiful into her hand. As soon as I felt her fingers curl around it, I let my hand trail all the way up to her elbow and smiled when I heard her breath catch.

"You going to family day this weekend?"

"Bree, you're asking me? I was the one that actually showed yesterday."

"Don't blame me; Harper wouldn't get out of bed with Brandon."

I was going to kill Brandon. I just had to find him first. "You ladies have fun, I'll see you later." I hugged Bree quickly and nudged my princess before making myself go back to my truck instead of finding Brandon. If punching him wouldn't win me points, killing him definitely wouldn't.

IT WAS RIDICULOUS, but I'd avoided being at my house as much as possible ever since I'd come home from work Monday night to find Harper and Brandon making their way into his room. Now, I was pretty much only here when I knew Brandon would be in class. But holy hell, if I could walk out of my room to see this every time I was home? I'd never leave. Harper was standing there in the tiniest bikini known to man, her body shaking slightly; I guessed it had something to do with the water that still clung to her skin. I couldn't stop myself from slowly, so freakin' slowly, taking in her practically naked body.

"Damn, Princess. You look"—God, I really needed to adjust myself— "wow."

"I was uh, just coming to get more towels."

I kept my eyes on her even though she'd covered her chest with her arms as I opened the closet next to me and pulled out a stack of towels. I dropped all but the top one and wrapped it around her shoulders. "How are you?" I brushed my fingers across her cheek, then down her neck, and watched as her eyes fluttered shut.

"Huh?"

I kept my eyes on her completely relaxed face until

I ducked my head under her jaw and kissed her throat, keeping my lips against her skin as I asked, "That good, huh?"

She pushed me back after a few seconds, and I couldn't help but smile at her fierce expression, which was becoming one of my favorites. "Why do you keep doing this to me?"

"What do you mean?" I tried to pull her into my arms, but she stepped back and, with the hand that wasn't gripping the towel to her chest, pointed at one of my arms.

"This! You can't keep doing this. I'm with Brandon now; you have to stop. No more notes, no more touches, no more putting your lips on me. This isn't fair to me. Do you have any idea how crazy you're making me?"

That Brandon shit had started to piss me off, but as soon as she asked that last question, I was smiling again. "Really now?"

"Chase, I'm serious. This has to stop."

Hell. No. "Give me one good reason why I should."

"I told you, I'm with Brandon now."

"I said a good reason, Princess."

"That's a perfectly good reason! And it's the only one you're going to get."

I watched as she bent down to pick up the towels and knew I needed to just tell her how I felt. I'd spent too much time confusing both of us—I needed to lay it all out there. "Harper."

She squeezed her eyes shut as she spoke to me, and I wanted to beg her to open them so I could look at her stormy eyes. "No Chase, please just—just don't. I really like Brandon. Besides, you have plenty of girls who are fine with being treated like shit by you. I'm not one of them. Go find another brainless bimbo to screw and get out of your system."

Holy shit; that hurts. I recoiled like she'd slapped me and didn't even try to stop her when she turned and walked back outside. She still didn't get it; she still thought this was just a game for me.

"Hey, there you are," Brad called, and I tore my eyes from the back door and over to him. "Whoa, are you all right?"

I nodded and looked back at the door.

"Um, okay. Well, before you run off again, I'm gonna grill some burgers in a bit. So why don't you stay until you gotta go in to work? I don't know why you've been gone so much, but whatever it is, we all miss having you around here. C'mon, we're all gonna be outside swimming and hanging out until later."

A shriek that was distinctly Harper sounded from the backyard, and I took off for the door in time to watch her get thrown in the pool.

"They're just throwing the girls in the pool, calm down."

"I know, I just . . ." Just what? Didn't want anyone touching her? Freaked the hell out when I heard her just then?

"Oh shit, man. Please don't tell me—"

"Don't worry about it, Brad. And yeah, I'll stay."

He sighed but didn't say anything else; I just shrugged out of my shirt and pulled a chair up to where the towels

I'd just given Harper were spread out. I had to grip the arms of the chair when Zach threw Harper into the pool again not thirty minutes later, but other than that, just sat around with everyone and tried not to make it obvious I couldn't keep my eyes off her. Bree and I were talking about this new prick she had with her and how she wanted to use my room *again* tonight, when Brandon ran up behind Harper and picked her up. I almost laughed when she kicked at him, but then he kissed her, and the laugh died.

He asked something too low for me to hear, but I definitely heard her response. "Not at all, I'm yours for the next three days." I watched as he walked them into the house and caught sight of Brad watching me and shaking his head slightly before looking back to the grill.

Bree was still asking for my room as I stood up quickly. "Whatever, Bree, I'll leave it unlocked."

I stalked back toward the house, and Brad stopped me with a hand to my chest, "Bro, you should really think about what this could do to you and Brandon before you go startin' shit."

I shrugged off his hand and gave him a warning glare. "Maybe you should shut the fuck up and mind your own business."

Before he could say anything else I went into my room and pulled out my sketchpad for a while before getting in the shower and getting ready for work. I hopped in my truck and wasn't even out of the neighborhood before I saw her. I had to do a double take, but I'd know that girl anywhere. I rolled down my window and slowed as I came up next to her and studied her hunched-over posture. "Harper?"

She didn't look up and didn't stop walking. What the hell was she doing? Why was she out here?

I threw my truck in park and jumped out before quickly rounding the front and going right to her. "Harper what are you—are you crying? What's wrong?"

She sniffed and wiped at her face roughly as she tried to walk around me. "Please leave me alone."

Hell no! "What happened?" *Who the hell made her cry? Because I sure as shit didn't; and why is she alone?* I grabbed her arms gently, making sure that I would not be able to bruise her again, and hunched down low to try to look in her eyes; she just turned her head away. My hands started to flex, and I forced them to relax. *Brandon, who the hell else? That's it, I'm going to kill him for real this time.*

"Nothing happened, Chase, so just let me go."

"Like hell. You're crying and walking through a dark neighborhood. Talk to me."

"Why are you even out here?"

I wanted to ask her the same thing. "I'm going in to work. Now tell me what he did."

"Don't act like you don't know. You tried to warn me; you knew he would do this." Her phone rang, and after ignoring the call, she shoved it back in her pocket.

"Princess, I promise you I have no idea what you're talking about, but I'll kill him for hurting you. Please tell me what happened." I let go of her arms, only to wrap one around her, bringing her closer to me, and with the other

I tilted her chin up so I could look into her heartbroken gray eyes. *Oh my God, Harper, what did he do to you?*

A short cry escaped her, and her body relaxed into me as she cried softly against my chest.

"You're okay, Princess, I've got you. Tell me what happened, and I swear I'll do everything I can to make this better for you." I ran my now-free hand up and down her back and tightened my hold on her when her phone rang again.

"Can you take me to the dorms, please?"

"You sure you want to go there?"

She nodded against my chest, and I knew Brian was right. I was in love with her. I wanted her in my arms forever, I wanted to take care of her when she was sick, hold her when she was upset, and kiss her senseless during the happy times. I took a deep breath and reluctantly let her go. It was not the time to push her into anything. She was upset over another guy, and I didn't want to be the rebound.

"'Kay, get in the truck, Princess." I helped her into the passenger seat and saw her body go rigid when her phone rang again as I got into the driver's seat. "Is that him calling again?"

"Yep."

"Are you going to answer it this time?"

"Nope."

I scooted across the seat, cupped her face in my hands, and wiped away the last of her tears. "Tell me what happened."

Before she could say anything her phone rang again, and she answered it this time. "What, Brandon?"

Oh hell. I was glad not to be on the receiving end of that. No more cute fierce looks; she looked like she could kill someone. I went back to my side and started driving toward the dorms.

"Seriously? You're really going to play that game with me?—I left." She started silently crying again and shook her head quickly. "Please stop calling me, Brandon."— "Why don't you ask Amanda? I'm sure she'd be more than happy to *show* you why I left." Not two seconds later, she ended the call and held the power button until she could turn her phone off.

Amanda? Who the hell is Amanda? I stayed silent for a few minutes before reaching over and grabbing her hand. Thank God she didn't remove hers. "Who's Amanda?"

"Apparently she's some girl he's sleeping with. Bree and I saw her on Monday with him and a group of guys."

Uh, I'd have known if Brandon were cheating on Harper. Even with avoiding the house. "Why do you think he's cheating on you?"

"I was getting back in my suit and his phone kept going off! I wasn't going to look, but I swear it went off like fifty times—okay not really fifty, but a few. It just seemed like a lot—whatever! So, anyway, I just leaned over to see who they were from, and there was a picture of this chick's shaved vaj!" My eyebrows shot up, but I didn't interrupt her. "So I opened his texts, and there was another picture of her boobs and her face, and she was saying things like, '*I can't wait 'til tomorrow*' and '*I can't wait to feel your lips all over me again*' I feel so stupid."

"You shouldn't." *Oh my God, what am I doing?* This is the perfect opportunity to get her away from Brandon, but if she was this upset over the possibility of his cheating, I knew I wouldn't be able to be more than what I already was for her. She needed to get over Brandon on her own another way, then come to me; but not from something she *thought* was happening. "I can't believe I'm about to say this, but I think you're wrong, Harper."

"Excuse me? I know what I saw, Chase!"

I pulled up outside her dorm and put the truck in park before turning to look at her, "I'm not saying that, but he wouldn't do that to you. That's not the kind of guy he is, but even if he were, he would have told one of us. We tend to brag about girls we're with. And as much as I hate him for it, all he does is talk about you."

"Do you realize how all over the place you are? A week ago, you were telling me not to go on a date with him, and now you're defending him?"

Yeah, I realized it; and yeah, I was driving myself just as crazy as I was driving her. "I'm not doing it for his benefit, trust me. I don't want you with him, that hasn't changed; I just hate seeing you hurt like this."

She looked at me curiously for a few moments before removing her hand and reaching for the door handle. "Thanks for the ride, Chase."

"Are you going to be okay? Do you want me to stay with you?"

"I'll be fine, I'm tougher than you think. Go to work; I'll see you around."

I watched her walk inside before putting my car in drive again; once I pulled into the shop's parking lot, I pulled my phone out of my pocket and called Brandon.

"What?"

God, he sounded rough, "Just thought you'd like to know where Harper is."

"What'd you do to her?"

Thank God I was already stopped or I would've slammed on my brakes. "What did I do to her? I'm not the one who had her crying!"

"I know that, Chase! I feel like shit enough as is; but you have her. Why do you have her?"

Had her. *Had.* And I pushed her away. Again. "Don't blame me for being there to pick her up when you broke her heart. She's in her dorm room, by the way; you're welcome for getting her there safe."

"Damn it"—I heard his keys through the phone and knew he must be getting ready to go over there—"Chase, I didn't do anything, I swear—"

"I know."

"You have no idea what Harper means to me."

My stomach tightened, and I ground my teeth together as I pulled the phone away from my ear. When I was sure I wouldn't snap at him, I brought it back, "I'm pretty sure I have an idea. I gotta get in to work. Talk to you later."

"Thank you."

The sincerity in those two words didn't help the jealous knot in my stomach one bit. "Uh-huh, see ya." I hung up, tossed my phone on the passenger seat, and rested my head against the steering wheel. *What the hell is wrong with me?*

"CHASE! WHERE WERE you this morning?"

I looked up from waxing my board to see all the guys from the house and one of Bree's booty calls making their way toward me, "Stayed at my parents' last night."

Six boards dropped near me, and Derek snatched the wax from my hand before going over to his own board. "Thought we were going to be short you and Brandon. If it weren't for Harper finally kicking him out of their bed, I don't think he would have come with us."

Their bed? If she's moving in, I'm kicking him out. Okay, maybe not, but still. I'd had more than enough time of bitching to Brian and my parents about what had happened last night to know I'd made the wrong move by helping them out. I ground my jaw and searched until I found another piece of wax to finish up.

"She that good that you can't even leave the bed to go surfing?" Drew snickered, and Brandon and I both froze. "Bet that whole virgin thing was just a play; girls like that are freaks in—"

"Swear to God, you talk about my girl like that one more time, and you won't be talking anymore, got it?"

I wanted to be happy Brandon was defending her rather than talking about her in a way I know Drew was searching for, but the fact that Brandon was defending her instead of me just made my already pissed-off mood explode. "That little body sure does feel good in my arms though."

Brandon sat back on his heels and turned to look at me. "The hell did you just say?"

I smirked and went back to waxing my board. "Having her run back to me and fall into my arms last night was just what I needed. I'd missed being able to hold her."

His hands fisted on his legs, and I tried to contain my smirk from going into a full-blown smile. "I don't know what your deal is, but I'm tired of this bullshit with you, and I know you're lying, so just give it up."

"Chase," Brad hissed, and when I looked back at him, he was shaking his head. "Stop."

"You can think I'm lying all you want"—I glanced back over to a red-faced Brandon—"you know I'm the one that had her since I called to tell you where she was. Just think about all the time in between when I got her and when I called you. Don't believe me? Go ahead and ask *my* princess what we were doing before I called you last night."

I'd barely gotten the last word out before Brandon was knocking me over and holding me down in the sand with one hand against my throat, the other fisted in the air, "Let's get this straight right now. You didn't want her, I made sure of that before I pursued anything with her. Now she's mine, and I don't care that it's been a week since I met her. I'm telling you I am *never* letting that girl go. Don't talk about her, don't go near her, and don't push me because I swear, brother, I am five seconds from ripping into you even though I know you're full of shit."

I couldn't swallow or speak, and he knew it, so when he felt I had gotten the message, he let up and started to sit back up; too bad I wasn't ready for this little heart-to-heart to be over yet. "Damn, the way she moans my name, though."

"Chase!" Brad barked, and Brandon's fist connected with my temple faster than I thought possible. *Shit, that one hurt.*

Blinking back the black spots in my vision, I stopped his next punch and got him in the ribs before Derek and Zach were pulling him off me while Brad and Drew kept me on the ground.

Bree's booty call walked past us, carrying his board and shaking his head. "Thought we came out here to surf. While your little catfight is entertaining as hell, I'd rather be in the water."

Brad, Drew, and I all started laughing; I liked this kid.

"Chase, you are beyond stupid. Next time, I won't try to stop him." Brad looked up to Drew and nodded over to Brandon's group. "Get lost." When he was gone, Brad loosened his grip and let me sit up; his back was to the other guys, and he was looking past me at something while talking low. "Is it because she's a virgin?"

I shook my head.

"Because she didn't want you?"

"At first."

"And now?" I didn't respond, and he sighed. "It's just her?"

I nodded. "Everything about her."

"I hate to say this, but Brandon is right. How many

times did he ask you before he did anything about it?" I growled, and he held up his hands. "I'm just saying man, you blew it. Stop making one of your best friends miserable because you missed your chance."

Thank God Brad had stopped talking when Brandon walked past us to grab his board. Brad stood and watched Brandon walk out toward the water before offering me a hand to pull me up as well.

"Come on, let's surf. You'll both get over what just happened, and we'll all go back to the house and have a hell of a party tonight. Maybe you'll find another chick." I glared up at him, and he stood up and took a step away. "Or maybe not."

The waves were perfect that morning, and we were able to surf for hours. It was just what I needed after what had happened on the beach, and by then I had needed what happened on the beach for a week. It wasn't enough, but it would keep my head on straight for a while at least. Like Brad predicted, all bad moods were gone within the first half hour, and I tried not to let the sight of Brandon practically lying on Harper when we all came up the beach get me pissed off again. Who was I kidding? Of course it pissed me off, but I just tried to look the other way. I stuck my board in the sand and toweled off while Harper talked to someone on her phone. I watched her easy smile and thought back to kissing the corner of her mouth in the shower that night, and wished I had just kissed her then, or even before that.

Next thing I know, Harper took off running away from our group, and I couldn't figure out if I wanted to chase after her or ask Brandon what he'd done now. Before I could decide, I saw her crash into some guy and start talking to him while he kept his arms around her. *Who the fuck is this?* Brandon stood up and walked calmly over to them, but when I saw his hands curl into fists, I looked down at mine and realized I was doing the same thing. I dropped the towel on the sand near the rest of the group's and stood waiting to see what would happen. After all, I hadn't gotten as much of a fight as I'd been wanting.

I watched as they all made their way back over to us, and I couldn't help but glare at this guy I'd never seen before. I already had my best friend dating her, I didn't need whoever this son of a bitch was who couldn't take his eyes off her chest coming into the mix. Brandon must've been real pissed, because instead of standing with Harper, who was currently holding on to this new prick's arm, he came and stood directly next to me.

"Who's this clown?"

"Her best friend from back home. Carter." He sighed and crossed his arms over his chest as he continued to burn holes through him.

"Carter. Clown. Same thing."

Brandon snorted, and Harper looked at us. "And that's Chase. He's Bree's brother."

Clown held his hand out, and I didn't even bother looking down at it. I just kept my eyes on him and almost smirked when his arm dropped, and he took two steps away. *That's right, prick. Step back.* Brandon grabbed Harper and sat down on the main blanket, and I took my seat next to him so I could continue glaring. For once, I was glad Brandon was here with her. Princess kept leaning forward and touching Clown's arm, hand, or leg, and each time, Brandon pulled her right back into his chest. Did she not see the way this guy was devouring her? I sat silently while he said things about Harper he really shouldn't, and even insulted Brandon. When he tried to turn around Brandon's being one of my housemates as us being partners, I swear I almost laughed out loud at how hard he was trying to piss us off. I was trying so hard to hold back, my whole body was shaking with silent laughter, but then he said the one thing that should never be said in front of Brandon, or me, and I went rigid.

"Consider this your warning, tool, the minute you touch *my* girl, I will end you."

Oh fuck this. Brandon and I both started to stand, but my fierce princess grabbed the clown's arm and practically started dragging him away before he was able to stand and follow her. Brandon started going after them, but I put a hand on his shoulder. "Don't, let her handle it."

We watched as she clearly ripped into him, and I couldn't help but smile. She really was something else. Brandon laughed, and whispered softly, "That's my girl."

Right. His. Because I'd messed up, like Brad said. With a heavy sigh, I turned and went back to sit on the blanket and attempted to ignore Harper, Clown, and Brandon for the rest of the afternoon. I wanted to punch Brandon in the face when he invited him over to the party that night. But hell, I'd be at work, and, anyone was invited. So I gritted my teeth and kept quiet until I finally left.

"MOM, DAD—I'M HERE, so stop having sex."

"That was earlier." Mom laughed as she leaned around the kitchen to look past the bar.

"Ugh, Ma, seriously? I was joking, I don't wanna know about that."

"Well! You asked for it."

I gagged and took a seat at the bar. "So what's on the agenda for today?"

"Just hanging out." She shrugged. "How are you? You sure have been spending a lot of nights here, which is weird and all because you know, I could have sworn you had your own house."

"If you don't want me here, I won't—"

"Oh hush, Chase, you know we want you here. But it's odd, don't you think? You have this massive house, and yet you're sleeping here most nights? What's going on, baby boy?"

I bit on the inside of my cheek and drummed impatiently on the marble countertop. "Well, uh . . . Harper?"

Mom's eyes got wide, but she stayed silent, even holding up a finger when my dad walked in so he wouldn't speak.

"She's dating Brandon."

"Huh, well good for her. Brandon's such a darling boy; he'll be good to her."

My hands stopped drumming, and I held them out, "What? No. I mean—yeah, he will. But that's not a good thing!"

"You know what else I could've sworn?" she asked as

she grabbed some cups from the cupboard. "You saying she was just another girl."

"Because she— well now . . . the point is, she's not."

Mom squealed and clapped after putting the cups down, "I knew it! So why didn't you do anything about it?"

"I don't know. Because I'm an idiot? I thought she'd be better off without me, I still do, but I basically handed her over to him. And now they're together, and I'm kicking myself every day. I swear if I have to watch them walk into his bedroom one more time, I'm going to throw him out."

"No you won't."

"I know I won't, but I want to."

"So fight for her." Dad shrugged. "You're never going to get her if she doesn't know you want her."

"It's useless; she thinks I just want to get her out of my system."

"Well maybe if you just—"

"Mom, I already told her. I told her I knew I'd never meet another girl like her, and at the same time I told her she needed to find someone who deserved her, and that it wasn't me. I'm telling you, I already screwed myself over with her."

"That's it then? You just give up?" Dad asked.

"No, I don't know what I'm gonna do; I just know that I want her."

"Want who?" Bree asked, and I turned to see her and my princess, who looked slightly uncomfortable and whose cheeks were turning red as she looked at me.

That girl, right there. I want her. More than anything. "More like a what, I'm starving, and Mom wasn't going to make breakfast until you got here. 'Bout time you showed up."

"Oh, Harper, honey! It's so good to have you back here!" Mom rounded the corner and pulled her into a big hug. Harper's arms hung limp at her sides for a few seconds before awkwardly going around Mom's waist.

"I hope it's okay that I'm here. Bree said it's family day, so I wasn't going to come, but she didn't really give me an option."

Thank God for that.

"Of course it's okay! You're always welcome, especially on family day." Mom winked at me, and I rolled my eyes. "Bree, honey, I need your help in the kitchen though . . . alone."

Wow, Mom. Subtle. Harper looked worried, and I wanted to tell my mom she'd just made it worse rather than helping like she'd thought. But then Harper came to stand right next to me, and I couldn't be annoyed with Mom anymore.

"Chase, maybe I shouldn't be here."

"Trust me, she wants you here. Her pulling Bree in there has nothing to do with Bree's bringing you, I promise."

She worried her bottom lip and shifted her weight a few times before looking up at me from under those impossibly long lashes, "Is it okay with you that I'm here?"

I hopped off the barstool and pulled her close to me, and she swayed into my chest. "It's more than okay, Princess." I leaned down to whisper in her ear and felt her shiver against me. "I'll always want you here with me."

Harper inhaled sharply, and her hands flew up to my stomach to push me back, but I held her close. "Chase, please. I need you"—her head dropped so that her forehead was resting against my chest to look at her hands, which were now curling against my abs—"um, I need you to uh, please . . . just let go of me."

"One day, Princess,"—*please God let me be right about this*—"one day." I released her and sat back on the barstool. She took a few calming breaths and gave me one more glance before sitting on a barstool two down from me.

The rest of the day passed way too quickly. Harper became comfortable with my parents before breakfast was finished being made, and not long after she was done trying to avoid looking at me and staying away. By the time breakfast was over, she wasn't leaving my side, and I definitely wasn't complaining. We had a lazy day of just sitting around watching TV, and I couldn't hold back my perpetual smile when she sat down on the couch with me, or an hour later, when she started to stretch out and I pulled her feet into my lap and she didn't move them back. Instead, she just nudged my stomach with her foot and gave me a small smile before looking back at the TV. To me, this was perfect, and I never wanted it to end.

BRANDON SHUFFLED INTO the kitchen the next morning, and I smiled to myself, knowing that Harper was alone in her bed in the dorm.

"Morning."

He grunted and grabbed a coffee mug, "Whoever made 8:00 A.M. classes on Monday was seriously disturbed."

My brow furrowed, and I looked back at the microwave clock. "Bro, hate to break it to ya, but it's almost eleven."

"I know, I just got back from it. Doesn't mean I'm actually awake yet."

"Nice. Guess it's a good thing Harper wasn't here to keep you up all night then."

"I'm not gonna talk to you about her." He sighed and finished pouring the coffee.

"Don't need you to now that I'll have her all to myself on Sundays. Yesterday was . . . perfect." Okay, yeah, I was laying it on thick. The day really had been perfect, but not like I was making it out to be.

"Chase, I'm serious brother, don't—"

"You really should see the way she lets go when you're gone."

He put the coffee mug down hard enough that some of the liquid sloshed over the side, and he gripped the edge of the counter, "What is your deal? What do you gain from pissing me off?"

"Other than Princess underneath me when you're not around? Not a damn thing."

"You son of a bitch! If you ever touch her, I will kill you. Do you get me?"

"Little late for that one." I watched as he tried to control his anger. "Does she moan that loud when she's with you, too?"

"Are you serious right now?" he roared, and slammed a fist down on the counter.

I shrugged and began walking out of the kitchen. "I'll take that as a no." He was breathing heavily and obviously trying to talk himself out of this fight, but I needed it. *I still hate that he has her, and I need the reminder that I never will.* "Looks like you're underperforming, brother. Better step your game up before she stays in my bed for good. 'Cause those moans and little noises she makes? God . . . sweetest fuckin' thing you've ever heard."

Brandon was already rounding the island before I'd finished with the last sentence, but this time I was ready for him. He was a skilled fighter, yeah. But this wasn't the ring he was used to, this was over a girl I knew he had fallen in love with just as much as I had; so he wasn't thinking strategy. He just wanted to hit something. And that's exactly what I'd been hoping for. He grabbed the collar of my shirt and slammed me up against the wall. I'd been expecting a blow to the head, but he smashed his fist against the wall near my head instead.

"I will end you if you touch her! Stay the hell away, Chase!"

I waited until he took a step back before landing one on his jaw. Payback. "Sorry, no can do."

He slowly looked back up at me, worked his jaw a couple times, and spit blood in my face. "You can, and you will. She's mine. I'm not doing this with you; you're like a brother to me." Brandon took a step back and shook his head before turning toward his hallway.

"No wonder she comes running for my bed. Obviously, you can't finish what you start."

He froze midstep and stayed like that for a couple seconds before turning and charging at me. He plowed into me, and I felt like all the air was knocked out of me from having him land on top of me. Before I could take a deep enough breath, he rolled off and punched me hard in the stomach.

"Stay. Away. From Harper!"

"Not my fault—" I wheezed and tried to take a deep breath—"you can't make her—scream your name."

Just as Brandon leaned back to deliver another punch, arms were around him and pulling him back. He turned and kicked my side as Derek and Drew pulled him away. "We are done! You hear me?"

I struggled up and winced at the pain in my stomach. *God, these guys really need to quit stopping the fights.* Brandon ripped his arms from the guys and scrambled up quickly before Zach was there, helping the first two keep him back, and Brad was in my face, pushing me toward my hall.

"You're such an ass, Chase. Why can't you just leave him alone?"

"Because he's with my entire world."

Chapter Six

"WHAT ARE YOU working on today?" Princess leaned over the back of the couch to look at my sketchpad.

I flipped it onto my stomach so the drawings were covered and turned to smile at her; her face was so close to mine, I could smell the mint from her gum, and it took everything in me not to lean in and taste her.

"Hey now! That's not nice. Is this one top secret?"

"Maybe, or maybe I just don't want you looking at my drawings." Not true, the way her face had lit up as she spent time going over every single one of my pieces from the sketchbooks I had at my parents' had made me fall in love with her that much more.

How she hadn't figured out I was a tattoo artist yet made me laugh at the time, but I was glad I got to see her reaction, glad that she was fascinated rather than disgusted. I wasn't bringing in money like Brandon, and while I loved what I did, I know some people looked down on it. Instead, the biggest smile I've ever seen crossed her face, and her stormy eyes got even wider when I brought down the sketchpads, and she'd spent hours going through them.

"Seriously? Rude." Her fingers came up to just behind my collarbone, and I swiftly moved from under her hands and knelt on the couch so I was facing her and pressing her hands down into the cushion.

"Now *that's* not nice. Your pressure-point training isn't fair."

"It's perfectly fair! It's the only way I can win at anything around you guys! All any of you have to do is pick me up, and it's over."

I raised an eyebrow at her seconds before I let go of her hands, grabbed her waist, and hauled her over the couch. She gasped, and I could tell she was getting ready to let me have it. Those hands of hers went up to hit another point I'm sure, but I let my body stretch out on top of hers, and her mouth snapped shut, her hands stilled on my chest. I leaned in close to whisper not even an inch above her lips. "Good girl. Now, if you're done trying to hurt me, I'm gonna go back to what I'm working on."

She nodded, and I sat up and prayed she didn't notice my hard-on. I picked the sketchpad up off the floor and got comfortable. Harper stood up, but I grabbed her hand and brought her ass right back next to mine, keeping my eyes fixed on the pad of paper on my lap.

"I said I was going back to what I was working on, not that I was ready for you to leave my side."

"Chase, I'm just going to—"

"Sit here with me."

Even though I was still grabbing one of her hands, the other came up to our joined hands, and she started nervously playing with her fingers. "So it's okay if I watch you?"

I finally looked up into her wide gray eyes, and said softly, " 'Okay' is an understatement. Please don't leave."

Her only response was to remove her hand from mine, bring her legs up onto the couch, and rest her chin on her knees as her gaze went to the pad of paper. They widened even more, and her face lit up. God, I seriously loved her reactions to my work.

Bree walked in as soon as I started back drawing, and I was glad she hadn't come in while I was lying on top of Harper. I could only imagine how that would have gone over. "We're having a movie day since it's all stormy outside. Any requests?"

Princess shook her head as she studied the latest piece, and I smiled. "Whatever you pick is fine, I'll be working."

Mom and Dad walked in with bowls of popcorn, and the three of them went about deciding what to watch first. Harper's eyes never left the paper; I'd have to draw something for her one of these days.

Harper fell asleep just minutes into the second movie, and I knew I should get down on the floor so she could lie down, but having her right next to me for the last couple hours had been more than perfect, and I only got her for one day out of the week; I wasn't about to give that up. I grabbed the pillow next to me and put it on my left leg before gently pulling her down. She went easily and immediately curled up against me. Her arms and legs were covered in goose bumps, so I took the blanket off the back of the couch and draped it over her. She grabbed at it subconsciously and pulled it tighter around her before stretching out and drifting back off. She looked so beautiful when she slept, and I wished I hadn't wasted time that first night with her, I wish I had woken up so I could watch her just like this. I could spend every early morning for the rest of my life watching her sleep, and it still wouldn't be enough.

One of her hands came out from under the blanket to grip the pillow, and the blanket slid down to just under her perfect breasts. I almost covered her back up since I knew she'd been cold, but I let my gaze travel up her throat to her face; her mouth was barely open, those incredibly long eyelashes I loved were resting against her cheeks, and her long hair was falling wildly around her face, shoulders, and chest. I knew I'd never forget this moment, but I never wanted to forget exactly how she looked that very second. I flipped the page on my sketchpad and took a deep breath before starting to replicate everything that was my princess. I just hoped she didn't wake up and freak out about this.

The movie was almost over by the time I was finishing and a loud explosion caused Harper to jerk awake.

"It's just the movie," I said low to reassure her, and let my fingers trail across her cheek. "Don't move yet, Princess."

"Don't move? Why?"

"I'm almost done; give me another minute or two."

She stilled but thankfully didn't ask any more questions. I finished up the drawing and slid out from under the pillow to kneel on the ground in front of her. Her breath caught and her eyes heated and I couldn't help but look down to that perfect lip that I'd just spent time re-creating. I wanted to kiss her so freakin' bad; this beautiful girl had no idea what she did to me. It was no longer a matter of just wanting to kiss her, I needed to kiss her, needed to know exactly how those lips would feel against mine.

"Why couldn't I move?"

Her words broke through, and I stopped my advance on her, "Oh, um. Well . . . here. Just don't freak out, okay? I wasn't trying to be creepy."

"You're not supposed to tell someone not to freak out—those words alone cause them to freak out."

"Okay, well then don't hit me or use your pressure-point training on me again." I took a deep breath and held the sketchpad in front of her and watched as her cheeks went bright red, and her mouth popped open. "Shit"—I took it away and wondered how I could have thought it would be a good idea to show her that—"I knew it was creepy."

"Chase, that wasn't creepy. Can I see it again?"

Um. Hell. No.

Her wide eyes held mine and pleaded with me. "Please."

Okay, now that look definitely wasn't fair. I would give her anything she asked for if she looked at me like that. I gave her the paper and tried to smile, but I was still freaking out over being a freakin' creep and drawing her while she slept. "I'm sorry, but you looked too perfect. I couldn't let that opportunity pass."

Her cheeks went red again, but I forced myself not to take it away as she spent minutes that felt like hours going over the drawing. "Chase, it"—she cleared her throat and shook her head slightly—"it's incredible."

"Yeah?" I wasn't sure if she was saying that to make me feel better, but the way she looked up at me and smiled the sweetest smile I've ever seen come from her pushed the last of the worries aside.

"Yeah."

Her eyes bounced back and forth between mine, and like she suddenly realized how close we were, they went down to my mouth, and I heard her next intake of breath. When she looked back up into my eyes, I could see the indecision in hers and wanted to beg her to choose me. I don't know who started leaning toward the other first, but just then a string of explosions sounded from the TV, and we both jerked away from each other. I looked back up at the TV, then over to my parents and Bree; I'd completely forgotten where we were and who we were with. My mom was smiling widely and trying to keep her eyes off us, and I exhaled loudly as I looked back over at my princess.

"I um, I have to . . . I'm gonna go get some water."

I shook my head and pushed her back onto the couch. "I'll get it, Princess, just stay there." By the time I got back into the living room, she was on the large chair with Bree, and I wondered if I'd just hurt any chance with her again. "I gotta go in to work; see you guys later." Handing the glass to Harper, I squeezed Bree's shoulder, then went to kiss Mom on the cheek.

"Chase, don't leave; everything will be okay," she whispered softly.

"I can't be around her right now, Mom. See you later."

I drove home to waste time before going in to the shop and regretted it as soon as I walked in. All the guys were sitting around the couches eating and watching the game; Drew was the first to speak up.

"Holy shit. I think I'm starting to forget what you look like."

"Funny. Who's winning?"

"Oh man, Chase!" Zach said, and held a fist up while he tried to swallow whatever he was eating. "You missed a *hilarious* party on Friday. You know that Carter kid? Princess's friend?"

I already didn't want to hear this story. I hated that clown.

"Get this. Homeboy takes Princess outside and kisses her right in front of *all* of us, starts declaring his love for her and goes to kiss her again when Brandon and Derek stepped in and took care of it. He freaked when Brandon wouldn't fight him and got all loud and pissy; Brad ended the entire party because of it."

"Good." I huffed and glanced at Brandon like he was insane. "He kissed her, and you didn't do *anything*?"

He started to speak, but Derek interrupted. "He handled it how he should have, and apparently it worked for Princess, too. I heard her moaning the next morning."

My body went rigid, and Brandon tensed as he glared

at Derek. "Shut the hell up; you know not to talk about her like that."

Derek held his hands up and smiled. "Just sayin', she sounded more than happy with whatever you two were doing."

"Shut up, man; you can talk about your girl all you want, but leave mine and what we do out of it."

My hands curled into fists, and Brad stepped right in front of me and started pushing me out of the living room, talking quietly, "Don't, Chase. We're not going through this shit again. Just leave it alone. They're dating, so it shouldn't be shocking to you. You've got to start being okay with this."

She was a fucking virgin, and he took that from her. I didn't have to be okay with anything! I wanted to go back in there and beat the shit out of him more than anything, but with all of them standing around, I wouldn't have even gotten one hit in. I thought about the time I'd just spent with her, and everything I'd just found out. Clown's kissing her Friday, she's screwing my best friend on Saturday, and leaning in to kiss me today? She's gonna make me feel like shit for the few girls she'd seen me with and tell me she'd just be another girl for me? Look in a fucking mirror, Princess. Because, obviously, I'm just one of many guys for you.

"CHASE!"

I groaned and hated the fact that despite all I'd found out about her, all I wanted was to take her in my arms.

"What, you're just not going to talk to me now?"

I kept walking down the hall and only stopped after she planted herself right in front of me, hands on her hips.

"Why are you being like this?"

Really? She really wanted to know why I was being like that?

"Did I do something to offend you? You haven't said a word to me since Sunday. You have been so bipolar lately, I don't even know what to expect from you."

I raised an eyebrow at her; she didn't know what to expect from me? At least I was completely honest. Well, maybe not, but at least I wasn't going around acting like some innocent virgin when I was really screwing everyone.

Harper's cheeks turned red suddenly, and now I had no idea what we were even talking about. Wasn't she just mad at me? What was the embarrassment for? She blinked her eyes rapidly a few times and narrowed her eyes at me. I almost laughed. My fierce little princess was back.

"Whatever. I'm done trying to figure you out. If you want to be an asshole, go right ahead. But don't keep acting like there's nothing wrong between us on Sundays."

Oh my God, really? This wasn't about me being an asshole, it was about the way I thought she was acting with every other guy! "We're back to this now?"

"It's a freaking miracle. He speaks."

"You think I'm confusing? God, Harper, that's rich. This coming from the girl who repeatedly told me to stay away, but fell into my arms at the first sign of trouble with her boyfriend? Do you want me to back off, or don't you?"

I took a step toward her, and another when she stepped back. I leaned in close and whispered softly in her ear, the way I did when I wanted her to sway toward me; and I wasn't disappointed this time either. "Why keep fighting the inevitable, baby? You want me. Even now, your body is shaking because you're trying to keep yourself from touching me." I brushed my fingers across her hand and watched her arms instantly get covered in goose bumps. "One touch from me, and you're covered in goose bumps. Tell me now that you want me to go away."

"You're such an ass. I just don't understand why we can't be friends all the time. I don't want to be your friend on Sunday and the girl you don't acknowledge every other day of the week. I want the same thing every day. So you decide what that is and let me know."

She tried to move past me, but I slammed my palm against the wall, blocking her from leaving the hallway. "I'll tell you, if you tell me."

"Tell you what?"

"I feel like I'm just one in a group of Harper's many guys, but I'm not getting the benefits. So tell me, if I act like your friend, will I get to fuck you, too?"

One second I was trying not to laugh from the thought of her actually getting a punch in, the next my back was slammed against the wall, and Brandon was directly in my face, his forearm pressed against my throat.

"What the hell did you just say to her?" His face was getting red, and he shoved into me harder. Once again, I couldn't speak, so I spit in his face.

The pressure was gone from my throat, but before I

could breathe deep enough, his fist went into my stomach; I swung my right arm, but the dumb-ass moved directly into the path of my left hook, like he always did.

"Oh my God, stop!" Harper's worried voice was probably the only thing that could break through at a time like this, but the confrontation was long overdue.

Brandon's leg came up, but before he could plant it in my stomach, I swiped his other leg out from under him. I only got in one more hit that wasn't blocked before Brandon's fist met my jaw, and my mouth filled with blood. I spit it onto his face and pulled my arm back, but was grabbed from behind before I could follow through with the crack to his temple. My arms were suddenly pinned behind my back, and I was pulled off Brandon at the same time Derek used his body weight to keep Brandon from getting up.

I struggled against Brad and Zach as they walked me to the other side of the living room. "Calm the fuck down, Chase. Seriously, I am so sick of this shit." Brad huffed and pulled me back another few feet until the three of us were in the master bedroom. "You have got to cut this shit out! He didn't do anything to you, and you're ruining your friendship with him over a girl who doesn't want you."

"Like hell she doesn't; you don't see her when she's with me."

"Whoa, wait." Zach blurted out, his eyes wide. "What?"

Brad pushed him out of the room before slamming the door shut. "I don't care if this is your house, Chase, you're done with this. Leave Harper and Brandon alone. They're good together, and you know that."

"No, I don't fucking know that! She was a virgin, and not even a month and a half into their relationship, she's not? He's supposed to take care of her and he's not!" I opened the door to leave, and he planted both hands on it and slammed it again.

"Like you wouldn't do the same given a chance with her? I doubt you two would have even lasted this long, and you probably wouldn't be half as decent about it! Brandon doesn't let any of the guys talk about her like that, and he never talks about what they do. Whether they're screwing or not is between them, and he's keeping it that way. You should at least be thankful for that. He's not making her out to be some whore; he's protecting her still despite what they're doing! You're the king of talking about all your conquests. I can't see you being tight-lipped about someone like Harper."

I shoved him away from the door and pointed in his face. "You don't know *anything* about her or what she is to me. You got that? I'm not giving up until she's mine."

"You're ruining any chance with her by trying to fight her boyfriend almost every day!"

I heard Brandon, Derek, and Drew all yelling from the other side of the house and flung the door open, stomped down the hall, and pushed against Zach when he tried to stop me from getting out in the living room. Derek and Drew were doing the same with Brandon, and he looked pissed. *Good.*

"So, I heard you know now!" I called over to Brandon. "She feels real good underneath you, doesn't she, *brother*."

Zach and Brad started yelling at me to shut up while Brandon was saying he was going to kill me, and Derek and Drew were yelling at him to calm down. He tried to charge again, and the guys took that as their opportunity to force him back down the hall and to his room.

"Go!" Brad shoved me toward the front door. "Get out of here until you calm down!"

Leave, or sit here and listen to them screw each other? Yeah, no thanks. "Gladly."

I wasn't scheduled, but I went to the shop anyway and told Brian the whole thing. He was siding with Brad. Bastard.

"Chase, bro, you've got to fight for her, but fight smart. You're taking a step forward with her every Sunday, but then you do shit like this and take two steps back."

"I just can't stand the thought of them being together, it—God it just pisses me off all over again thinking about it."

My phone rang, and I answered without looking, "Yeah?"

"Chase!" Bree screeched. "What the hell did you do to her?!"

I sighed deeply and leaned against the counter at Brian's station. "I didn't do anything to *her*." *Brandon, on the other hand. . .*

"Brandon just showed up here at the dorm, looking for Harper. She's not here, and obviously she's not with him, and he was ranting about you when he left. So what. Did. You. Do to her?"

"Shit, she was at the house with Brandon when I left! Where would she go, Bree?"

"I don't know, Chase! What did you do to her?"

I ran out of the tattoo parlor and shoved my keys into the ignition of my truck. "I didn't do anything to her, I did—shit, I said something to her."

"What did you say?"

"I was being an ass, she was mad because I was ignoring her, and I said something about the fact that she has a list of guys, and I'm just one of them, but I'm not getting the benefits of fucking her, too."

Bree gasped and relayed everything to someone she was with, "Chase Grayson! You are such an asshole! Why would you even say something like that to her? You know she's a virgin! No wonder she left! You embarrassed her *again*!"

I huffed a laugh, "Virgin. Right."

"What is that supposed to mean?"

"Was, is more like it. I heard all about her and her friend from back home, and how she's screwing Brandon."

"I don't care what you heard, you're wrong! She doesn't even like Carter! He kept trying to kiss her, and she was pushing him away and telling him to stop! And she's not having sex with Brandon, you dumb-ass! She and I talk about everything, so I know exactly what they are and aren't doing, and I can assure you she is *not* having sex with him! You are such an asshole, I can't believe I'm related to you. Find her and make this better!"

"What do you mean she's not having sex with Brandon?"

"I mean exactly what I said. What does it matter to you?"

I pulled the phone away from my ear and cursed loudly. "Bree, if he finds her, let me know. I have to go." I ended the call and dropped it into one of the cup holders. "Son of a bitch!"

"Harper." I breathed and bit back a groan when those gray eyes flashed their hurt before she could turn to walk the other way.

I'd already gone back to my place by the time Brandon called Derek to see where he'd taken her Thursday night, so I knew she was safe, just like I knew she had spent an entire weekend in a hotel room with Brandon. But I wasn't going to keep assuming anything about her. She'd spent entire weekends with Brandon in his room, and according to Bree, she was still a virgin. So I was praying a hotel room didn't change that. Bree called out Harper's name, and I knew I only had a few minutes before she would be gone for most the day. I grabbed her hand and pulled her to a stop.

"Princess, stop walking and just talk to me."

"Why? So you can let me know again how much of a slut you think I am?"

"I don't." God, could I have been more of a dick to her? "I don't think you're a slut. You just caught me on a bad day."

"Let me guess, Chase; you hurt me because you were just so damn mad . . . am I right?"

Her bruises flashed through my mind when she threw that line back at me, and I felt sick. I backed her into the wall and brushed the hair that had fallen in her face back so I could look at her stormy eyes. "This is why I told you I would never be good enough for you, all I do is hurt you, Princess."

"This isn't about your being or not being good enough for me. I just want to be your friend, and you're making that impossible."

"Friend." That one word hurt so much, I could barely make it out to be more than a whisper. Could she not see that I needed all of her or none of her? Because being friends with her just left me with the hope that I could change that, and I was aware that, for her sake, I never could. Her eyes did that pleading thing again, and I knew I was gone. *Anything for that look. Always.* I grabbed a fistful of hair in exasperation and spoke on a rough exhale. "Okay, fine, we're friends. But I need you to stop approaching me around my house and at school."

She recoiled like I'd slapped her. "What? Then that puts us exactly where we've been the last three weeks; that doesn't change anything."

"It needs to be that way." I turned away as I tried to force myself to say something to make her run. *Let her go man, just let her go.* The ache that instantly speared my chest halted my thoughts, and I turned to face my world again. "Sundays are the only day I get you. Those are the only days when you're here with me." She started to speak, but I stopped her, "No, I know you're not here *for* me . . . but you're here. And he's not; I need these days with you, Harper. But every other day, you're his, and it's not a good idea for us to be around each other then. So stay away. Please."

"Chase . . ."

"If you think acting like you don't exist isn't the hardest thing I've ever done, you're wrong. I hate not talking to you, I hate not bickering like we're an old married couple, and I hate not spending every day right next to you. But this is how it has to be. Brandon hates me, and, Princess, trust me when I say he has every reason to. So if after everything I've done to you, you'll still even consider being my friend, then it has to be Sundays only."

"Brandon won't care if we're friends."

Ah, Princess, you are sassy and sweet as hell, but you aren't dumb. "I know you're not that naïve." Mom and Bree walked out the front door, and I sighed, knowing the majority of my only day with her would be spent *without* her. "Now go have lunch with Mom and Bree, then get your ass back here so I can have my few stolen hours with you."

"Chase?" she asked after walking a few feet toward the entryway, her back still to me.

"Yeah, Princess?"

She took a deep breath and looked over her shoulder, capturing my eyes with hers. "Will you please stop hurting me . . . in every way?"

Fuck. I can spend the rest of my life making up for everything I've done to her, and I still won't forgive myself for the shit I've put her through. I walked quickly up to her and pulled her into a tight hug, trying to memorize the way she felt in my arms. I inhaled her vanilla scent and wished I could promise her that I would never do anything to hurt her again, but we both knew that would be a promise I could never keep, "Go eat, sweetheart." I squeezed her tight before releasing her and turning to walk up the stairs.

Chapter Seven

"HI, HONEY! I wasn't expecting to see you tonight. Aren't your friends having a party?"

"Uh, yeah? Why wouldn't you be expecting me? It's New Year's Eve."

Mom's eyes went wide, and she gave Dad a quick glance, "Well, you haven't been around much. We only saw you for about an hour on Christmas . . ." She trailed off and looked at me for an excuse.

I didn't have one; well, I did, but I didn't feel like sharing with them. Brandon had taken my princess to Arizona for the first half of winter break. He'd taken her *home*. I knew he loved her, and I knew they were serious. But I wasn't ready for them to be this serious. I'd spent every free moment surfing or at the tattoo parlor these last two weeks, so I could try to do anything *but* think of Harper. And as soon as Mom started crying on Christmas because Harper's presents were still under the tree,

I was gone. I already had to deal with the fact that they were gone and falling more in love with each other, and I didn't need my family reminding me of that. But she was coming home tonight, thank God, and my sister had made her promise to be here for New Year's. I'd have her for two weeks without Brandon, and I couldn't wait.

Looking back up, I noticed that Mom and Dad were still waiting. I shrugged. "I've been busy, but I'm not anymore."

They hugged some more people who walked in, and I did the polite *hellos,* but I didn't care about everyone showing up tonight, just one.

"Are Bree and Harper back here yet?"

"I don't even know if they're coming here; I thought they were going to your house."

My house. I didn't want to spend New Year's Eve with Harper and a bunch of wasted coeds. "I'll text Harper. I don't want them going to that party tonight."

You gonna be at the house tonight?

"Chase, honey."

"Hmm?"

"You know, she and Brandon are getting really serious, do you think . . . maybe?"

I looked up to my mom and cocked my head, "Maybe what, Ma?"

"Maybe you should stop waiting for her? What you're doing to your friendship with Brandon, over a girl who's in love with someone else—it isn't worth it, honey."

My phone vibrated, and I looked down, *Princess: Nope, going to hang with the family.*

Perfect. I smiled to myself and looked back up to my parents. "When it comes to that girl, Mom, nothing else matters. So no, I don't think I should stop. Love you." I kissed her cheek and went upstairs to find Harper's present.

I grabbed the wrapped box that held the ring I'd passed walking to my truck a few weeks ago, and hoped like hell she'd accept it. Other than hearing her tell Mom and Bree about how much she loved orange lilies, this trinity symbol was the only thing I knew Harper loved. I didn't know what it meant to her, but no matter where we were, if she had something to write with, it ended up somewhere. Napkin, paper, her wrist . . . anywhere. So finding a ring that entwined into a trinity symbol on top was the perfect gift for her. Or so I hoped.

I paced my floor for what seemed like hours until I heard Harper, Bree, and my parents talking excitedly in the room next to mine. I sat down on my bed with a huff and closed my eyes as I listened to her voice. God, I'd missed that voice. I'd missed everything about her. Ever since Thanksgiving week, when I'd almost given in and kissed her, and she'd asked me not to, I hadn't even touched her, and the distance was making me crazy. These last two weeks had been the longest I'd ever gone without seeing her, and I didn't know if I'd be able to keep my distance when I finally saw her again.

As soon as I heard my family say they'd give her time to get settled in, and the door closed, I took one last deep breath and headed to Bree's room. I knocked softly as

I pushed open the door, and I swear my heart stopped when I saw Harper sitting on the floor.

"Hey, Princess."

Her eyes went wide when she looked up at me. "Chase, I didn't think you were going to be here."

Shit, I should've told her I'd be here, too. "I asked if you were coming to the house."

"Right, I just figured you meant your house."

I watched her watching me and tried to figure out if she was happy to see me or not. The room got thick, and my eyes flashed down to her chest, which was rising and falling quickly; this couldn't just be me. I wasn't dumb, I knew she was in love with Brandon—anyone in the room with the two of them knew that. But the way she reacted to me definitely wasn't the way she reacted to Brad, or Bree's boyfriend, Konrad. She bit her bottom lip softly, and a light blush covered her cheeks. God, she was beautiful. I finally noticed all the presents lying around her and remembered why I'd come in here in the first place. Pushing away from the door, I walked over to her and sat down close enough that I could feel her body heat but not so close that I was touching her.

My hand shook as I handed her the ring, and my voice was rough and low, "Merry Christmas, Harper."

I'd been holding my breath while she stared at the tiny, wrapped box, and huffed a small laugh when she finally asked, "Why?"

"Because you're my favorite, remember? When I saw it, there was no way I couldn't get it for you. Please open it."

With the way my heart was pounding against my chest, I had no doubt she could hear every beat as I watched her face when she lifted the lid of the box. She gasped, and her eyes went wide as she studied it. When she looked up at me, I was relieved to see the awe there as she shook her head, and asked, "How did you know?"

"You doodle it on everything put in front of you."

She nodded, and choked out, "Chase . . ." Her head dropped, but not before I saw the tears falling down her face. Damn it.

"Don't cry, Harper. If you don't like it, or you don't like that it's from me, I'll take it back."

"I love it; please don't take it."

Then why are you crying and breaking my heart? "Then what's wrong?" I placed two fingers under her chin and tilted her head back so I could look into her eyes and brush away her tears. My breath caught at finally touching her again, and my heart started hammering when her eyes fluttered shut for a few seconds.

"I've never had this before. Not just the presents . . . the love that your family has for me. I've never had it until now, and it's so overwhelming. I don't know what I did to deserve it, and I don't know if I show them that, too."

"You do. Trust me." I looked at her beautiful, tear-streaked face and wiped away more tears that escaped her stormy eyes. There were so many things I wanted to say to her right then. *I love you. I want you to be mine.* "You're special, Harper, it's not hard to love you." I had to leave before I said more, which would send her running from me again. Without another word, I stood up and left the room.

I went back to my room and tried to talk myself into leaving now that I'd given her the ring, but then the shower turned on, and I groaned as I flopped onto my bed. I raked my hands over my face as I tried to do anything but picture Princess in the shower, but that wasn't happening. I wanted to thank my sister for getting Harper to wear bikinis and thought of the handful of times I'd seen her at the beach or lying out by the pool at my place. Those suits didn't leave much to the imagination, and those images mixed with the running water were making my already pain- fully hard erection, throb. It'd been months since I'd been with anyone, and even before then, Harper had starred in every one of my fantasies. This one wasn't any different. I quickly undid the button and zipper on my jeans and nearly groaned again when I finally grabbed myself.

"Chase"—someone pounded on my door—"your dad said you're in here, and he needs our help bringing some stuff into the house."

You've got to be shitting me. I liked Konrad, he was good to my sister, and he fit in our family well. But I was going to knock him the fuck out for this.

"Chase, buddy," Dad's voice came from the other side of the door, "c'mon. Got a lot of ice chests and food that need to be brought in."

Well, that killed any fantasy of Harper I might have been having. I adjusted myself and fixed my pants before opening the door. "All right, let's do this."

The last load was small enough for two, so Konrad went to find Bree as my dad and I went back to finish bringing the last of it in. I'd decided leaving was my only option if I wanted to have any sort of control around Princess, but then I saw her standing there behind Bree and Konrad at one of the poker tables, and I knew I wasn't leaving anytime soon. She looked amazing, even more so than usual; a brief flash of how I'd been picturing her not ten minutes earlier went through my mind, and I fought with the idea of grabbing her and taking her to my room to actually live it. My eyes snapped up to find her watching me, and her cheeks went red as she dragged her gaze back to the poker table.

I noticed an empty seat at the table and made my way toward it, slowly taking in every inch of her on my way over. I caught a flash of silver and looked at the hand closest to me to find my ring on her finger. My chest swelled, and I couldn't stop myself from grabbing her right hand to run my thumb over the ring before dropping her hand and going to sit.

The games were passing quickly—I wasn't winning, but, thankfully, I wasn't losing much either. Splitting my time so the majority was spent watching her, and the rest was actually focusing on the hand I had, and the bets people were placing was a sure way to lose everything I'd just put down. But it was worth it just to be able to look at her for the first time in two weeks.

"I'm running to the bathroom." Konrad stood up and stretched. "Take my place, Kid, but please God don't lose any more of my money."

I'd never understood why he called Harper, "Kid," but it's not like I was one to judge when it came to giving her nicknames. I watched her sit down, and her eyes glazed over as she looked at the cards. God, she was horrible at any card game, but it was cute to watch her try.

"You better just hand over all his chips now, Princess; they won't be here by the time he gets back anyway." I smirked at her and loved the way her ever-present blush crept back up her cheeks.

Bree leaned in to whisper in her ear, and I watched closely as she and Harper spoke quietly. My smirk died when Harper's face drained of color, and a murderous glare followed by a deep ache filled her eyes. What the fuck had Bree said?

Konrad came back before we even got around to showing our cards, and I watched Harper avoid looking at me as she quickly got up and walked away from the table. What the hell? I glared at my sister as she flirted with her boyfriend. She was sitting there having a good time when she'd clearly just hurt Princess? I looked for Harper and found her talking to my parents before slowly making her way toward the kitchen.

I put my cards on the table, tossed my chips at Konrad to make up for what Bree was losing, and got up quickly. "I'm out." Harper placed five beers on the kitchen island from one of the coolers, and I just shook my head. "Nu-uh. If I'm not drinking, you're not drinking."

Her eyes darted in my direction before going back to the beers. "Well then, why don't you have one?"

"Because I don't drink anymore."

She put a hand on her hip and finally turned to face me. "Since when?"

Since when? I stopped looking around the kitchen and looked directly at her. *Has she not noticed everything I've changed for her since meeting her?* "Since I was a jackass and hurt my princess."

Her eyes went wide, and I heard her next intake of breath, "Huh . . . I didn't realize."

"You're the one that told me I should stop."

"But I didn't mean you had to, Chase. You're grown; you can do whatever you want."

"I know. Nothing good ever came from drinking, though." *And if I kept it up, I'd never get you.* Not like I had her then . . . but it would have pushed her even further away.

She blinked quickly and looked back down to the beers she'd been collecting. "Do you want to split one? Nothing will happen from half a beer, right?"

Nothing would happen from three, but there wasn't a point in starting anyway. I smiled at her and tried to mimic her voice. "I guess my little body can handle half a beer."

"You're so dumb. Help me with these, I'm hanging out at your mom's table."

We went back to their table, and I pulled up a chair right next to Harper's, so we were always in some kind of contact. I watched as she leaned in to my mom, and I thought about how perfect she would be in this family, as my wife. That thought slammed into me, and I had to lean back as I let it wash over me. Every feeling Harper had stirred up in me was beyond anything I'd ever experienced, but I'd never once thought about marriage until just then. Even so, I knew that if I could marry Harper, I would in an instant. I watched her laugh with my mom, and her eyes flashed over to catch mine for a few tense moments before going back to the table. *It's official. I'm completely gone on this girl.*

Everyone started leaving the numerous poker tables set up around the house to find a spot where they could see one of the TVs for the countdown to midnight, and I frowned when my princess got up without a word or glance in my direction and found her way toward Bree. I saw her take one look at Bree and Konrad making out with each other and laugh to herself as she shook her head. She brought her right hand up to look at the ring I'd just given her, and what happened next was what finally made up my mind. She bit down softly on her bottom lip, her cheeks barely turning pink, and smiled the sweetest smile as she looked at it before dropping her hand and glancing back to the TV. I'd just had one of those freakin' lightbulb moments when I realized I would give anything to marry her, and I still hadn't kissed her. But after watching that, I wasn't waiting any longer.

I walked up behind her, grabbed around her waist, and pulled her back into the dark hallway. She gasped but slammed her mouth shut when I turned her so her back was against the wall and her eyes looked up to meet mine. I cupped her face in my hands and allowed my thumbs to brush over her cheeks as I studied her dark eyes. Her mouth opened slightly, and even with everyone in the house counting down to midnight, I could hear her intake of breath before I finally, *finally* pressed my mouth to hers. She locked her body up for a few seconds before relaxing and wrapping her arms around my neck. When she began moving her mouth against mine, I knew I could die happy.

I let my tongue trace against that bottom lip of hers I loved so much and groaned when she opened her mouth to me. I led us roughly back to the opposite wall, let go of her face, and grabbed her hips to bring her between my legs. She went willingly, and when one of my hands pressed against the small of her back to push us closer together, she moaned into my mouth and arched her body into mine. Her hands slid down from around my neck to fist into my shirt and pull me closer, and I smiled before nipping at her bottom lip and taking her mouth again. By the time we pulled back from each other, we were both breathing hard, and I rested my forehead on hers while I tried to catch my breath.

She put a hand to her chest but didn't say anything and would no longer look at me. She was looking straight down. I needed her to look at me, I needed to know what she was thinking. That kiss hadn't been what I was hoping for when I decided to finally kiss her. It was more. It'd been hungry and passionate and like we couldn't get enough of each other. *So why won't she look at me?*

"Harper."

Her eyes snapped up, and my stomach dropped. She looked like someone had just crushed her. I'd never felt so alive, and she looked like she was on the verge of bursting into tears.

"I will think about that kiss for the rest of my life." I gently pushed her away from me and watched the pain flash through her eyes as I wondered if I'd just made the biggest mistake of all when it came to this girl. I dropped my arms, walked quickly out to my truck, and got away from that house as fast as I possibly could. If she regretted that, I knew that I wouldn't be able to handle it, so I didn't want to know.

"Chase, stop."

I froze and hung my head before turning to look at Brad. "Yeah?"

"What is going on with you lately? I'll admit it's been nice the last few weeks not having you and Brandon fighting around here all the time, but you've been snapping at everyone and avoiding all of your housemates for the last few weeks, and now when I see you . . . you just look like a zombie. What's going on?"

"Nothing."

Before I could reach for the doorknob, he put a hand on the door and spoke again. "We used to be friends, but whatever's happening with you lately has you burning all your friendships, including ours."

"I don't know what you want me to say, man. You know what's going on with me, and you're taking Brandon's side."

"No one's taking sides—you're just going about it the wrong way. You're causing unnecessary shit, and it makes it hard to be in a room with the two of you."

"Well, there you go. That's why I'm always gone."

"Do you realize how dumb all this is?" He waved a hand toward the rest of the house. "This is your fucking house, and you're never here! Look, man, I know you like her—"

"Love her." I cut Brad off, and his eyes widened.

"Uh . . . all right. I know you *love* her, but you missed your chance—for now at least. Right now, she's with Brandon, and if there's ever going to be a 'you and Harper,' then you need to stop doing what you've been doing."

"There will be," I said softly toward the front door. "I know she wants me, too."

"Well shit, I hope she does, Chase! I've never seen you care about a girl for more than a handful of minutes. You don't even look twice when Natalie comes around anymore, and she was the only lay you had more than once. I know Harper means something to you; I'm not blind! But if you're so sure she wants you, too, then don't fuck up the friend you have in Brandon to get with her."

"Brandon's in just as deep as I am, so I'm pretty sure that's not possible."

"Well, you need to figure something out. Because how it's been isn't the way to go about this."

I sighed roughly and finally turned to look at him. "Are we done here, Dr. Phil?"

Brad's head jerked back slightly, and he shook his head, "Seriously man, what the fuck has gotten into you?"

"Look, I'm sorry, I know I'm being a dick lately I just—I don't know how to explain it . . . if someone were dating Sarah, what would you do?"

"My Sarah?" When I nodded, he continued, "Beat the shit out of him and take her back."

I raised my eyebrows and continued to look at him.

"But that's different, bro. Sarah and I have been together for two years, you aren't even *with* Harper."

"I know, but if she said yes, I'd marry her today."

"Chase"—he looked at me like I was crazy—"you don't even really know her!"

"Yeah, I do, and I'll do anything to have her. You can think it's crazy all you want, but you can't act like you haven't seen what she's done to me without even trying. She hadn't even realized I'd stopped drinking for her. I haven't had or thought about another girl since the end of August, and the same with alcohol. And the funny thing is, I don't even care. I could care less that I've missed every party over the last four months. None of that matters anymore; she does. And one of these days, she'll be mine." *I hope.*

He held up his hands and took a step away, "All right, man . . . all right. Just try to be smart about it, yeah?"

I smirked and nodded as I opened the front door. "I'm taking my cues from her."

I hadn't seen or heard from Princess in almost a week since kissing her on New Year's Eve, and every day Brian made me kick myself for leaving after the kiss. He'd even had Marissa come down to the shop to lecture me about kissing her and leaving, and how I'd probably hurt her more by doing that. I wasn't sure if they were right, but I sure as hell was about to find out.

On one of the Sundays, I'd heard all the girls talking in the kitchen about flowers, and Harper had gone on about orange lilies being her favorite. I'd known I couldn't just get her some, but hearing her talk about them never left my mind, and I'd sketched up a large drawing of four orange lilies for her as a tattoo. She knew I had a tattoo for her, and I knew she wanted one, but I refused to tell her what it was unless she came to get it; and I'm pretty sure the only reason she never did was because Brandon would have stopped her. It's just such a damn shame he's still in Arizona right now. I hopped in my truck and pulled out my phone.

So . . . you ever going to come get that tattoo?
Princess: When are you free?
Seriously?
Princess: :) Make me an appointment. I'll be there
We open at four today. Come in then
Princess: Do I get to know what it is first?
You can see it when it's done. I'm warning you now, it's going to take hours.
Princess: Chase, I swear, if you put something I hate on my body . . . I'll kill you
I promise you'll love it
Princess: Don't make me regret this
See you in a couple hours Princess

Hell. Yeah.
I cranked the engine and took off for the shop to start

on the outline so I'd have everything ready by the time she got there, and was almost done when Brian came in.

"Thank the good Lord above. Chase has come to his senses and finally gotten him some ass!"

My expression deadpanned as I looked up at him.

"Or maybe not."

"You would be correct with the latter," I mumbled as I went back to the outline.

"Then what was up with the goofy grin?"

"Princess is coming in for her tattoo."

"Oh no shit? I gotta tell Riss!"

I snorted and looked back up to him. "Do you tell Marissa everything?"

Brian took a massive bite of a burrito and looked at me funny, "Uh . . . yeah."

I just shook my head and went back to the outline.

"Riss said this is huge," he said around another big bite, "and that it means she's either not that upset with you or wants to see what will happen."

"That's nice, Bri."

"And Riss wants to know if you're gonna kiss her."

I dropped the pen and looked up. "Brian, I don't know man. I didn't think she'd agree to it in the first place; I don't know if she'll even show up. Tell Marissa if she wants to be in on it so bad, she can come watch." Brian took another bite, nodded, and started tapping on his phone. "No don't *actually* tell her that! I don't want to freak Princess out! Which means you can't act like you know who she is, either. I swear, she'll probably run away screaming if she sees you smiling at her the way you do when I talk about her. She's gonna think you're a freak, Bri, so just be cool."

"I can be cool"—he shrugged—"I'll be so cool she'll be like 'man that guy's so fly,' and she'll leave your ass for me."

I choked on my gum and had to wait a couple minutes before responding. "Did you just say 'fly' in a thug voice? Shit, all you're missing is the grill, real O.G. over here." I laughed and dodged the balled-up foil from the burrito he threw at me. "And leave me for you? Please. Brian, you have massive hair, look like you haven't shaved for days, and are covered in tattoos and piercings. Like I said, she'll run away screaming."

"Psh, nah, you be trippin'."

"You are so white. Leave me alone. I want to finish this before she shows."

"You can bet your ass I'm gonna be texting Riss a play-by-play once she does!"

I just shook my head. "As long as you stay away, you can do what you want."

Thirty minutes later, I was done and sitting with Brian when my Princess walked into the shop. She was in sweats and still looked more beautiful than any other girl I'd ever seen.

"Holy shit, is that her?" Brian asked, and I nodded as I stood up. "Damn, I'm gonna need to take a stalker picture of her to send to Marissa; your girl is hot."

"You're so fucking dumb. Remember, stay invisible. You may know about her, but she doesn't have a clue about you." I walked to the front and took what felt like my first real breath in days when she smiled at me. I grabbed her hand and led her back to my station. "I can't believe you actually came."

"I know. I'm kind of freaking out."

Shit. "Then I'm not going to do it, Princess. I'll do it whenever you're ready."

Her eyes went wide, and she shook her head quickly. "No, no. I want it today, but I'm afraid it's going to hurt, and it's really hard not knowing what it is. Can you please just let me see it?"

Uh, no. That was the deal. "I'm not going to lie to you and say it won't hurt, but it's different for everyone. Some people hate outlines, some hate shading. Some people don't feel a thing, and some hate the entire process. I told you, you'll love what it is. But it's a surprise; I can't tell you."

She bit her lip and looked around for a few seconds before looking back at me. "I'm trusting you with this, Chase."

I put a hand around the back of her neck and pulled her close to me. "I know, Harper, thank you." I kissed her forehead and forced myself back to lean up against my counter so I wouldn't press my lips to hers. "Where do you want it?"

"Um . . . you said it was big, right?" I just nodded. "Can I know how big? Because the location depends on the size."

"Turn around."

"What? Why?"

I laughed when her eyes went wide again and put my

hands on her hips to turn her body away from me. "Because I already have the outline ready to go, I'm about to grab it to get the farthest points, and I don't want you to see it." I grabbed tracing paper and laid it on top of the outline, marked the points, and turned her back toward me. "This big."

"Okay, I want it here." She grabbed the paper from me and held it up on herself. "I want it to start on the far left side of my stomach and wrap around my left hip."

That's almost exactly where I had pictured it on her, too. I had to take a deep breath when I realized I was about to freely touch her, and reached for her shirt to roll it up so it would be out of the way. "Lie down on your side." Once she was on the table, I tugged the left side of her sweatpants down slightly as well, and my heart started hammering about the same time she sucked in a quick, audible breath. "I'll keep everything covered, I promise. I just need this side farther down." My voice came out deep and husky, and I tried to shake it off; I'd done tattoos in more intimate places than this on women, and it'd never affected me like this.

"Chase?"

"Hmm?"

"You said it's going to take hours?"

"Yeah, probably three. As you can see, it's big, and the shading is really detailed. That part will take the longest. This is where you need to trust me. I'm about to put the outline on, so please don't look." She squeezed her eyes shut and made the cutest scrunched-up face I'd ever seen. "If you ever need me to stop, just tell me, okay?"

" 'Kay. I'm ready, let's do this."

Once the outline was on and how I wanted it, I set up the machine and inks and put on my gloves. I turned to look at my princess, and I couldn't help but just stare at her for a few moments. God, she was perfect. I heard someone clear his throat and looked up to see Brian nodding and giving me a thumbs-up. I shook my head and flipped him off before rolling my chair over to her and squeezing her hand. "You picked the perfect spot; this is gonna look awesome."

"It better."

I smiled and started on the outline. Her body relaxed soon after I started, but when I looked over almost half-way through the outline, her hands were still clenched into fists. She was doing amazing so far, wasn't flinching or making any pained noises. But inking the girl that meant the world to me with *this* tattoo had to be a better moment for me than kissing her, and I wanted her to enjoy it, too. "You okay?"

"Yep, just pay attention to what you're doing."

I laughed. Did she really think I'd mess this up on her? I finished the outline, fixed the machine to start the shading, and went back to giving my princess her lilies. I tried to ignore the way my heart was pounding and jeans felt like they were tightening as I continued to work on her, but the way her body felt, all I could think about was ripping off my gloves and exploring every inch of her without them. It definitely didn't help when I looked up to see her biting her lip and her chest rising and fall-ing in a calculated pattern. She started moving her body slightly, like she was uncomfortable, and hell if I didn't start thinking of every way I could *make* her comfortable.

"Princess, you gotta stop moving." *For the love of God, please stop moving, or I'm taking you right here in the middle of a tattoo parlor.*

She froze and whispered an apology, and I tried to think of surfing to clear my mind and get back into my zone. Halfway through the shading, I kept hearing something that wasn't the music playing in the shop, wasn't the gun, and wasn't my phone. I looked up and tried to figure out the noise but couldn't hear it anymore. When I bent back over Harper I could hear it again and stopped the gun before I leaned closer to her and smiled to myself.

"Are you humming?" Good God she was cute.

Her eyes shot open, and she froze. "Maybe."

I barked out a laugh and took off my gloves as I went back to my counter and looked for my phone. I grabbed it, my headphones, and walked back over to her as I pulled up iTunes and handed it to her. "You're doing great; I'll be done soon." Without thinking about it, I kissed her neck softly, but thank God she only started blushing as she put the headphones on.

An hour later, I was done, and I had to admit, it looked perfect. Even better than how I'd imagined it on her. I loved watching her as she looked at my sketches, and though I was nervous as shit, I couldn't wait to see her reaction to this one. I put the gun up and took off my gloves, and when I turned around, her eyes were still closed, and she was once again moving to whatever song she was listening to. Deciding to push my luck further, I leaned my body over hers and kissed her lips quickly.

Her eyes popped open, and she pulled out the earbuds. "Am I still moving too much?"

"No, Princess, I'm all done. Are you ready to see it?"

"You have no idea!"

I huffed softly. So damn cute. "Close your eyes again, I'll let you open them when we're next to the mirror." I helped her off the table and led her over to a large mirror, positioning her so she'd be able to see it perfectly. I took one last deep breath and leaned close to whisper in her ear, "Open your eyes, Harper."

For a few tense moments she met my gaze in the mirror before letting her eyes travel down. She gasped, and my body went rigid as I watched her wide eyes and dropped jaw. She stepped away from me, and closer to the mirror, and I felt like I was holding my breath as she just stared at her left hip. Still without speaking, she turned to face me, stepped close, and ran a hand through my hair, her other hand coming up to the side of my neck.

"Please tell me what you're thinking." *Because, swear to God, I'm about to go crazy guessing.*

Without warning, she kissed me hard, and I thought I'd freakin' die. To have this, have her kiss me . . . meant everything. I deepened the kiss, and freaking Brian and Jeff started yelling for us to get a room. Harper pulled back and her face was bright red as she bit her lip to contain her smile and looked at the ground. I grabbed her hand, led her back to my table, and finished putting the ointment and wrap over her lilies. She still hadn't said anything, but I'd take that kiss as a confirmation that she liked it.

"What made you choose those?"

I looked up and smiled at her. "I heard you talking to Bree and Mom about them being your favorite. And ever since that day, all I've wanted to do was get you orange lilies, but I knew I'd probably get punched again. This was my way around it."

"It looks amazing, Chase, thank you."

Thank God.

I shrugged, but she grabbed each side of my face and pulled me down so I was less than an inch from hers.

"I'm serious. I love it, thank you."

I kissed her softly and skimmed my nose across her cheek, breathing in that soft vanilla scent that was distinctly my princess. "God, you're beautiful, Harper."

Her gray eyes were shining, and her smile widened, but just as I started to lean in, her phone rang, and we both froze for a few seconds before she reached into her pocket and pulled it out.

"Hey, babe," she answered.

You have got to be kidding me.

"Um, it's not done yet. Can I call you after?"

I held my breath and watched as her eyes got that crushed look like she'd had after I'd kissed her on New Year's Eve. Son of a bitch.

"I love you, too. Have fun tonight."

And that ended it. Right there. She couldn't kiss me

and talk to her boyfriend, telling him she loved him while I was still standing there. I stepped away from the table and tried to shake off the feeling like she'd just punched me in the stomach.

She pulled the phone away from her ear and looked up at me, "Chase—"

No, fuck no. I can't do this with you. I couldn't be a dirty secret for her. I wanted her, but I didn't want her to fucking play with me. "So you'll need to go buy some antibacterial soap to clean it."

"Please talk to me."

"I'm trying." I grabbed a piece of paper and turned back toward her, looking everywhere but at her. "Look, here are some aftercare instructions. Don't take the wrap off for at least an hour. If anything looks wrong, give me a call." Dropping the piece of paper on her stomach, I stepped away and looked over to see Brian at the front just watching us with a confused look on his face. He handed someone a binder and pointed to the back of the shop before making his way over there.

"Chase!"

I finally looked back at her and gritted my teeth as I spoke again. "I have another appointment, and he's waiting. I'll see you later."

She nodded and shook her head on an exhale. "What do I owe you?"

"Nothing. It was a gift. But I'm busy, so please go." Without another glance in her direction I turned and went to the back room to meet Brian.

"Dude, what the fuck? All looked good the last few hours, so why do you look like someone just killed your dog?"

"Brandon just called her—"

"Oh, fuck me."

"Yeah." I sighed heavily and sank down onto one of the couches we had in the back. "She dismissed him and whatever, but she called him babe told him she loved him . . . *all* while keeping one hand around my neck to keep me close to her."

"Slut."

"Shut the fuck up, Bri. I just . . . I'm not going to do this with her anymore. I want her to be mine, not a secret to be kept while Brandon's away, one that she feels guilty about after." Brian's eyebrows raised, and he just stared at me. "What?"

He shrugged as he searched for the words he wanted to use. "I guess I just didn't think she really meant that much to you. You've grown up a lot in the last few months; I know I bullshit with you a lot about the girls that come in here for you or that you used to be with, but it's awesome to see this from you. I mean, it sucks that all this has been the result of a girl who's with your best friend, but good to see you grow up, man."

I huffed and looked around, "Uh, thanks . . . I guess?"

"You know what I mean. So does this mean you're done messing with Brandon?"

"I don't know. Fighting with him keeps my head on straight that she's with him and not me. I just know I'm done pushing it with her. I thought it was worth it, just to have her for any amount of time . . . but I can't keep playing this back-and-forth with her."

"Yeah, all right." He nodded, then smirked. "I bet you don't last a month until you're chasin' her again."

"Then I'll have to make sure I'm not around her for over a month."

"That's what I thought. Gotta get back to my next guy, see you out there."

Chapter Eight

I PULLED INTO the empty driveway of my parents' house and was glad everyone was out of town for the weekend. I was doing work on Brian's leg in a couple days, and the sketchpad that had the drawing on it was here, but I'd been avoiding seeing my family and Harper since I walked away from her in the parlor a week ago.

I heard the TV seconds before I saw Harper lying on the couch. Her eyes went wide, and I froze. I was gonna kill Brad; he'd texted me almost an hour ago saying they all had left for LA, and Harper was with them.

"I thought you were going to LA?"

"No, I told Bree I was sick."

"Are you?" I took a step toward her but forced myself to stop and look over her from where I was. She looked fine, better than fine, actually.

"I'm fine, I just wanted to be alone."

I snorted. "Well, I'll be gone in a few minutes. I just

need to grab a few things. How's the uh—how's the tattoo?"

"Beautiful. Can we talk about that night?"

Uh. No. I turned and headed for the stairs, "There's nothing to talk about."

"Yes there is; you completely shut down, and you've been avoiding me ever since!"

I forced myself to keep walking even though I knew she was following me. "I'm not avoiding you; I just have nothing to say."

"Why are you treating me like this? What did I do?"

Dated my best friend, for starters. "Nothing!"

"So this is what *you* do then? You make girls feel like they're special for a few days, then treat them like they're nothing?"

Oh, hell no. I turned, and she had to stop quickly so she wouldn't run into me, "You're really gonna put this on me? One minute you're kissing me, the next you're talking to your boyfriend and telling him you love him!"

"What did you want me to do? Not answer it?"

Yeah, that's exactly what I wanted you to do. She was looking at me like I'd lost it, and I realized there was no way for her to see my side since, clearly, I meant next to nothing to her, "It doesn't even matter, Harper, so drop it."

"It does to me! I'm so tired of this roller coaster with you. I never know which Chase I'm going to meet up with that day. Is it going to be the cold Chase or the funny and caring Chase? Will it be the one who's with four girls in one night, or the one that tells me how beautiful I am, does amazingly sweet things for me, and notices stuff about me that no one else does?"

You. Are. Shitting me. She thinks I'm the bipolar one? And does she still not see how I've changed everything for her?

"You're all over the place, I don't know how to act around you, I don't know what you want!"

"I want you! All I've ever wanted is you."

"Then why are you trying to hurt me again?"

"Because it's easier that way," I answered honestly, "You're with Brandon. Do you know what it's like watching you with him? Wanting you so bad, but knowing he's who you should be with?"

"But what if I want you?"

No, no. No more games. "Harper, don't."

"I'm so in love with Brandon, but I can't help what I feel for you, and I know you know what I'm talking about. Whatever this is between us . . . it's been there since we met. It's like I can't get enough of you, but all you do is push me away. It's all you've ever done!"

"Because I'm not what you need, Harper!"

"Then why did you kiss me, Chase? You knew it would change everything, and it did. So tell me, why did you do it?"

Such a frustrating girl! Does she really want to do this now? After every back-and-forth game we've played over the last four and a half months? I closed the small distance between us as I spoke—half of me yelling to just leave, the other half wanting nothing more than to take her in my arms. "I needed to. You're all I can think about, and it drives me crazy! I would have given anything for that kiss, and I knew I wouldn't get that chance again, so I had to. I had to know if you felt something, too."

She threw out her arms and let out an exasperated huff. "Was that not obvious? Is it not obvious that I'm in love with you?"

I didn't waste time crushing my mouth to hers. I'd waited so long to hear those words come from her. She moaned, and her body melted into mine, her legs going weak. I grabbed behind her thighs and wrapped her legs around my waist as I pushed her against the wall in an attempt to get our bodies closer together. The kiss deepened, and I begged her to say it again.

"Chase," she whispered against my lips before grabbing my face to look into my eyes, "I love you."

My heart was pounding against my chest. Months of wondering and waiting, and it was finally out there. She pressed her lips firmly to mine, and I growled against her mouth, "God, Harper I love you, too, so much."

I pushed away from the wall, and keeping her legs around my waist, walked us into my room and lowered us onto my bed. Her hands left my hair and started pulling at my shirt. A soft sound of frustration sounded from the back of her throat, and I pulled away from her long enough to grab the back of the collar to pull my shirt off and throw it to the ground. Harper sat up slightly, and our mouths slammed together before I pressed her against the mattress again. Her hands ran over my bare chest and stomach, and all I could think about was everything I'd wanted to do to her while I'd been giving her the tattoo. Leaning back long enough to give me room to take her shirt off, I threw it to the floor as well and kissed her soft lips once more before making a line of kisses down to the orange lilies wrapping around her hip.

Harper sucked in a soft gasp when I gently bit down on her hip, and I smiled against her skin as I took off the skintight black workout pants she was wearing and tossed them aside as well. Add those to one more thing I didn't want her wearing around anyone but me. I made another trail up her stomach and sucked on a hardened nipple through her bra before pressing my body against hers, her legs already wrapping around my back.

"I want you."

My head fell into the crook of her neck, and I groaned—as if everything else didn't already show how much I wanted her as well, the painfully hard erection I was currently sporting was making it that much more obvious. I bit softly on her collarbone as I tried to make myself stop before this went any further. "I don't have any condoms here, Princess."

"I don't care."

I laughed. *God, this girl will be the death of me.* "Don't say stuff like that, I'm only so strong."

She grabbed at the button on my jeans, and her shaky, fumbling hands had me thinking Breanna was still right about my Princess. I grabbed her hands and pulled them away, just before she confirmed those thoughts. "Please, Chase, I don't want to wait any longer. I want you to be my first."

I leaned away from her and rested on my knees. "I can't."

Her eyes went wide with hurt. "You don't want me?"

"Of course I do!" *God, can't she see that?*

"I don't—I don't understand." Her stormy gray eyes bounced back and forth between mine for a few moments before they filled with an understanding, and her cheeks darkened. "It's because I'm a virgin."

Shit, she has this so wrong. "Not in the way you're thinking. Trust me, I want to make you mine."

She cupped my face and pulled me down to her as she whispered, "Then please."

"Princess, you can't want it to be me. With what I've done . . . I don't deserve to be given something like that."

"It's yours. I'm tired of ignoring what I feel for you and denying myself what I want."

Her eyes fell down to stare at my chest, and I watched as they slowly looked back up to mine. I waited to see if there was any indecision in them like the days before. But there was only complete trust. "You're sure, Harper?"

"I want you. All of you."

I pressed my lips softly to hers again and stretched my body on top of hers as our kisses slowed, and her shaky hands reached for the top of my jeans again. Resting on my forearms, I took my weight off her so she could undo the button and zipper and slowly push them and my boxer briefs down. I helped kick them the rest of the way off and pulled her up to reach behind her and find the clasp for her bra. Once that and her underwear were on the floor with the rest of the clothes, I took my time studying every inch of her, learning what made her moan and her eyelids flutter shut, and memorizing every noise she made when I'd suck on her breast or trail my fingers against her heat.

Her heavy breathing cut off quickly, and her body locked up when I finally pushed inside of her, and I would give anything to have taken away her pain as a short, pained cry burst from her chest. But what she was giving me meant the damn world. When her body relaxed, we began to move against each other again, our mouths finding each other's desperately, as I slowly made love to my princess. I held both of her hands in one of mine above her head on the pillow and whispered in her ear that I loved her as she came again just moments before I followed. I collapsed onto the bed, rolling so she was in my arms, and we were on our sides as our breathing calmed and we continued to kiss softly and pull each other closer.

Not more than five minutes later, Harper fell asleep wrapped up in my arms. I pulled the covers over us before pressing my lips to her forehead and vowing to love, and take care of her, forever.

THE SOFT SCENT of vanilla registered in my mind at the same moment I felt the tips of Harper's fingers trailing up my arms and over my shoulders. I cracked open my eyes to see her mess of hair covering my pillow and her shoulder, and I couldn't help but smile. Waking up to her in my arms was perfect, and though I wished I could have watched her sleep . . . watching as her stormy eyes roamed over my tattoos was just as good.

"Feels good."

Her eyes flashed up to mine, and she grinned softly before looking back down to my shoulder. "I've wanted to do this since that first night in your bed."

"Why didn't you?"

"Well, you were a little intimidating, and plus, you not so subtly let me know I wasn't the kind of girl you would ever be with."

Uh, fuck that. All I remembered was trying to scare her off and her looking at me like I disgusted her. "What did I say?"

"I don't remember exactly, you were just freaking out because you thought you'd let a girl stay over and proceeded to tell me you didn't let girls you would screw stay with you." She paused and chewed on her bottom lip for a moment before looking back up to me, and softly asking, "Speaking of . . . is it okay that I'm here?"

"I've never been happier than when I just woke up with you in my arms." I gently kissed all over her face before kissing her swollen lips. "You're the only girl I've ever fallen asleep with, and I want to keep it that way. You're not just some girl. I'm in love with you, Harper, I wouldn't want you anywhere else." *And, God, I want you here forever.*

She smiled wide and sat up to kiss me hard, catching me off guard and causing both of us to laugh before deepening the kiss. She pushed on my shoulder, and I fell to my back, keeping my hands on her naked body as she climbed on top of me and arched her body against mine. I moaned and grabbed her hips to press us closer together as she ground her hips onto me again. I was making a trail down to her breast when the loudest growl came from my princess. And that shit had nothing to do with how we were currently attacking each other. We both burst out laughing as she fell onto my chest, her hair falling in front of her face as her shoulders shook from laughter. Guess my girl was hungry.

"Is there any way you didn't hear that?"

"Not a chance." I moved the hair away from her face and kissed her hard before moving her off me and onto the bed, "I'll go make breakfast; I'll be right back."

"Okay, I'll come help."

No you won't. You just gave me you, I'm about to spoil the shit out of you. "Let me do this for you, Princess," I said softly as I pushed her back onto the pillows and kissed her jaw. "Stay here, I want to see you just like this when I get back."

She saluted me before curling up in my comforter. *Smart-ass.*

I got out of bed and started looking for our pile of clothes when I heard her gasp. I whirled around to see her stormy gray eyes even wider than usual. "What's wrong?"

"Chase"—she blinked a few times and shook her head slightly as she looked back up into my eyes—"you're beautiful."

"Beautiful, huh?" I'm pretty sure what I was staring at just then was the only thing that I'd ever seen that could be described as beautiful. I climbed back onto the bed and crawled over her, kissing her softly, and whispering against her lips, "Trying to take away my masculinity, baby?"

"So sorry," she said between kisses. "I meant. Rugged. And handsome. And so, so sexy."

I laughed and kissed her cheek before getting back off the bed. God, she was cute. I grabbed my jeans and pulled them on, looked at her staring at me while lying in *my* bed one more time, then went to make breakfast for my princess.

I hadn't even made it down the stairs when I heard her phone ringing. By the time I made it to the couch where she'd been when I came in last night, it had stopped, and I couldn't find it. Walking into the kitchen, I started the bacon and turned on the coffeepot as her phone dinged a few times. Just as I'd finished whisking together the eggs and milk to make an omelet, it began ringing again. I jogged into the living room and dug around the couch, finally finding it in the blanket.

Brandon.

I took a deep breath as I watched her lock screen come back up displaying eleven missed calls, four voice mails, and eight texts from Bree, and six missed calls, five voice mails, and ten texts from Brandon. Her phone dinged again—*and there's voice mail number six from him*. I ran back into the kitchen to take the bacon off the skillet, and, swear to God, he called again before I could finish. I wanted to delete all of them but knew I couldn't. I just didn't know what this would do to us. New Year's Eve and the tattoo parlor flashed through my mind, but I pushed those images away. Last night wouldn't have happened if she didn't want to be with me. She told me she loved me, and I had no doubt she did.

We'd just have to deal with this, and the sooner, the better.

I grabbed the phone and ran up the stairs and to my room, taking another deep breath before opening the door and praying to God that when she broke the news to Brandon, he didn't somehow suck her into staying with him. Her eyes lit up, and the sweetest smile you've ever seen crossed her face momentarily before falling when she saw whatever expression I currently had.

"You might want to answer that when he calls again." I dropped the phone next to her and tried to give her a reassuring smile, but it felt like more of a grimace as I turned around and went back out the door to finish cooking. As I was passing the entryway I felt my pocket vibrate and grabbed my phone to find five calls from Breanna, two from Brandon, and twenty-two texts from both of them begging me to check on Harper because she hadn't picked up her phone and was sick and alone. The most recent from Bree was saying everyone was going to leave LA in a couple hours. *Fucking awesome.*

When I got back upstairs with the food, Harper had the comforter over her head, and I almost wished she would put it back over when she pulled it down. That crushed look was in her eyes again, and though I knew this would be hard for her since it wasn't a secret she was in love with my best friend, that look was terrifying me. I put the plates between us and ate silently as I watched her holding a piece of bacon and staring at the covers. Almost ten minutes of her in that exact position, and I was about ready to beg her to reassure me that we would be okay. I felt like such a girl, but I had one of those ominous feelings in my gut, like this wasn't about to go my way.

I placed my hand on her back and rubbed small circles against it as I finally begged her to say something.

"Brandon will be back in a couple hours."

"Shit." I fell back against the headboard and rubbed my palms down my face, I didn't want to deal with Bree and everyone's being home; but I really didn't want to have him here yet. "I thought he wouldn't be back 'til tomorrow night."

"He got scared when I didn't answer the phone. Bree told him I was sick and alone, and since no one could get ahold of me . . ."

"Bree called me a few times, begging me to come check on you. Looks like they're all heading home today, too."

"Chase"—she turned to look at me, her eyes wide and terrified—"what should I do?"

"I can't answer that for you, Princess. No one can." Her question had the ache in my chest already starting, and God I didn't want to ask her my next question. Even though I would have told you that just thirty minutes ago I knew what the answer was, by then I was worried that I didn't. I looked at her hands, which she seemed so fascinated with all of a sudden, and forced it out. "Who do you want?"

"I don't know!" she blurted out, and looked back at me. "I want you, Chase, but I can't hurt him. I won't hurt him any more than I have. I love him too much."

My jaw dropped, and the air left my body. *What the*

hell? Does that mean . . . ? I should have known, but I—I couldn't. *What the hell am I supposed to do without her?*

"No matter who I choose, people will get hurt. And then what happens if I leave him? He lives in your house, Chase. He'll have to see us together, and it will kill him. I can't do that to him! He loves me, he hopped the first flight he could because he was scared for me and wants to come back to take care of me. How am I supposed to tell him I'm in love with someone else after that? If I left him for you, it would be bad for us. He'd come after you, the guys in the house would take sides. We would be miserable. My body craves you, Chase, but I feel like I'm being torn in two. I just—I need a few weeks to think about this. Can you please give me that?"

But I love you, too. Couldn't she see that? Couldn't she see she was crushing me? I ground my jaw to keep from saying any of that. If I wanted to win her, I couldn't force her to choose me; she needed to come to me on her own. "Are you going to ask him to give you time, too?"

"No, I can't."

The fuck did she just say? "So you're just going to go back to him? Pretend like last night never happened? You're so worried about hurting everyone else, do you even realize you'll be hurting me?" I got off the bed. "Damn it, Harper, don't you see that? I'm the one that will have to watch you with your boyfriend while waiting for you to figure out what you want!" I didn't look at her again as I walked out of the bedroom and slammed the door shut.

I stormed down the stairs and paced back and forth

in the living room before deciding to go back upstairs to just grab my shit and leave. But before I knew it, I had the phone to my ear.

"'Mmm 'lo?"

"Bri, put Marissa on the phone."

"Chase?" he grumbled. "Fuck man, do you know what time it is."

"No; put Marissa on the phone."

"Shit, are you crying?" He sounded more alert now.

"No I'm—" I rubbed my hand over my eyes and pulled it back to find them wet. "Just put her on the damn phone!"

There was shuffling before I heard Marissa's groggy voice; I knew that Brian had put me on speaker, but I couldn't bring myself to care anymore. *I'm losing the only girl I will ever love; not much else matters.* "Chach, what's wrong? Brian said you're crying?"

"I'm losing her, Riss, I'm losing Harper, and I don't know what to do. I'm five seconds from leaving again, but I need to know if I'd fuck up everything for good by doing that."

"Well, what happened?"

"I slept with her last night—"

"What?" they both yelled.

"—and now Brandon's coming back, and she wants me to give her time, but I know she's just saying that. She's going back to him, like nothing between us ever fucking happened!"

"Hold up! Rewind. You slept with her?" Marissa sounded a little more composed now, "Okay, either Brian hasn't been keeping me updated or some serious shit went down yesterday, so tell me everything." She covered the speaker, and whispered to Brian, "I'm gonna punch you in the throat if you didn't tell me this."

"Riss, he didn't know, so give him a break." I stood at the bottom of the stairs and looked up as I told them everything that led up to what happened last night and everything that happened this morning; the ache in my chest growing as I relived it all. "I can't lose her. But she basically just threw last night in my face now that her boyfriend is coming back, and once again, I'm nothing to her."

"God, Chase," Brian said, "when did you become such a fucking girl?"

"I know"—I sighed—"I freakin' feel like it."

"Screw you, babe!" Marissa shouted, and suddenly she was talking loud enough I figured I was off speaker. "Chase, she loves you. You aren't *nothing* to her, she's just confused. She doesn't know what to do. Her boyfriend is coming back, and she just admitted to his best friend that she's in love with him too *and* lost her v-card to him. She's probably freaking out. If she said she needs a few weeks, then give the girl a few weeks. But don't just leave her, Chach."

I snorted at her nickname for me. "Do you think this is all one big game to her?"

"No way. If it were, she wouldn't have a problem leaving you."

Just before I could ask how Marissa was sure she wouldn't, the worst sound in the world sounded over the running water of the shower. "Fuck."

"What? What happened?"

"I can hear her crying." I ran a hand through my hair and grabbed a fistful as I pushed off the wall. "I gotta go to her, Marissa."

"Damn straight you do! This is just as hard for her, probably harder because she's the one who has to choose."

I stumbled halfway up the steps at that. "I don't know what I'll do if she chooses him," I said honestly. "I need her."

"I know, Chach."

"Gotta go, thanks Riss." We said good-bye, and I tossed the phone on my bed, which just that morning had been a major part of my favorite moment in my life, and, I was afraid, would only ever be a memory.

I opened the door to my steam-filled bathroom, and the pained sobs that filled the room pierced my chest.

Oh, Princess.

Harper was holding herself up against the tile wall when I stepped in behind her, and I didn't know how my heart could break any more. Grabbing around her waist, I turned her toward me and pressed her close to my body as hers shook with hard sobs. The thought of losing Harper had tears falling down my face for the second time that morning—before that day, I couldn't remember the last time I'd cried. But after that night with my princess, I didn't know how I was supposed to go through life without her. I gripped her harder to me when her sobs quieted, and looked down at her puffy red eyes when her head tilted back to look up at me.

She looked at me for what felt like hours before speaking, her voice rough and scratchy from crying. "Why are you in here?"

Where else would I be? My whole world was crashing down, and I was trying to hold on to it for as long as possible. "Because you need me, and if this is my last hour with you, I'm not going to waste another second of it."

I bent to touch my lips softly to hers and was met with a hungry kiss that quickly escalated. I hadn't taken the time to get out of my jeans when I got in there, and they were soaked, but we furiously worked at getting them off, all the while bringing our mouths back to each other's and pressing our bodies closer. The hot water pelted down on us as I pushed Harper against one of the shower walls, the steam so heavy in the bathroom that there was nothing but my princess and me. Slowing down so I wouldn't ruin, or ever forget this, I pulled away to look at her. Her bottom lip was trembling, the tears still falling from her passion-filled eyes as she watched me memorize every bit of her. I cupped her cheeks, wiping away tears and water from the shower before sucking on her bottom lip and taking her mouth with mine.

Her hands went up my chest, around my neck, and into my hair as I used the wall for leverage in lifting her up, wrapping her legs around me, and positioning myself at her entrance. I groaned, and a muffled cry left her when I pushed in and began to slowly make love to her for what I prayed wasn't the last time but had a sinking feeling would be. Like I'd told her, if this was my last hour with her, my last time with her . . . there was no way I'd waste a moment of it. She climaxed, gripping the tensing muscles in my back and shoulders seconds before I followed. Not willing to end the moment, I just stood there with her in my arms, our foreheads pressed together, eyes locked on each other, and I hoped she understood that I was hers, completely and undeniably, forever. That if I had all of this to do all over again, I would change everything. And that in any life, in any situation, I'd choose her. Every time.

An hour and a half later we were sitting in my truck, outside my house, and I was gripping Harper's hand like a lifeline. We hadn't said a word since I'd told her why I was in the shower, but there wasn't anything to say that we hadn't been showing each other—that I loved her, and always would. And I had no doubt she loved me, too. It had been there in her eyes; but so had that look like someone had just crushed her heart, and I was terrified that her love for me wouldn't be enough to keep her with me. But now, I knew I had to let her go for however long she needed to make a decision that could potentially change everything.

All too soon, she reached into her purse and grabbed the keys to Brandon's Jeep, so she could go pick him up from the airport.

When she grabbed for the door handle, I said, quietly, "Harper, I will love you for the rest of my life."

She sucked in a quick breath but didn't turn to look at me, and before she hopped out of my truck and away from me, she whispered softly, "You will always be in my heart, Chase Grayson."

I felt like I was dying as I watched her start up his Jeep

and leave me sitting there. I tried to tell myself that we would figure this out, and she would come back to me. But as I turned my truck back on and headed toward the beach, I found it harder and harder to convince myself that she would be mine; and after an hour on the beach, I ended up talking myself into begging her to choose me instead.

Brandon's Jeep was outside my house by the time I'd come back, as was most everyone's, and after hearing Princess's voice coming from the kitchen, I headed toward her and the smell of Chinese food, fully intent on pulling her to my room and *showing* her why she should be with me instead. I rounded the corner into the living room and saw Brandon and Harper, Harper in nothing but one of his shirts, laughing and flirting with Brandon.

My footsteps faltered, but I couldn't make myself stop anymore; it hadn't even been three hours since I'd been making love to her up against my shower wall, and she was wearing nothing but his shirt? Harper's laugh instantly cut off when she saw me, and I watched as her jaw dropped, and her eyes got wide. They flashed quickly to Brandon, then back to me, and that was all I needed to know. Apparently, she hadn't needed a few weeks, just a few hours. Brandon nodded at me, and with a hard nod back, I forced myself to my room and away from them so I could grab my board, sketchpads, and as much of my other shit as possible, so I could avoid seeing them like that again.

So I could avoid seeing them—period.

Chapter Nine

"CHASE, HONEY?"

I closed my sketchbook and sighed. "Yeah, Mom?" I swear if she brought up—

"Sweetheart, we really should talk about whatever is going on."

Yep . . . she was bringing it up again.

"You're not even *mostly* living out of our house, you're living here. Granted we don't see you much since usually you're surfing when we get up, then at the shop at night, but I'm not that dumb. You're living here."

"You're not dumb at all, Mom."

She set two mugs of coffee down on the table and sat next to me. "I was hoping you'd say that!" She laughed and pushed on my shoulder, but her laugh died when I continued to sit there with my arms crossed over my chest, "Okay, well since I seem to be awesome enough to be graced with your presence today"—I snorted when she rolled her eyes—"I'm gonna make you sit here and talk to me."

"You're gonna make me," I deadpanned, and raised an eyebrow at her.

"Don't push me, Chase Austin Grayson. In all seriousness, your father and I are so worried about you. I was less worried when you were at your own home, but with you here and seeing how you're pushing yourself—"

"Shouldn't you be the one telling me that I need to push myself?"

"Not the way you have been! With the exception of three days, including today, over the last few weeks, you get up at dawn to go surfing, come home only to shower and change, then go to classes. Then you go straight to the shop, and you're home after your dad and I are already asleep! And throughout all of this, you've just . . . lost you. The few times I have seen you, you look dead. You disappear completely on family days; Bree said she hasn't even *seen* you in weeks and that Brad, Brandon, and the rest of the guys are really getting worried about you because you don't talk to them or surf with them anymore . . . ? Chase, what is happening with you?"

I made a mental note to tell Bree to shut the hell up. "Mom, I don't know what you want me to say. I've just been busy."

"I call bullshit," Dad said as he joined the conversation, looking like he was about to leave for work.

"Morning to you, too, Dad."

"And you can drop the attitude, too. She said we're worried about you, and we are. You're an adult, you have your own house; so trust me when I say I have no problem telling you that I love you, but if you don't tell us what's going on and start respecting us, you can move right back out and into your house."

Is he serious? I just sat there staring at both of them for a few minutes before deciding that he was and sighing heavily. "I've been thinking about moving."

"Okay?" Dad drew out the word. Obviously, he wasn't getting it.

"No, I mean *moving* moving. Like, moving away from San Diego."

Mom gasped. "What?"

"After graduation."

"Why?" Mom's eyes were filling with tears, and Dad's eyebrows were scrunched together.

"It's just something I need to do." I shrugged. "Something I want to do."

"Why would you *need* to move away?" She started to cry, and I unfolded my arms, reached across, and grabbed her hand.

"Mom, it's fine. It won't be forever. I ju—" I broke off quickly and sat back.

"Son."

I looked back to my dad and sighed "I can't be around Harper and Brandon. I can't be around her at all while she's with him. It's just too hard. And she's pretty much a part of this family, and I can't handle that right now. I'm in love with a girl who will never want me, so for now, I need to go."

"But how long will be enough for you to be okay with

it? What if they stay together? You can't stay away forever!" Mom was on the verge of hysterics.

"I don't know." I looked up to my dad for help, but he was just shaking his head at me, arms crossed over his chest. "I don't even know if I *will* move. It was just a thought. Mom, seriously, please don't cry."

"Just a thought?" She wiped under her eyes and let her hands fall to the table. "Chase, you're already cutting ties with everyone. This isn't a thought, you're already beginning to execute this childish plan of yours!" The chair legs scraped across the tile as she scooted away from the table.

"Ma."

She swatted my hand away when I reached for her and took off through the living room and up the stairs.

"If you want to be with Harper so bad that you can't stand to be in the same city as her and her boyfriend," Dad said, "then you need to fight for her. Not run from her." He grabbed his briefcase off the table and caught my stare. "Whether she's dating your best friend or not, she's close with you, and it would hurt her to have you leave regardless."

"I really doubt that."

"So you're going to punish your mother, me, your sister, and Harper by leaving because you won't man up and fight for what you want? That's not how we raised you, Chase." And with that, he walked out of the kitchen and out the front door.

"Kinda pointless to fight for what you want when what you want continues to break your heart," I whispered to the empty kitchen.

With a heavy sigh, I pushed away from the table and called Bree as I made my way to my truck.

"WELL WHAT DID you expect me to say? Everyone's worried about you, and you don't show up to family day anymore. You're making Mom sad!"

"Nothing. You say nothing, Breanna. I have my own reasons for doing what I'm doing, and I really don't need you going to Mom and telling her everything you see or don't see here, and I sure as shit don't need you telling her what the guys are saying about me."

Her eyebrows shot up, and she sucked in a deep breath, but before she could throw her attitude back at me, all the air came whooshing out of her body, and she bit down on her bottom lip, which had started to tremble. *Damn it.*

"Bree," I said softly, and rested my forearms on the kitchen table she was sitting at so I was eye level and closer to her.

"You're my big brother, and I'm worried about you." She took a shaky breath in, and her eyes glassed over when she looked up at me. "I'm afraid you're getting into bad things with the way you've been acting. Your temper is through the roof, and your mood swings are epic lately. And that's *when* we see you. Most the time, you're gone. I'm worried about what you might be doing . . ." she trailed off.

"Hey." I kissed the top of her head and hugged her hard before going back to resting on my forearms. "I'm not getting into anything bad, I swear. Nothing illegal, nothing Mom and Dad would be pissed about. I'm just having a hard time dealing with stuff, and I seem to be taking it out on everyone."

"Well, what are you dealing with?"

I shook my head, "Nothin' you need to worry about. I'll figure it out, and I'll try to be around more—come to family days and shit."

"'And shit.' Nice." She snorted and blinked back the rest of her tears. "All right. If you say there's nothing going on, then there's nothing going on. And I'll try to keep my mouth shut about you around Mom and Dad."

"I'd appreciate it. Love you, brat."

Her smile got wide. "Love you too, punk."

Just then, all the hair on my arms and the back of my neck stood on end, and I wished I had gotten out of there sooner, or that Bree would have been at her dorm rather than my house. I straightened from leaning on the table and tried not to react when I heard her voice.

"Uh, good morning." Harper said softly.

Bree's smile got even bigger as she leaned over in the chair to look past me. "Morning, doll! How'd you sleep?"

I didn't want to see her, but I couldn't stop myself from glancing over my shoulder quickly before looking back at Bree.

"Pretty well," Harper responded. "You?"

"Excellent." Bree sounded like she was in a daze, and it didn't take a genius to know why.

"Ugh, seriously Bree? Save it until I'm gone at least." I wasn't dumb, I knew my little sister wasn't a virgin, but I didn't want to know about it.

Without another glance at my princess, I took off for the master bedroom and slapped my hand against the door a few times before Brad opened it. His eyes narrowed, and he straightened so we were almost eye to eye, and instantly I knew what he was doing, and my body automatically tensed in preparation. Brad and I had met while working out and training at the same gym, McGowan's, right after freshman year started at San Diego State University. We were always thrown into the ring together to spar since we were almost identical in height and weight, and had been friends ever since. We'd fought a little here and there in what they called "The Underground" in Southern California. Not exactly legal, great pay, and kept quiet so law enforcement wouldn't find out. We'd also met Brandon through McGowan's once he moved here, and had all formed what Bree likes to call a bro-mance through fighting and surfing. I knew I could never actually win a fight against Brandon—the asshole was unstoppable in the ring—and, let's face it, he's fuckin' huge. Only two inches taller, but he's got forty pounds of muscle on me. So I never expected to win a fight against Brandon, but that's not why I started them. I just wanted an opportunity to punch the guy I'd come to love like a brother since he was with the girl that had quickly become my everything to me. Brad, though . . . I knew that Brad and I came out pretty even when it came to fighting. We'd been thrown in the ring enough times, never knowing who'd win, and at that moment he was ready to beat the shit outta me from the look of him. But I was done fighting.

I forced my body to relax but noticed Brad's hands had clenched into fists, and he was still glaring.

"Shouldn't be taking it out on you." I shrugged.

"Brandon doesn't deserve your bullshit, either."

"I know; he's not the one I'm mad at."

Brad's eyes went wide, and his fists unclenched as he stepped away from the door. He sat on the couch he'd put in his room, and I sat on a chair he had pulled up in front of the TV for gaming. "It's been nice to not have any fights between the two of you, but your disappearing wasn't what anyone wanted either."

I nodded. "Finding it harder and harder to be near them, she's all I think about anymore. But I know I'm the one who fucked up. I should've never pushed her away."

"I don't get you, man. You change your life for her, ruin your friendships for her . . . then you disappear for a few weeks, and now you're just giving up; but you're still in love with her?" Before I could respond, he shifted forward in the couch, and his voice got low. "Did you see her that weekend?"

My eyes snapped up to meet his, and my mouth fell open, but nothing came out.

"Look, I didn't want to tell you she was staying because I knew you were going to be running by your parents' house. That probably makes me just as much of an asshole to Brandon as you've been, but you and Harper needed to work this out. And with the depressing bullshit you'd been pulling, I knew you would have stayed away from her. So, did. You. See her?"

We continued to stare at each other before I leaned

back in the chair with a groan and raked my hands down my face. "I love her."

"Know that."

"She loves me, too." I kept my eyes trained on the ceiling and kept talking. "Spent that night and the next morning with her."

"Shit, Chase."

"And, well, you know everyone came back early. Princess got scared, and went back to Brandon."

"And you disappeared."

"Yep." I sighed heavily and looked back at him. "She said she needed time, but I know she doesn't. I've messed things up with her too much from the beginning for her to come to me."

"So what are you gonna do now? Keep staying gone?"

"I don't know. Told Mom and Dad this morning that I was thinking about moving away from San Diego after graduation to get away from them. But I just caught a glimpse of her for the first time in weeks, and I don't think I can do that. I just can't stay away from her."

The door flew open, and Brandon didn't even enter the room fully as he yelled, "Harper fainted, and she's not waking up."

My heart skipped a beat, and I was out of the chair and racing after him, with Brad right behind me before I fully registered what he had said. When I got to the kitchen, my princess, my entire world, was lying on the ground covered in sweat. Her eyes were wide open and bouncing between Bree, Brandon, Brad, and me.

Brandon went down on his knees next to her, and I

gripped the island next to me. I wanted to be the one to make sure she was okay. "She's awake?" he asked Bree.

"She's okay, Chase," Brad said low enough so only I could hear, and clapped my shoulder once. "She's fine, calm down."

There was a loud thud, followed by a moan from Harper. "Ow."

I gripped the counter harder when Brandon reached for her, and her eyes locked on him. "Brad, get the couch ready for her."

He walked away from me, and I worked on controlling my breathing as I watched my best friend take care of her. I wanted to hate him, but I couldn't. Harper asked if she'd fallen asleep in the kitchen, and for the first time since Brandon had rushed into the bedroom, I felt like laughing.

Bree laughed, but it sounded shaky. "Not quite. You passed out."

"I did?" Harper's already-wide eyes got even wider, and she looked scared.

"Yeah, Harper," Bree responded. "Scared the crap out of us, too."

Brad came back into the kitchen. "Couch is ready, so get her over there."

Brandon went from his knees to a crouch and looked up at both Brad and me, but we were already stepping toward her. We'd all seen Brandon carry Harper more than enough times, and Lord knew I could carry that girl; but I hadn't seen her go down, and none of us knew what was wrong with her. So with me at her head and shoulders, Brad holding her legs and Brandon carrying her body, we walked her over to the couch.

"I'm fine," Harper groaned, and tried to sit up once we had her on the couch. "You're all being ridiculous."

Brandon looked at her like she was crazy and pushed her gently back down. "Sweetheart, you were out for—"

"I get that, but I'm fine now." She sighed and rolled her eyes at the same time her stomach growled loudly. She smiled and pointed at her stomach. "See, I'm fine."

It felt like I couldn't breathe. Something as ridiculous as her stomach growling, and all of a sudden all I could see was us in my bedroom, her naked body on top of mine as she arched against me. That had been the best morning of my life, and I would give anything to go back and replay it over and over.

"Uh, Brad?" Harper's voice snapped me back to the present, and I saw her wince as she looked at Brad holding a small towel to her leg. "Could you ease up? You're hurting me." Her face fell when she saw him stand up with the bloody cloth. "What the—"

"You dropped your mug, and a big chunk sliced your leg pretty good," Brandon hurried to tell her what happened, and his head dipped in to kiss her neck. Harper's eyelids fluttered shut, and she inhaled deeply.

The pain in my chest intensified, and once I knew she was all right, I couldn't stand to be in the room with them anymore. I hung my head and stepped away from all of them, wishing for the thousandth time I could go back in time to when I first met that gray-eyed girl and do everything differently.

I walked back into Brad's room to grab my keys, and when I turned to leave, he was standing in the doorway. "You leaving again?" When I just nodded, he asked, "For how long this time?"

"I don't know, man, I'll probably keep staying at my parents. Watching her go in and out of his room would kill me. But I'll be around." He pointedly looked at the keys in my hand, and I raked my free hand over my face. "Have to get to class, then to the shop. You guys surfing at our spot tomorrow?"

"Always."

"All right, I'll be there."

Brad grinned, and I made my way past him and to the hall. Brandon was making breakfast in the kitchen when I went past him, and I tried not to grit my teeth when he spoke.

"Where've you been, bro? I haven't seen you for more than ten seconds since I got back."

"Just been busy with the shop." I shrugged. "Mom and Dad's house is closer to work. It's easier just going back there." I heard Bree and Harper talking down the hall toward Brandon's room, and looked up at him. "She okay?"

"Harper? She'll be fine. Bree said she hasn't eaten since yesterday morning; I'm guessing that's it."

I looked back at the breakfast he was making her and thought about the only time I'd ever cooked for her and how my life had turned to shit while I was doing it. "Well, take care of her."

Brandon's eyes widened before narrowing as his brow

bunched together, but before he could say anything else, I took off for the front door and left for school.

"No fucking wonder your parents kicked you out of their house."

My eyes widened, and I looked over at Brian and another artist, Jeff.

"If this is how you looked all the time, I'd kick your ass out, too," Brian finished as he moved aside some papers and hopped onto my counter at the shop. The door opened, and Jeff and I looked over to it, but Brian just sat there with a shit-eating grin. "Oh, by the way, Riss is coming to tell you off."

"You're serious, Brian? You called your wife to come yell at me?"

"Chachi!" Marissa snapped, and I groaned. "It has been a month. A month! You have two choices: grow a pair and ask her if she's made up her mind yet or get over the bitch."

"Marissa," I growled in warning.

She smiled impishly. "That's what I thought. So go ask her."

"I can't!" I flung my sketchbook onto the counter and crossed my arms over my chest. "She's made up her mind. That's it."

"No, she told you to give her some time, and you have. You're still freakin' miserable, you're only moving back into your house because your parents kicked you out of theirs, and she can't get out of what she did like this."

"Like what?"

"She can't tell you she needs time to decide just for you to ignore the issue completely. That's letting her get off easy. She cheats on her boyfriend and goes back to him without consequences? Fuck that, Chach. Your girl needs to face the shit hole she's made, and she's never going to if you just sit here wanting her from a distance. Otherwise, she's just going to keep doing it, whether it's with you again or someone—"

"I'm the one who pushed her into all this! I pushed her away, pushed her right into his arms. She didn't do anything, I'm the one who created this mess. So stop talking about her like she's a whore!"

"Well, if it talks like a whore, spreads its legs like a—"

"Marissa!" I uncrossed my arms and stepped right up to her. "Swear to God, if you know what's good for you, you'll shut the fuck up. Now. I don't give a shit that you're Brian's wife or that you're a woman. You don't fucking talk about my girl like that again. No matter who she chooses tonight. You got me?"

She smiled wide and bounced up and down on her toes a couple times before throwing her arms around my neck. "You're going to talk to her tonight? Chachi, I'm proud of you, and we're here for you no matter what happens!"

"What the hell? Just—what?" Brian and Jeff laughed at me as I stood there with my arms hanging limply at my sides, "Bri, your wife's bipolar!"

Marissa leaned back slightly but kept her arms around my neck. "I've heard all your stories about her, I don't think she's a whore. I just think she's confused and in love with two guys. But you needed to go talk to her." She hugged me tight again, and I chuckled softly as I hugged her back.

"So all that bullshit was to get me to go talk to her?" I let go and stepped away from her, watching as she went to Brian's arms.

"Well, it worked, didn't it?" she asked smugly. "You said tonight."

"Yeah . . . thanks, Riss. Next time try a different approach though, yeah?" I kissed her forehead, smacked Brian across the head, and clapped Jeff's shoulder before grabbing my keys and phone. "I don't have any appointments tonight. See you guys tomorrow."

"Good luck, Chach!"

Marissa's words had me remembering what I was about to do, and I took a deep breath in. I had a feeling I'd need a lot of luck to get through the night.

I called Brad, and he said the girls still weren't back from family day, so I drove to my parents' house and had to take another deep breath in and out when I saw Bree's car sitting in the driveway. The ache in my chest was already making itself known, and I hoped this wouldn't end in a way that ruined me forever.

Bree's laughter came from the kitchen, and I drifted in that direction to find her at the kitchen table, Harper standing right behind her with a bag of chips in her hand, both staring at Bree's laptop. Bree noticed me first, paused whatever they were watching, and folded her arms across her chest as she sent an impressive glare my way. Princess still had her eyes glued to the screen.

"Well, look who decided to join the party. Mom and Dad are already asleep."

I kept my eyes on Harper as she slowly looked over to my sister, then up to me. Her gray eyes widened, and the bag of chips slipped from her grasp.

"I was busy." It's not like Mom and Dad didn't know *why* I'd been avoiding today. "Harper, can I talk to you?"

"Uh, yeah. Yeah I guess." She started walking toward me and her face paled drastically, her arm shooting out to grip the counter. "Whoa."

"Are you okay?" Bree was out of her chair, and I was rushing toward Harper when she held up a hand to stop us.

"I'm fine, I just got dizzy for a second. Thought I was going to faint again."

My hands clenched into fists. I needed Bree to not be here; it was taking everything in me to not go up to her and hold my princess. To check her myself and make sure she was okay. *Is she sick?* I hadn't seen her since over a week ago, when she fainted in the kitchen of my house, and even now she still looked like she might fall over at any second. Bree and Harper spoke softly to each other before Harper said she'd be back and stepped toward me again.

I turned without a word and walked halfway down my parents' driveway before turning to look at her.

Her eyes took me in, and even in the dark, I could see the color come back to her face, along with the blush I loved so much. She bit down on the corner of her mouth and shifted her weight a couple times before saying, "Hi."

I blew out a breath I hadn't realized I'd been holding. *A month without talking at all, and all she can say is 'Hi'?* "Hey, Princess."

"Where have you been?"

"Working a lot, classes, surfing. That's about it."

She nodded and looked away, then down before talking again. "Your family misses you."

This was it. This was where I needed this to go. I steeled myself, and shakily asked, "Do you?"

Her eyes snapped back up to look at me, and I hated the pain I saw there; but it gave me the smallest sliver of hope. "Of course I do, Chase."

"Harper, I've given you more than enough time. I can't stand to stay away from you anymore, so I need to know who you choose."

"You're really going to do this now?" she hissed, and looked at the door before taking a step closer and speaking low. "Bree could be listening from the front door!"

"Yes, now." While I still had the balls to do this! "I need to know."

"Chase, how can you even ask me to choose between you two?"

What?

"You left me, like you always do. You expected me to think you still wanted me after you've completely avoided me for a month?"

Seriously? What. The. Fuck. I threw my arms out and looked at her like she was insane. *Does she not remember anything she's told me?* "I was giving you time! You asked me to give you time!"

"I didn't want you to avoid me like the plague, I wanted you to fight for me. To show me that you loved me like you said you did."

Could she honestly even question my love for her after what happened between us? "I do love you, Harper, and that's why I gave you that time to think about things without my interfering."

She stepped back, and I closed the distance again. Her eyes held mine, and I watched as they filled with tears. "I'm sorry, Chase, but I can't."

Oh, shit. "No. No, no n—"

"I can't be with you. I love Brandon; I'm sorry."

No! "Baby, don't say that. I will fight for you, I will. Please just give us a shot."

"A part of me will probably always love you, too, but I can't take chances with you, Chase. You'll leave me one day, and it will kill me when you do."

"Wha—No! I wouldn't, I swear I wouldn't." Did she not understand that she meant *everything* to me? I pulled her into my arms and held her as my body started shaking. I couldn't lose her. I'd been preparing for it, but I couldn't handle it.

"You can't stay with any one girl, that's just how you are. And that's fine, Chase, it's fine. You're with different girls every night, but when I think about love, I think about forever. You can't give me that, so I'm not going to hurt myself by only having you for a short time."

Tears stung my eyes, and it became painful to breathe. After everything, she still thought I was living my old life? She still hadn't realized I'd changed everything for her? I've never claimed to love anyone other than her, I'd never even thought of loving anyone but her. I would give her the world if she asked for it. And she thought I just wanted some fling with her?

I cupped her cheeks and brought her face from my chest so I could look at her, but she was a blurry mess from the tears that were threatening to spill over. "I haven't been with anyone but you since you started dating Brandon. I knew then there would never be anyone else like you, and I wasn't going to waste time being with someone else."

Princess shook her head slightly, went up on her toes and kissed the corner of my mouth before beginning to move out of my arms. "I love you, Chase."

"Baby, please. Don't do this!" I gripped her hand, not willing to let her leave yet. I couldn't just let this end like this.

"I have to, I'm sorry."

"Why? Why can't you be with me?" When she didn't answer, I swallowed back bile and asked the one thing I'd been worrying about most in the last month. "Are you sleeping with him, too, Harper?"

"Why does that matter?"

"Please"—I shut my eyes as I prepared myself to ask again—"just tell me if you are sleeping with him."

"I've only been with you," she whispered softly, and all the air left my lungs as she pulled away and began to walk away from me. I looked up at the same time she stopped walking, her body going rigid before she gasped.

"What? What's wrong?"

"I have to go," she shouted, and took off running for the house.

I stood there in shock for a few moments before forcing myself back to my truck and driving to Brian and Marissa's. I had no idea what had just happened; all I knew was that she'd just shattered my world.

Marissa answered the door, and, with one look at me, her jaw dropped, and she quickly covered her mouth with a hand. "Oh, Chachi."

My mouth opened, but nothing came out, and I hung my head as my tears fell to the concrete.

"Brian should be home soon," she said softly, and stepped back from the open door. "C'mon in; you can crash here tonight." Marissa called Brian to let him know I was there and sat on the chair across from the couch I was on. "Do you wanna talk about it?"

I shook my head. I didn't know if I even could talk about it.

"What are you gonna do, Chach?"

"Wait—" My voice was low and rough as I spoke around the lump in my throat. "Wait for her. I'll always wait for her. It'll always be Harper for me, I'm never going to stop wanting her to be mine."

"Chach—"

"Riss, I won't give up on me and Harper. I can't."

Chapter Ten

I'D FULLY MOVED back into my house the day after Harper had shattered me. I'd been prepared to stomach seeing her and Brandon together, see them going to and from his room and her in nothing but his shirts. But I hadn't seen her at all. It'd been a week, and while I saw Brandon a few times, he was always alone. I'd seen him yesterday morning when he was coming into the kitchen, and I was leaving, but it ended the same as it always does lately. Completely silent. I didn't know what to say to him anymore, so I didn't say anything. Before, I'd hated him for getting the girl. Now that I'd had her, and she'd left me for him again, I couldn't stand to see him without wanting to die.

I went through my everyday forced routine. Surf in the mornings, now with Brad and the guys again even though Brandon had been missing over the last week. Class during the day and work at night. I was standing outside my last class of the day, trying to kill time by talking with some old buddies, when I was knocked into one of them.

"What the he—" I broke off when I turned to see a mess of auburn hair and wide gray eyes staring at me. "Princess?"

Without saying anything, she bent down to grab her phone, which had dropped into the middle of the circle she'd just plowed into, and turned to leave. Fuck that.

"Harper, wait up!" As soon as I caught up with her, I grabbed her arm and turned her so she was facing me. "You're not even going to say hi now?"

She dropped her head, and a shaky "Hi" came from her.

Why won't she even look at me? I placed a knuckle under her chin and lifted up, and my chest tightened when I saw that her eyes were filled with tears. *Why the hell is my princess crying?* "Baby, what's wrong?"

Her cheeks went red, and she blinked her eyes rapidly to hold back the tears. "Nothing, it's just allergies or something."

Bullshit. She looked side to side quickly, and I figured my touching her wouldn't fly with Brandon if he saw us, so I took a step away and let my head drop to stare at the space between us. "I haven't seen you around my house much. I know you don't want to be with me, but don't feel like you can't be there, I won't bother you and Brandon."

"That's not why I haven't been there. I um, I broke up with him."

My head snapped back up, and I stared deep into her

stormy eyes. "You did? When, why didn't you tell me?" Was it twisted that I couldn't help but hope that I was finally going to get what I'd been wanting for over five months?

"A little over a week ago. But it hurt me more than I could ever explain to do it, and I need time to get over that. I can't just rush back to you because Brandon and I aren't together anymore."

I can't just rush back to you . . . Does that mean she plans to come back to me? Hope surged through my body, and I cupped her pink cheeks in my hands as I bent down, so I was closer to her eye level. "I love you, I'll give you all the time you need." *Shit, stop assuming.* "Unless. Unless you don't want me anymore?"

I held my breath as she grabbed my left hand and pressed her cheek harder to it. Her eyes drifted shut, and she took a deep breath in. "I've told you, I will always love you, Chase, but I'm still not sure you won't eventually leave me. Because of that fear, I don't know if I can be with you. And some things have changed since we talked last, so you might change your mind about me altogether."

"That's not possible."

She removed my hands from her cheeks only to wrap herself up in my arms. I exhaled deeply and started to thank God when she kissed my throat and buried her head into my chest, but then she whispered, "I wish that were true."

What do I have to do to convince this girl that I love her more than anything? Tears suddenly clouded my vision, and my voice cracked as they spilled over. "It is, Harper. I love you so damn much, why can't you see that?"

Her wide eyes started watering as well, and her jaw started quivering. The next thing I knew, she was out of my arms and walking away. "I have to go; I'm sorry."

"Harper, please. Please don't just walk away. Talk to me, baby." She didn't stop and didn't look back at me. "Princess, please stop walking." Nothing; she kept her head down and continued away from me, and I was terrified that if I let her go, I'd never get her back. "Harper, please talk to me!"

She turned suddenly, but I didn't stop walking until I was directly in front of her.

"I will," she promised. "We *will* talk, but right now I have to go." This time she cupped my face to wipe away my tears.

"Promise?" When she nodded, I whispered, "I love you," before kissing the inside of her wrist and watching as she stepped away from me. I was so focused on Harper I didn't notice anyone else was there until Bree touched my arm. My eyes flashed between the two of them, and I tensed up for their reaction at saying that out loud in front of my sister. But they both just smiled at me, and my body relaxed until I looked around and noticed we'd caught other people's attention. Ducking my head, once again I quickly walked away from the girl I loved.

"You like it?"

Brad smiled as he looked in the double mirror to see the ink I'd just finished on his back. "Yeah man, Sarah will love it."

I put ointment on the tattoo and covered it before Brad pulled his shirt back on and hopped up onto the table. I wanted to make some comment about how Brad was whipped for getting Sarah's name on the back of his shoulder, but Brian had already done the piece on my arm that had "Princess" hidden in it. So I didn't have much room to talk.

Jeff walked up to my station and threw a soda at Brad and me before opening up his own and sitting on my counter. It was a slow night in the shop, and Brian was the only one with an appointment . . . and it was his brother.

"We going surfing tomorrow?" Brad asked before taking a long drink.

"Yep. Do you know if Brandon's going?"

Brad shrugged his shoulders. "I swear, you two switched places, you're getting back to yourself, and Brandon's disappeared, well . . . except for lunch the other day."

"Yeah, but he left as soon as I sat down." And Brad was so wrong. I wasn't getting back to myself, I was just hoping that every day was the day I would finally get to take Harper in my arms again. But with each passing day, that hope had slowly started to fade.

"You're not still fighting, are you? I mean neither of you have Harper, so there's no point." My expression deadpanned, and I shot a warning glare at Brad, who raised his hands in surrender and smirked. "Hey, man, you know I'm still pulling for you. I want you to be happy. But it's the truth."

I rolled my neck and sighed deeply. "We haven't

fought since he went back home over winter break. But we've only talked once since he got back, and that was the morning Princess fainted."

"Well, I wouldn't talk to you either if you had fucked my girl," Jeff huffed, and dodged my empty soda bottle. "Well, I wouldn't!"

I'd fucked plenty of girls. And what Princess and I had could never be considered a fuck. "He doesn't know."

"Yeah he does!" Brian called out from his station, never looking up from his brother's calf. "Hell, even when you two fought all the time, he was still in here getting work done. Now your boy's peaced out. Your girl dumped him, and he's avoiding you now more than ever? Trust me, bro, he knows."

"I doubt it." Brad said at the same time I shook my head, and said, "There's no effing way. He'd beat the shit out of me if he knew."

"Exactly," Brad agreed, and pointed his empty bottle at me. "You shoulda seen the way he went after Chase. Not saying Chase didn't deserve it, but he was beyond pissed. And that was before anything happened."

"He knows," Jeff disagreed. "Otherwise, he wouldn't be avoiding you."

"He's avoiding everyone." I tightened my hold on the back of the chair I was leaning against. My heart had started racing with the possibility of Brandon's knowing what had happened between Princess and me. I quickly glanced around the shop to make sure we were the only ones in there, and my gaze settled on her name on my arm.

"I just don't get why you're still waiting for her," Jeff said. "You've been waiting for months, and now she breaks up with her boyfriend and . . . how long has that even been?"

I gritted my teeth as I answered, "Over a month and a half." And no . . . I hadn't been keeping track . . .

"Month and a half," he continued. "and she barely talks to you. Just get over the girl already."

"He loves her!" Brian called from his station, and I snorted a laugh. He'd listened to me bitch and whine about Princess for over half a year, and he still backed me up in my feelings for her.

"Whatever!" Jeff said exasperatedly. "It's been a month and a half since she said they'd 'talk,' and that still has yet to happen."

I continued to stare at her name on my arm as I thought about the few times I'd seen her since she told me she'd broken up with Brandon. It'd been a handful of times, maybe a little more, but almost all of them were glimpses as we passed each other. She'd said she would talk to me, and I'd given her plenty of time for that. But her birthday was in two days, and I had a plan. "It'll happen." I looked at Jeff, then over to Brad, who nodded. "I'll make sure it happens."

I ONLY HAD one class tomorrow, but it was Harper's birthday, and I had a surprise planned for her. So on my way out of my last class, I stopped by my professor's office and handed over the paper due, saying I'd be out of town. I'd just left his office when I saw Harper rush into the bathroom, her hand covering her mouth. Looking around to make sure no one was around, I pushed opened the door and heard her getting violently sick in one of the three stalls. Her backpack had been discarded on her way to the stall, and she hadn't even closed the door.

Walking up behind her, I leaned against the side of the stall and rubbed large circles on her back until she was finished.

"Go away," she groaned as she flushed the toilet.

Not likely. I did step away, but it was only to wet a few folded-up paper towels and bring it to her. "Here you go, Princess."

She grabbed it and wiped her mouth before standing up and turning to look at me. "Thanks."

I looked over her, but she didn't look sick. She looked beautiful. Absolutely beautiful. "Are you okay? Do you want me to take you somewhere?"

"No, I'm great."

"Great? You just threw up, Harper."

She took a deep breath in and held it as she returned my stare. With a subtle shake of her head, she looked back down and moved past me out of the stall and over to the sink to rinse her mouth. "I know, and now I feel fine."

"If you don't want me to take you, at least let me call Bree so she can take you home." I thought about my conversation with Dad this morning, and added softly, "Speaking of, when were you going to tell me you moved into my parents' house?"

She turned off the faucet and put a piece of gum in

her mouth, chewing a few times before asking, "Does that bother you?"

"Not at all, but I just found out this morning that you've been living there over a month. I would have come around more if I knew you were there and not hiding from me in your dorm."

"I haven't been hiding from you, Chase."

I almost snorted. Jeff had been right last night—I'd barely talked to her in the last month and a half. I knew she wanted time, but she always seemed to run in the opposite direction from me. My head dropped, and I stared at her backpack sitting between us. "You sure about that?"

She was quiet for a few moments, and when she finally said something, her voice was soft and shaking slightly, "I've just been busy, and you haven't been around much either. You haven't come to a family day in months."

"As before, Harper, I'm giving you the time you asked for."

"Oh."

Yeah.

She picked up her backpack and walked past me, and when I turned to look at her, she was looking at me expectantly, her hand on the handle of the door. I followed her outside, and remained silent until I caught her looking up at me from the corner of my eye.

"Harper, can you tell me one thing?"

"I'll tell you anything, Chase."

I touched her arm to stop her and waited until she was looking at me with those wide gray eyes. "Have I—have I missed my chance?"

Her brow furrowed. "What do you mean?"

"I mean with you, *us*. Did I miss my chance?"

My chest tightened painfully when she closed the distance between us and wrapped her arms around me. The night on my parents' driveway when she kissed me softly before telling me she was staying with Brandon flashed through my mind, and I held my breath and gripped her tighter when she answered.

"I'm sorry that you would even have to ask that. I wish you knew how much I love you, Chase, it's just been a hard time for me. I didn't know you were still giving me time; I figured I'd already lost you." Her voice broke at the end, and I almost thanked God out loud.

"Aw hell, baby. That's not possible." I kissed the top of her head and squeezed her tighter to me. "What's been going on? Is it still because of Brandon? Or did something else happen?"

"We need to go, Harper."

I dropped my arms and stepped back when I heard my sister's voice. Once again, I expected Bree to freak out, but she just stood there with a soft smile on her face.

Harper looked up at me and touched my arm softly. "See you."

"Bye, Princess."

I watched her walk away from me again, but this time I promised myself it would be the last time. Tomorrow, she would be mine.

I hoped.

Chapter Eleven

I'D GONE TO Los Angeles early in the morning to get everything I needed for Harper's surprise and barely made it to school in time after dropping it all off at Brian and Marissa's. I laid the bouquet of orange lilies onto the chair that was propping open the door to Breanna and Harper's class and stood back, hidden from view. Not more than five minutes later, the girls were walking up. I watched as my princess looked up, then did a double take at the chair. Her footsteps faltered as she walked slowly over and picked up the bouquet. Her body straightened as she turned around and scanned the crowd before picking the note out and moving the bouquet to the crook of her arm while she read it.

When she turned back around to look through everyone again, she had the widest smile on her face, and it took everything in me not to go to her. Bree took the note from her and shook her head slowly before looking around again as well. As soon as they walked into the classroom, I pulled out my phone.

You look beautiful today

Princess: Were you watching me?

Maybe. I finally got to give you your lilies

Princess: You already gave me my lilies a few months ago, remember?

I couldn't forget that day even if I tried

Princess: Well, you could have given these to me yourself, you know. I would have liked to see you

It was worth it to see that smile on your face

Princess: :) Thank you for my flowers. I love them

What are you doing for your birthday?

Princess: Dinner with your fam tonight, movies at the house after. You're invited

I'll see what I can do

I wouldn't be there. But I sure as hell hoped she loved her surprise.

Since I'd missed it this morning, I went surfing with Brad and Drew before going back over to Brian and Marissa's to help get everything ready for that night. I couldn't help but laugh when I saw Brian knee deep in lilies.

"Good look for you, Bri."

He pointed a bunch of lilies at me and glared. Coming from a man of his size, mass of hair, tattoos, and piercings . . . that shit was hilarious. "Watch it, Grayson! I'm doing this for you!"

"And I appreciate it."

"Chachi?" Marissa came running into the living room. "Do you think we got enough flowers? We can go scope out some flower shops around town."

My eyes widened as I looked around their living room. "Uh, Riss. We bought every orange and white lily they had at the flower market. I think we're good." My phone rang, and I answered without looking, "Yeah?"

"Hey, sweetheart!"

"Hey, Ma, what's going on?" Since Mom and Dad had sent me back to my house, I hadn't seen or talked to Mom much as Harper was usually with her. Hopefully, that was all about to change.

"Well, um, I don't know if you know . . . because you know . . . well maybe—"

"Mom, just say it."

"It's Harper's birthday, you know."

I smiled widely. "Oh yeah? Huh. That's good."

"Are you rethinking your feelings for her?" She sounded panicked, and I took my phone away from my ear to look at my screen for a second.

"Hell no. What's going on? You okay, Ma?"

"Oh that's good . . . that's real good."

Seriously, why is she being so weird?

"Well, we're all going out to dinner tonight for her birthday, and I know she'd love it if you were there."

"Yeah, look, I'd like to, but I just can't. I'll be busy tonight." If she hadn't started to weird me out so much, I might have told her my plans; but she just wasn't acting like my mom.

"I hope you don't give up on you and Harper, sweetheart."

"Mom." I spoke softly into the phone. "I haven't. I promise. I have things I need to do tonight though . . . all right? If it eases your mind, I've decided to stay in San Diego after graduation."

She blew out a relieved breath, "Oh thank God. All right. Well, if you change your mind, we're going at six tonight."

"Six. All right. Love you, Ma."

"Love you, too, honey."

We got all the flowers put together before I had to go in for my first of two appointments at the shop; and by the time I was done with the second, I was rushing to get the lilies, so they were covering every surface in the living room and breakfast bar at my parents' house. I walked into the kitchen in search of anything I could scarf down quickly and a book sitting on the end of the kitchen table caught my eye. I did a double take when I saw the title and froze.

What. The. Hell.

I took a tentative step in the direction of the table, praying my eyesight had just declined significantly, and I wasn't reading it correctly.

What to Expect When You're Expecting was there, right in front of me. "This better be a fucking joke," I whispered to the empty room and noticed the top of a white bookmark peeking out of the top about a fourth of the way through. Taking a deep breath, I flipped to the page and saw that the bookmark was actually an ultrasound picture.

I was going to kill Konrad.

I pulled the ultrasound photo out of the book and let the book fall to the table again as I stared at my niece or nephew. The front door opened, followed by gasps and a low whistle before I heard it shut. I turned and was yelling before I could storm out of the kitchen and see my family. "Are you fucking kidding me? How could you guys keep this from me? Where the hell is he? I swear to God, I'm going to kill him!"

"Chase!" My dad bit back at me, and took a protective step in front of Princess, Mom, and Bree. "Calm down. What is going on?"

Calm down? Calm down? Is he serious? "I saw the books, I saw the effing ultrasound pictures!"

Dad straightened his body and crossed his arms over his chest, one eyebrow raised. "And?"

"And? *Dad!*" I flung my arm toward the girls, pointing with the photo. "Bree's knocked up, and all you can say is 'and'?"

Bree crossed her arms over her chest, making her look just like Dad. "Please. I'm not as stupid as you. *I'm* not pregnant."

"Breanna!" Mom hissed, her eyes wide.

Not as stupid as me? Wh—just . . . what? "Then what the hell is this?" I shoved the photo directly in front of her face and held it there with a shaky hand until Harper pulled the picture out of my hand. Her voice was soft and controlled.

"It's mine, Chase."

I looked over to my princess and was about to apologize for blowing up on her birthday when what she said finally hit me. *It's mine, Chase.* The book, the ultrasound picture . . . were hers? *My princess is pregnant?* But she'd told me she'd only been with . . . *oh holy shit.* My legs started shaking as everything started clicking in my mind. I couldn't stop the wide grin that crossed my face as I realized the girl I loved more than life itself was carrying *our* baby.

My gaze left her worried expression to travel down her body until I hit her slightly rounded stomach. *Holy shit.* How had I not noticed before tonight? "You're pregnant, Princess?"

"Yes," she answered softly.

I glanced up and smiled at her before looking back to her stomach, which she had just placed her hands on. "Is it—is it mine?"

"Of course it is."

A surge of warmth spread through my body. I knew what she was saying. I knew what this meant, but I couldn't stop asking her, "We're going to have a baby?"

"Yes."

I grabbed the ultrasound picture in her hand, my fingertips barely grazing her baby bump. "This is our baby?"

"Yes."

Glancing back up at my gray-eyed princess, I studied her beautiful smile as the tears started pouring down her face. "We're having a baby," I said out loud.

She laughed and nodded as she watched me.

I huffed a laugh and ran a shaky hand through my hair, grabbing a fistful before letting go and looking from

Harper's stomach, to our baby's picture, and back to her stomach. That was us. This baby was ours. And Harper's smile was saying more than her words could. This beautiful girl was mine.

"I love you so much." I took the last step toward her and brought my mouth down roughly to hers.

She wrapped her arms around my neck, and I straightened, lifting her from the ground as we moved our lips against each other. For the first time in almost three months, I felt alive again, and I never wanted to go back to a life without Harper in it. I set her back on the ground and kissed her one more time before dropping to my knees so I was eye level with her stomach. I gently ran my hands over the small bump, and my breath came out in a huff. I couldn't believe I'd had no idea. Lifting her shirt enough to see the bump, my heart took off as I looked at her tattoo of orange lilies wrapping around so they barely touched the edge of where her bump was.

Mine.

Leaning forward, I gently kissed her small bump twice before running my hands over it again and standing up to cup her face in my hands. "Why didn't you tell me?"

Harper shrugged, her gray eyes glistening with tears. "I was scared; I still am."

"You don't have to be scared," I whispered, and kissed her nose softly. "I'll take care of us," I vowed. *Always.*

She looked around to my parents and sister as she grabbed my hand. "Can you guys excuse us for a minute?"

I followed her up the stairs and to my room. As soon as we were in there, her next inhale was audible as she just stared at the bed for a few moments before going to sit on the edge of it. I fell into the middle of it and pulled her with me so we were lying down, me on my back, and her curled onto her side against me. We stayed silent for a minute, and I grabbed her hand, so I could link our fingers together before bringing it down to kiss her palm.

"I can't believe we're going to have a baby."

Harper exhaled harshly, and my body locked up. "About that . . . Chase—"

"No." No way was I going to let her do this to us again. "Don't do this again, please."

"Just hear me out, okay?" She leaned up on her elbow and looked directly into my eyes, "You're twenty-two, you're about to graduate from college, I don't want to take your life from you. If you want to live your life, I won't stop you. Just because this baby is yours, don't think that means you're forced to be with me . . . with us. I want you to be with us, don't get me wrong. But I will let you go if that's what you need."

I knew she was being serious, but I couldn't stop smiling at her. "Are you done?"

"Yes."

Good. My turn. Since apparently you still haven't figured this out. "Harper, I love you more than I could ever explain. Meeting you changed my world. Even when I thought you would never be mine, I couldn't continue to live a life I knew you hated. The night you told me you loved me was the best night of my life, up until tonight. I never want to let you go again, I want to be with you for the rest of my life. I want to marry you someday, Harper."

I paused when her gray eyes widened. "I would do anything for you. I don't know what to do to make you believe me, but I'll spend forever trying to show you."

"You want to marry me?" she asked softly.

More than I want to breathe. "You have no idea how much."

"Not just because I'm pregnant?"

I brought her back down so she was lying on my chest and tilted her head back to kiss her lips softly. "Not at all. I gotta admit, it's a little bit of a shock, but I've always thought about being with you and starting a family. And even though it's sooner than I thought it would be, I'm so freaking excited that it's happening. When should we be expecting him?"

"Him?"

"Yep, it's gonna be a boy."

She laughed softly and ran her fingers through my hair, "I'm due October 4."

I quickly added up the months and grinned again. "So six months, huh? Do you want to take next year off from classes?"

"I can't go back to school."

I squeezed her shoulder. "Of course you can, I'll help you."

"No, not that. I know you would." She took a deep breath and rolled off me and onto the bed, grabbing my hand. "I told Sir that I'm pregnant."

"And?"

"He uh—isn't going to pay for school anymore, and he said I'm not welcome back home."

"Bastard," I mumbled softly. "Are you serious? We'll figure it out. If you want to finish school, we'll make it happen."

"Really, I don't even want to go back after this semester. That's not why I'm sad. I just hate how he is. I hate how he resents me for having been born."

I pulled her closer to me again to run my hand up and down her side. How anyone could hate this girl, especially her own father, is beyond me. "It's not your fault. He's a douche, and it's his loss for missing out on an amazing daughter."

"I was afraid you'd resent me, too," she admitted into my chest, "for getting pregnant. You wanted to stop, and I pushed you."

"It's not like you had to push hard, I wanted you so bad." I laughed, but she remained silent as she traced patterns onto my chest. "I don't resent you, Harper, I never will."

She leaned up to kiss me soundly, and we lay there silently until my sister opened the door to let us know they were going to turn on a movie. When the door shut again, Harper didn't move, and neither did I.

"Harper, I want you to be mine—and not just because we're having a baby though I'll warn you, I'm about to tell everyone that we are." Her eyes brightened, and I smiled at her before kissing her nose. "But I want to be able to hold you in public, I want to show everyone that you're taken, and you belong to me. That you'll always belong to me. Are we done torturing each other by staying apart?"

"Are you done leaving me?" she countered, and I

rolled over to rest above her, my mouth less than an inch from hers.

"I'll never leave you again, sweetie."

"Then I'm yours."

She reached up to kiss me and I smiled through our kiss. *Finally. This girl is mine.*

"BRANDON, WAIT UP!"

He hesitated for a second before continuing to close the door to his Jeep. Both hands scrubbed down his face before falling to the steering wheel.

"We need to talk."

We still hadn't spoken to each other since the morning Harper fainted. All the guys in the house knew she was pregnant and that we were together, but Drew had been joking about Harper's "Buddha belly," and next thing I know, Harper's hyperventilating. I'd freaked out, trying to figure out what brought it on all of a sudden, and when I looked up I saw Brandon walking away from all of us. I don't know what her reason to Brandon was when they broke up, and I didn't know if all of our joking about it was the way he found out. But I owed it to him to talk to him about it.

"I don't have a whole hell of a lot to say to you." He kept his eyes trained straight ahead of him, the muscle in his jaw ticking.

"Harper's pregnant."

He snorted. "Know that. And I know the baby is yours."

"I'm sorry you had to find out the way you did; I should have come to you first."

"Not really necessary since I've known. She told me the day she found out."

I blinked quickly. "So you knew all that time, and you never said anything to me?"

"Wasn't my place to tell you, Chase, it's your baby. Harper needed to be the one to tell you."

"No, not that." I shook my head and took a deep breath, "I—I hated that you had her. I hated that I'd pushed her away in the beginning and told you she was available. And I just acted like a dick to you because of it. I started fights with you just because I wanted a chance to hit you. And you knew . . . for what? Two months? And you never did anything?"

"Three months."

"What?"

He turned to look at me, his eyes glassy. "I knew for three months. As soon as I came back from Arizona, I knew. You couldn't go more than a day without trying to start shit, and I come back and you won't even say a word to me and look like you're dead . . . and she couldn't stop looking at that ring you gave her. I didn't know she was pregnant yet, but I knew I'd already lost her."

My gut churned with guilt. "And you did nothing?"

"What, Chase? What could I have done to make things different than how they were? She was in love with you, too. You'd already slept with her. She was already pregnant! I couldn't fucking change anything. I couldn't change the way she felt for you! So what's the point of beating the shit out of you when it would change *nothing*?"

I watched as the tears rolled down his face, and, for the first time since all of this started, I felt sick. All I'd wanted was her, and I never considered how that would hurt my brother. All I cared about was how I felt like I was dying without her. "I'm sorry."

"You were like a brother to me." Before I could respond, he turned to glare at me again. "But I'm sure you can understand why I'm saying we're done."

Trying to swallow past the lump in my throat, I nodded and took a step back when he turned his Jeep on.

"Chase." He cleared his throat and shook his head once. "That girl means everything to me. Which means her baby does, too. I will never do to you what you did to Harper and me. But know this. If you do not take care of them, and cherish them . . . I will not hesitate again to beat the living shit out of you. You get me?"

"I got you. I love them, I'll always take care of them."

With a hard nod, he threw his Jeep into drive and took off.

Chapter Twelve

"You got everything ready for today?" Brad asked as he jumped up onto the counter and brought Sarah between his legs.

"Pretty sure." I took the last bite of my apple and threw the core into the trash. "Called the dealership, called the B&B . . . everything should be good to go."

"Harper's gonna love today, Chase." Sarah said with a wide smile on her face. "So sweet of you to do all this for her. But she's going to think you're gonna propose with how the day is set up!"

I grinned. "I already know when I'm going to propose, and it's not today."

"When?" Her eyes brightened, and she bounced up on her toes a few times.

"You'll see." I shrugged and caught the bottle of water she threw at me. "I'm not telling anyone, it's a surprise."

"Whatever. So you're going to find out if it's a boy or a girl today?"

"Guess so, she's due October 4, so she's sixteen weeks today, and her doctor said we should be able to . . . but I already know—" I broke off, and the massive grin I'd been sporting fell as Brandon walked into the kitchen.

"It's not like I don't know what's going on," he said without looking at anyone as he grabbed a bottle of Gatorade and two bottles of water. "You don't have to stop talking because of me."

Brad's eyes bounced back and forth between the two of us, and Sarah was covering her mouth while she slowly shook her head, her eyes full of pity as she watched Brandon.

After he'd grabbed a couple of protein bars and put everything in his bag, he finally looked back at us, his gaze resting on me. "Or maybe you do." Without another word, he left the kitchen, and Brad hung his head.

I pushed away from the counter and followed after him. "Brother—"

"I thought we'd already decided we weren't that, either."

Grabbing his shoulder, I stopped him before he could reach the door. "Look, I'm sorry! I'm sorry I did this to you."

He turned to look at me, his brow raised high. "You're sorry. So, what . . . we go back to being cool again?"

"I don't know, man. But we can't do this."

"And why can't we? You couldn't stand to let me have *one* normal day with her. Have I done anything to you since she and I broke up?" He paused, but I didn't respond. "No. I haven't. You dealt with it by being an ass, so let me deal with this my way. And my way doesn't include acting like you didn't steal my girl from me."

"I didn't steal Harper!"

He opened the door and took a step outside, his shaking hand gripping the outer knob. When he looked back at me, his eyes were flat and lifeless. "You stole my entire world."

"Chase"—I turned to see Brad leaning against the wall—"you need to give him space. He's right, you were the biggest dick to him while he was dating her. Now that you have her, you can't act like the two of you can just go back to being the way you were. He needs time to get over what you guys did to him. You know he told Derek he planned to marry her?"

"No"—my eyes narrowed—"what's your point, Brad?"

"His best friend and the girl he wanted to marry, stabbed him in the back. He has every right to try to ruin this for you, or at the very least to beat you into next week. And he's stepped back . . . so let him step back. What you're doing is just twisting the knife."

I nodded and sighed heavily. "Fuck."

"Yeah. Well, you're about to find out if your son is actually going to be a son. And you planned a weekend I know Sarah is seriously jealous of." I snorted, and he clapped my shoulder. "So cheer the fuck up. Because if Harper sees there's something wrong, she's going to want to know what it is. And you can't tell her about this shit; she hates herself enough as it is."

"I know." No need to remind me that the woman carrying my child still loved someone else.

It didn't take much for my mood to change again. Seeing Harper and being able to pull her into my arms always made everything right again. And knowing I was about to see our baby for the first time had everything else just slipping away. I met her doctor and talked with her about everything I'd missed so far and what to be expecting, and about took off running for the ultrasound room when it was time for that part of the appointment. Princess had just laughed and gripped my hand to keep me by her side, and I'd continued to cling to her when the doctor turned off the lights, and the ultrasound started.

And all I could think was *holy shit*.

The air had left my body in a rush when our baby appeared on the screen and a lump formed in my throat. My mouth opened, but nothing came out, and when the heartbeat filled the room, it took everything in me to not break down right there. *This baby is ours*. I turned to look at Harper and saw her eyes glistening through the dark in the room as we listened to our baby's racing heart.

"I can't even believe how perfect a position your baby is in right now! That is unreal." The doctor laughed. "Now, did you *want* to find out the sex of the baby, or do you want it to be a surprise?"

"I already know." My princess glanced back at the screen and smiled softly when I squeezed her hand and laughed.

"I told you, baby," I whispered. "I told you it would be a boy."

We both looked at Dr. Lowdry. "It is a boy, isn't it?"

"Oh, he is definitely a boy." She laughed again, and I watched as our baby boy moved around on the screen.

I looked back over at my beautiful girl and kissed her softly, keeping my lips brushing against hers as I told her, "I love you and our son so much, Harper."

When I pulled back, I saw that her eyes were glistening, and a few tears had fallen down her face. Using my thumbs, I brushed the trail of wetness off her cheeks and was rewarded with a heart-stopping smile.

After the doctor handed us the ultrasound pictures, I continued to stare at our son as Harper and I left the building. I'd known for months that I was in love with the girl walking next to me, and I'd known that I would give anything to make her mine, forever. But I wasn't expecting to fall in love with her all over again, or to have this instant love for our baby.

When we got to my truck, I grabbed around her waist and hauled her back to me, my mouth crashing down on hers. Harper laughed softly, and her arms went around my neck as I walked her slowly backwards 'til she was against my truck. Our kiss was slow and heated as I tried to show her how happy she was making me.

I broke the kiss on a huff and looked into her smiling gray eyes, "That was . . . that was absolutely amazing!" I laughed and kissed her hard once more.

Her hands found their way into my hair as she pulled back. "Having you there made it so special, all I could think about the last two times was how I wished you were there to experience it with me." Harper's eyes filled with pain when she whispered, "I'm sorry it took me so long to tell you."

"No *sorrys* today. I love you, and we're having a son." *Holy shit, we're really having a son.* I smiled and pushed some hair away from her face. "Today is only allowed to be an *I love you* day." When she nodded, I opened the door and helped her into the truck before running around to the driver's side and getting in.

Out of the corner of my eye, I watched as my Princess looked over the pictures with a wide smile. I only hoped the rest of today kept her smiling just as big.

We stopped for Mexican food, but thank God Harper was too distracted by the appointment to notice I could barely touch my lunch. My palms were sweating, and I was praying that the rest of the day wasn't too much too soon for her. I hadn't been lying to Sarah and Brad. I already had an idea in mind for a proposal to the only girl in the world that would ever matter; and it wasn't going to happen that day. But everything I had planned for that day could definitely scare her just as bad as a proposal this soon would.

I was so stressed, I couldn't even hold Harper's hand as I drove us to the Ford dealership I'd had her dream car sent to. So I kept the music up loud enough that there wouldn't be much room for talking and kept my right hand on the steering wheel, so I wouldn't go to grab her hand. There was no way she could miss my shaking if I did.

As soon as I pulled in, Harper's head stopped moving in time with the music, and she instantly stopped singing, "Uh . . . ?"

I had to clear my throat before I could talk to her as I turned to grin at her. "So I've been thinking, you're going to need your own car soon, and I happen to know that you want a blacked-out Expedition."

"Chase . . ."

"I *may* have had one brought to this dealership."

"No you didn't." Her already wide eyes got even bigger, and her jaw dropped as she looked around at all the cars.

"I said I may have. Never said I did."

She backhanded my arm before opening her door and hopping out of the truck. I blew out one last shaky breath as I rounded the front of my truck and pulled her into my arms. She was chewing on her bottom lip and looking around me before finally meeting my eyes. "Are you being serious?"

I smiled and pressed my lips to her neck. "I am. But we can look around and see if there's something else you want."

"Babe! I can't buy a car."

Shit, here goes nothing. "Maybe not, but *we* can."

"You want to split it?"

A short, hard laugh escaped my lips at her adorably confused expression. "Not exactly. Okay, you can tell me if this is moving too fast, but since I plan on marrying you soon, I wanted to put you on my bank account so you have access to my money."

"Chase"—her face had fallen, and I felt like I was holding my breath—"I don't need you to do that, and I don't need you to buy me a car."

"I know, Princess, but I want you to have access to it. I make decent money at the shop, but Bree and I were also left a lot when Dad's parents died. So I have more than enough in savings to take care of the three of us and to buy you a car. It's not a big deal."

"I know you want to, and to be honest, it kind of excites me that you want to share all that with me. But I'm saying . . . I *really* don't need you to. If we're going to share your bank account, then we should share mine, too."

"Harper, that isn't necessary." Exhaling in relief, I pulled her into my arms again and thought I'd heard her wrong when she told me how much she had saved up. *Uh . . . come again?* It wasn't as much as I still had for us, but I'd inherited the money I had in savings. Almost all bills, except for the house, came from what I made from the shop, so I rarely pulled any money out of savings. *She'd made* that *from working on base?* "Are you serious? Just from working on the base?" When she confirmed with one stiff nod, I whistled low. "Well damn, babe. That's great, and if you want to add it to our accounts, that's fine. But I'd rather not touch that money; we can save it for emergencies, and just let me take care of you."

I'd been expecting some sort of argument, or at least hesitancy. But she just shrugged with an, "Okay," and kissed me softly as she melted into my arms.

"You ready to look for a car?"

"Nope! No need to look. I already know I want the Expedition!"

She jumped out of my arms and grabbed my hand as she started walking off in the direction of the cars in the lot. I laughed and pulled her toward the showroom instead. Harper test-drove the completely blacked-out SUV and fell in love with it, just as I was hoping she would. We went through the process of buying it, and I swear the guy helping us scoffed when I said we would pay for the car right then. *Ass.* Once we were done with his stubborn ass, we drove separately to the bank and started the much-shorter process of adding Harper to my accounts and putting her savings into what was now *our* savings account. She was smiling brightly and bouncing along, and I wondered why I'd ever been worried about the day.

My family already knew what I had planned for it, but you could see the relief in Mom's and Dad's eyes as Harper excitedly showed them her new car and told them all about joining our bank accounts. When we were sitting at the table for dinner, we told everyone we were having a boy, and Mom had immediately ran to the kitchen to get the baby-name book, and we started through it right then. We must have highlighted three dozen different names before shutting the book for the night, and I watched as Harper lovingly ran her hands over her small stomach and talked to our "Gummy Bear," as she'd come to call him. God, I was so in love with her.

After dinner, I packed my bag and threw it in my truck before giving Brian a call at the shop.

"Hey, man! Shit, took you long enough to call, Riss is freaking out texting me every ten minutes wanting to know how everything went."

I snorted a laugh. "Tell her to calm her ass down. Everything went great, we're—" inhaling deeply, I shook my head at the ridiculous smile I had on my face—"we're having a boy."

"Yeah?" He laughed loudly and shouted the news to whoever was in the shop before coming back. "Hate to break it to ya, Chase. But I've been thinking, and I've decided you're seriously confused and just *think* that this is your baby."

My heart stopped, and my smile quickly fell. "The fu—"

"I mean," he cut me off with a snort, "everyone knows it's my baby. You're just in denial."

As soon as his words registered, I laughed out loud. "Seriously, I was about to go kick someone's ass."

"Just sayin', I even told Riss. That baby is mine."

"All right, I'll let Princess know, too."

"Damn straight you will! As long as we're all on the same page, we'll be good."

"You're such a dumb-ass." I laughed again. "Tell Marissa that the rest of the day went well. Harper's really happy, and we're about to leave for the last part of tonight, er, this weekend."

"You lucky bastard. All right, have fun but make sure my baby mama doesn't overdo it."

I shook my head. "See you Monday."

We hung up, and I jogged back into the house and into the living room, where I wrapped my arms around Princess from behind the couch.

My lips skimmed that sensitive spot behind her ear before I whispered, "Can you do me a favor?"

Her head had rolled to the side, and her arms were covered in goose bumps. "Anything."

"Go pack a bag for a few nights and meet me down here in ten minutes." Lightly nipping on her ear, I lowered my voice even further. "You won't need many clothes."

Her eyes flew open, and she turned to look at me, an odd expression passing over her face. "Are we going to your house?"

I wanted to ask what had freaked her out so much but decided I might not want to know since Brandon was at my house. Whether it had to do with him or not, I'd been making sure he and Harper didn't see each other anymore and really didn't want to discuss him with her. "Nope, but it's a surprise, so I can't tell you."

Her face relaxed, and she rolled her eyes with a light laugh. "You and your surprises. Okay, ten minutes, and I'll be ready."

While she was packing, I called Brad and told him about the appointment, the sex of the baby, and made sure everything was all right at the house. By the time I was hanging up, Princess was coming down the stairs with a *very* small bag, and I couldn't help but smile. Apparently, she'd taken my words seriously.

Since we'd gotten together, Harper and I hadn't slept together . . . in any way. We would curl up on her bed in my parents' house and talk until she fell asleep, and I'd quietly make my way back to my room. I knew my parents didn't care—after all, she *was* already pregnant. But even though she'd taken time between breaking up with Brandon and telling me about the baby, I was terrified of pushing her away like I'd done so often during the school year. And she hadn't asked if I would stay with her, so I'd continued to let her sleep alone.

But this weekend, I had other plans. I know I'd told her not to bring many clothes, but that'd been a joke. All I wanted was to fall asleep with her and wake up the same. If she was still uncomfortable, I'd gladly sleep on the floor if that's what she needed. But I figured it might be uncomfortable for her either at my house with her ex, or at my parents' with them there. So I was taking us for a weekend of just us. And hoping I didn't screw it up.

"Oh my God," she whispered, and slowly scrambled out of my truck once I was parked, unable to take her eyes off the restored Victorian house in front of us. The sign out front showed it was a bed-and-breakfast. "Chase, I don't know how you're ever going to be able to top today. Finding out we're having a boy, buying me a car, joining our bank accounts, and this?"

"I promise I'll always try to top this, but I did want today to be perfect." Kissing her forehead softly, I grabbed our bags and went inside to check us in. As soon as we were in our room, I wrapped my arms around her and pulled her close, waiting until her eyes met and locked with mine. "I know what I said earlier, but don't think we have to do anything this weekend. All I wanted was to have three nights of just you and me; I don't expect anything."

"I know you don't"—her voice was breathy as she grabbed for the bottom of my shirt and lifted it until I had to take over for her—"but I want this, too, Chase."

I sucked in air though my teeth when the tips of her fingers ran gently down my bared chest and stomach until they came to rest on the top of my jeans. Her eyes clouded over when she ran her fingers just inside my waistband, only to remove them and reach for the button. I would do anything to have her this way, but I needed to know she wouldn't regret this later. Grabbing her hands, I stilled them and bent slightly to look at her. "You're sure, Harper?"

She huffed softly, and her head tilted to the side as she pointed to her rounding stomach. "Um?"

"Just because we're having a baby doesn't mean we have to do anything."

"Chase. I didn't mean it like that. But yes, I am sure. Now stop trying to stop me and let me love you."

Shaking my head, I let out a short laugh and rested my forehead against hers before straightening and letting go of her hands. Her fingers and knuckles brushed against my growing erection as she undid each button and slid my jeans down before doing the same with my boxer briefs. I swear I groaned at one point. How was something as simple as her taking my pants off already having me breathing roughly? As soon as I kicked my pants away, I was grabbing for her shirt and giving her the same torture she'd just given to me. My knuckles skimmed across her small baby bump, and when the tips of my fingers caressed up the side of her breasts, I was rewarded with hearing her breath catch and her body instantly become covered in goose bumps. It took everything in me not to touch her where my body was craving, but I was happy to see I wasn't the only one struggling with keeping still as I pulled her shorts and underwear off her body. Her hands were clenched into fists, and if I hadn't looked up to see her gray eyes turn to liquid silver and her teeth sink into her soft bottom lip, I would have been afraid I'd been rushing things again.

Stepping away from her, I shamelessly ran my eyes over her beautiful body, and once again my chest filled with love when they caught sight of my work on her hip, and her little Gummy Bear bump. She finished her visual exploration of me seconds after I'd finished mine of her, and I bent down to press my lips to her growing belly and tattoo before standing to take her lips in mine. She moaned, and her hands came up to my neck as she deepened our kiss. Lifting her gently, I carried her over to the bed and deposited her in the middle before crawling on top of her.

Minutes that felt like hours—and still not nearly long enough—were spent touching every inch of each other with hot kisses and memorizing hands. As I made a trail of openmouthed kisses up her body, she grabbed my cheeks and begged me not to make her wait any longer. She grabbed my length and guided it to where she wanted it most, whimpering softly when I pushed inside her. Her eyes had fluttered shut momentarily, and opened on a gasp when I slid out and back in. I made love to her slowly, letting my lips graze hers softly before making their way back down to worship her neck and breasts, and when her head dropped back, and her body tightened as she came, I rolled us over so she was on top and lowered her body to kiss her again as she continued to move on me. Her breathing picked up again, and she intertwined our fingers, holding our hands down firmly on the bed as she sat up slightly and rolled her hips against mine over and over. I gritted my teeth and removed one of my hands from hers to grip her hip and help in her movement as she cried out her next orgasm, and I followed her into it.

"CHASE, WHERE'S MY baby mama?"

I turned to look at Brian and laughed. "Probably out with my mom and sister."

"Well, get her ass in here! I miss my baby boy."

"Bri, she was just here a couple days ago."

He looked at me like I was missing something. "Yeah . . . and?"

"And apparently nothing," I snorted, and looked back down to the rib cage of the girl I was working on. "You doin' all right?"

"Uh-huh!" she said tightly, and blew out quickly.

"If you need me to take another break, just let me know." She'd already taken one, and all I was doing was a name. I could easily have this done in ten minutes, fifteen tops. But not even halfway in she said she was going to pass out, and she needed ten minutes just to calm down. I'd advised her not to get her first tattoo on her ribs, but people will do what they want.

"N-no. I'm—I'm okay."

Hell no, she wasn't. I lowered my voice as I continued

on, trying to calm her. "We're almost done. Promise."

The bells above the door sounded and I glanced up to see a Kat Von D look-alike walk into the shop.

"You lookin' to get work done?"

"No," her husky voice said confidently as she walked right up to my station. "I'm Trish, and I start today."

I nodded but kept working. "Chase, good to meet you. Brian just stepped into the back for a second. He can show you around." Other than Brian, Jeff, and me, we'd had one other artist, Frankie, but the guy was usually so stoned out of his mind he couldn't work even if he did show up. Jeff had finally gotten rid of him a few weeks ago, but we'd been struggling with just the three of us, and he'd hired someone new while Harper and I had been in Dana Point. He hadn't said anything about its being a girl, though.

"Hey, homie!" Brian called out to her as he walked back in. "You bring your stuff with you today?"

"It's on the way, I left it in my girl's car, and she had to run an errand. She'll be here in a minute."

"All right, well I see you met Chase. Chase, this is the new chick." *No shit.* "Let me show you around the shop and get you in your station."

Thank God I'd pulled the needle away from the girl I was working on, because Trish touched my shoulder, and I jerked away from her hand. "Good to meet you, buddy."

"Yeah." *Fuck. Hot chick working here?* I honestly didn't care if she was a model; it wouldn't change the fact that the only person I wanted was Princess. But I knew from our conversations she still didn't really believe that I'd wanted only her since I met her. And I just hoped this didn't make her insecurities with our relationship grow.

I finished the small tattoo, covered it, and got her out the door before I went to where Brian and Trish were hanging out. As soon as I sat on Brian's counter, the door opened again, and Trish smiled wide as she ran over to it. Following her path, I saw a butch-looking girl standing there only to catch Trish as she crashed into her and kissed her hard. I blew out a relieved breath and smiled to myself. *She's gay. Thank. God.*

"That's hot," Brian said next to me, and I looked at him like he was insane.

"Bri, the other chick looks more like a guy than you do."

"Don't be jealous of my hair, bro. You just wish you could pull this off."

"You look like Troy Polamalu. Trust me when I say I'm not jealous."

He kicked at my leg and nodded when the girls walked up to us.

"Brian, Chase . . . this is my girlfriend, Erin. Erin, these are some of the guys."

Erin set a box I'm guessing had Trish's needle in it on the counter and roughly shook our hands. "You guys take care of my girl for me."

"Will do." The door opened again with a girl and a guy walking in holding hands. I stood and began to make my way toward them, turning toward Erin and Trish as I passed. "Good to meet you."

After I handed a couple books of our work to the new-lyweds wanting matching tattoos, Brian came up beside me, and whispered, "Dude, she looks like Kat Von D. Shit, that's hot."

"I'm gonna tell Riss you're hard for our new girl."

"Dude . . . Riss would think she's hot, too. She'd appreciate my taste in women."

I snorted. "Yeah, all right." Marissa was cool, but Brian had cheated on her right after they got married, and while I can't imagine why she'd stay with his lying ass after that, she was always getting on Bri whenever he checked out girls. He was terrified of losing her, we all knew that, so I knew he wouldn't touch another girl again. But he had that look-but-don't-touch philosophy, and I knew one day it was gonna set Riss off all over again.

We shut up when Erin and Trish walked past us with their arms around each other, and as they got to the door, shared a *long* kiss good-bye.

"Still hot," Brian whispered, and I just shook my head.

"Bro." Trish looked at me and laughed through her smile. "That's it! I gotta meet her."

"I don't know." I raised an eyebrow and sucked in air through my teeth. "You might try to take her from me. Lord knows Brian's already claimed the baby as his."

"The baby *is* mine!" he said loudly and caught the wrapped-up burrito Jeff tossed over to him.

We'd just barely opened the shop, and I had clients coming in a little over an hour, but other than that, we were dead. As was common in the early afternoons. Trish had been working for a few days, and after Brian and Jeff had told her about their wives, they'd turned it around to me and Princess and basically told her everything about our relationship up 'til now. And I mean *everything*. But with how much the other guys loved her, too, Trish was dying to meet the girl who changed me.

"Get my baby mama here!"

Jeff swallowed the bite of taco he'd just taken, before adding, "If Brian gets this baby, can your next baby be mine?"

"So dumb. I don't know how your wives or Princess put up with you guys." But I still pulled out my phone and gave her a call, and when she answered, I couldn't stop the wide smile that crossed my face at hearing her voice, and Trish started razzing me with Brian about it. "Hey, Princess, can you come by the shop?"

"I'm going to dinner with Bree in a little over an hour, but I can swing by really quick. Did you need me to bring you anything?"

"Just yourself. Brian's mad because you haven't been around." I didn't mention he was currently giving me puppy eyes. I rolled my eyes at him and shoved him away as he tried to take the phone from me. "And we have a new artist, she wants to meet you after hearing all our stories about you."

She laughed softly and sighed. "I was just there last week! I'm leaving right now; see you in a minute."

I mouthed to the guys and Trish that she was coming. "I love you."

"Love you, too, Chase."

I would never get enough of hearing her say that.

Trish and I were in my station, and I was telling her about how I'd come to give Harper her nickname, when my girl walked in. God she was gorgeous. Her stomach was getting bigger, and I loved it. Ever since the bed-and-breakfast, we spent every night in each other's arms, and I would always pull her shirt up so I could trace random patterns across her growing belly. To be honest, it was the best part of my day. She'd already be asleep since I worked late most nights, but she'd wake up so we could talk an hour or so about everything and nothing and just enjoy each other without anyone else around.

Harper stopped walking suddenly, and an odd expression crossed her face. My brow scrunched momentarily until the expression vanished, and I held my hand out to her. "Come here babe!" As soon as she was close enough, I pulled her into my arms and kissed her soundly before turning her toward Trish. "Harper, this is Trish. Trish, this is my beautiful Harper."

"Chase," Jeff called from behind me, and I turned to face him. "Guy just called in wanting a finger tat. Can you fit him in before your other appointment comes in?"

"Yeah, when will he be here?"

"He's already on his way, just a few minutes. Hey, Harper." He smiled and took her from me to wrap her in a big hug.

"Do I see my baby mama?" Brian boomed as he walked out of the back, and I laughed as he hugged her close and kissed her cheek. I knew I didn't have to worry about Princess and Brian. She loved him and Marissa, but she responded to him the same way she responded to Brad. And besides, as soon as Brian released her, she sank right back into my arms.

"Where have you been?" Brian asked, and pouted miserably. "You're keeping my son away from me now?"

"Never," she teased. "Why else would we be here?"

"'Sup, little BJ."

"Uh . . ." Harper cocked her head to the side. "BJ?"

"Yeah, Brian Jr., that's what we're naming him."

Fucking hell. Harper, Jeff, and I all started cracking up. "Did you already ask Marissa? I'm pretty sure she doesn't need another Brian to take care of," I teased as I pulled Princess into my arms and pressed my lips to her neck, my hands trailing across her stomach. *Mine.*

Brian and Jeff started arguing over who got our next kid, and I loved how Harper interacted with my friends. She was so relaxed with these guys, and to be honest, I'd been worried about that. I knew she loved my work, but loving what I do and being all right with the guys I worked with are two completely different things. So to have them all instantly accept each other was a huge relief.

The call-in walked into the shop, and I gave Harper one more kiss before going over to talk to him. Tattoo was simple and would take no time at all, he just wanted his wife's initials on his ring finger. I turned to look at Princess talking to Trish and smiled to myself, knowing that she was already tattooed on me. I wanted to tell her, but it had just never come up, and though she knew I'd been in love with her all this time, I had no clue how she would react if she knew I'd drawn that up so soon after meeting her.

After giving the guy the call-in a book of different fonts, I walked back over to where the girls were talking, and Trish smiled wide at me. "Hey buddy, great girl you've got here!"

"Yeah, isn't she? You gonna stay and watch, babe?"

Harper turned and after a brief look at me, looked down to the ground. "No. I need to go meet Bree. I'll see you at home."

"All right, let me walk you out." As soon as we were outside and next to her SUV I pulled her into my arms again. "Thanks for coming, they've all missed you."

Nodding twice, she started searching through her purse.

What the hell? "You okay?"

"Not really. No." She sighed heavily and finally looked up at me. "I don't like Trish."

"What? Trish is awesome." I swear her and her girlfriend should switch places, she acted just like Brian, and if she didn't look like a Suicide Girl, I would swear she *was* a guy. "Why don't you like her?"

"It might have been the fact that she refused to return my greeting, *or* that she let me know she was going to "take care" of you while I'm not around."

I laughed and squeezed my arms tighter. This was just another thing I loved about Harper. She didn't bullshit the way some girls did. If she was mad, she let you know. And while I didn't like that she was uncomfortable, I'm not gonna lie. It felt real good knowing she was jealous.

"Aw, Princess, she's just joking with you. You don't have anything to worry about. She's gay."

"I promise you, she isn't."

"Yeah she is; she told me yesterday."

"Okay, Chase. I really do have to go, I love you. See you when you get home."

Kissing her soft lips, I pulled away slightly to catch her gaze. She still look worried when I brought one hand up to cup her cheek. "Cheer up baby, I love you, too."

I watched her pull away and walked back into the shop. Catching the call-in's attention, I took him back to my station, where Trish was still sitting.

"Dude." She smiled and jerked her head toward the door. "Your girl is head over heels in love with you."

The corners of my mouth tilted up. *Feeling was definitely mutual.* "I'm a lucky man."

"I'd say, even pregnant, she's fucking hot."

Brian, Jeff, and the call-in all grunted agreement, and I glared at them before teasing Trish. "You got your own girl, so stay away from mine."

She shrugged and jumped off my counter to go help people who were done looking through art on the wall, and I gestured for the call-in to sit in the chair. "Let's do this."

Chapter Thirteen

PULLING MY VIBRATING cell out of my pocket, I checked the messages and saw there was a text from Trish. I suppressed a groan and silently prayed shit wasn't hitting the fan at the shop. This was my first night off since Princess and I had gone to the bed-and-breakfast well over a week ago. And I wanted nothing more than to finish hanging out with my family and take her to bed.

Trish: Hey buddy . . . gf is working graveyard 2nite. Wanna come over 4 dinner when I get off?

"Are you kidding? Of course we did! That lady was hilarious, there was no way we weren't giving her money." Standing up from the table, Breanna started showing us a dance this homeless lady had been doing earlier when she was out with Konrad. I laughed and tapped out a quick text back to Trish.

Can't, sorry. Spending time with Princess

"Chase, you should go find that woman," Dad said on a laugh. "She would probably teach you to dance for a few bucks."

I snorted. "At least I don't look like a dying fish when I dance." I glanced at him meaningfully, and he started laughing at the same time Harper gasped loudly and gripped my arm.

"You okay?" I turned to look at her, and she was looking straight down. Looking at her line of sight, I couldn't see anything wrong and looked at my parents, who seemed just as confused as I was.

"Say something, Chase."

The hell? I leaned closer to her, trying to look into her eyes, "Sweetie, what's wrong?"

Harper started laughing and glanced at me quickly before looking straight down again, "He's kicking! He's kicking whenever you talk!"

Oh my God. My knees hit the ground, and I pushed my way in between Harper's legs while letting my hands cover her rounding stomach. My heart was racing, and I had to take two deep breaths before leaning in close, my nose almost touching her belly. "You kicking Mom?" I kept my voice low, and said slowly, "C'mon, Gummy Bear, Daddy wants to feel you kick, too. I love you so much—" A light nudge hit my hand, and my head shot back to look at my princess. "Oh my God!" Bringing my head back to her belly I swear I fell in love with our son even more while I continued to talk to him. Each time, I was rewarded with a soft nudge, and I couldn't help but laugh shakily at how amazing it was.

Mom, Dad, and Breanna all took turns feeling GB kick, all while I spoke softly to him. Once Bree was done, I went back to kneeling in front of Harper, but I didn't feel him kick again.

"I think he rolled over," Harper whispered, and I stood up, pulling her with me to capture her lips with mine. "That was incredible!" She laughed against my mouth, and I smiled.

"My thoughts exactly." Without looking back at my family, I grabbed her hand and started towing her toward the stairs. " 'Night, everyone."

Harper giggled and turned to wave. "Good night!"

They all called out good nights, but I didn't slow down for anything. As soon as we were in my room, I shut the door and locked it before pushing Harper up against it. "Babe—" I growled against her mouth, and she leaned away, running her thumb over my lips.

"I know, Chase. I love you, too, so much."

"That was amazing. Thank you, Harper. Thank you for our son, thank you for loving me."

"Always," she whispered, and brought her mouth back to mine, our lips moving against each other slowly.

Lifting her shirt over her head, I dropped it next to us and immediately went for her bra. Her hands started undressing me as I pulled down her tight workout pants.

She had just gotten the button on my jeans undone and was going for my fly when I removed her hands and turned us, walking her back toward the bed. After laying us down, I made a trail from her lips to her ear. "Let me love you tonight, Princess."

Without waiting for a response, I kissed and sucked my way down her body, lifting her legs so her feet were planted on the bed, and her knees were bent. Trailing my fingers along her wet folds, she sucked in air and whispered my name. Hearing Harper say my name that way— seeing the way her head would fall back and body would arch off the bed when I ran my tongue over her heat, and feeling as her body tightened and shuddered around me as she came—was perfection to me. And that perfection was mine.

"COME ON, GUMMY BEAR, you gotta wake up for Daddy. Kick for me, buddy."

Harper laughed softly, and her hands went into my hair. "I'm telling you, babe, he's asleep. He's not gonna wake up."

"You'll wake up for Daddy, won't you? You don't want me to go to the party; you want to kick the crap out of Mom's belly while I talk to you, don't you?"

Still nothing.

I sighed and ran my nose back and forth across Harper's stomach. Graduation was on Sunday, so the guys at my house were throwing one last Friday night party . . . and I didn't want to go. I'd started working a lot more back when Harper and Brandon were dating, so I hadn't even been to a party in who knows how long; and it just didn't interest me anymore. Besides, Princess wasn't going, so if she wasn't going, I definitely didn't want to go. She'd been pushing me out the door, saying I needed a good weekend with my friends, and, as a last attempt, I told her that if I could get GB to kick for me, I didn't have to go. But five minutes of talking to her swollen stomach, and he hadn't so much as rolled over.

Harper tugged on my hair gently, and I reluctantly stood up. "Go to the party, Chase. Have fun."

I grumbled, but cupped her cheeks and kissed her soundly. "I'll be back later tonight."

"Just have fun. I'll see you tomorrow."

Shaking my head, I kissed her forehead and unlocked my truck. "I need you in my arms when I fall asleep tonight, Princess. I'll text you when I'm on my way back here."

Ignoring the urge to turn my truck back around to go be with her, I reasoned that at least I could grab the solitaire engagement ring I'd bought Harper last week. I had everything planned to propose after graduation on Sunday, and it felt like the next day and a half would drag by. Princess was always saying she didn't need to be married just because she was pregnant. But what she wasn't getting is that I couldn't wait to marry her. I wanted to be with her forever and didn't see the point in waiting to start my life with her.

I'd just gotten done showing Sarah and Brad the engagement ring before stowing it away in my desk and locking my room back up when my phone started chiming. *Trish.* I sighed and opened up the texts. Almost every night over the last two weeks, she'd tried to get me to come hang out at her apartment either after work or for the night when she wasn't working. She said her girlfriend was always working graveyard shifts, and Trish was cool and all—but I knew Harper still couldn't stand her, so I'd continued to say no. You'd think after two weeks of that she'd get the hint. Apparently not.

> *Trish:* U should come keep me company. I'll make you dinner
>
> Can't. Sorry
>
> *Trish:* :(u gonna make me spend another night alone?
>
> Where's your girlfriend? Graveyard shift again?
>
> *Trish:* . . . yep
>
> Sorry dude. Having a party at my place. Catch you Monday

Shoving my phone back in my pocket, I made my way through the house toward the kitchen. Drew and some girl I'd never seen were doing shots, and I grabbed a bottle of water out of the fridge, working hard not to shake my head at everything happening in the house. I couldn't remember how I'd ever found these entertaining. But I was already counting down the minutes until I could go back to my parents' house. I'd already been here for almost five hours, and I figured if I gave it another hour, Princess wouldn't think I'd missed out on anything because she wasn't here.

Brandon walked past me to grab a beer out of the fridge, and I tensed when he came back to hop on the counter next to me. We hadn't talked in almost a month, but when he didn't immediately try to hit me, I started to relax a bit.

"What's going on?"

"Not much," he said gruffly, and took a long drink. "Think I'm gonna go hide in my room soon. These just aren't as fun as they used to be."

"Agreed. I'll be going to my parents' in a bit. You going back to Arizona as soon as the year's over?"

"Nah. Mom bought a house in Carlsbad, she and Jeremy move here in a week."

"Huh." My eyebrows shot up. "That's good then."

He nodded, and we fell back into an awkward silence. A couple times he'd start to say something before stopping himself. And just as I was about to tell him to spit it out, he shakily asked, "How's uh—how're Harper and the baby?"

My chest tightened, and guilt ate away at me. Every time I thought of them, I couldn't help but smile—a fact Brian, Jeff, and Trish teased me about relentlessly. But with Brandon, I just had the need to apologize. "They're really good. Look man, I'm—"

"Don't apologize." He drained his beer and hopped off the counter, turning slightly to look at me. "I—I hate what you did. To be honest, I don't think I'll ever get over it, but I . . ." He trailed off and took a deep breath before looking me in the eye. "I forgive you. I know you love her, and I know she loved us both. All I want is for her to be happy. And if she's happy with you, then that's all I need."

I stared at him for a long time, trying to figure out exactly what to say. But nothing seemed right. When he started to turn away, I called out, "Thank you, brother. That means a lot."

With a hard nod, he turned and made his way toward the hall his room was on. I was still sitting there dumbfounded when someone gently punched my arm. Looking to my right, I saw Trish, and my head jerked back, "Hey, dude."

"Cool that I'm here? Didn't feel like being alone while Erin was gone tonight."

"Yeah, sure. Parties are always open to anyone."

She looked around before asking, "Where's Harper?"

"At my parents'. She didn't think she should be here since she's pregnant. Sorry, I know you just got here, but I wanna get back to her so I'm gonna leave in an hour or so. Can I get you a drink, though?"

"Nah, I'm good. Can I just have a sip of your water?"

I handed it over without a word and turned when loud cheers came from the dining room. *Keg stands. Seriously? Can't they do that shit outside?* Trish handed my water back to me, and I took a long drink.

"So hey"—she nudged my arm—"I was wanting another tat. You gonna do this one, too?"

"Sure, sure. What are you wanting?"

"Some lyrics from a song, right under my left boob."

Aw hell. Harper's gonna flip. "Uh, all right. We'll see." I drained my water and showed her the empty bottle. "I'm gonna get another one, you sure you don't want one?"

She eyed the empty bottle, and her eyes flashed over to mine. "Yeah sure, I guess I'm thirstier than I realized."

"You skank! He's having a baby!"

I worked at opening my eyes, but my lids felt heavy. Too heavy. And my head was pounding like I had a wicked hangover. *What the hell? I didn't even drink last night. Did I?*

"Can you please give us some time alone?" a husky, feminine voice asked.

"Get out of his bed! Konrad, let me go, I'm gonna kill her! Chase, you asshole, wake the fuck up!"

The fuck? I felt something tighten around my waist. Harper? Still trying to force my eyes open, I turned and had barely cracked them open when I saw her.

Not Harper.

Holy shit.

My eyes widened, and I scrambled away from Trish, my head pounding in protest, and I grabbed it as Bree started screaming again. "What the fuck is going on?" I yelled, and forced my eyes open again to look around. I was in my bed, in my house. Konrad looked like he wanted to kill me as he held a bucking Breanna to his chest.

"Chase, make them leave please." Trish moaned and wrapped an arm around my waist, and I pushed her away.

"What the fuck are you doing in my bed?" I looked

around wildly. "Where's Harper? Oh my God, what the hell happened?" I groaned and gripped my head again as I struggled to get out from under the comforter and off the bed. I tripped out of the comforter and landed hard on the floor; when I looked down, I saw I was only in my boxers. Glancing up as Trish rushed out of the bed and over to me, I saw she was wearing my favorite shirt and underwear. Nothing else.

Oh God, no. No, no, no.

"Baby, are you all right?" Trish asked as she squatted in front of me. Her arm reached out toward me, and I smacked it away.

"The fuck, Trish! What are you doing in my bed? Why are you wearing my shirt?"

"I'll kill you, you evil bitch!" Bree screeched and bucked harder against Konrad.

It felt like my skull was being split and I groaned as I tried to hold it together, like that would somehow stop the pain. "Harper, oh God, Harper. What happened? What did I do?"

I tried to remember going to bed with Trish . . . I tried to remember going to bed period. *I can't remember anything past*—another shooting pain went through my head as I tried to stand—*Shit, I can't even remember my last solid memory of last night!*

"Chase—" Trish reached out for me when I stumbled into my desk, and again I smacked her arms away.

"Do. Not. Touch me." I glared at her, and my breathing became rougher. How could I have done something like this to Princess? "What. The hell. Happened?" When she didn't respond right away, I yelled, "Why the fuck were you in my bed?"

"How can you do this to me, Chase? You're going to pretend like I mean nothing to you just because your sister caught us?"

I turned to see my sister sobbing; Konrad's nostrils were flaring as he held her tight and continued to shoot daggers my way.

"You bitch!" Breanna cried, and wiped angrily at her eyes as she looked back up at Trish. "Tell him the truth! *Tell him!*"

My eyes widened, and I turned to Trish while still cradling my head and trying to steady my breathing, so I wouldn't vomit everywhere. "What, Trish? What's the truth?"

She shook her head and shrugged. "Your sister's psychotic. I don't know what she's even talking about."

Before I could say anything about that, Konrad beat me to it, "You fucking whore! Say another word about her, and I swear to God, I will forget about all my views on hitting a woman. Tell him that Harper was here! That she's the one that found you two!"

I dropped to my knees and started dry heaving. *Oh God. Harper was here. She was the one that found us. Oh my God, what have I done?*

"The sooner that little slut found out, the better. She was ruining Chase's life!"

"Get out!" I yelled between heaves. "Get the fuck out of my house!"

"Chase—" Trish began again, but I cut her off.

"Get. *Out!*"

After another minute, the door to my room shut, and the only sound were Bree's sobs and her repetitive words. "How could you, Chase?"

I couldn't have. I wouldn't have done that to Harper.

"Where's Harper?" I groaned as I shakily got to my feet and began grabbing at my discarded clothes. "Breanna, please, where is Harper?"

"She left with Brandon."

All the air left my lungs at Konrad's words, and I tripped trying to get into my shorts. Slowly, I lifted my head 'til I was looking at them. "W-what?"

"She was crying and going to leave, so Brandon took her away from here. And you should be damn thankful for that. I want to beat the shit out of you right now, but Brandon looked like he was ready to kill you."

"Chase," Bree cried. "Why? How? How could you do this to her? I thought you loved her."

I dressed and looked for my phone. As soon as I found it, I tried calling Harper twice, but it went straight to voice mail. "I wouldn't," I finally responded. "Bree, I wouldn't. I love her, and I would never have done anything like this to her."

"Then why—"

"I don't know, Breanna! I don't remember anything after—anything after—*damn it!* I don't remember what happened last night!" I don't even remember fucking drinking! I tried Harper's cell again and patted my pockets until I found my keys. "You said Brandon took her? Did he take her to the house?"

Konrad shook his head. "Harper said she couldn't face your parents. I don't know where they went."

"I have to go find her."

"Chase," Konrad said roughly, as I reached my door. "Don't do this to her. Don't lie to her. If you love her, let her go. Don't pretend like nothing happened."

"I wouldn't do this to her!" With that, I stormed out of my room and house. As soon as I was driving, I tried Harper one last time before calling Brandon.

"I warned you," he growled in way of greeting.

"Please tell me she's there."

"I have her, but she needs this time to herself. She's not in the car with me."

"Where are you? I need to talk to her!"

"Like I said"—his voice lowered—"she needs to be by herself. Leave her alone."

"Brandon—"

"I fucking warned you!"

A sob broke through, and I pulled off into a nearby parking lot, threw my truck into park, and hunched in on myself. "I don't know what happened—"

"Bullshit! You told Harper to meet you at the house this morning, then this chick comes walking out? Jesus, Chase! You should've seen Harper when she ran to your room and saw you. You just crushed her."

"Told her to—what? No, I just woke up to Bree yelling!"

"You don't deserve her. All this time, and you've just been playing games. For what, Chase? You make our lives miserable, you get her, then you just throw all that away?"

"No, no! I don't remember last night at all."

Brandon remained quiet for a long time. "I told you to cherish her. To cherish them."

"I do! I—I honestly don't remember last night at all! Did you see me with her? With Trish?"

"I went to sleep after you and I talked."

"We talked?" I searched my still-throbbing brain for anything. But nothing.

"Chase, don't play dumb!"

"I don't remember anything!" I yelled and gripped my hair with the hand that wasn't holding the phone.

"I told you my mom and Jeremy were moving here. We talked about you and Harper! Jesus," he hissed. "Why am I even going along with this?"

It took a few minutes before anything started coming to me, but then flickers of images flashed through my mind. "You forgave us," I whispered.

"Up until about an hour ago, I forgave both of you. Now? I swear, Chase, if I see you anytime soon—"

"You'll beat the shit out of me, I know. Bro, I wouldn't do this to her."

"Save it. I don't want to hear it. You *crushed* her." After another few silent minutes, he whispered, "She deserves so much better than you."

I wanted to defend myself again, but what was the point? I'd just woken up to Trish. I shook my head, not understanding anything. *She's gay; she has a girlfriend! And what the hell happened last night?* "I know she does," I admitted softly.

"For a while, I thought I hated you for taking her from me. She was happy with you, though, so I couldn't. But now, all I can think of is destroying you for hurting her. Again."

Tears fell silently. I had destroyed her. Destroyed us. And I'd pushed her right back into Brandon's arms. He'd never hurt her—all he ever did was take care of her. "Please . . . please bring her back to me."

Brandon sighed heavily. "When she's ready to see you, I will."

"Keep her safe."

"Always."

I ended the call and shut my eyes as tears continued to fall.

What the hell have I done?

By the time I got to my parents' house, Harper still wasn't there, and I still couldn't remember all of last night. I remembered Zach's hitting on Trish when I walked back with fresh bottles of water until she dismissed him by saying she was happy with her girlfriend. Not that he'd let it go that easily, but by the time he walked from where Trish was leaning up against the island and I was sitting on the counter a couple feet away, everything started to blur. I vaguely recalled a fight breaking out in my living room, and Derek and Brad rushing toward the fight. But I did not remember their breaking it up, and not a thing after that.

Walking into the living room, I found Konrad and Bree on the couch opposite where my mom and dad were sitting. Bree and Mom were crying, and all of them looked like they wanted to beat my ass.

I knew the feeling.

Chapter Fourteen

"HARPER?" BREE CALLED, and rushed to the entryway.

All the air left my body, and I struggled to take in a breath. It'd been over nine hours since I had gotten off the phone with Brandon, and though Bree had been texting him most the day, I was terrified Harper wouldn't be coming. But she did; she'd come back. Thank God. Bile rose in my throat, and I forced it back down as flashes of waking up next to Trish flew through my mind.

God damn it.

I heard Harper and Bree make their way into the living room and was somehow able to lift my head to look at my world—and what I saw made me want to die. Her eyes were red, her cheeks splotchy, and she looked like someone had ripped out her heart.

Me. I did that. I'm the one who put that look on her face.

I started to stand, but Dad pushed me back down,

and I couldn't even try to fight against him. It felt like someone had shot me in the chest, and with the pain radiating through my body, I didn't know how I was alive— let alone breathing. I watched as Harper hugged Mom tightly for a few moments and wanted to yell at everyone to leave, I wanted to be the one holding her. *Needed* to be the one holding her. Her eyes flashed over to me quickly when the others started leaving the room, and in the split second they held mine, I felt all of my pain mixed with hers. *What have I done?*

"Baby—"

"Don't. Call. Me. That." Her eyes flattened out as she spoke through a clenched jaw.

"Harper, please, I messed up," I choked out, and didn't care about the tears falling down my face anymore. There was no point in trying to stop them now. "I don't remember anything, you have to believe that I wouldn't do that to you." My voice gave out again, and I forced the lump back down. I'd hurt her so many times before, but all of that had been to save her from me. Not now, though—not this time. I wouldn't do that to my princess.

"Why her, Chase? The one person I hate! How could you do this to me? How could you do this to our baby?"

I flinched back as if she'd slapped me. "I didn't. I mean—I don't know, I don't remember anything!" *God, why can't I remember the rest of last night?* "I was at the party and the next thing I know I'm waking up to Breanna and Konrad screaming at me, and Trish is in my bed with me. But I swear I wouldn't touch her, I wouldn't touch anyone. I love you!" Didn't she see that? After all this time, couldn't Harper see how much I loved her and all I'd do for her?

One of Harper's eyebrows rose shakily, and even through her pained expression, I could see the disgust in that look. "You really expect me to believe this? You *know* how I feel about her, Chase, then you invite her to a party I just happen not to be at? Everyone thinks you came back to me last night, and yet she walks out of your room this morning wearing your shirt, and you were practically naked in the bed?"

God, I would never have touched that woman—*any* woman—but especially not Trish. "I didn't invite her, she invited me over again, and I told her no, with the excuse of the party. I didn't know she was going to show up."

"Why did you have to have the party as an excuse? Why can't I be excuse enough? You should have told her a long time ago that she needed to stop, that you were in a relationship and going to be a father, and her flirting with you wasn't okay! Instead, you let her continue to flirt with you and invite you over to her place in the middle of the night. When I was around, she would be hanging off your arm, and you think I'm going to believe that you didn't sleep with her when I *wasn't* around?"

"I thought she was gay! But I wouldn't sleep with her, baby, you have to believe me!"

"You're still sticking with that?" She looked expectantly at me as if waiting for another answer, and scoffed when she didn't receive one. "That is exactly why I don't believe you—you can't even tell me the truth when you know I've seen the pictures."

My body froze. *Pictures. There are pictures?* "What pictures?" She didn't respond, just continued to sit in the large chair staring at me. My body shot off the couch, and I was yelling before I could stop myself, *"What pictures, Harper?"*

"Come on, Chase, they were taken with *and* sent to me from your phone."

I struggled with getting my phone out of my pocket and began scrolling through my pictures, and checking the texts to Harper when I didn't see anything new. All I could see was what I'd sent her this morning, after waking up, and normal stuff before that. "I don't see anything."

Princess sighed and started messing with her phone, and I swear I stopped breathing as I waited for her to be done doing whatever it was she was doing. Her phone repeatedly chimed, and once it died down, her shaky hand held it out to me. I didn't want to see whatever was on that phone . . . I didn't want to, but I had to. I reached forward to grab it and flipped back and forth between the two pictures a few times to make sure I wasn't imagining things. My stomach tightened, and I thought I was going to throw up right there. I gasped for air, and my legs gave out on me; the pain from hitting the ground was welcomed as the worst nightmare of my life became a reality.

"Oh God. No. No, no I wouldn't have."

"Well, you obviously did."

I couldn't have! "I don't remember this, I wouldn't do this to you! You know I love you!"

"Maybe you were just that drunk."

Drunk? She knew better than anyone that I hadn't had anything to drink since the end of August. "I didn't drink last night, I swear! Ask Bree!"

"Chase"—her voice came out soft and so calm it broke my heart more—"just stop lying to me."

"I'm not lying!" I moved closer to her and put my hands on her thighs, forcing them not to grip her too tight. "Please believe me!"

She took my hands off her, and it felt like another shot to the chest. "Chase, if you still want to be in the baby's life, I would love that. But I can't continue to be in this relationship. Besides, we both know it was doomed from the beginning."

No, no, no—"No it wasn't!"

"I can't trust you, Chase. Especially after this."

"Harper. We. Are not. Breaking up. I was going to propose to you after graduation tomorrow!"

She looked at me with a pained expression. "We need to. You obviously still want to live your old life, and I need to not have to worry about what you're doing when I'm not with you."

The fuck I do! "I don't want my old life! I don't want anything without you! You are my everything, Harper. You and our baby are my everything." She was leaving me, my world, my heart—was leaving me. Sobs tore from my chest, and my head dropped into her lap as my body shook violently.

"Maybe sometime later, after you've had a chance to think about what you really want, we can give us a shot again."

My hands tightened into fists around her shirt in a pathetic attempt to somehow keep her with me. "Princess please, *please* don't do this. I can't lose you."

"You don't have to," she whispered. "We can remain friends, you can be at all the appointments, and I will continue to live here if that's what you want. But, Chase, you have just shattered my heart over what will probably only be one night with Trish. Because of that, I can't be yours right now. I can't be the naïve girlfriend at home with a baby while you're off with other women."

"I won't be, I only want you." God, if I had a selfless bone in my body, I would have told her she's right and let her live a life she deserved. She needed someone like Brandon, someone who would take care of her even after we screwed him over. Not me. Even without trying, all I do is hurt her. *She deserves so much better than me, but fuck, I can't lose her.*

"It's going to take a lot for me to believe you again, Chase, but I'm willing to give you the opportunity to earn my trust again. We're going to have to start over as friends, though."

"I don't want to be your friend, Harper!"

"It's that or nothing, Chase."

"Baby, I'm so sorry. I promise, I wouldn't have done that to you, I don't remember anything from last night." Even with the pictures, I could hardly remember anything after Trish showed up.

"I told you, I'll give you a chance if you want it. But I need a few days before we can try to be friends. I really— I'm hurting, Chase, I feel like you just confirmed every fear I've ever had of being in a relationship with you. And I'm still not sure how to begin to deal with this."

I was at war with myself—part of me was yelling to let her go so she could be happy, the other was dying inside at the thought of not having her to myself. I cupped her cheeks and kissed her deeply. "I will get to the bottom of whatever happened. I love you, Harper, more than you can ever imagine." I caught her lips again with my own and prayed that this wouldn't be the last kiss we shared.

System of a Down came blaring through my phone, and I went to hit ignore, knowing it was someone from work. When I caught sight of the name, I did a double take and took the call, standing up and storming off into the kitchen as I yelled into the phone, *"What the hell did you do to me? Do you have any idea what you've done?"*

"Chase—how can you talk to me like that after what we shared last night? Everything you promised me?" Trish asked, sounding hurt.

Shared? Promised? I didn't—*Fuck!* "No!" *There's no way I would have done something like that to Harper, no fucking way.* "You just ruined my life, do you understand that?"

"I-I-I'm sorry, I—"

"Don't fucking apologize to me! Harper is the only person you should be apologizing to, but understand that if you *ever* contact her, or me for that matter, again, I will make the rest of your life a living hell!"

"Cha—"

I hung up before she could say any more and threw my iPhone against the wall as hard as I could. The case shattered, and Princess flinched as a chunk flew right past her head. "Oh God, Harper. I'm sorry!" I walked quickly toward her and watched as she shrank into the chair, her face pale and body shaking. *Oh my God, I'm scaring her.* I couldn't have made things any worse if I had tried. "I have to go, before I mess this up more." I brushed my knuckles along her jaw, hating that she flinched when I touched her and trying to memorize her face. "I'm sorry for everything. I can't say that enough, Harper, I'm so, so sorry. Please don't end us, though. I will earn your trust again somehow, just don't do this."

"Don't make this harder for either of us; you know how I feel. Let's give it a few days, and we'll see if we can start again as friends. No matter what happens to us, Chase, I want you in his life."

But I wanted to be in her life, too. My world meant nothing if it didn't have both of them in it. My stomach churned, and my vision blurred as I realized this was it, the moment I'd always wanted her to find but had always dreaded—when she realized she was better off without me. "I love you, Princess," I whispered before kissing her one more time and walking out the door.

My body shook brutally with a new round of sobs as soon as I was in my truck, and I slumped against the steering wheel. This is what she needed, but I couldn't let this happen. I was too selfish to let her go; I needed her more than she could ever imagine. Before I met her, I'd thought my life was perfect. But, in reality, it was meaningless, and would go back to being just that if she was gone. Every ounce of my being was yelling at me to go back into my parents' house, pull her into my arms, and make her forget about what had happened. But if I was to ever get her back, I needed to give her the space I knew she needed. I scrubbed my hands down my face and cranked the engine over, I had to get out of there before the idea of kissing her senseless started sounding better and better.

While I drove, I thought about everything that had happened in the last year with her, and I couldn't believe one girl had changed me so completely. My chest rose and fell quickly as I thought about everything I'd done wrong when it came to her, wishing I hadn't wasted so much time being an asshole to her, and at the same time wishing I had continued to push her away. But how do you continue to push away your reason for staying on this earth? My chest tightened as my heart and mind continued to fight for two different outcomes. I didn't know which side was winning out. I just knew I wanted her—and I wanted her forever.

Thoughts of my conversation with Brandon in the morning kept creeping back, and though I wanted to push them away, I knew he was right. I knew he was what was best for her. Hadn't I always been the one saying that? To her—to everyone? Brandon wouldn't do this to her, he wouldn't crush her over and over again, but I didn't know if I had the strength to leave her for good. She was mine—she would always be mine.

I lifted my hips slightly to reach for my phone in my back pocket. When I didn't feel it, I started going through all my other pockets. Nothing. Where was my phone? I needed to call her. Even if she didn't answer, I needed to tell her I loved her and that I wasn't giving up on us, I never would. I felt around on the passenger seat, again turning up nothing. I looked in the rearview mirror and out the windshield. No cars around me, and the light up ahead was still green. Leaning over, I ran my hand over the floor on the passenger side but didn't feel anything. I swear I had just—Trish . . . I threw my phone against the wall. Fuck, I'd left it at Mom's. I sat up quickly, deciding it was a sign, and I needed to go back and take Harper into my arms and talk everything out.

I saw the lights out of the corner of my eye before I heard the horn. My eyes darted up to see the red light before I turned my head just in time to have my entire body rocked and the sound of crunching metal fill my world.

MY EYELIDS FEEL heavy as I slowly blink them open. There is a heavy ringing filling my ears, and it feels like a crushing weight is sitting on my chest. I try to lift my arms up to my chest to remove whatever it is, but I can't make them move. Slowly, things start coming to me. The sound of a continuous horn, searing pain throughout my body, the smell of smoke, and something that smells close to rust and salt filling my nose. My head falls forward, and I realize I've closed my eyes again. Forcing them open, I see my blue shirt covered in blood. *Why am I covered in blood?* I start to panic; my chest heaves up and down roughly once, and the movement forces me to cough out a cry of pain—blood trickling past my lips and onto my lap.

I try to take a steady breath in, but it feels wrong, it feels like I'm breathing in fluid. Choking—I'm choking on blood. Another cough, and more blood falls past my lips. I somehow lift my head enough to see a massive grill where my window and door are supposed to be. Flashes of a red light, bright headlights, and a loud horn. *Oh God. God no, please no.* Tears form quickly, and I shut my eyes against the blurred grill and pain that is slowly leaving. I don't want the pain to leave because in its place I feel nothing at all. Please, God—please I'll take the pain, just don't take me. I don't want to die. Don't take me from Harper and our baby.

"You'll always have my heart, Chase Grayson."

"Princess? God, Harper—what have I done? I don't want to leave you and GB. God, please don't make me leave them. I'll do anything."

"One of these days, Princess, I promise you."

"I would never be desperate enough to want you."

"We'll see."

"I love you, Princess, I'll always love you."

"No. I don't deserve you, either. You need someone who will cherish you, protect you, and take care of you. Someone that realizes they'd never be able to find another you in the world, no matter how hard they looked."

"Chase . . ."

"That first night, I did realize I would never meet another girl like you. But you deserve someone who has waited for you as long as you have waited for them. And

no matter how much I wish I could be that guy, I can't, Harper."

"I'll never leave you—I'll always be with you."

"Was that not obvious? Is it not obvious that I'm in love with you?"

"Say it again."

"Chase, I love you."

"Tell GB I love him . . . every day."

"I've never been happier than when I just woke up with you in my arms. You're the only girl I've ever fallen asleep with, and I want to keep it that way. You're not just some girl. I'm in love with you, Harper, I wouldn't want you anywhere else."

"And know that I've loved you since the beginning."

"Why are you in here?"

"Because you need me, and if this is my last hour with you, I'm not going to waste another second of it."

"I'm sorry for the time I wasted, but I'll cherish every second we had together."

"You're pregnant, Princess?"

"Yes."

"Is it—is it mine?"

"Of course it is."

I don't know what is real and what isn't anymore. I swear I can feel Harper in my arms, smell her light vanilla scent. I can hear her soft laugh, which was always reserved for the dark, as if we are curled around each other in bed. I can feel her lips on my throat and her hands in my hair. God, please, don't take me from her! How can this be happening to me?

More flashes—*Harper holding a baby. Our baby.* A painful cry tries to work its way out of my chest, but all that comes out is more blood as I hang limply against the seat belt. I try to take another breath but don't feel the relief of it. There is nothing; this is it. My time is running out, and I wish more than anything that I could have one more day with her. To cherish her and worship her, to tell her and GB a million times that I love them. The vision starts blurring, and I cling to it like it can keep me alive. I'm not ready to go, I'm not ready to lose her. I try, futilely, to take more breaths, but there is no air, just more fluid. *Harper in a wedding dress, she looks beautiful, her smile brighter than the sun, and she is looking directly next to me. Turning, I catch sight of Brandon at my side just before everything goes black.*

"Take care of my family, brother. Please."

"Chase!"

She sounds so close.

"Chase!"

"Live, Princess, for me. I love you."

Acknowledgments

As ALWAYS, a big thank-you to my husband for dealing with my crazy. I get extremely involved in my characters' world, and I love that even though he looks at me like I'm insane, he takes the time to listen and ask about what I'm writing. Love you, babe!

Thank you to the girls of Book Broads! This book is dedicated to you, because without you, I would have never had the courage to write Chase's story. I understand this is a difficult story for many. Trust me, it was difficult for me, too. But the Book Broads helped me realize that even though we all miss Chase something fierce, we still needed more of him, and he deserved to be heard.

VERY big thank-you to my amazing editor, Tessa Woodward from HarperCollins; and to my incredible agent, Kevan Lyon from Marsal Lyon Literacy Agency. You ladies are incredible, and I don't know what I'd do without y'all!

Amanda Stone, not only are you my best friend, I don't know what I would do without you being my slave driver and always getting on me to actually write this book. It's one thing to ignore the shiny place, better known as Facebook; it's another entirely to sit on the phone with you for five hours talking about everything and nothing and being silent as we write. Love you, Sef!

Kelly Elliott . . . I swear where would I be without our weekly lunches? Probably going insane in a corner of my office! I love you and am so thankful for your friendship and our weekly vents!

Thank you to my BRGs: Colleen, Kim, and Lisa. Y'all helped me more than you could imagine by giving me an escape, and, Colleen, everyone reading this book has you to thank for giving me the drive to write the shower scene!

A.L. Jackson—a massive thank you to you for starting our writing sprints! Those first three were what got me to finish this book, so thank you, I love you BIG, BB!

To all the bloggers, friends and amazing readers who have helped with the cover reveal and sharing teasers and pictures, THANK YOU! I love y'all so much!

**Keep reading for more fabulous
stories from Molly McAdams.**

FORGIVING LIES

Chapter One

Rachel

"CANDICE, YOU NEED to focus. You have got to pass this final or they aren't letting you coach this summer."

She snorted and her eyes went wide as she leaned even closer to the mirror and tried to re-create her snort. "Oh my God! Why didn't you tell me how ugly I look when I do that!?"

I face planted into the pillow and mumbled, "Oh dear Lord this isn't happening." Lifting my head slightly, I sent her an unimpressive glare. "Snorts aren't meant to be cute. Otherwise they wouldn't be called something as awkward as 'snort'."

"But my –"

"Final, Candice. You need to study for your final."

"I'm waiting on you." She said in a singsong voice. "You're supposed to be quizzing me."

I loved Candice. I really did. Even though I currently wanted to wring her neck. She wasn't just my best friend; she was like a sister to me and was the closest thing to family I had left. On the first day of kindergarten, a boy with glasses pushed me down on the playground. While he was still laughing at me, Candice grabbed his glasses and smashed them on the ground. That's playground love. And since that day we've never spent more than a handful of days apart.

By the time we started thinking about college, it was just assumed we would go away together. But then my parents died just before my senior year of high school started; and nothing seemed to matter anymore. They had gone on a weekend getaway with two partners from my dad's law firm and their wives, and were on their way home when the company jet had engine failure and went down near Shaver Lake.

Candice's family took me in without a second thought since the only relatives I had lived across the country and I hardly knew them; if it weren't for them I don't know how I would have made it through that time. They made sure I continued going to school, kept my grades up and attempted to live as normal of a life as possible. I no longer cared about graduating or going away to college, but because of them, I followed through with my plans of getting away and making my own life. I would forever be grateful for the Jenkins family.

I applied to every college Candice did and let her decide where we were going. She's been a cheerleader for as long as I can remember, so it shouldn't have surprised me when she decided on a university based on the football team and school spirit. And granted, she was given an amazing scholarship. But, Texas? Really? She chose the University of Texas at Austin and started buying everything she found in that God-awful burnt orange color. I wasn't exactly thrilled to be a "longhorn" but whatever got me away from my hometown was fine by me . . . and I guess Austin was that place.

When we first arrived I remember it felt like walking into a sauna, it was hot and humid; of course the first thing Candice said was, "What am I going to do with my *hair*?!" Her hair had already begun frizzing, and not more than five minutes later she was rocking a fro. We got used to the humidity and crazy weather changes soon enough though, and to my surprise, I *love* Texas. I had been expecting dirt roads, tumbleweeds and cowboys – let me tell you I have never been so happy to be wrong. Downtown Austin's buildings reminded me of Los Angeles, it was unbelievably green everywhere and had lakes and rivers perfect for hanging out with friends. Oh, and I've only seen a couple of cowboys in the almost three years we've been here, not that I was complaining when I did. I had also worried with Candice's recent burnt orange fetish, people were going to be able to spot us like Asian tourists at Disneyland. Thankfully, the majority of Austin is packed with UT Longhorn gear, and its common to see a burnt orange truck on the road.

Now we were a little less than two weeks away from finishing our junior year and I couldn't wait for the time off. Normally we go to California to see Candice's family during the winter and summer breaks, but she was working at a cheer camp for elementary-aged girls this summer so we were getting an apartment that we planned to keep as we finished our senior year.

That is, if we ever got Candice to pass this damn final.

Before I could even ask my first question, Candice gasped loudly, "Oh my God, the pores on my nose are huge."

Grabbing the pillow under me, I launched it at her and failed miserably at hitting anything, including her. At least it got her attention. Her mouth snapped shut, she turned to look at the pillow laying a few feet from her, then turned around with a huff to walk back to her desk.

Finally. "Okay, what is—"

"So are you ever going to go on a date with Blake?"

"Candice!"

"What?" She shot me an innocent look. "He's been asking you out for a year!"

"This—you need—forget it." I slammed the book shut and rolled off my bed, stretching quickly before going to drop the heavy book on my desk. "Forget it, we'll just see if we can get our deposit on the apartment back. I swear to God, it's like trying to study with a five-year-old."

"You never answered my question."

"What question?"

"Are you going to go on a date with Blake?"

I sighed and fell into the chair at my desk. "One, he's your *cousin.* Two, he works for UT now, that's just . . . kinda weird. Three, no."

"It's not like he's your professor! He isn't even a professor, period. And do you realize that if you marry him, we'll actually be family?"

"Marry? Candice—wait . . . how do you even jump from me going on a date with him, to marrying him? I'm not going to marry your cousin, sorry. And I don't care if he's a professor or not, it doesn't change the fact that he works for the school. Besides, he's not even my type."

"Not your type?" She deadpanned and one perfectly blonde eyebrow shot straight up. "I seem to remember you having the *biggest* crush on him when we were growing up. And I know he's family, but I can still say that he's gorgeous. I'm pretty sure he's everyone's type."

I had to agree with her on that. Blake West was tall, blond, blue-eyed and had a body like a god. One of these days he was going to show up on a Calvin Klein billboard. "I had a crush on him when we were thirteen. That was eight years ago."

"But you'd had a crush on him for years. Years. You were devastated when he moved away."

"And like I said, I was thirteen. I was ridiculous."

Blake is five years older than Candice and me, but even so, all of my childhood memories included him. He was always at Candice's house to hang out with her older brother, Eli, and we followed them everywhere. I'd viewed both Eli and Blake like awesome, older brothers until the day Blake saved my life.

Okay, that's a little dramatic. He didn't actually save my life.

I was nine at the time, we'd been playing on a rope swing and jumping into a little lake not far from our houses. When I'd gone to jump, my foot slipped into the foot hole and I ended up swinging back toward land headfirst, screaming the whole way. Blake had still been standing on the bank and caught me, swinging me into his arms before I could make the trip back toward the water.

In that moment, he became my hero, and I fell in love. Or, at least, my nine-year-old version of love. My infatuation for him grew over the next few years, but he never saw me as anything other than his "little cousin's best friend". I'm sure if I'd been older, that would have been a blow to my ego, but I just kept following him around like I'd always done. When he graduated from high school, he immediately joined the Air Force and moved away from me. I remember throwing a few "my life is over" fits to Candice, but then I got boobs and hips and the other boys my age started noticing me. And then it was something along the lines of, "Blake, who?"

He's been out of the Air Force for four years now and had pretty much been off the grid until this last fall when he moved to Austin and started working at UT as a personal trainer. Candice had flipped out over having her cousin near her again. And I'd just straight flipped out. But then I saw him. He looked like freakin' Adonis standing there in his god-like, too beautiful for his own good, glory. Every straight female in a mile radius seemed to flock to him, and he loved every second of it.

That is why I refused to go on a date with him.

"Rachel." Candice snapped.

I turned my wide gaze to her.

"Did you even hear me?"

"Not unless we're done talking about Blake."

"We are if you've decided to say 'yes' to him."

I rolled my eyes, "Why is it so important to you if I go on a date with him or not?"

"Because he's been asking you out all year! He's my cousin and you're my best friend and I love you both and I want to see you two together."

"Well, I'm pretty sure you and Blake are the only two who feel that way. I have absolutely no desire to date a guy that has women literally hanging on him all the time." Stupid Air Force turning him into sex on a stick.

Suddenly she was sporting her signature pouty face. "Rach? How much do you love me?"

"Nope. No, I'm not going."

"Are you saying you don't love me?" I was already shaking my head to say no when she turned on the puppy eyes and continued, "So will you please do this for me? Pleeeeaaasse? I thought you were my best friend."

I can't even believe we're doing this right now! "If I go on *one* date with him will you drop this forever?"

She squeaked and did a happy clap, "Thank you, I love you, you're the best!"

"I didn't say I would, I said if."

"But I know you'll go."

"He works for the school!" I whined, going back to my original argument. Even though he wasn't a professor at UT, he did work there as a personal trainer and helped out in the athletics department. Since I was majoring in Athletic Training and Candice in Kinesiology and Health Ed, we saw him almost daily in classroom type settings. That just—didn't sit right with me.

"Rachel," she sighed and twisted back around to face me. "Seriously that is getting old. He already checked it out and it's a non-issue. Stop acting like you don't want to date him."

"I don't! Who wants to date a man-whore?"

"He isn't a—well . . . eh." she made a face. "Well, yeah."

"Exactly!" Blake was rumored to be screwing most of the females he trained as well as . . . well . . . he was rumored to be screwing pretty much any female he passed. Whether the rumors were true or not was up for debate. But seeing as he didn't try to squash the rumors, and the horde of bimbos was never far from him; I was leaning toward them being true.

"You haven't dated anyone since Daniel, you need to get back out there."

"Yes I have. Candi, just because I'm not constantly seen with a guy like you are, doesn't mean I don't date."

I had gotten kind of serious with Daniel at the beginning of our second year here. But apparently six months was too long to make him wait to have sex and he ended up cheating on me. I found out two days after I'd given him my virginity.

Asshole.

After him I've gone out with a few guys, but they didn't last much longer than a date or two and an "I'll call you later". Not that there was anything wrong with those guys, I was just more interested in being done with school and Texas than getting my "MRS" degree or risking catching a disease.

I sighed to myself and headed toward our door.

"Are you going to find Blake?!" Candice was bouncing in her seat and her face was all lit up like a kid on Christmas morning.

"What—Candice, no. It's after midnight! I'm just done talking about this. I'm going to wash my face so I can go to sleep. And I'm not gonna hunt him down either, *if* he asks me out again, then I'll say yes." I grabbed my face wash and was reaching for the knob when someone knocked on the door. I don't know who I was expecting it to be, but I wouldn't have thought Blake West would be the one standing there in all his cocky glory. From the look on his face, there was no doubting he heard part, if not all, of our conversation. What the eff was he doing in our dorm?

He pulled one long stemmed red rose –that was unexpected– from behind his back, looked over my shoulder and his cocky smile went completely serious. "Hey, Candi. Do you mind if I steal Rachel for a few minutes?"

I turned around to look at her and she was grinning like the Cheshire Cat. *Traitor.* I looked back at Blake and he let out a short laugh at my question mark expression.

"That is, unless you're busy or don't want to. It looks like you were headed somewhere." He looked pointedly at the hand that wasn't holding onto the door.

It took me a few seconds to look down at my hand and realize he was looking at my face wash. "Oh . . . um, not.

No. I mean. Busy. Not busy. I'm not busy." Wow, that was brilliant.

Blake's lips twitched and his head fell down and to the side to hide the grin he was failing at keeping back.

Trying not to continue looking like a complete idiot, I took a deep breath in and actually thought about my next question two different times before asking it. Okay fine, I thought about it four times. "So, what can I do for you?" Yeah, I know. Now you understand why that required a lot of thought.

"I was wondering if I could talk to you for a few minutes."

"Uh, you do realize it's almost one in the morning, right?"

His head lifted and he looked slightly sheepish. That look on this man was so different than anything I'd ever seen and I almost didn't know how to respond to it. "Yeah, sorry. I think I fought with myself for so long on whether or not I should actually come up here and talk to you, it got a lot later than I realized." He jerked the rose up in front of him like he'd just remembered it was there, "This is for you, by the way."

"And here I was thinking you just walk around holding roses all the time." I awkwardly took the rose from him, looked at it for a few seconds, then let it hang from the tips of my fingers. "So, Blake . . ." I trailed off and searched his eyes for a second before his flashed and he took a step back.

"Can I talk to you out here for just a minute? I promise I won't keep you long."

Yeah, well, the fact that I've turned you down for the amount of time it takes to make a baby and now you're standing at my dorm room door at one in the morning is kind of creepy. But of course, we have history, you're incredibly hot now and I'm thinking about as clearly as Candice does. So, sure. Why the hell not? I followed him out into the hall and shut the door behind us, but stayed pressed up against it.

"Rachel," he ran a nervous hand through his hair and paused for a second, as if trying to figure out what to say, "the school year is about to end and you'll be going back to Cali over the summer. I feel like I'm about to miss any chance with you I may have. And I don't want to. I know you liked me when we were growing up. But Rach, you were way too young back then."

"I'm still five years younger, that hasn't changed."

He smirked. "You and I both know a relationship between a thirteen and eighteen-year-old, and a twenty-one and twenty-six-year-old are completely different."

So? That doesn't help my argument right now. "Well you and I have both changed over the last eight years. Feelings change –"

"Yes," he cut me off and his blue eyes darkened as he gave me a once over. "They do."

I hated that my body was responding to his look. But honestly, I think it'd be impossible for anyone not to respond to him. Like I said. Adonis. "Uh, Blake. Up here." He smiled wryly and dear Lord that smile was way too perfect. "Look, honestly? I have an issue with the fact that you're constantly surrounded by very eager and willing females. It's not like I'd put some claim on you if we went on a couple dates, but you ask me out *while* these girls are touching you and drooling all over you. It's insulting that you would ask me out while your next lay is already practically stripping for you."

His expression darkened and he tilted his head to the side, "You think I'm fucking them like everyone else?"

Ah frick. *Um, yes?* "If you are, then that's your business. I shouldn't have said that, I'm sorry. But whether you are or not, you don't even attempt to push them away. Since you moved here, I've never seen you with less than two women touching you. You don't find that weird?" Seriously, am I *really* the only person who finds this odd?

Suddenly pushing off the wall he'd been leaning against, he took the two steps toward me and I tried to mold myself to the door. A heart-stopping smile, and bright blue eyes now replaced his darkened features as he completely invaded my personal space. If he weren't so damn beautiful I'd karate chop at him and remind him of personal bubbles. Or go all Stuart from MADtv on him and tell him he's a stranger and to stay away from my danger. Instead, I tried to control my breathing and swallow through the dryness in my mouth.

"No, Rachel. What I find weird, is that you don't seem to realize that I don't even notice those other women or what they're doing because all I see is you. I look forward to seeing you every day. I don't think you realize you are the best part of my weekdays. I moved here for this job before I even knew you and Candice were going to school here, and seeing you again for the first time in years—

God, Rachel you were so beautiful and I had no idea that it was you; but you literally stopped me in my tracks and I couldn't do anything but watch you.

"And you have this way about you that draws people to you . . . always have. It has nothing to do with how devastatingly beautiful you are –though that doesn't hurt–" he smirked and searched my face, "but you have this personality that is rare. And it bursts from you. You're sweet and caring, you're genuinely happy and it makes people around you happy. And you have a smile and laugh that is contagious."

Only men like Blake West could get away with saying things like that and still have my heart racing instead of laughing in their face.

"You're not like other women. Even though these are the years for it, you don't seem like the type of girl to just have flings; and I can assure you, that's not what I'm into, nor what I'm looking for with you. So I don't see those other women, all I'm seeing is you. Do you understand that now?"

Holy shit. He was serious?

"Rachel?"

I nodded and he smiled.

"So, will you please let me take you out this weekend?"

For the first time since he came back into my life, he actually looked unsure of himself. I was still in complete shock, but I somehow managed to nod again and mumble, "Sure, where do you want to go?"

He smiled wide and exhaled in relief, "It's a surprise."

I frowned. How did he have a surprise planned if he

hadn't even known I was going to say yes? "And by surprise, do you mean you have no clue?"

"No, it's just a surprise."

I started to turn into Candice and whine that I wouldn't know what to wear, but was interrupted by a huge yawn making me sound more like Chewbacca. I covered as much of my face as possible with the hand that wasn't holding the rose and laughed awkwardly. "Oh my word, that's embarrassing."

His laugh was deep and rich, "It's late and I stopped you from going to sleep. If for some reason I don't see you for the rest of the week, I'll pick you up at seven on Friday. That sound all right?"

"That sounds perfect. I'll see you then, and uh, thanks for my rose." Before he could say anything else, I turned the knob, gave him a small smile and backed up into the room and shut the door in his still-smirking face. "Holy hell." I whispered and let my forehead fall against the door.

"Tell. Me. *Everything!*" Candice practically shrieked and I turned to narrow my eyes at her.

Like she hadn't been listening.

"We're going on a date Friday. That's about it."

"That is *so* not all that was said, Rachel! Ohmigod did you swoon when he said all he's seeing is you?"

"Swoon, Candice, really? This isn't one of your romance novels." And yeah . . . I did kind of swoon. "And that's exactly why I don't tell you. You eavesdrop anyway, what's the point in going over it all again?"

"Because I want details of how he looked at you, and how you reacted to him."

Oh dear God, this was going to be a long night.

WHY BLAKE THOUGHT we wouldn't see each other the rest of the week was beyond me, because sure enough he was the first person I saw when I walked into the athletics center the next afternoon. And surprise, surprise . . . he only had four girls around him today. That's not including the one he was stretching out on the ground.

Candice's constant talking faded out as I watched him explaining why he was stretching those particular muscles. But I knew the girl wasn't paying attention, all she could care about was that he was practically in between her legs.

The girl on the ground said something I couldn't hear, and the runway beautiful, mocha-skinned girl standing closest to me practically purred as she reached for his forearm, "Well, that's just because Blake's so good with his . . . *hands.*" The other four girls started giggling and I wanted to gag.

Blake's head shot up and I realized I must have actually gagged out loud. *Whoops.* Our eyes locked for a few seconds before he quickly looked at the girls surrounding him and his position with the one on the floor. When he looked back at me, his blue eyes were pleading, but I just shook my head and walked off toward the back to get my out-of-the-classroom part of my course over with.

"Hey." Candice nudged me, "Don't get upset about that. They aren't the ones who have a date with him on Friday."

"I'm not upset about that." I'm upset about the fact that *that* pissed me off. What, did I expect him to change overnight just because we were going to go on one date? Or did his words last night really have me thinking I'd imagined his robot bimbo herd all year? And sheesh, why did I care at all? I didn't even want to go on a date with him! Not really . . .

An hour and a half later, and I'd successfully avoided all of his gazes I could feel like lasers on my back. But when I turned to put some equipment away, he was right there and there was no way I could avoid Blake in all his real-life Calvin Klein model-ness.

"You're mad." He guessed and began taking the equipment out of my arms and putting it in the closet.

"Um . . . not? And I can put this away myself."

"Rachel, I told you. I only see you."

"Yeah, no, I heard you." As soon as everything was put up, I turned away only to quickly turn back around and face him. "Look, Blake, I don't think Friday is a good idea."

"Why isn't it?"

"Well, it's—you know . . . it's just not. So thank you for your offer. But once again, and hopefully for the last time, I'm not going to go on a date with you. If you ever move back to California, I really hope this doesn't make family dinners awkward."

The corners of his lips turned up slightly. "All right. You done for the day?"

This was the first rejection he'd taken well, and it threw me off for a moment, "Um, yes?"

"Let's go then."

"Whoa, wait. Go where? Its Wednesday, not Friday. And I said no anyway."

"You said no to a date with me. The date was on Friday. So we aren't going on a date. We're just going to go walk, hang out, whatever you want. But it's not a date." He stepped close enough that we were sharing the same air and his voice got low and husky. "If you want to call it something, we can call it exercising, or seeing Austin. You can hardly count that as a date, Rach."

I was momentarily stunned by the effect his voice and blue eyes had on me, "Um." I blinked rapidly and looked down to clear my head. "I've lived here almost three years, I don't need to see the sights."

"Perfect, I don't get out much other than to come to work, so I do. You can be my tour guide."

"Blake –"

"Come on, Rachel."

Not giving me an option, he grabbed onto my arm and began towing me out of the building. I caught sight of Candice and she waved excitedly as she watched us leave.

Why was she smiling? I sure as hell wasn't smiling, and Blake was practically dragging me away! He could be hauling me off to slaughter me and leave my remains on a pig farm for all she knew, and Candice was just going to sit there and wave like a lunatic? Playground. Love. Over. Best friend card officially revoked.

As soon as we were outside, I yanked my arm free and continued to follow Blake as he made his way off campus. Well, at least he was right about one thing, I couldn't count this as a date. No way would I wear baggy sweats cut off at my calves and a tight tank on a date.

"Are you still mad?"

I glanced up to see his stupid smirk that I seriously hated right now. "Why would I be mad? I was just dragged out of a building to go *walk* with a guy I turned down for a date."

His smirk turned into a full-blown smile, "Still mad." He confirmed and looked ahead, "Although I always did find your temper adorable, let me know when you're not."

Thirty minutes later and I was getting tired of following him around. Tour guide my non-existent ass. He wasn't looking at anything. He was walking with a purpose and hadn't looked back at me since he'd asked if I was mad.

"So, this has been awesome and all. Are you going to tell me where we're going now?"

"Are you going to tell me what you're mad about?"

"I'm not mad!"

He slowed his pace so he was directly next to me and I was surprised to see him looking at me completely serious. "Yes you are, Rach. If you didn't want to go on the date on Friday, you would have never agreed, and you wouldn't be following me right now." I opened my mouth but he cut me off, "You would have gone back to your dorm and you know it. I was two steps ahead of you the entire time, you could have turned back if you were really mad at me."

"You didn't even give me an option to say no!" He raised an eyebrow and I huffed. "All right. Fine. Maybe I am mad."

"And you're mad at me."

"Yeah, Blake, I am."

"But not because I pulled you out of the building."

Oh my word, he was so infuriating! "Uh, yeah, I'm pretty sure that's why I'm mad. Are you going to start telling me I'm not hungry either? Since you all of a sudden seem to know me so well?"

He pulled me to a stop and moved to stand directly in front of me, tipping my head back with his fingers, "You're mad because of the girls around me when you walked in this afternoon."

"I—"

"And I told you I only see you. I'll tell you that over and over again until you understand that. They mean nothing, nor do I notice anything other than the fact that they talk like they're in middle school."

"I don't care about them the way you think I do. When I saw it, it just reminded me why I never wanted to go on a date with you in the first place. Nothing more, nothing less."

"You're lying, Rachel." I could smell the mint from his gum and feel his breath on my lips, and suddenly I was wondering if I *was* lying. There must be something in his gum that puts me in a daze. "It's fine to admit you were getting jealous. I hate seeing the way Aaron looks at you, and you work with him every day."

I was so not getting jeal– wait. What?! Aaron's gay. I leaned away from his nearness and started to tell him when I realized we were on top of a bridge surrounded by a bunch of people just standing there looking toward the side like they were waiting for something. I pointed toward the people, "Uh . . . am I missing something?"

Blake looked a little smug as he glanced at his watch, then the sky. "Nope, give it a couple minutes. We got here just in time."

Aaron, his sexuality and the fact that Blake gets jealous over my flaming gay friend completely forgotten, I looked at the sky then pulled out my phone to check the time. There was nothing special about the time from what I could tell. As for the sky, it was nearly dusk, and although it was beautiful I didn't know why that was anything worth noting either. Glancing at the people and the street around us, I turned and saw the street sign and did a double take. We were on Congress Avenue.

"Oh no. No, no, no, no, no!" I started backing up but ended up against Blake's chest. His arms circled around me, effectively keeping me there. I felt his silent laughter.

"I take it you know about this then. Ever seen it?"

"No, and there's a reason. I'm terrified of—" Just then, close to a million bats took flight from underneath the bridge. A small shriek escaped my lips and I clamped my hands over my mouth, like my sound would attract the bats to me.

There was nothing silent about his next laugh. Blake tightened his arms around me and I leaned into him more. I'd like to say it was purely because my biggest fear was flying out around me, but I'd be lying if I said his musky cologne, strong arms and chest had nothing to do with it either. This was something I'd wanted for years, and I almost couldn't believe that I was finally here, in his arms.

I continued to watch in utter horror and slight fascination as the bats that seemed to never end continued to leave the shelter of the bridge and fly out into the slowly darkening sky.

Minutes later, Blake leaned in and put his lips up against my ear. "Was that really so bad?"

Forcing my hand from my mouth, I exhaled shakily and shook my head, "Not as bad as I'd imagined. Doesn't change the fact that they are ugly and easily the grossest thing I've ever seen."

"But now you can say you've faced one of your fears."

"The biggest."

"See?" He let go of me and started walking again in the direction we'd come. "You up for a drink?"

I realized I was still shaking so I nodded my head and followed him. "Just one though."

We walked for well over half an hour while Blake tried to recreate my shriek from seeing the bats and I accused him of doing that with every girl so he'd have an excuse to put his arms around her. The air between us was much more relaxed this time as he asked about life after he'd joined the Air Force. I told him all about the end of middle school and high school, but never once mentioned my parents. I wasn't sure if he knew about them or not, but there was no point in bringing up that hurt. Besides, if he had known, he hadn't even come back for the funeral. Just as we were passing the school, Blake slid his hand down my arm and intertwined our fingers.

"Rachel, why did you finally agree to go out with me?"

When I looked up, I was surprised at his somber expression. I would have expected something a little more taunting. "Do you want me to answer that honestly?"

"I'd appreciate it. I've asked you out for . . . shit. I don't know, nine months now? No matter what I say, your answer is always 'no'. Until last night."

"Well." I looked down at the sidewalk passing beneath our feet.

"You can tell me, it's fine. You never were one to hide your feelings. And your hate for me lately has been a little more than apparent. I'm already expecting the worst."

"I don't hate you. I just don't exactly like you . . . anymore." I squinted up at him and nudged his side with the arm he still had a firm grip on.

He gave a little grunt with a forced smile.

"Um, Candice is always bugging me for turning you down. She said she would stop if I agreed to one date with you." I know, I know, I could have made something up that wasn't so harsh. But I didn't. If I hadn't looked back down, I probably would have missed the pause in his step.

"Figures." We walked for a few more minutes before he paused and turned to me. "I'm not going to make you go out with me."

"You aren't, I said I'd go."

He raised an eyebrow, making it disappear under his shaggy hair. "You also told me earlier today that we weren't going anymore. I'm just letting you know I'll stop. All of it. Asking you all the time, what I did today. And I'll talk to Candice."

"Blake—"

"No, Rach, I should have stopped a long time ago. I'm sorry you felt pressured into it last night. I want you to *want* to go on a date with me. I don't want you to go just so she'll drop it or because you want me to quit asking. Which I will." I couldn't tell if he looked more embarrassed or hurt.

Is it ridiculous that I want to comfort him? "I want to go."

"No, you don't."

Okay, still somewhat true. "I didn't . . . before." Ugh, who am I kidding. He knows I'm lying anyway. "Look I don't know what you want me to say. You can't exactly blame me for not wanting to go out with you." He looked as if I'd slapped him, I hurried on before I could chicken out with the rest. "I mean, come on Blake, you were rumored to be screwing all these students, co-workers and faculty. And not once did you try to shut down those rumors. Add to that, the Blake I grew up with is completely gone, now you're usually kind of a douche. Why *would* I want to go out with someone like that?"

"Rumors are going to spread no matter what I do. The more I try to stop them, the guiltier I look. Trust me. As for you thinking I'm a douche . . ." he trailed off and ran a hand through his hair, "try seeing it from my side. The only girl I've wanted for years now, and can't get out of my head no matter what I do, repeatedly blows me off like I'm nothing."

Did he say *years*?

Letting go of my hand, he turned and headed toward the dorm instead of Spider House Café, like we'd originally planned. "Come on, I'll walk you back to your dorm. I won't make you do this, Rachel."

"Blake, why can't you just be like this all the time? If how you were growing up, last night, and the last hour, was how you always were . . . I probably wouldn't have ever turned you down."

He huffed a sad laugh, "Yeah, well . . . obviously I've already fucked that up."

I watched him walk away from me and squeezed my eyes shut as I called after him, "You know, you kinda traumatized me tonight. I feel like you owe me a beer." Peeking through my eyelashes I saw him stop, but not turn around. "And maybe dinner on Friday night?"

When Blake turned to face me, his smile was wide and breathtaking.

Chapter Two

Rachel

DRINKS WITH BLAKE had actually been more fun than I would have thought, and we'd ended up spending Thursday afternoon and evening together as well. He seemed to slip back into the Blake that Candice and I had spent years following around. On Friday, when I stepped into the Athletic center, I was met with three red roses and a heart-stopping grin. He'd said regardless his reasoning on Wednesday afternoon, he was counting the bats and bar on Wednesday, and movies on the couch in my dorm room on Thursday, as dates. So Friday night would be our third, and deserved three roses.

I'm not gonna lie, I totally did the *aww, you're so sweet* girly thing as I took the roses from him and kissed his cheek in front of the circle of girls he was doing pretty well at fully ignoring. When Candice dragged me out of the center not even an hour later to go get a pedicure and have me start getting ready for the date, she pressed me for every single detail of my time with Blake thus far. She was really rooting for this whole actually being related thing.

He'd been sweet, attentive, and completely down to earth. But I was glad he was still giving me my space. Even being alone in the dorm room for three movies, he never once tried to pull me into his arms and had yet to try to kiss me. Which Candice was taking as a bad sign, I rolled my eyes at that assumption. Now that Blake was finally getting his dates, he was letting me take this at the speed I wanted; and I couldn't be more thankful.

But then Friday night was just . . . odd.

Blake had picked me up in his silver Lexus convertible and taken me to The Oasis, a restaurant sitting on the lake with the most amazing view as the sun set, which had begun just after we'd arrived. I honestly don't think I've ever seen anything more beautiful, and just as I began to tell Blake that, our waiter arrived to take our drink order. Without a word, Blake handed him both menus and placed our order for our food and drinks. I hadn't even looked at the menu yet. The food was just as he said it would be, to die for. But from the way he continued to treat me I was expecting him to cut my meat and feed me himself by the time our food got there.

Conversation was at a standstill until we were back in his car.

"Want to go for drinks again?" He asked suddenly, halfway back to campus.

Obviously he had missed how awkward the last hour had been. "Two margaritas are more than enough for me. I'm good."

His laugh had boomed throughout the small car, as his hand fell onto my upper thigh and gave a little squeeze. "Okay, no drinks. Anything else you want to do?"

"Um . . ."

"Do you like horses?"

"Horses?" That wasn't something I'd been expecting. "Of course I like horses."

"So how about we go for a carriage ride down 6th Street before I take you home, sound good?"

"I don't know."

"Rachel, did I do something? I feel like we've gone back a few steps."

"No, I'm sorry . . . I'm just tired. I've felt off all day, is it okay if you take me back?"

"Of course, there's always tomorrow!"

I'd stifled a groan and smashed myself as close to the side of the car as possible. The entire way back he kept his hand on my thigh, and continued to rub his thumb back in forth. In an effort to not smack it away, I'd crossed my arms under my chest and resorted to burning imaginary holes in his hand. After we got to campus he walked me all the way to my room before trapping me against the doorframe and leaning in. I'd turned my head away at the last minute but that didn't seem to faze him. Grabbing my hips and pressing his body closer to mine, he started kissing a line down my neck; and I swear he smelled my hair before groaning. I'd tried not to gag.

"Blake, please? Can we not do this?"

He'd pulled back and his blue eyes had flashed. "Fine." The way he looked at me from under his eyelashes caused a chill to run down my spine. And not a good one. "I'll see you later." Without another word he'd pushed off me, turned and stalked down the hallway.

"RACH, WAKE UP and tell. Me. *Every*thing!"

Cracking my eyes open the next morning, I looked at a too-perky Candice and groaned. "Where were you when I got back last night?"

"With Jeff," she dismissed his name with a wave of her hand, "now tell me about your date!"

"Wow, Jeff too, huh? Good one, Candi."

"Don't stall!"

Pulling myself up so I was resting on my elbows, I didn't even feel like sugar coating the prior night. "It was awful."

Her eyes went wide, "What do you mean? What'd you do?"

Bitch. "Why is it that I had to do something?"

"Um let's see," she started counting on her fingers, "One, you didn't want to go out with him in the first place. Two, unlike Wednesday and Thursday, Blake didn't text me after to tell me about your time together. Three, you didn't want to go out with him in the first place."

"You already said that." I pointed out.

"Exactly, that's a big enough one that it counts for two! So what happened?"

I sighed and flopped onto my bed. "It was just weird, it's like we had nothing to talk about. Which was crazy because we talked the entire time we were together on Wednesday and Thursday. And, he didn't even let me see a menu, he ordered for me. Like I was a three-year-old or something."

"Is that all?"

"Well, yeah. Oh! And when we were on our way back he just started acting like the night had been completely normal and not awkward in any way. Then we got back, he pushed me up against the door and started kissing me neck. I kind of asked him to stop and he got weird. Like creepy, scary, weird . . . and then he just up and left. I don't know, the whole night was just a bust."

Candice didn't say anything, she just sat there staring at me.

"What?"

"Are you insane? You told him to stop kissing you?!"

Really? That was all she got from what I told her? "Yeah, we had a bad date, why would I want him to kiss me? Maybe if it had gone something like the first two nights I wouldn't have—"

"No, no. Rachel. Oh my God. We need to fix this. I can't believe you still managed to mess up the date after everything I went over with you yesterday!"

"Wow." I shook my head and let my arms give out so I face-planted into my pillow again. I was so dumbfounded I didn't even know what to say anymore.

After running to the café to grab a quick breakfast, we made our way back to *hopefully* study for finals that were next week. But from the way Candice had tried to lecture me on all I probably did wrong on the date during breakfast, I'd doubt much studying would take place if it involved her.

Not even two minutes after getting back into our room, there was a knock on the door. And surprise, freaking surprise. Blake West. With *four* red roses.

"You do realize it's not even nine on a Saturday." I answered. And yes, I laid the California bitch tone on thick.

Blake didn't miss a beat, and his smirk didn't falter. "Morning, Rach. Can I take you out to breakfast?"

"Oh, we just ate!" *Darn.* I didn't even try to sound disappointed.

Candice gave me a look that I pretended not to notice.

"Well that's okay," his smile was full of easy confidence. "How about we go grab some coffee instead?"

"I actually need to start studying for my finals."

"All the more reason for coffee now, it'll keep you awake."

Dear lord what was it with him and Candice? Do they not get hints? Must come from her mom's side of the family. "Sure why don't we all go? Candice you want to get coffee?"

"Nah, I'm good. I just texted Eric to come over in a few to help me, um, study."

Traitor. I looked back at a victorious looking Blake, "Could you give me a couple minutes?"

"See you down there." He handed me the four roses, winked, and walked down the hall.

"Eric today, huh? I'm sure you two will get tons of studying done. Maybe I should stay and help you, you can't afford to fail this thing.

"You better go!" She looked me over and raised an annoyed eyebrow. "Please tell me you're going to change."

I looked down at my yoga pants and off the shoulder Iron Maiden concert shirt. "Ha! No, definitely not. It's early in the morning, and we're just getting coffee. Which means I get to stay skanked up."

"You do not stay skanked up when you're trying to get the man of your dreams to fall in love with you! You stay skanked up if no one is going to see you! You know this, Rachel."

Love? God this whole dating her cousin thing was making her more dramatic than usual. I threw my long, dark hair up into a cute messy bun, grabbed my purse and sighed heavily. "See you later."

Blake didn't say a word to me as I slid into the passenger seat of his car, and continued to stay silent as we drove to one of the Starbucks near campus. The only acknowledgment he made of my presence was to put his hand high up on my thigh again, and hold tight. Too tight. And not much changed once we were finally in the shop. Conversation didn't happen, his hand was back on my thigh, and we had four different stare downs.

I only won one of those.

At least he let me order my own coffee. That was honestly the only good part of this morning.

I was barely able to hold in my sigh of relief when my phone chimed.

"Who is that?" Blake's eyebrows were pulled down, and he seemed more than a little annoyed.

Only checking the text preview on the lock screen I shrugged, "Oh it's just a friend, he wants to get a study group together tonight." I started to put my phone back in my purse when his hand shot out and grabbed onto my arm, effectively keeping it suspended above my purse.

"Well, it's rude to keep him waiting. Aren't you going to answer him?" He looked like he was struggling to keep himself in check.

I tried to pull my arm back and he finally released it. Sheesh, what was his problem? It was just a text. "Sure, I guess."

"Just let him know you can't go."

"Excuse me?"

He leaned forward and his eyes narrowed. "I'd prefer you study with Candice."

Now I was getting mad. He didn't own me, he definitely wasn't my boyfriend, and this was Aaron. The same gay guy that Blake didn't like "looking at me". "And since when do you get to decide who I hang out with? Look maybe I've been giving you the wrong impression over the last few days, but we aren't together. You have no say in what I do."

Like a switch had been flipped his face went back to his smooth, sexy self. "You're right, actually I think it's a good idea for you to study with some other people besides Candice; I'm sure you wouldn't get anywhere with her."

Wait, what? The sudden change in his mood made me almost feel dizzy. It's like I had my own personal Dr. Jekyll and Mr. Hyde sitting next to me.

When I could finally get my mouth to stop opening and shutting like a fish, I shook my head and exhaled roughly. "Speaking of, I really need to get back to campus." I stood to leave without giving him the chance to say no.

Without another word, Blake followed me out to the car. We didn't say anything on the drive back but he put his hand on my thigh again. Was I imagining how tight he was holding it? When we arrived at the dorm, he parked in one of the spaces rather than letting me out in front. I grabbed the handle to open the door and he pushed down on my thigh gripping it tighter. I turned to look at him and was surprised to see he still looked light and easy going.

"I'll get the door for you. Wait here for just a second."

Crap, I hope he wasn't going to walk me to my room, I'd bet Candice still had Eric in there with the door locked. As soon as he released me, my thigh throbbed from the relief of pressure he'd had on it and I almost wished I'd been wearing shorts so I could look at the damage I was making myself believe he'd done. The passenger door opened and I stepped out without looking up at him. We walked without saying anything and I made sure to put some distance between us. I was relieved when he began to slow down as we reached the main entrance of the dorm.

"Well, thanks for the coff—"

He caught me around the waist, pushed me up against the wall and kissed me roughly, interrupting my good-bye. Before I had time to realize what was happening and push him away, he pulled back and started backing up toward his car.

"I'll see you later." He winked then turned away from me.

I have no idea what my face looked like, I couldn't even pin down an emotion. I was disgusted, annoyed, confused and pissed. It took a second before I was able to compose myself. I shook out my arms and walked up to my room.

I didn't know if I was ready to tell Candice about this, or if I even wanted to. Knowing her, she'd somehow turn it around so that I had done something wrong, or that I didn't know how to kiss. Needless to say, I was dreading facing her. Luck was on my side, Eric must still be in there because the door was locked, and on the mini white board attached to our wall in Candice's writing were the words, "<u>DON'T</u> come in." I texted Candice, asking her to put my laptop and books outside while I went to the bathroom so I wouldn't be subjected to a flushed and rumpled Candice and Eric. After I picked those up, I went back to the common room and pulled out my phone to finally text Aaron back.

Sounds good. What time and where?

Aaron: 7p @ Starbucks

Great like I wanted to go there again. I sighed, cracked open a book and tried to not think about Blake.

WITH THE STUDYING I'd done before the group, and the five hours with them, I felt fully prepared for this final, and was glad it was on Monday. Once that was out of the way, I only had two days left of easy finals and this year would be over.

I was still wired from all the espresso I'd sucked down in the last few hours and since it was a twenty-four hour Starbucks, I decided to stay in the café and write in my journal. After my parent's accident, Candice's parents tried everything to get me to talk. I think they were afraid I would never come out of my depression. Her brother Eli had been the only one that had known how to handle me—so to speak. He'd been home from college for the summer when the accident happened, and unlike his first few years away, came back every weekend to see me once school started back again. He would hold me while I stared off into space, and never spoke a word. Eli's form of healing was my favorite since it was silent, but we all knew he couldn't be there for me forever. One night when I got home from school there was a journal on my bed with a note from Candice's dad, George. He suggested using the journal to write to my parents like they were still here. At first it freaked me out, but I told him I would try, and I'm glad I did. Even I could see the difference in myself. I wrote to them every day, even if it was just a few lines. But I viewed it as a way of continuing our family time. Every night after dinner while I was growing up, we'd pile up on the couches, turn on the TV and talk about our days while watching whatever shows were on that night. So that's what I did. I just told them what was going on in my life like I would if they were still here.

When I finished a couple hours later, I put everything in my purse and called out goodbyes to the too-awake baristas. As soon as I pushed open the door and walked out into the muggy night air, my phone went off and the words on the screen caused me to stumble and a chill to shoot through my body.

Blake: You look beautiful tonight.

Instead of bolting for my car like any sane person, I looked around until I found him. Well, running to my car wouldn't have helped much; he was parked right next to it and leaning against the driver door of his shiny little Lexus.

How did he know I was here? If he didn't know I was here, what is he doing here at two in the morning? Oh my word, he's been following me! No, that's ridiculous; come on Rachel get a grip. He is not following you, frick I really need to stop thinking the world and everyone in it revolves around me. He just happened to be here and saw your car. That's all. Right? Right.

I took a few steps closer to the cars and took a deep breath as I dropped my phone back into my purse, trying to calm myself down. "Hi, Blake."

"I was starting to think you would never leave, I've been out here for hours."

Oh God, he had been waiting for me! Those words were creepy enough, but paired with the sexy, innocent smile they seemed even worse. I meant for my voice to sound strong and annoyed but it was barely a whisper, "Why are you following me?"

"Following you? I'm not following you. Candice told me you were waiting for me to pick you up from the study group. Jesus, Rachel, you look like you've just seen a ghost; are you all right?"

"Candice said what? No, I was definitely not waiting for you; I drove myself here. That should be obvious, since you're parked next to my Jeep." I didn't know what was going on, but I wanted to get out of there and away from him. Now.

"Yeah, but your car isn't starting. Which is why I'm here." He said every word slowly like I was a child or something. "Don't you remember Rachel? You called her almost three hours ago, but she was busy so you told her to call me. Are you feeling okay? Come on, get in the car I'll get you back to your room."

"I am *not* getting in your car, I'll drive myself back!" With that I took the last few steps to my car, got in, locked the door and put the key in the ignition. I turned it but nothing happened. There wasn't even a click. What happened to my car? I knew I hadn't called Candice. And even then, if I'd wanted Blake to pick me up I would have called him myself. Someone tapped on the window and even though I knew who it was, I still jumped.

"Come on, Rach, this is dumb. Just get in the car I'll take you back. I'll get your car towed in a couple hours."

There was no point in trying to call someone else. It was two in the morning, everyone was asleep, and I definitely couldn't walk back at this hour. I let out a big sigh and opened the door.

"That's my girl, come on let's go." He helped me into his car then got in beside me, this time he didn't put his hand on my thigh.

The short drive to the dorm seemed to take forever, and besides asking me a few times if I was feeling all right; there was no conversation. Blake seemed genuinely concerned about me. Had I called Candice? Did I just forget about everything while I was writing to my parents? Is that why I went in to write to them in the first place? Maybe all the studying mixed with my caffeine high that was turning into a major crash had my mind all jumbled. I must have just forgotten. It would have been easy to grab my phone and check the recent call history, but something inside me tightened and I knew it would be the wrong thing to do. We finally reached the dorm, and just like this morning, Blake parked in the lot. Aces.

"Are you sure you're feeling okay?" He asked for the fifth time since we got in the car, "You freaked when you saw me."

"I'm fine, really, don't worry about me. I probably just forgot and lost track of time in there." I tried to make my smile convincing, I didn't want him to walk me to my room. I got out of the car, ducked my head back in to thank him and saw he was getting out too. Crap. Well, at least this would give me time to tell him I needed some space.

"You don't really think I'm going let you walk up there by yourself, do you?"

"Of course not," I muttered, "I was just trying to be

polite. It's late and you've already been waiting on me for hours . . . apparently."

He just laughed as he walked toward me, put his arm around my waist and led me to my room. When we got there he reached out to open the door for me; at least the good bye would be short. But my happiness was short lived; he walked me into the empty room and then turned to shut and lock the door behind us.

"Where's Candice?" I couldn't stop my voice from shaking. How weird that just Thursday I'd spent hours alone with him in this room and had felt comfortable and enjoyed my time with him. But now, being in here with him felt . . . wrong.

"She didn't tell you when you talked? All she told me was she was busy." He said a little too innocently.

I turned to face the room again to see if her laptop or cell were around, if they weren't I was going to call her immediately. Before I could find—or hopefully *not* find–everything, Blake came up behind me and began kissing the back of my neck.

"Uh, Blake? Can you not do that right now? I need to find out where Candice is."

Instead of stopping, he turned me around, pushed me up against my wardrobe, and resumed his place on my neck. I tried pushing him back, but it was useless. The guy was a rock and he wasn't budging.

"She'll be back when she's ready to come back." He breathed between kisses and little bites.

Well I wasn't about to wait for that to happen, I wanted him out of my room now, "Okay, I'm really ti—"

He quickly moved up to my lips, shutting me up, and his kisses became rough and possessive. Just as they'd been this morning, only these weren't lasting three seconds. We were close enough to the door that he reached out to flip off the lights and caught me around my waist again before I could take advantage of the break in his strong hold. He started backing me up toward the bed, and I pushed as hard as I could against the hand holding my head in place. His only response was to push against me harder. My bed was high enough that it hit at the small of my back and helped me stay standing when he tried to push me down. When I didn't immediately fall onto the bed, he pulled my head back to look at me, giving me the break I needed.

"You need to leave. Now!" my arms had been caught between us, but with the new space I put them against his chest and tried to push him back farther. Instead of moving away, he got a smile that turned my body to ice, and my arms to jello. This is what I'd imagine a crazy person looks like.

"You don't mean that," he growled as he pulled my face back to his.

Did he really think I was just playing hard to get? I wanted him off me! He let go of my waist and began searching for the bottom of my shirt, but even though my waist was free I still couldn't move; I was caught between him and the bed. When he found it he didn't waste time traveling up to grab my chest. I could feel him getting excited and it made me want to throw up. His lips moved back to my neck.

"Please. Stop." I hated how small my voice sounded.

"This would be over sooner if you'd just lie down and shut up."

Grabbing both sides of my waist he lifted me onto the bed, pushed me down and climbed on top of me. I tried to tell him to stop again, but nothing was coming out except for my rapid breathing. My body was shaking violently and I was dangerously close to hyperventilating. He bit my bottom lip causing me to gasp enough that he could slide his tongue into my mouth. Blake's knees were pinning my legs to the bed and I bucked my hips and pushed against his shoulders, but he still didn't move. He gathered both my wrists in one hand and pinned them above my head. Tears pricked at the back of my eyes, I tried to move my head to the side so I could scream for help but he moved with me as he thrust his tongue in my mouth over and over again. I froze for all of five seconds before biting down on his tongue as hard as I could. He flew back with a pained cry and I tasted blood in my mouth. I was going to throw up. Before I could scream, his free hand slammed down on my throat and his face was directly above mine again. He growled as his blue eyes turned to ice and he just stared at me as I gasped for air.

"You're going to regret doing that, sweetheart." He vowed and my vision blurred from my tears, the outer edges were turning black as I struggled to stay conscious.

Blake's breathing deepened and the look that crossed his painfully handsome face terrified me. My mouth opened and shut, but I couldn't pull in any air and I couldn't make a sound. My arms gave up their fight seconds before my bucking hips did the same, and soon I could hardly focus on Blake at all. I prayed that someone would come and save me as the hand that had been holding my hands down on the mattress slid down and cupped me through my thin yoga pants.

I felt his hot breath on my ear, "I'll make sure you never want to fight me again, Rachel."

The hand that was cupping me went up and slid under my pants and underwear. I tried to roll away but it was taking everything in me to stay awake. Tears spilled over and fell down my cheeks. Just as my mind started shutting down, the hand clasped around my throat was gone and I began gasping for air.

Waves of dizziness washed over me, and the blackness slowly faded away. I heard the distinct sound of his zipper over my gasps and sobs and my head shook slowly back and forth. I felt like I was underwater and couldn't find my way to the surface. His hand closed around my throat again and I frantically tried to pull in air and claw at his hand, but it was useless. My arms lost function quickly and the edges of my vision were going black again, and I begged the darkness to come quicker. I didn't want to be conscious through what he was doing. I didn't want to remember this. The sweet numbness began claiming me, and at that moment, the most beautiful sound in the world came from outside the door.

Candice's voice.

Blake was off the bed and putting himself back in his shorts in seconds while I wildly tried to take in as much oxygen as possible. He roughly pulled my pants up just as the key could be heard in the lock and took the few steps toward the door to flip the light on before coming back to my side. When the door opened, Blake was standing at the side of my bed looking down at me, the light brush over my throat and solid glare was clearly a warning. But I was still on the verge of fainting, now from trying too roughly to inhale.

Candice said goodbye to whomever she'd been talking to as she shut the door. "Oh, hey, cuz! I didn't mean to—" Blake turned to look at her and Candice's eyes went wide when she saw me, "Oh my God, Rachel, are you okay?!"

She rushed over to me, but Blake touched her arm and pulled her slightly away. "She was attacked by a couple guys outside Starbucks tonight. She called me about half an hour ago, she's in shock but she'll be okay."

"What?!" Candice screamed and tears instantly filled her eyes.

What? No. No, no, no. My head shook back in forth as I choked on a sob and my breathing got even faster and heavier. I tried to tell her that was wrong. That he was lying, but all that came out was ragged sounds of my breathing.

I could see Candice and Blake's mouths moving, but I couldn't hear anything else. Everything tilted to the side and the blackness came back full force. I reached out for Candice but missed her arm as the dark claimed me.

TAKING CHANCES

1

MY FACE WAS stretched in a wide grin as I looked around
my bedroom one last time. I was doing it, finally going to
live my life however I saw fit to live it. I'd grown up with
only my dad, and I loved him, but he didn't know how to
be a parent. The only part he seemed to get was the word
"no." I promise I'm not just being a whiny teenager, that
really was about the extent of our conversations. He is
always around me, rarely talking to me and always silently expecting me to be perfect. Not that I could blame
the way he is, he has been in the Marine Corps since he
graduated high school, and apparently he's really good at
what he does. The guys that came through his units re-
spected him, and he always exuded pride for them. He'd
kept me home-schooled which resulted in me going to
work with him every day and doing my work in his office.
I learned early on that if I didn't understand something, it
was just better not to ask. He'd look up at me from under

his lashes with a raised eyebrow, sigh, and then go back to whatever he was working on. I was expected to finish by the time he started drills in the morning so I could go out there with him, but he still never said a word. The only interaction I really ever had was with his Marines. If anyone were to ask, I would let them know in a heartbeat I was raised by a bunch of immature jarheads that I adored, not by my father.

And now, after eighteen years of struggling to achieve a perfection that couldn't be reached in my father's eyes, I was finally going to let loose, have the college experience—whatever that was—and hopefully find out who I am in the process. I could have easily gone to a college here, but to say that my dad was strict would be the biggest understatement of my life, and I wanted to experience things I knew I wouldn't be able to if I stayed here.

"Are you sure you want to do this Harper? There are plenty of excellent schools in North Carolina."

I kept my eyes trained on his. "I'm one hundred percent certain Sir, this is what I need to do." Did I mention I'm only allowed to call him "Sir"?

"Well," he looked past me at my window, "it will be different around here." He turned and walked out of the room.

And that's as good as it was going to get, to be honest, it was one of the longest conversations we had in a few months. Four sentences. It was surprising that he could talk to his guys all day long, but we start talking and he's out of the room within minutes.

My phone chimed and I smiled again, my "brothers"

weren't thrilled I was leaving for California. I'd been getting calls, texts and messages on Facebook since last night begging me not to go. Now that I was older and closer in age with most of them, the guys no longer tried to raise me; they saw me as their sister or friend and taught me everything I needed to know when it came to other guys like them. It always made me laugh that most of them preferred to spend time with me rather than heading off base during their liberty, but I think they liked that I wasn't one of those girls that tried too hard to get their attention. Not that they didn't like that kind of attention, but apparently I was a nice break from the rest of the women they dealt with.

J. Carter: DON'T LEAVE ME! I'm going to go insane without you here to keep me company.

Me: I'm sure you'll be fine Carter. Prokowski and Sanders seem to be taking it a little harder than most too . . . you can comfort each other ;) Or you can always take up one of the base skank's offers. They're sure to keep you better company than me.

J. Carter: I think I got herpes just thinking about them.

Me: Ha! Ew. I gotta go, Sir's done loading up my bags in the car.

J. Carter: I'll miss you something fierce Harper. Have fun, don't forget about me.

Me: Never.

Jason Carter was twenty and had been in Sir's unit for about a year, he and I had become close quickly. He was my best friend and if I was on base when they had liberty, he was always one of the guys that opted to spend time with me rather than hunt down women with some of his other friends. I had always been sad whenever one of the guys transferred to another base, unit, or finished their time in the Marine Corps. But I'm pretty sure Carter would have been one that would kill me to see go, so I wasn't surprised that this was the sixth time he's asked me not to leave within the last hour. He couldn't have said it better, I would miss him something fierce too. I glanced around the house I'd grown up in one last time before meeting Sir in the car. That house was definitely something I wouldn't miss.

Almost twelve hours, two cars and two planes later and I was standing in my dorm room at San Diego State University. My new roommate hadn't checked in yet, but from the e-mails we'd sent back and forth over the last few weeks, she lived close and would be moving in a few days from now. I picked my side of the room and hurried to settle in before taking a shower and falling onto my bed. Glancing at my phone I noted it was almost two in the morning and groaned, if I was back home I'd already be on base with Sir. It had been a long day of traveling and unpacking and it took all the rest of my energy just to curl up in my comforter and fall asleep.

"Harper? Haaaaarperrrrrr! Wake up!"

My eyelids opened just enough to see a smiling face directly in front of me. I shot upright and brought my arms up, my entire body already tense.

"Whoa, whoa! It's me, Breanna!"

"Do you have a death wish? Don't do that!" She'd better be happy I had still thought I was dreaming, growing up with my dad meant always being on the defensive when waking up.

She giggled and sat on the edge of my bed, "Sorry, I've been trying to wake you up for the last five minutes."

Weird, I was usually a really light sleeper. "I thought you weren't coming 'til Sunday?"

"Well technically I'm not, all my stuff is still at home . . ." She gestured to the still bare other half of the room, "but my brother and his buddies are throwing a huge party tonight and I figured I'd see if you wanted to go."

The closest I'd ever come to a party was the stories I heard from the guys on base. I tried not to show my excitement and shrugged indifference. "Sure, when is it?"

"It doesn't start until nine or so, so we still have a few hours. Want to grab dinner?"

"Dinner? What time is it?!" I grabbed my phone and didn't even look at the time, all I could see was the twenty missed calls from Sir. "Crap, I need to call Si—um, my dad back. But after that I'll get ready and we can head out."

Breanna didn't move from my bed so I decided to just

let her stay there, I'm sure after she heard him yelling she'd leave. I caught the time just before I hit the send button and gasped. I'd slept for almost 16 hours, he was gonna kill me. As assumed, he answered on the first ring starting off in a disapproving lecture about not letting him know I'd made it to California and that I was okay, not answering my phone, and how bad of an idea it was to let me come here. I murmured apologies at all the appropriate times, and tried to ignore Breanna's laughing at the conversation. We may not ever talk, but when he was pissed, it wasn't something to take lightly.

"Oh my God, time to cut the apron strings, don't you think?"

I blew out a sigh of relief that the conversation was over, "Yeah, well, I'm all he has left."

"Where's your mom?"

"She died."

Her hand flew to her mouth, her eyes wide. "I'm so sorry! I had no idea!"

"Don't worry about it," I waved her apology off, "I never knew her."

She simply nodded.

"I know my dad though, this is just the first time I've ever been away from him, and I think he's worried. Now that he knows I'm alive, I probably won't hear from him again for a while."

Breanna still wasn't talking. This happened every time I told someone I didn't have a mom. Instead of trying to tell her not to worry about it again, I got up and got dressed for the party. Thankfully, my thick auburn hair was already naturally straight so I was ready in no time. Grabbing my purse, I turned to see Breanna's horrified expression.

"Wh-what?"

"Is that what you're going in?"

Shrugging, I looked down to my long jean shorts and black and gold infantry shirt. "Yes?"

"Oh no." She was now looking in my wardrobe, checking all my clothes. "Okay you and I are both a size two, how tall are you?"

"Five feet two." Yes, I know. I'm incredibly short.

"Just barely shorter than me . . . hmm. Okay come on, we're going to my place to get you changed."

"Is there something wrong with this?"

She raised one perfectly shaped blond eyebrow at me, her blue eyes narrowed, "Let's just say I'm going to throw out your entire wardrobe and take you shopping tomorrow, because we obviously don't have time tonight. I'm guessing we have to get some make-up while we're at it?"

I nodded. To be honest, I'd never felt like I'd needed make-up. Not saying that I think I'm really attractive or anything, just never saw the need. I'd been blessed with a smooth complexion and had wide gray eyes hidden behind long dark lashes. I always thought anything else would have been too much. Plus, I'm sure Sir would've had a fit if I'd ever bought any.

We grabbed some sandwiches from a deli and before I knew it, I already had my make-up completely done and Breanna was holding different outfits up to my body. She settled on a faded, torn denim mini skirt that looked like it would barely cover my butt, and a black spaghetti strap.

"Okay put these on, and no peeking yet!"

"Is there something else to go over this undershirt?"

"Undershirt? No, that is the shirt!" She looked at me like I was crazy before walking into the bathroom.

Thankfully, the spaghetti strap was pretty long allowing me to pull the skirt down enough so I didn't think my butt was showing, but I'm pretty sure I'd never been this exposed outside of my bathroom in my life. If she was a couple inches taller, how on earth did she even wear this thing?

"Ooo. MUCH better!"

"Are you sure? I feel like I'm naked." I was still trying to tug the skirt down.

"Hah! No, you look hot, I promise." She spun me around until I was facing a mirror.

"Oh, crap." Sir would kill me, but I had to admit I think I liked it. Just as I thought, the skirt barely covered a thing, and it was impossible not to have cleavage in this shirt. I guess I had a nice chest, but when almost every top you own is from the Post Exchanges on base, there isn't ever an opportunity to see anything. I turned to look at my backside and smiled a little bit before facing forward again. "Oh my God, look at my eyes!"

"I know, don't you love them?"

"You're a genius Breanna." I looked at my smoky lids, and even thicker eyelashes making my eyes look like dark thunderstorm clouds.

"Well it's pretty easy when the model has your face

and body. Mind if I steal your lips and eyes for the night?"

I laughed but was still mesmerized by my new reflection. "I can honestly say I've never worn anything like this, and this is my first time ever having make-up on."

"Are you serious?" She looked appalled.

"My dad is a career Marine. I've never even *touched* make-up. Hell, I haven't even been to a mall." I giggled when her face dropped to one of horror.

"I guess this means you won't be opposed to me taking you shopping tomorrow then?"

"If you can make me look this good for a simple party, I'd let you pick out all my outfits."

She squealed and clapped, turning to grab her clutch. "Yay! Okay, let's go snag a couple guys."

I stopped walking, eyes wide. I don't know how to talk to a normal guy, let alone snag one. "Uh, I'm not exactly great with the opposite sex. Like, I've never had a boyfriend or anything."

"Whoa, what?!"

"What part of Marine for a father didn't you understand? I don't think I've ever even talked to a guy that wasn't a Marine."

"Okay, timeout. Are you being serious? Have you ever been kissed?" She gasped when my lips pressed into a hard line. "Oh honey, I promise to fix at least that by the end of tonight."

My cheeks flamed as I quickly followed her out to her shiny graduation present of a car.

"HEY BREE!"

"Hi Drew." Breanna hugged an already intoxicated looking guy that opened the door. "Drew this is my new roomie Harper, Harper this is Drew."

"Nice to meet you," I mumbled. Before I knew what was happening I was being lifted up in a bear hug. I gasped but refrained the urge to kick him.

"Always a pleasure to have fresh meat here," he said with a wink before putting me down.

"Easy tiger, she's off limits to you!" She mock glared and poked him in the chest.

"Aww, come on Bree, don't be a cock block."

Raising an eyebrow I almost smiled at him. He wasn't even attractive and was holding a blow up doll.

"Nu-uh, no one that lives in this house is allowed to touch her. I know how you all are. So play nice, kay?"

Drew grumbled and walked away to refill his plastic cup. Breanna leaned in to speak in my ear, "I'm not gonna lie and tell you they aren't all like that, practically every guy that lives in this house is just as bad as him, and most of the guys that will be here tonight are too. I'll tell you who's safe and who isn't."

I smiled at her, "Thanks Bree, I'll owe you." Not that I needed her to tell me to stay away from guys like him. Sir let me around the Marines not only because they were like the brothers I never had, but he knew I would never end up falling for someone who would talk like that in front of a girl.

She scrunched her brows together and teased me, "Duh. Want a drink?"

Agreeing, I walked with her to a group hovered around one of the kegs. After getting a beer and forcing half the cup down to get the bad taste over with as fast as possible, I followed her out to the back yard to meet more people. I don't remember most of their names, but I got picked up and carried around more times than I cared to count, and was gawked at by every guy I met. Bree assured me it was because I looked good, but I was already wishing I'd worn a sweatshirt and jeans and cursing my tiny frame. Breanna seemed so at ease with the way guys were touching her and raking their eyes over us, and I didn't understand how she could do it. I no longer felt beautiful, I felt exactly like what Drew called me. Meat. I was halfway through my second beer of the night when I was pulled onto the dance floor by Bree and a few others.

I'd never felt so out of place in my life. Just watching the way these people were groping each other was making my cheeks burn, I tried to follow Bree's lead but I ended up just stumbling around from people rubbing up against me. I turned my head to see the most recent encounter and found myself being glared at by the most beautiful blue eyes I'd ever seen. Taking in the rest of him I could see I'd gotten in the way of his dry humping with a busty blonde and tried to quickly move away. Pointing to the kitchen when Bree tried to stop me, I slowly made my way through the packed bodies and out of the living room.

"What's up Harper?"

I turned to see Drew standing beside me. "Uh, nothing. Just had to get out of that," I said pointing over my shoulder.

"You don't like to dance?"

You call that dancing? "Not really my thing."

Drew put an arm on each side of me trapping me against the counter and pressing his body into mine. "Is there anything else I can I interest you in?"

Not you. "Is there a bathroom I can use?"

As soon as I asked, a bunch of guys started chanting and I turned to see what the fuss was about. My eyes about bulged out of my head when I did. The same guy I'd last bumped into on the dance floor was now taking shots out of a girl's mouth, running his tongue and lips all over her neck and chest between each one. When he sprinkled more salt on her, I realized why he'd been licking her. After the third one he looked right into my eyes and winked before putting his mouth to the fourth glass. I shook my head and didn't even wait for Drew to respond, I went off to find the bathroom on my own. After opening the doors on two couples having sex, I finally started asking more people where to find one. Once I got in, I locked the door and tried to calm myself. I may have heard disgusting stories from my brothers trying to get a rise out of me when I was young, but hearing it and seeing it are two completely different things.

I stayed in the bathroom until people started pounding on the door and dashed down the long halls trying to avoid looking at the doors to the other rooms I'd already opened. When I rounded a corner I ran right into a broad muscular chest and almost fell on my butt before he caught me.

"I'm so sorry, I—" I shut my mouth when I looked up and saw those deep blue eyes again.

He smiled and I momentarily got distracted by his perfectly straight, white teeth and full lips. Cocking his head to the side, I saw the recognition flash across his face that was soon replaced by a sexy smirk. By the way my heart started pounding, I was sure he'd perfected that look years ago. "Now who are you?"

I blinked and tore my gaze from his mouth and tried to move around him but his hands were still holding me in place.

"What, you're too good to tell me?"

I thought about the two girls I'd seen him with, and for the first time since running into him, realized there was a new blonde with her arm wrapped around his waist. Wow three girls within half an hour. I raised an eyebrow at him, "Apparently."

He and the tall blonde both scoffed. After releasing my arms he crossed his in front of his chest exposing even more muscles and a good bit of half sleeve tattoos on both arms. His stance may have looked intimidating if his face didn't appear so shocked and amused. "Excuse me Princess?"

Narrowing my eyes I started to shoulder my way past him, "You're right, *excuse* me."

He let me pass and I made my way back outside, to where most of the activities happening didn't make me want to shut my eyes and turn away. Bree said we'd be here all night, and I know it's childish, but all I want to do is hide out. I found a couple chairs in a dark corner of the backyard and plopped into one. It's obvious I'm not going to be a fan of parties. I pulled out my phone and texted Carter.

Me: So . . . I don't understand why you guys get so excited about parties

J. Carter: You at one?

Me: Yep.

J. Carter: Are you drinking?

Me: A little.

J. Carter: . . . please be careful. I know better than anyone that you can take care of yourself. But you've never had alcohol before. Don't let anyone hand you an open drink, and don't set yours down ever.

Me: Okay Mom.

J. Carter: I'm serious Blaze. Be careful.

I smiled at his nickname for me. I was known for blushing.

Me: I will. Miss you already.

J. Carter: Same here. No one left this weekend, we're all too upset knowing you're gone.

Me: I doubt that. You're probably on a date right now, already forgetting about me.

We texted for hours and I realized the party had thinned out immensely by the time Breanna found me.

"Harper! What are you doing out here by yourself? I've been looking for you forever."

"Sorry, guess I'm not as good at this as you."

Huffing, she fell into the chair next to me. "You'll get used to it, once you know more people you'll have fun. Did you talk to anybody?"

I shook my head, "After I left you I only saw Drew and some other guy."

"There were a lot of guys here, you're saying you only saw two in the last few hours?"

"Not that, he just . . . stood out I guess." Not only because he'd given me a nickname I'd lived with and hated my entire life, but he is easily the most attractive guy I've ever seen. He had that bad boy model look going for him, and unfortunately he knew it.

"Really? And who is this mystery guy?"

"Apparently he isn't really a mystery." I laughed, "I saw him with three different women in like thirty minutes. He was kind of a jerk too." Not exactly, but I didn't like his entitled attitude.

"Sounds like my kind of man!"

I looked over at her, shocked.

"Kidding Harper! Kidding, oh my God you are too fun to mess with. Well, not to say I didn't have my hands all over a few guys myself, but at least that was over the course of four hours." She laughed and stood up, offering me a hand. "Come on, practically everyone's already gone."

"Are we going back to the dorms?"

"No way, crazy! I never drive if I've had anything to drink within the last three hours. It's a rule."

"Sooo . . . where are we going then?"

"Well first we're gonna find my brother, and then we'll crash in his room."

"What? No! I'm not sleeping in his room."

"Chill Harp, it'll just be you and me in there. I always get his room after these parties." She pulled me across the lawn toward the back door.

I groaned and tried to keep up, almost losing my flip flops on the way.

"YYYEEEAAAH, Bree and fresh meat are sleeping over tonight!" Breanna bounced over to where Drew and another guy I didn't recognize were pouring shots and grinning while staring at my chest.

"Well, well. If it isn't the princess."

My body tensed and I frowned when I saw him approaching. Narrowing my eyes, I plastered on a fake smile. "I almost didn't recognize you without a tramp attached to you."

Drew and the other guy snickered.

Leaning into my ear he harshly whispered, "Would you like to change that? I'm not up to my limit tonight yet."

Gah, why did he have to be so hot? My body was practically humming with how close he was. I leaned away and replied with the most innocent expression on my face, "Oh I'm sorry, but I don't have any STDs, I'm not your type."

Drew started choking and Breanna spit her next shot all over the counter. Sputtering and choking, she finally composed herself enough to chime in, "Chase, you better stay away from my roommate. I told the guys she's off limits."

I tore my eyes away from his to look at Bree, "You know him?"

Everyone started laughing except for the guy standing next to me. His eyebrows were raised and his perfect mouth was slightly open. I guess women don't turn him down often.

"Well I'd like to think so, he *is* my brother."

Oh. Crap. Heat instantly spread to my cheeks and I took a step away from him. Now that I'd been informed, I realized I should have known it. They had the same blond hair, blue eyes and killer smile.

"Wait, Harper is this the guy you said was a jerk?"

My eyes widened and I looked at the ground.

"You said I'm a jerk?" Chase laughed and turned to the bar, "She's the one that just practically called me a dirty man-whore."

"Don't be rude to my friends Chase!" Breanna took another shot then punched his arm, I doubt he felt it though.

Without saying anything else I went back outside to my chair in the dark corner of the yard, and stayed there until the music was turned off. As a rule, I don't let guys push me around, but I felt horrible that I'd said that to my new roommate's brother. Not to mention we were currently at his house and about to stay in his room. I planted my face in my hands, elbows on my knees and groaned at myself. I should have just kept my mouth shut. As if he knew I was thinking about him, Chase fell into the seat next to me. I removed a hand and looked into his dark blue eyes.

"You hiding?" That stupid sexy smirk was there again.

"Is it that obvious?"

He looked around the empty backyard, then glanced back to me, "A little." He stretched out his long legs and sank farther into the chair, "Tell me, what's a princess like you doing at my party?"

I bristled and literally had to bite down on my tongue. "I'm not sure what you mean, but I was invited." It came out a little harsher than I'd meant it to, but I wasn't about to apologize for that.

His smirk was gone, and he looked pissed, "You don't have to be invited to come to the party, but if you didn't notice, you don't exactly fit in here, *Princess*." He sneered.

My mouth dropped open with an audible pop, I quickly shut it. He was right, I didn't. But seriously? Rude. At least when I was snide, you could hear the sarcasm.

"If the way we are disgusts you so much, feel free to stay at school next time." Standing quickly, he shot me one more glare before turning away.

Aces. I've been here a little over a day, and my time here in California was already starting off so well.

"Chase," my voice stopped him, "I'm really sorry, I was out of line."

He turned to look at me, head cocked to the side.

When he continued to look at me with a confused expression I went on.

"I was raised not to back down to people, but what I said was too much. So, I'm sorry. I don't know you, I shouldn't judge you."

A huff of a laugh escaped his chest and I saw the corners of his mouth slightly tilt up. He shook his head, still looking confused and now a little stunned before he took off around the side of the house.

This was going to be a long night. If I had any idea where we were, I'd try to walk back to campus.

"Haarrrrrppppeeeerrrr!" I looked over to see Breanna stumble out the back door. "Harper, come inside, everyone's gone!"

When I got close she hooked an arm through mine and led me into the living room. "So did you kiss anyone tonight?" She raised both eyebrows and it looked like she had to struggle to keep them there.

"No," I muttered.

The same guy she'd been taking shots with when I left yelled from the kitchen, "I can help with that!"

I shook my head and started to answer when Bree spoke again. "No, no, no. I told you guys, she's off limits!"

"Come on Bree, what's your deal?"

She leaned forward and fake whispered, "Cause she's *pure*. Completely. Pure."

My jaw dropped and I grabbed her wrist as she went to tap my lips with her finger. "Breanna!"

Putting her hand back to her own lips she held one

finger in front of her mouth. "Shh! Harper don't tell them!"

A little late for that. I was completely mortified. I wanted to be angry at her, but she could barely stay standing, I doubt she would remember any of this tomorrow. Looking up, I saw four guys standing there staring at me with wide eyes before busting up laughing. I needed someone to kill me. Now. No, first I needed to get out of here. Then someone needed to kill me.

One of the guys I hadn't met was wiping tears from his eyes, "Oh my God! Princess, is she serious?"

Glad to see they all adopted my favorite nickname. Was there something about me that just screamed *Give me a nickname*? I couldn't even respond, my throat had closed up and I thought I would actually cry for the first time in years. Unhooking my arm from Breanna, I made a beeline for the front door, intent on trying to find my way back to campus. I stopped when I realized Chase was blocking the hall that led to the entryway, he was the only one in the room not laughing. Instead, his lips were mashed together and he was shooting daggers at his sister.

"Please. Move."

He moved, but it was to grab my shoulders and steer me back toward the living room. What was he doing? I dug my heels into the carpet trying to scramble back in the other direction.

"Don't touch me!" I hissed.

"Just trust me," he growled in my ear, walking me past everyone still laughing at Bree's slip.

When we hit a hallway I hadn't been down tonight, one of the guys from the kitchen yelled, "Looks like Chase is gonna take care of that problem for you Princess!" That brought on a new round of hysterics.

Chase paused for a second, cussed under his breath and started forward with me again. When we got to the end of the hall he stopped in front of a door, and pulled out a key to unlock it before towing me in. When the light flipped on, I blinked until I realized we were in a bedroom, I gasped and tried even harder to get out of his grasp. If I could just turn a little, I could have him on the floor in a few seconds. But his grip was firm, I couldn't budge at all.

"No! Get off me!"

"Not until you stop trying to hit me!"

I stopped but stayed tense as he waited for almost a minute before releasing my arms. Once he did I turned on him and backed away.

"Calm down Princess." He sighed sounding uninterested, "I'm not going to do anything to you."

"I really wish you would stop calling me that," I said through gritted teeth.

He rolled his eyes and went to a drawer, after throwing a pair of basketball shorts at me he walked back to the door. "Put those on, I'll be back."

"Why?"

"Did you want to sleep in that skirt?" He bit his bottom lip, his eyes glued to my legs. "I swear I won't mind it, I figured you'd be uncomfortable though."

"Breanna said I would be in a room with her tonight,

and if that's not happening I'd rather just go back to the dorm."

"I can assure you she'll be sleeping in the bathroom. I'll give you a minute to change, I'll be right back."

"I am not sleeping with you in here."

"Look, you're seriously hot, that alone is going to have them chasing after you. But top that off with the few words you've even said that shows me just how snarky and sweet as hell you are, that is one hell of a tempting combination. Trust me when I say they're going to want to change what they just found out about you. So if you don't mind, I'd rather make sure that doesn't happen."

He slammed the door shut and not more than three seconds later I could hear him yelling at the guys in the kitchen and telling Breanna to fend for herself tonight. I was standing there in his basketball shorts and Bree's spaghetti strap when he walked back in and locked the door.

"That was rude, she's your sister. She should be in here too."

He looked at me incredulously, "Are you serious? You're gonna defend her after she just spilled that?"

I shrugged my shoulders and put the skirt on a chair, keeping my back to him so he couldn't see my cheeks flaming again. "She's drunk. I'm sure she didn't realize it."

"That's not an excuse." His voice was soft as he pulled down the covers, "Come on Harper, get in."

The way his voice wrapped around my name sent a warm shiver through my body and I had to fight to keep

my eyes away from his now-bare chest as I crawled into
his bed. Even the quick glance at his sculpted chest and
abs had my heart racing. After he flipped off the lights, I
felt the bed sink down from his weight and I sat up.

"What are you *doing*?"

"What do you mean?"

"You can't get in here with me!"

He chuckled, "It's my bed, I'm sure I can do what I
want."

I know he couldn't see me, but I glared at him anyway.
Flipping the cover off me, I grabbed a pillow and sank
down to the floor.

"Get back in the bed Princess."

I scoffed at my nickname but didn't say anything. I
could feel his eyes boring into my back and after what
felt like an eternity, heard him sigh and the bed shift. I
wanted to ask for a blanket but was too stubborn to ask.
Next thing I knew I was in the air.

"Oh my word! Put me down!"

He dropped me onto the bed and crawled over me.

"Chase! No!"

"Calm down, I'll stay on my side. We can even put a
pillow between us if it'll make you feel better." He snickered.

I grumbled and scooted to the edge of the bed. Obviously I've never been in a bed with a guy before, and the
fact that he was inches away had my whole body shaking.
"I swear if you touch me, I'll go Lorena Bobbitt on you."

It didn't take him long to figure out what I was re-
ferring to. He put a pillow over his face to muffle his

booming laugh. "Oh my God! Princess! You're my new favorite!"

"That wasn't a joke."

His body was still shaking with silent laughs as he moved closer and trailed his fingers up my arm. "One of these days, you'll be begging for me to touch you."

I couldn't tell if my next shiver was out of pleasure or disgust but I still growled at him and slapped his hand away. "I'm serious Chase. I'm not like all those girls I saw you with tonight."

"That's an understatement." He rolled back to his side of the bed and sighed, "Get some sleep Princess, I'll see you in the morning."

MY EYES SHOT open the next morning when I felt something squeeze me. Looking down I saw tattoos trailing down to a muscled forearm that was wrapped securely around my waist and gasped when I remembered I'd slept in Chase's bed last night. I jumped out from under his arm and off his bed in a move so fast it had my head spinning. My heart took off again as I took in Chase's shirtless body. His tattoos expanded up his shoulders and for some reason I wanted to trace them with my fingers and splay my hands across his well-defined abs and chest. Dear me, this man was gorgeous.

Chase sat up cursing until he realized who I was. "Jesus Princess! You almost gave me a heart attack. I thought I had a girl in here." He flopped back onto his pillow, raking his hands over his face.

That snapped me back to reality. "Chase?"

"Hmm?"

"Sorry you didn't seem to notice, but I *am* a girl."

He dropped his hands and scowled at me but still proceeded to slowly take in my body. My cheeks were bright red by the time he looked back up. "I noticed last night, trust me." My question mark face must have prompted the rest of his response. "I meant, I thought I let a girl stay the night with me."

"Uh . . . ?"

"Someone I'd been with Princess. I thought I banged a girl and let her stay here."

"Oh."

He snorted. "Sorry, is that too much for your PG ears?"

"No, I just don't understand why that would be a bad thing."

Sighing deeply he propped himself up on an elbow and looked directly into my eyes. "Girls I screw around with aren't allowed to come in my room, let alone stay the night. This is the only place that is mine, and I'm not about to share it with them."

"So you sleep with women and then make them leave?" I didn't even want to ask *where* he slept with them.

"No, I *screw* women . . . and then make them leave."

I shook my head and walked toward the door, "You're a pig."

He laughed once without humor and watched me leave.

When I got out to the living room I saw Breanna at the kitchen table with a housemate, as soon as they saw me the conversation stopped. I hadn't known I could feel even more awkward, guess so.

Looking at me sheepishly, Bree stood from her chair and pulled me toward the living room. "Harper, I'm so sorry. Brad just told me everything." Her voice broke at the end. "I swear I would never intentionally do something to embarrass you. I know we just met but I've been looking forward to living with you and I can't believe I hurt you like that after just meeting you."

"Really, it's fine. I've heard enough stories that I figured you didn't know what you were doing."

"It's not fine! You should hate me."

I nodded and looked over at Brad who was grinning at me. "Well I don't plan on seeing any of these guys ever again, so there's no use in making you suffer with me." I smiled at her, trying to make light of the situation.

Although I was still humiliated, I'd never been one to hold a grudge, and I wasn't about to start now. I had wanted to come start a new life here, and even though I seem to have taken five steps back, I was still determined to make this the best experience ever. Embarrassing moment or not, it's not like I had a lot of options here. Either let this get to me and cower away from people, or hold my head high and push forward.

She still looked sullen and it was making me uncomfortable. "Well at least people don't think I'm a whore."

That brought on a smile which turned into a light laugh. "You're a glass half full kind of person, aren't you?"

"Definitely."

Hugging me tightly before walking back to her cup of

coffee she said, "At least let me buy you one new outfit."

"Hah! I won't stop you. Are you sure you're up for that today though? I figured you wouldn't be up for much of anything after last night."

"Sweetie, I'm *always* up for shopping. Go change, I'm ready when you are."

I walked back into Chase's room to find it empty, after shedding his basketball shorts I quickly stepped into Bree's skirt. Before I could pull it up, the door swung open and Chase walked in.

"It's really a shame you don't let anyone see that sexy little body."

Blushing fifty shades of red, I pulled them up and turned to face him.

"Calm down, you don't have anything I haven't seen before." He cocked his head and raised an eyebrow making it disappear under his shaggy blond hair. "Not saying I wouldn't want to see yours."

"Bite me." I pushed past him toward the door.

"Is that an invitation?"

"Not even close."

He grabbed my waist, and pulled me against his chest, his nose skimming along my jaw, "One of these days Princess, I promise you."

I turned to scowl at him once more, "I would never be desperate enough to want you." Okay that was a lie; my breaths were already quickening just feeling his sculpted body pressed against mine.

His smile was slow and sexy, "We'll see."

BREANNA AND I were lying on our beds in the dorm room after an epic six hour shopping trip at an outdoor mall. As promised, I let her pick out all my outfits, and she paid for one of them. Now that we were done, I was regretting how much money I'd spent, but I'd just bought fifteen different shirts, four pairs of jeans, a couple pairs of ultra-short shorts and skirts, three sexy but cute dresses and five pairs of shoes. After that was done we headed to Victoria's Secret, and I blushed my way through the entire store while she picked out all my new underwear, bras and sleeping clothes. Our last stop of the day was at Sephora where we basically purchased my own make-up counter after Bree swore to teach me how to put it all on. And for all that? I think I did pretty well. The only thing Sir had let me do growing up was work at one of the Post Exchanges. Not that kids my age were generally allowed to, but everyone knew our situation so I started there when I was twelve and had saved every cent.

"I'm. So. Exhausted."

"It was so worth it though! Now you're finally ready for college."

Looking at the garbage bags full of most of my old clothes I laughed and let my head fall back onto my pillow. "I think you're right."

"Now we just need to get you comfortable being around cute guys and you'll be golden. What's your type?"

Your brother. "Um, I'm not sure I have a type."

"So no preferences? Hair color, eye color, skin color? Athlete, geek, musician?"

Rugged surfer, with dirty blond shaggy hair, impossibly blue eyes, the most breathtaking smile you've ever seen and cover him in tattoos. I'll take that, please? "Nope, none. We'll just have to start from scratch."

Just thinking about his tattoos had me biting my lip and fantasizing again about tracing them with my fingers. He was exactly the kind of guy Sir would hate, so naturally I was drawn to him.

"Hey Bree?"

"Yeah?"

"There's kind of something I've wanted to do for a whi— You know what, never mind."

She sat up on her knees bouncing, "No you don't! You have to tell me now. You've wanted to do what?"

"Well there's a lot of things. But it'd probably be a bad idea to do them all at once. I should spread them out, and think about them more."

"I'm waiting Harper."

I sighed and scooted up against the wall, "I want to get a couple piercings."

"Pfft, I thought you were about to say something juicier than that." Figures she wouldn't be excited, each of her ears had four piercings.

I frowned at her.

"Okay, okay! What piercings do you want?"

"Um, I don't know what they're called. But here, and here." I pointed a finger to my upper lip, and another to my ear.

"Oh cute! Your lip is called a Monroe, and your ear is

a tragus. I actually really want my lip pierced too! Do you want to go get them done together sometime?"

I looked down before stealing a sideways glance, "Could we maybe go right now? Eighteen years of not being able to do what I want, I'm kind of impatient."

"Harper, I'm pretty sure we're going to be best friends." Without another word she shot off her bare mattress and headed for the door. Guess that means we're going.

I'm really glad she knew the area, because she drove right to a tattoo parlor, and after chatting it up with the piercer, we were sitting in his room picking out the studs before I could even think about this possibly being a bad idea. To my surprise, I wasn't even nervous 'til I was sitting on his chair and he was putting the markers on me. "Oh my God, Breanna I need your hand."

She laughed and sauntered up to me.

"Don't laugh, you're next." That shut her up.

"Okay deep breath in." The piercer said, "Annnnd blow out." After he finished putting the one in my ear, he opened up a new packet and got to work on my lip. "Another deep breath in . . . and blow out."

My eyes were watering, but thankfully it was done. I glanced in the mirror and a huge smile crossed my face, I absolutely loved them.

"Oh my God those are perfect for you! Ahh. I'm so excited for mine now!" Bree had also decided to get her tragus pierced so we both were getting two, but she and the piercer had agreed her bottom lip would be better for the way her mouth was set.

Another ten minutes and hers were done, I made her eat her words when she grabbed my hand at the last minute and squeezed until I thought I'd never get the circulation flowing again. We paid the guy and ran to her car, looking into the visor mirrors before we left.

"Are your parents going to mind?"

"What? No way. Have you seen my brother? They love his tattoos so they aren't going to care about this. Besides I'm pretty sure I couldn't get them mad at me even if I tried." She laughed, "Let me guess, daddy's gonna be pissed?"

"Ha! Yeah, I'm almost positive he's going to try to rip them out. Good thing I'm not going home for ten months!"

"Ten months?! What are you doing for winter break?"

I shrugged, "Stay here. It wouldn't be much different than being there. We don't spend much time together if we're in the same house."

"Jeez Harper, you had the most depressing childhood didn't you?"

"Not really, I mean it's all I've ever known. I thought it was normal until a few weeks ago when you and I started e-mailing." I think I need to stop talking about my past, because I always seem to depress everyone. "So . . . dinner?"

She smiled and turned to glance at me, "You read my mind roomie, let's grab some burgers then we can stay at my house tonight. We'll move my stuff into the dorm tomorrow."

FROM ASHES

1

Cassidy

"Do you even know anyone who's going to be there, Ty?"

"Just Gage. But this will be good, this way we'll be able to meet new people right away."

I grumbled to myself. I wasn't the best at making friends; they didn't understand my need to always be near Tyler, and when I'd show up with bruises or stitches, everyone automatically thought I was either hurting myself or Tyler and I were in an abusive relationship. Of course that wasn't their fault; we never responded to them, so the rumors continued to fly.

"Cassi, no one will have any idea about your past, the last of your bruises will be gone in a few weeks, and you're gone from there now. Besides, I hate that you don't have anyone else. Trust me, I understand it, but I hate it for you. You need more people in your life."

"I know." I instinctively wrapped my arms around myself, covering where some of the bruises were. Thank God none were visible right now unless I stripped down to my skivvies, but I couldn't say the same for some of the scars. At least scars were normal on a person, and the worst of them were covered by my clothes, so I just looked like I was accident-prone.

"Hey." Tyler grabbed one of my hands, taking it away from my side. "It's over, it will never happen again. And I'm always here for you, whether you make new friends or not. I'm here. But at least try. This is your chance at starting a new life—isn't that what that favorite bird of yours is all about anyway?"

"The phoenix isn't a real bird, Ty."

"Whatever, it's your favorite. Isn't that what they symbolize? New beginnings?"

"Rebirth and renewal," I muttered.

"Yeah, same thing. They die only to come back and start a new life, right? This is us starting a new life, Cass." He shook his head slightly and his face went completely serious. "But don't spontaneously burst into flames and die. I love you too much and a fire wouldn't be good for the leather seats."

I huffed a laugh and shoved his shoulder with my free hand. "You're such a punk, Ty; way to kill the warm and fuzzy moment you had going there."

He laughed out loud. "In all seriousness"—he kissed my hand, then met and held my gaze for a few seconds before looking back at the road—"new life, Cassi, and it starts right now."

Tyler and I weren't romantically involved, but we had a relationship that even people we'd grown up with didn't understand.

We grew up just a house away from each other, in a country club neighborhood. Both our fathers were doctors; our moms were the kind that stayed home with the kids and spent afternoons at the club gossiping and drinking martinis. On my sixth birthday, my dad died from a heart attack—while he was at work of all places. Now that I'm older, I don't understand how no one was able to save him; he worked in the ER, for crying out loud, and no one was able to save him? But at the time, I just knew my hero was gone.

Dad worked long hours, but I was his princess, and when he was home, it was just the two of us. He'd brave tiaras and boas to have tea parties with me; he knew the names of all of my stuffed animals, talked to them like they would respond; and he would always be the one to tell me stories at night. My mom was amazing, but she knew we had a special relationship, so she always stayed in the door frame, watching and smiling. Whenever I would get hurt, if he was at work, Mom would make a big show of how she couldn't make it better, and I'd have to hang on for dear life until Dad got home. She must have called him, because he would run into the house like I was dying—even though it was almost always just a scratch—pick me up, and place a Band-Aid wherever I was hurt, and miraculously I was all better. Like I said, my dad was my hero. Every little girl needs a dad like that. But now, other than precious memories, all I have left of him is his love for the phoenix. Mom had let Dad have his way with a large outline of a phoenix painted directly above my bed for when I started kindergarten, a painting that's still there today, though Mom constantly threatened to paint over it. And although I tried to keep a ring he'd had all his adult life with a phoenix on it, my mom had found and hidden it not long after he died, and I hadn't seen it since.

My mom started drinking obsessively when he died. Her morning coffee always had rum in it, by ten in the morning she was making margaritas, she'd continue to go to the club for martinis, and by the time I was home from school, she was drinking scotch or vodka straight out of the bottle. She made time for her girlfriends but stopped waking me up for school, stopped making me food, forgot to pick me up from school—pretty much just forgot I even existed. After that first day of being forgotten at school, and the next day not showing up because she wouldn't leave her room, Tyler's mom, Stephanie, started taking me to and from school without a word. She knew my mom was grieving, just not the extent of it.

After a week with no clean clothes and a few rounds of trial and error, I began doing my own laundry, attempted to figure out my homework by myself, and would make peanut butter and jelly sandwiches for both of us, always leaving one outside her bedroom door. Almost a year after Dad's death, Jeff came into the picture. He was rich, ran some big company—his last name was everywhere in Mission Viejo, California—but up until that day I'd never seen or heard of him. One day Stephanie dropped me off and he was just moved in, my mom already married to him.

That night was the first time I'd ever been hit, and it was by my own mother. My sweet, gentle mother who couldn't kill a spider, let alone spank her own daughter when she misbehaved, hit me. I asked who Jeff was and why he was telling me to call him Dad, and my mom hit me across the back with the new scotch bottle she'd been attempting to open. It didn't break, but it left one nasty-looking bruise. From that point on, I never went a day without some kind of injury inflicted by one of them. Usually it was fists or palms, and I began welcoming those, because when they started throwing coffee mugs, drinking glasses, or lamps, or when my mom took off her heels and repeatedly hit me in the head with the tip of her stiletto . . . I didn't know if I would still be alive the next day. About a week after the first hit was when I first got beat with Jeff's socket wrench, and that was the first night I opened my window, popped off the screen, and made my way to Tyler's window. At seven years old, he helped me into his room, gave me some of his pajamas since my nightshirt was covered in blood, and held my hand as we fell asleep in his bed.

Over the last eleven years, Tyler has begged me to let him tell his parents what was going on, but I couldn't let that happen. If Tyler told them, they would call someone and I knew they would take me away from Tyler. My hero had died, and the mom I loved had disappeared down a bottle; no way was I letting someone take me from Ty too. The only way I had gotten him to agree was agreeing myself that if he ever found me unconscious, all promises were off and he could tell whomever he wanted. But that was just keeping Tyler quiet; we never had factored in the neighbors . . .

After the first three years of the abuse, I stopped sneaking out to Ty's house every night, only doing so on the nights when it was something other than body parts hitting me, but Tyler was always waiting, no matter what. He kept a first aid kit in his room, and would clean up and bandage anything he was able to. We butterfly-bandaged almost all the cuts, but three times he forced me to get stitches. We told his dad I tripped over something while going for a run outside each time. I'm not naïve, I knew his dad didn't believe me—especially since I was not one for running, and the only time I was involved with sports was watching it on Ty's TV—but we were always careful to hide my bruises around him and he never tried to figure out where I actually got the cuts from. I'd sit at their kitchen table and let him sew me up, they'd let me out the front door when they were sure I was okay, and Tyler would be waiting by his open window as soon as I rounded the house. Every night he had something ready for me to sleep in, and every night he would hold my hand and curl his body around mine until we fell asleep.

So when Tyler kissed my forehead, cheek, or hand, it never meant anything romantic. He was just comforting me in the same way he had since we were kids.

"Cassi? Did I lose you?" Tyler waved his hand in front

of my face.

"Sorry. Life, starting over. Friends, yeah, this, uh—will be—I need to . . . friends." I'm pretty sure there was English somewhere in that sentence.

Ty barked out a laugh and squeezed my knee, and after a few silent minutes he thankfully changed the subject. "So what do you think about the apartment?"

"It's great. Are you sure you want me to stay with you? I can get my own place, or even sleep on the couch . . ." My own place? That was such a far-fetched idea it was almost funny; I didn't even have a hundred dollars to my name.

"No way, I've shared my bed with you for eleven years, I'm not about to change that now."

"Ty, but what about when you get a girlfriend? Are you really going to want to explain why I live with you? Why we share a dresser, closet, and bed?"

Tyler looked at me for a second before turning his eyes back to the road. His brown eyes had darkened, and his lips were mashed in a tight line. "You're staying with me, Cassi."

I sighed but didn't say anything else. We'd had a version of this argument plenty of times. Every relationship he'd ever had ultimately ended because of me and the fact that we were always together. I hated that I ruined his relationships, and whenever he was dating someone I would even stop coming to his room and answering his calls so he could focus on his girlfriend instead. That never lasted long though; he'd climb through my window, pick me up out of bed, and take me back to his house. We never had to worry about my boyfriends, since I'd never had one. What with Tyler's possessiveness and all, no one even attempted to get close enough to me. Not that it bothered me; the only guy I'd ever had feelings for was too old for me and had only been in my life for a few short minutes. The moment I'd answered the door to see him standing there, my stomach had started fluttering and I felt this weird connection with him I'd never felt with anyone, and even after he was gone I'd dreamed about his cool intensity and mesmerizing blue eyes. Ty didn't know about him though, because what was the point? I'd just barely turned sixteen and he was a cop; I knew I'd never see him again, and I didn't. Besides, other than my real dad and Ty, I had a problem with letting guys get close, strange connection or not. When my already-disturbed world turned completely upside down the minute a new man came into our house . . . trust issues were bound to happen.

Tyler had decided to go to the University of Texas in Austin, where his cousin Gage, who was two years older than us, was currently studying. I'd heard a lot about Gage and his family from Ty over the years, since they were his only cousins, and I was genuinely happy he was going. Gage was like a brother to him and Tyler hadn't seen him in a few years, so their sharing an apartment would be good for Ty. I wasn't sure what I was going to do when Tyler left; the only thing I did know was that I was getting away from the house I grew up in. I just had to make it another month until I turned eighteen and then

I was gone. But Tyler, being Tyler, made my future plans for me. He crawled through my window, told me to pack my bag, and just before he could haul me off to his Jeep, he told Mom and Jeff exactly what he thought of them. I didn't have time to worry about the consequences of his telling them off, because before I knew it we were on the freeway and headed for Texas. We made the trip in just over a day, and now, after being here long enough to unpack his Jeep and shower separately, we were headed to some lake for a party to meet up with Gage and his friends.

Gage's family wasn't from Austin; I didn't know where in Texas they lived, but apparently they had a ranch. After hearing that, I'd had to bite the inside of my cheek to keep from asking what Gage was like. I understood we were in Texas now, but already Austin had blown my expectations of dirt roads and tumbleweeds away with its downtown buildings and greenery everywhere. I just didn't know how I'd handle living with a tight-Wranglered, big-belt-buckled, Stetson-wearing cowboy like I'd seen in rodeos and movies. I'd probably burst out laughing every time I saw him.

When we came up to the lake and the group of people, I sucked in a deep breath in a futile attempt to calm my nerves. I wasn't a fan of new people.

Tyler grabbed my hand and gave it a tight squeeze. "New beginning, Cassi. And I'll be right here next to you."

"I know. I can do this." His Jeep stopped and I immediately took that back. *Nope. No, I can't do this.* I had to think quickly of where every bruise was, making sure my clothes were covering them all, even though I'd already gone through this at the apartment. I just didn't want anyone here to know what kind of life I'd had.

I jumped out of Tyler's Jeep, took one more deep breath, and mentally pumped myself up. *New life. I can do this.* I turned and rounded the front and hadn't even made it to Tyler's side when I saw him. I don't know if I made a conscious choice to stop walking or if I was still making my way to Tyler and didn't realize it; all I could focus on or see was the guy standing about ten feet from me. He was tall, taller than Tyler's six-foot frame, and had on loose, dark tan cargo shorts and a white button-up shirt, completely unbuttoned, revealing a tan, toned chest and abs. His arms were covered in muscles, but he didn't look like someone who spent hours in the gym or taking steroids. The only way I can describe them is natural, and labor-made. His jet-black hair had that messy, just-got-out-of-bed look, and my hand twitched just thinking about running my fingers through it. I couldn't see what color eyes he had from here, but they were locked on me, his mouth slightly open. He had a bottle of water in his hand, and it was raised like he had been about to take a drink out of it before he saw me. I had no idea what was happening to me, but my entire body started tingling, and my palms were sweating just looking at him.

I'd seen plenty of attractive guys—Tyler looked like an Abercrombie and Fitch model, for crying out loud. But Mr. New couldn't even be described as something as degrading as *attractive*. He looked like a god. My breath was becoming rougher, and my blood started warming as I took an unconscious step toward him. Just then a tall, leggy blonde bounced over to his side and wrapped her arms around his waist, kissing his strong jaw. It felt like someone punched me in the stomach and I was instantly jealous of whoever this girl was. Shaking my head, I forced my eyes to look away. *What the hell, Cassidy? Calm down.*

"Cassi, you coming?"

I blinked and looked over at Tyler, who had his hand outstretched to me. "Uh, yeah." I glanced back at Mr. New and saw he still hadn't moved. The perky blonde was chatting his ear off, and he didn't even seem to be hearing her. I felt a blush creep up my cheeks from the way he was looking at me, like he'd just seen the sun for the first time, and continued over to Tyler.

Tyler pulled me to his side and whispered in my ear, "You okay?"

"Yeah, I'm fine," I reassured him, trying to slow my heart down for a completely different reason now.

He kissed my cheek and pulled away. "Okay, well let me introduce you to Gage."

Right. Gage. Tyler dropped my hand, only to put his on the small of my back as he led me over to Mr. New and the leggy blonde. *Oh no. No no no no no.*

"'Sup, man?" Tyler slapped him on the back and Mr. New slowly dragged his eyes from me to the guy who'd just hit him.

Gage's eyes went wide when he saw Ty. "Tyler, hey! I didn't realize y'all were here yet."

Oh. Good. God. That voice. Even with that small sentence I could hear the drawl in it. It was deep and gravelly, and easily the sexiest thing I'd ever heard.

"Yeah, we just got here. Cassi, this is my cousin Gage. Gage, this is Cassi."

Gage brought his hand out. "It's a pleasure, Cassi. I'm glad y'all are finally here."

My knees went weak and a jolt of electricity went through me when I shook his hand. From how he glanced down at our hands quickly, he'd felt it too. "It's nice to meet you too." Now that I was up close, I could see his bright green eyes, hidden behind thick black lashes and eyebrows. He was the definition of masculine. From his strong jaw and brow, high cheekbones, defined nose, and perfectly kissable lips, his looks screamed *man*. The only thing offsetting the masculinity were his boyish deep dimples, which had me hooked. Yep, *god* was the only word out there that fit him.

Our hands didn't separate fast enough for the tall blonde, so she thrust her hand forward. "I'm Brynn, Gage's girlfriend." Her eyes narrowed on the last word.

I shouldn't have, but I glanced at Gage again. His brows were pulled down in either confusion or annoyance when he looked at Brynn. *You have got to be kidding me,* I thought. I didn't care if it had been only two seconds since I first saw him, this couldn't be a normal reaction for two people just meeting to have with each other, and he had a freaking girlfriend. It hadn't even felt like this with the cop who came to my door that night, and I'd thought about him for almost two years!

I squared my shoulders and dropped Gage's hand, focusing on Brynn. "It's great to meet you, Brynn!" I hoped my smile looked genuine. I didn't need an enemy yet, especially if she was dating the guy I was going to be living with. But hell, I'm not gonna lie—I was already thinking of ways to get her out of the picture.

Tyler and Brynn shook hands, and she looked back at me, noticing that I was doing everything to keep from looking at her boyfriend. Tyler and Gage were catching up, and every time Gage would speak I had to force myself not to shut my eyes and lose myself in the way his voice caused chills to go through my whole body.

"So, Cassi, what do you say we go introduce you to the rest of the girls?" Brynn finally said sweetly.

Tyler looked elated; this was exactly what he wanted. "Sounds great," I said, and stepped away from the guys. It felt wrong to walk away, but I could feel Gage watching me as I did.

"You and Tyler, huh?" Brynn nudged my shoulder.

"What do you mean?"

"Y'all make such a cute couple." She wasn't complimenting, she was reaching.

"Thanks, but no. Tyler and I are best friends, nothing more."

"You sure about that? I saw the way he was looking at you, and he had his arm around you."

"We're just different like that. We've been best friends our entire lives."

"Right. Are you going to UT too?" she asked, sounding a little too curious.

"Uh, no. I'm not planning on going to school at all."

"So why are you here?" If it hadn't been for the curled-up lip, she would have just simply sounded interested.

"Honestly? I have no idea. Tyler packed my bag and threw me in his Jeep. Apparently Gage didn't care if I lived with them." I smirked and turned to begin the introductions with the girls who were now right next to us.

Gage

WHAT THE HELL *was* that? Nothing like that had ever happened to me. One look at Cassi and it felt like my world stopped. All I could think about was closing the distance between us. I don't know how to describe it, but I needed to go to her. Unfortunately, I was frozen in place, taking in the most beautiful girl I'd ever seen. Her long brown hair was windblown, and those wide honey-colored eyes made me want to get lost in them. She looked so sweet and fragile, I wanted to wrap my arms around her and protect her from seeing anything bad in the world, but something in her eyes told me she knew too well what the world was like and could take care of herself. Which is why it was so damn confusing that she clung to my cousin like he was a lifeline.

Tyler told me he was bringing his friend to live with us, and that she was a girl. I'd remembered hearing her name over the years, but whenever he spoke about her, it seemed like they were only friends, so why did he hold her hand and kiss her damn cheek? I couldn't even stop the growl that came from my throat when I saw it. Then freakin' Brynn. Girlfriend? Really? We'd gone on two god-awful dates last year and I told her before school let out that I didn't want any form of a relationship with her. I thought we'd been clear since she'd avoided me all afternoon until Cassi and Ty showed up.

When Cassi first spoke, I had to force myself to breathe. Her voice was soft and melodic. It fit her perfectly. She was petite and even with how short she was, those legs in those shorts could make any guy fall on his knees and beg. I couldn't stop thinking about how she'd feel in my arms, how she'd look in my truck or on my horse. And yeah, I'm not gonna lie, I'd already pictured her beneath me . . . but one look at her and there was no way not to.

After Brynn guided her away, it took a huge effort to stop watching her, but I didn't want to let on to Tyler that I was already completely taken with her.

"She's mine, Gage. Let's get that clear right now."

Okay, so maybe I'd been a little more obvious than I'd thought. "Thought you said y'all were friends."

"She's my best friend, but you'll see. She's mine."

I nodded and clapped his back, forcing my hand out of a fist. "I got you, man. Come on, let me get you a beer."

As the night wore on, I continued to get closer and closer to where she was. I felt like a creep, trying to be near her, but I couldn't stop it. I wanted to listen to her talk and laugh; I swear she sounded like an angel singing when she laughed. I almost groaned out loud—*Angel singing? What the hell is wrong with me?*

We were all sitting around the bonfire talking and

drinking. I was just a few feet from Cassi when she got up to head over to Jackie. If it hadn't been for what happened immediately after, I would have punched Jake in the face for touching her. With one hand he grazed the front of her thigh, and with the other he grabbed her ass, causing her to stumble and fall right into me, her beer soaking my shirt.

Her big eyes got even wider and she sucked in a quick gasp. "Oh God, I'm so sorry!" The sun was setting and it was getting darker, but I could perfectly see her blush. I'm pretty sure Cassi blushing was my new favorite thing.

I laughed and grabbed her small shoulders to steady her, not caring one bit about my shirt. "You all right?"

Her eyes focused on my lips, her teeth lightly sinking into her bottom one. I wanted to replace her teeth with mine and without realizing it, I started to lean forward. She blinked quickly and glanced up, then looked at Jake on my right. "I'm fine. I'm really sorry about your shirt."

Aw hell, this isn't normal. She's said all of two sentences to me tonight and I was about to kiss her? "Don't worry about it," I murmured as she righted herself and continued toward Jackie, only to be quickly pulled away by Tyler as he spoke in her ear, his arms around her.

"Damn, when you said your cousin was bringing a chick, I wasn't expecting her to be so hot," Jake said.

"Jake, touch her again . . . see what fuckin' happens."

"Whoa, got it bad for your cousin's girl already, huh? You gonna try to get with that?"

I eyed Cassi in Ty's arms and shook my head as I

brought my beer up to take another long drink. "Nope."

Yes, yes, I am.

"Well, if you're not, I sure as hell am."

"Jake," I growled.

"All right, all right. Chill, Gage. I won't touch her and you heard her . . . she's fine." Jake leaned forward to grab another beer out of the ice chest and settled back into his chair, his eyes already off Cassi and onto Lanie.

After a quick glance to see Cassi and Tyler still quietly talking, I got up and walked back to where all the trucks were parked. I took my wet shirt off and hung it off the bed of my truck before grabbing a clean one out of the backseat. When I turned around, Tyler was walking up to me.

"I'm real glad you're here, bro," I said.

"Me too." He took a long drink out of his can before setting it down on the tailgate. "We couldn't get here fast enough. Cali was really starting to wear on me; I was ready for someplace new. And hey, I know I've said this, but I appreciate you letting us room with you. I know you could've had anyone share your apartment with you, and he probably wouldn't have brought a girl with him."

"Don't worry about it, you're family. To be honest, I was kinda surprised when you said you were coming to Austin to go to school with me. After you started refusing to come to the ranch with Aunt Steph and Uncle Jim the last few years, I just figured you didn't like us much anymore."

"Nah, it had nothing to do with you. I just hated leaving Cassi behind. Sorry I made you think that though."

I took a deep breath, reminding myself Cassi *had* followed him to Texas. "Really? I don't get it, Ty, you said she was a friend. Then she follows you here, and now you're saying you wouldn't come visit because you didn't want to leave her? How come you never just told me how it really was with y'all?"

"It's complicated; we really were just friends. But she needed me; I couldn't just leave her. And I'm in love with her, man."

Holy hell. I felt like someone had just knocked the air outta me. How was I already so into this girl that it physically hurt to think of her being with Ty? With anyone, for that matter? Seriously. This was not. Fucking. Normal. "What do you mean she needed you?"

Tyler sighed and shook his head. "Like I said, it's complicated."

We both looked up when we heard girls squealing and splashing. Some of the guys were throwing them into the lake, and I couldn't stop myself from going to Jake when he picked Cassi up and threw her over his shoulder. My hands were already balled into fists for when he put her down. Her long hair was hiding her face as she pounded her little hands on his back.

"Put me down! I'm not wearing a suit!" She sounded so determined for a little thing that I almost smiled. Almost. "I'm serious, put me down!"

"Jake, I told you not to touch her. Put her down." I was standing right behind them then. Cassi grabbed the top of his jeans to push herself up and look at me, but Jake turned so he was now facing me. She was trying to kick him as well and his hands high up on her thighs had my hands fisting again.

"Come on, Gage." He sounded annoyed. "All the other girls went in."

"She doesn't want to—" Jake slid her down, causing her shirt to ride up high on her back. I choked on my next words, and at least two other people gasped behind me. *WHAT THE HELL?!*

Tyler grabbed Cassi and started pulling her away. He looked at her sympathetically, and when his eyes met mine they looked worried. Cassi's face was bright red again and her lips were smashed together tight as she let Tyler lead her to his Jeep.

Jake looked at me like I was insane; if it wasn't for the other guys having the same reaction, I woulda felt like it too. I turned and followed Tyler and Cassi to the Jeep, waiting until I was sure no one could hear us. "What the hell did I just see?"

Tyler helped her into the Jeep before going to the driver's side and opening up his own door. Cassi was looking straight ahead, her jaw still clenched.

"Ty, man, what was that?"

"Nothing. We'll see you whenever you get back to the apartment."

"That wasn't nothing!"

He sighed and stepped away from the door, leaning close so she couldn't hear him. "Look, we were trying to avoid something like this, but since you already saw, I'll explain it later. But this is exactly what I was getting her away from, so I'm going to take her back to the apartment now if you don't mind."

I didn't wait for anything else. I practically ran to my truck, grabbed my wet shirt as I put the tailgate up, hopped in, and drove back with them. A million things went through my mind on the way back to the apartment, and each one had me gripping the steering wheel hard. It was dark enough that I couldn't be sure what I'd seen, but it looked like bruises. Lots of them. I'd heard of people with some illnesses who are covered in them. I tried to think of what it could be and thought about her too-small frame. If her face didn't look so healthy, I would have been sure it was that. But the way Tyler talked about not wanting to leave her behind, I couldn't dismiss it either. I refused to think about the obvious; there was no way someone would hurt her. I'd hunt them down if they did.

Why was I so protective of her? I didn't know her from Eve, and we'd barely said anything to each other all night. I was hardly like this when it came to my sisters, and I loved them more than anything. I didn't know what it was about that girl, but she was already completely under my skin. And I wasn't sure if I liked that or not yet.

The drive took forever, and I let out a long sigh when I finally pulled into my spot. When they pulled up next to me, I jogged over to the passenger door and opened it. Cassi's face made me take a step back. There was absolutely no emotion there, and though she wouldn't meet my eyes, hers looked dead. I held my hand out to help her down, but Tyler pushed through me, glaring at me, and helped her out himself. He kept an arm around her as he led her to our place and took her right into his bedroom. I stood in the living room waiting for them to come out, but thirty minutes passed and the door still hadn't opened. With a heavy sigh, I turned and went to my bathroom to take a shower since I still smelled like the beer Cassi'd spilled on me. Thank God I hadn't gotten pulled over on the way home. When I got back to my room, Tyler was sitting on my bed.

"Sorry, Gage, she didn't want to talk to you when we got here."

"Is she sick, Ty?"

Tyler started. "What? No, she's not sick. Why would you—Oh. No. She's not."

Part of me was relieved, but now that I knew that wasn't it, I felt sick knowing what must've happened. "That why you never wanted to leave her?" I asked quietly.

"Yeah, that's why."

"Boyfriend?"

He shook his head.

"Parents?" I gritted my teeth hard when he nodded.

"Hold on a sec." Tyler walked quickly to the other side of the apartment, and I heard his door open and shut twice before he came back to my room, closing the door. "I wanted to make sure she was sleeping; she doesn't want you to know. But since you saw it, I have to tell you—I need to tell someone." He dropped his head into his hands and took a deep breath as his body started shuddering. "I haven't told anyone in eleven years. Do you know what it's been like, knowing what's happening and not being able to say anything?"

"Eleven years?!" I hissed, and made myself lean back against the wall so I wouldn't go after him. "This has been going on for eleven fucking years and you didn't tell anyone? What the hell is wrong with you?"

"She made me promise I wouldn't! She was terrified they would take her away."

"Did you not see that? Her entire back was black and blue!"

Tyler hung his head again. "That's not the worst it's ever been. She'd come over with concussions; a few times I made her agree to stitches. Swear to God, that girl is tougher than most men I know, because without any pain medication she'd let Dad sew her up right there in the kitchen. Then there were times she couldn't even get off the floor. When she was young, sometimes she'd lie there for hours before she could move; when we got older and got her a phone, she'd have to text me and I'd come get her."

I tried to swallow the throw-up that was rising in my throat. "It got that bad and you never said a word. What would you have done if they killed her one of those times, Ty?"

A sob came from where he sat hunched in on himself. "I hate myself for letting her go through that. But every time I tried to confront them, she'd flip out and make me leave, and when I would, that night or the next day would be one of those days where they'd beat her so hard she wouldn't be able to pick herself up."

"That isn't an excuse, you could have taken her away from them. Uncle Jim could have done something!"

"Look, Gage, you can't make me feel any worse than I already do! I'm the one who had to clean the blood off her, I'm the one who had to bandage her up even during the dozens of times when she should have gotten stitches. I had to buy a mini freezer for my room so I could have ice for when she came over!" He pulled his phone out of his pocket, tapped the screen a few times, and stifled another sob as he handed it over to me.

"What is this?" Whatever these fresh bruises were, they definitely weren't done by hands. The small rectangles looked familiar, but I couldn't place what I thought they were.

"Golf club. I didn't even know about this last time. She just told me about it on the way back here, and I took the pictures before I came in here. She said it happened yesterday morning before I came and packed her bags."

"Are there more pictures?"

He raised his head for a second to nod. "Ever since I got my first phone I've taken pictures every time she came over, and I always transfer them to my new phones so I'll have them. They're all backed up too. She wouldn't let me say anything, but I wanted to have photos in case . . ." His voice trailed off. There wasn't a need for him to finish that sentence anyway; I got the message.

Flipping through some of his pictures, I couldn't believe this was the same sweet Cassi I'd just met a few hours ago. Bruises of all shapes, sizes, and colors covered her body and it was killing me to look at them, but I couldn't stop. You could see all the ones that were fading slowly get covered up by new ones, and other pictures showed her back, arms, and face covered in blood. What killed me was that whenever her face was in the picture, she wore the same expression I'd just seen outside. No emotion, dead eyes, and absolutely no tears.

"What would they do to her?"

"You don't want to know."

Like hell I didn't. I was already planning on going to California with my twelve-gauge. "What. Would. They. Do?"

He was quiet for so long I didn't think he was going to answer. "When it first started, it was *usually* just hitting and kicking. The older she got, the more it turned into whatever they had in their hands or could grab quickly. Once that started, she only came over if it was other objects. She lived for the days when it was only hands."

"So what I saw tonight, you said it isn't the worst?"

"Not even close."

"What was?"

Tyler sighed and looked up at me, tears streaming down his face. "I don't know, there were a few that really stood out, but I couldn't name one that was the worst."

I just kept glaring at him; he needed a beatin' just for letting this go on for so long. She was seventeen or eighteen now, so she had been six or seven when this all started. And he'd known the entire time.

"A couple years ago, the cops showed up one night—"

"I thought you said she wouldn't let you call?"

"I didn't." He sighed and ran his hands through his

hair a few times. "The old lady that lived in between us heard her screaming one night, called the cops."

I shoved off the wall and flung my arms out. "You had a perfect opportunity and you still didn't do anything? *They* didn't do anything?!"

"Gage, I didn't even know the cops were called until she texted me hours after they'd left!"

"What happened?" I demanded, and forced myself back against the wall.

"Cassi opened the door, her mom and stepdad right behind her. None of her bruises were visible then and they all denied the screaming, including Cass."

Seriously? What the fuck?

"When the cops left, her mom took off her high heels, used the pointy heel part to hit her head repeatedly. There was so much blood when I got there, Gage, and she couldn't lay her head even on a pillow for almost a week after that. Another time her stepdad threw a glass of alcohol at her, she ducked, and it shattered against a wall. Since she didn't get hit by it, he grabbed her by the throat, dragged her to where it was, and just kept slicing her forehead, arms, stomach, and back with one of the pieces. She wore a scarf every day 'til the finger marks were gone. That's why she wears her hair with those things, what are they called? Bangs. She got those scars when she was ten and the one on her head isn't very noticeable anymore, but she still tries to hide it. She tries to hide all of them, but some she can't unless she wants to wear jeans and long sleeves in the summer."

I stood there in shock, trying to make the connection

between this girl he was telling me about and the girl I'd just met. Even with seeing the pictures it wasn't clicking for me; I couldn't imagine someone touching her, or her being so willing to let it continue. "You're a poor excuse for a man, Tyler." I opened my door and stood next to it, arms crossed over my chest.

He looked like he crumpled in on himself. "You think I don't know that?"

I couldn't say anything else to him. As soon as he was out of my room I slammed the door and fell on my bed. I wanted to make him stay in my room and go to her myself. Hold her and tell her I'd never let anyone else hurt her again. But for whatever reason she wanted him, and we didn't know each other so it would be even creepier than my trying to be close enough to hear her talk tonight.

My whole body shook as I thought about anyone laying a hand on her, let alone sharp objects. Sweet Cassi, she deserved parents and a man who cherished her. Not ones who beat her and a boy who sat back and let it happen. I swallowed back vomit for the third time since I found out what happened and forced myself to stay in my bed.

I closed my eyes and tried to steady my breathing, focusing on her face and honey-colored eyes instead of what I saw on her back and the images that Tyler's phone had seared into my brain. I thought about running my hands through that long, dark hair. Pressing my mouth to her neck, her cheeks, and finally those lips that were full and inviting. *Tyler doesn't deserve her. Not at all.* I thought about taking her in my arms and taking her to the ranch so I could keep her safe for the rest of her life. But she'd already been living a life she didn't choose, so I wouldn't choose for her either; I would wait for her to leave him and come to me.

2

Cassidy

WE HADN'T BEEN in Austin for more than six hours before someone saw the bruises. And not just anyone, Tyler's cousin, our new roommate, and the guy who wouldn't leave my every waking thought. I told Tyler not to tell him—let him make his own assumptions—but of course Tyler didn't listen and told him way more than he should have. I couldn't blame him though; I'd made him keep a secret no kid should have to. I know he thought I was sleeping, but even if I had been, Gage yelling at Tyler, or Tyler coming back into our room to hold me and tell me how sorry he was while he cried, would have woken me up. I'd learned long ago that if I cried, I got hit harder until I finally stopped, so I'd become a master at turning off my emotions. But I knew if I had opened my eyes to watch him cry, it definitely would have broken through that wall and I would have been crying right there with him. So I lay completely still, emotions turned off and eyes shut, while Tyler cried himself to sleep.

Once Tyler got in the shower the next morning, I slipped into the kitchen to start some coffee. We'd spent so many nights without sleeping over the years, we'd both started drinking it early on, and I was glad that now he didn't have to sneak an extra cup for me since his parents hadn't exactly known that I stayed the night all those years.

I shut the door quietly and turned to tiptoe across the hardwood floors when I saw Gage, and my heart instantly picked up its pace. He was dressed only in jersey shorts and shoes, his body still glistening with sweat. God, he looked amazing, and my breath caught at how perfect his body and face were. I'd barely caught a glimpse of him without his shirt on last night before Tyler had caught me staring, and now I couldn't make my eyes look away.

"Morning."

My eyes finally snapped up to meet his. In the light and this close, I could see the gold flecks scattered throughout the green of his eyes. They were the most beautiful eyes I'd ever seen. "Good morning, Gage."

"How, uh—how are you today?"

I sighed and walked over to the coffeepot. "I know he talked to you, I could hear you guys last night. I don't want you to be awkward around me now because of what you know."

"Cassi, those things should have never happened to you. He should have told someone."

I turned to find him right in front of me again. "I made him promise he wouldn't."

"Well he shouldn't have listened to you."

"You don't get it, Gage. You weren't there. I couldn't let him."

His eyes narrowed. "No, I wasn't there. But if I had been, something would have been done the first time it ever happened. Why didn't you say anything the night the cops showed?"

I shook my head; there was no point in trying to make him understand.

Gage put a hand on each side of my face and leaned closer. I swear I thought he was about to kiss me, like last night, and it didn't matter that I hardly knew him; I wanted him to. "You didn't deserve that, Cassi, you know that, right?"

"I do."

Before I could realize what he was doing, he brushed my swoop bangs back and traced his thumb over a scar from Jeff's glass. My body instantly stiffened and Gage's eyes turned dark as he looked at it. He slowly tore his gaze from the scar to my eyes and spoke softly. "Didn't deserve any of that."

I took a step back and turned to look at the almost-full pot of coffee.

He reached around me and brought down two mugs before pouring coffee in each one. "I'm sorry if you like cream," he drawled. "I don't have any here."

"That's fine." I breathed a quiet sigh of relief as I

walked over to the fridge and grabbed the milk. "I'll go to the store later and get some."

When I was done pouring it in, he put the cap on for me and put it back in the fridge. Walking back over to me, he put a finger under my chin and tilted my head up so I was looking at him. "How often did it happen, Cassi?"

My breaths started coming quicker. What was it about him that made me want to fall into his arms and not ever leave? It took his repeating his question for me to come out of my daydream. I was up against the counter, so I couldn't step back, but I moved my head away from his hand and stared past his shoulder into the living room.

He guessed when he saw I wasn't going to answer. "Every day?"

I still didn't respond; if it was a weekend, it happened at least twice a day. But that was something even Tyler didn't know. My body started involuntarily shaking and I hated that I was showing any sign of weakness in front of him.

"Never again, Cassi," he whispered while he studied my face.

My eyes flew back to meet his and my throat tightened. He sounded like he was in pain just talking about it and I had no idea why. But I'd be lying if I said it didn't make me want his arms wrapped around me. I cleared my throat and forced myself to continue to meet his gaze. "Cassidy."

"What?"

"My name is Cassidy."

"Oh." He looked a little sheepish. "My apologies, I didn't realize."

"No. Um, Tyler doesn't like it. He calls me Cassi. I just wanted to tell you my real name." Really I just wanted to hear it in his gravelly voice.

He smiled softly as he studied me for a minute and took a sip of his black coffee. "I like Cassidy, it fits."

Oh damn . . . yep. I was right in wanting to hear him say that. My arms were covered in goose bumps and I even shivered. Yeah—his voice was *that* sexy.

When I didn't say anything he walked around to the table and held out a chair, waiting for me to sit in it. We sat in silence for a while before I finally looked up at him again.

"This might be rude, but can I ask you something?"

One side of his mouth lifted up in a smile. "I think I already cornered the market on rude questions this morning, so go ahead."

And cue the freaking dimples! I got so lost staring at them I forgot to ask my question and his smirk went to a full-blown Gage smile. At this rate I'd need to start wearing a sleeping mask and earplugs around him in order not to make myself look like an idiot. Though I'd look ridiculous either way. "Well, um, Tyler said you live on a ranch?"

"I do."

"I was kind of thinking you'd look more like a cowboy . . ."

Gage's laugh bounced back off the walls, and I felt my

body relax just listening to it. "And how exactly were you expecting me to look?"

"You know, boots, hat, big belt buckle, super-tight bright blue jeans," I replied, a little embarrassed.

"Well I definitely have the boots, and the hats, but I don't think my sisters or Mama would ever let me dress like Dad."

"Oh."

"My dad even has the big mustache, looks like Sam Elliott."

It took me a second to figure out who that was, and then I laughed. "Seriously?"

"Swear, they could be twins."

"I'd love to see that. So where was your hat last night?"

He shrugged. "I leave all that at the ranch."

"What? Why?"

"I don't wear them as a fashion statement, and I definitely don't have any kind of work that would require them here in hippie town."

"Hippie town?" I deadpanned.

"Just wait until we go out anywhere. You'll see."

I nodded. "What kind of work? What kind of ranch do you have?"

"Cattle ranch, and whatever needs to be done that day. Taking care of the animals, moving the cattle to different parts of the ranch, fixing fences, branding . . ." He drifted off. "Just depends."

"How many cows do you have?"

"About sixteen."

Okay, I understand I don't know a thing about ranches,

but I figured you'd need more than sixteen cows to make it a cattle ranch. "You have sixteen cows?"

He huffed a laugh and smiled wide at me. "Hundred. Sixteen hundred."

"Dear Lord, that's a lot of cows."

He shrugged. "We'll be getting more soon, we have the land."

"How many acres is the ranch?"

"Twenty."

"Hundred?"

"Thousand."

"Twenty thousand acres?!" My jaw dropped. Why on earth would anyone need or want that much land?

"Yes, ma'am." He spun his mug around on the table.

"'Ma'am'? Really?"

One of his eyebrows raised. "What?"

"I'm not some grandma—I'm younger than you."

Gage rolled his eyes. "I didn't mean you're old, it's respectful." When he looked at my expression he shook his head and chuckled. "Yankees."

"Uh, get a clue, cowboy . . . I'm not from the North."

"You're not from the South either. Yankee." He smirked, and if I thought that was going to melt me, when he added a wink I knew I was done for.

"Are you going on about Yankees again, bro?" Tyler asked, walking into the kitchen.

Gage just shrugged and his green eyes met mine from under those dark brows again. "She didn't like that I called her 'ma'am.'"

"Get used to it, Cassi, we may be in the city, but it's different here."

I grumbled to myself and Gage laughed.

"So what are you guys talking about?" Tyler sat in the seat on my other side.

"Their huge ranch with too many cows," I answered.

"She's right about that, there are way too many cows there," Tyler said between sips of his coffee.

"You'd like it." Gage looked at me with an odd expression.

"Hell no, she wouldn't! Cassi doesn't like getting dirty, and she hates bugs. Your ranch would be the worst place for her."

Gage flicked a quick glare at his cousin, then looked back to me. "We have horses."

I gasped. "You do? I've never been on a horse!"

"Eight Arabians. I'll teach you to ride when you come to visit." He sat back in his chair and folded his arms, smirking at Tyler like he'd just won something.

Tyler and I both got quiet. My dad told me he was going to let me start taking riding lessons for my sixth birthday and buy me a horse for my seventh. Obviously those things never happened. Not that we didn't have the money, but my mom wouldn't even cook for me; no way she would let me do those things. It didn't help that even though I still loved horses, whenever I saw them I couldn't stop thinking about my dad.

"Did I say something wrong?" Gage looked confused but kept his eyes on Tyler.

"No," I said with a soft smile. "I'd like that."

After a few awkward minutes, Gage stood up and put his mug in the dishwasher before walking toward his room, "Well, I'm gonna take a shower. If there's anything y'all wanna do today, let me know."

Tyler scooted my chair closer to him. "You okay, Cassi? Is it because of your dad?"

"No, it's fine. I mean, I was thinking about him. But I just can't believe he's been gone for almost twelve years. I feel like I should be over it, I was so young when it happened, but I don't think I was ever allowed to grieve, and that's why it's still hard. I'm not looking forward to this birthday. I always thought when I got away from Mom and Jeff, I would finally enjoy my birthdays again, but I'm looking forward to it less than ever. I think we need to give me a new birthday, Ty." I huffed a light laugh. "No one wants a birthday on the anniversary of their father's death."

He pulled me onto his lap and held me loosely so he wouldn't hurt my back. "He was a great dad; you aren't supposed to get over him, Cassi, you'll always miss him. And no new birthdays, you're keeping the one you have and I'll make sure they get better and better every year."

I let him hold me for a few minutes before speaking again. "Thanks, Ty, I love you."

"Love you too, Cassi."

Gage

OH MY GOD, her dad died on her birthday? What else has happened to this girl? Okay, I'll admit I left the bathroom door cracked for a few minutes before shutting it and starting my shower. But the way they'd both got so quiet there at the end, I knew I'd said something I shouldn't have, and I figured Tyler would bring it up as soon as I was gone. I knew she'd be hooked as soon as I mentioned the horses, and she was; I just didn't know telling her I'd teach her to ride would take them back down memory lane to her dad, who was obviously nothing like her mom or stepdad.

Sitting there talking to her before Tyler had come in was the best morning I think I'd ever had, and it didn't even last ten minutes. She smiled so much it made my heart swell each time, and God, that laugh. I was right; it sounded just like freakin' angels. I wanted to die every time she'd start to relax into the chair. Her eyes would go wide for a split second and she'd sit right back up like she'd forgotten about the bruises on her back for a minute. I didn't have to ask her to know she was in pain; there was no way she could have been comfortable with what I'd seen last night. But even with that, her smile never faltered, and that may have killed me even more. She should have been depressed or crying or something. What kind of person goes through that kind of life, as recent as two days ago, and still finds reasons to smile?

When I walked out of the bathroom, she was still

curled up on Tyler's lap and I blew out a frustrated sigh. I needed to get over her soon, or living there with them was going to be a challenge.

"Hey, Gage?" Tyler called before I could shut my door.

"What?"

"You up to showing us around the city today?"

No. I want to show Cassidy the city, I want you to go the hell back to California. "Sure."

I shut the door behind me and had just finished getting my jeans on when Tyler walked in.

"You okay, man? We don't have to go out today, I was just asking. Or Cassi and I could go by ourselves. It's not a big deal either way, I just figured since you knew the area . . ."

I never asked Cassidy why Tyler didn't like her name. It was so perfect for her, and why would he even tell her he didn't like it? Seriously, how were we related? "No, it's fine, I just have a lot on my mind. I'll be ready in a minute, we can go whenever."

"All right, well I'm sure she wants to shower. So it'll probably be a while," he called as he walked back out of my room.

I grabbed a shirt and headed out to the living room. Tyler wasn't there, but Cassidy was sitting at the kitchen table, staring intently at her hands. "You okay, Cassidy?"

She jumped and looked up at me, her brows pulled together in confusion and hurt. She didn't say anything, just studied my face for a minute, before blowing out a deep sigh and standing up to walk toward their room.

"I'm sorry for reminding you about your dad. I didn't

know." I still didn't know. What did horses have to do with her dad?

Cassidy stopped walking and looked over her shoulder at me for a second, then continued to the door.

I stood there staring at the door, feeling like an ass, even after Tyler walked out of the room and started hooking a gaming system to the TV. Did telling Cassidy I'd teach her to ride really hurt her so much that the girl who asked why I didn't dress like a cowboy just disappeared? Everything in me screamed to go to her and talk to her, but the shower started, so I turned back to the living room. I told Tyler I'd watch him play and flopped onto the couch. I tried not to picture Cassidy in the shower while I listened to the water running, but that was damn hard, so I focused as much of my attention as I could on Tyler shooting people and tried not to think about her and the hard-on I was trying to cover with a pillow.

When Cassidy came out less than an hour later, her hair was wild and slightly wavy, and she had less makeup on than last night too. She looked beautiful. Without all that dark stuff around her eyes and stuff on her face, her honey-colored eyes looked even brighter and you could see a splatter of very light freckles on her nose. Not saying she hadn't looked gorgeous last night, because she had. She took my breath away. But I preferred this almost completely natural look. She was wearing green Chucks, jeans with the bottoms rolled up to her calves, and a worn black Boston concert shirt. *Boston. This girl is perfect.*

"Ty, I'm ready."

She still had yet to look at me since she walked in the

room, and though I wanted her to, I was enjoying being able to take her in. I noticed her bottom lip was a little too full for her top lip, and her nose couldn't have been more perfect if she'd chosen it herself. Her eyes flitted over to me quickly, then right back to Tyler; her cheeks got red and I couldn't help but grin. *There's no way she doesn't feel this too.* She started biting her bottom lip, and again I thought about what it would feel like to kiss those lips. I'd never wanted to kiss a girl this damn bad.

"Tyler!" She tapped his leg with her foot and he looked at her, then back at the screen.

"What's up?"

"I'm ready, are we going or not?"

"Yeah, just let me finish this match and we can go. Like eight minutes."

I had already sat up when she entered the room so she could sit on the couch with me, and she was eyeing it now, but instead turned and went into the bedroom. She stayed in there while Tyler played two more matches and didn't come out until he went to get her.

I took them all over Austin that afternoon, and while she was polite and would respond whenever I asked her a question, she wouldn't hold a conversation with me and made sure she was always by Tyler's side, farthest away from me. Maybe I was wrong about her feeling whatever this connection was, because she definitely didn't seem like she was having a hard time not touching me. It was all I could do not to grab her hand and keep her by my side.

When we were on the way back, she asked if we could

stop by the grocery store, and we let her take over the shopping after her third eye-roll at our food choices.

"Don't worry," Tyler whispered as she compared packages of ground beef, "she's been cooking for herself since she was six; she's better than my mom."

I hadn't been worried, and now that added just one more thing I wished I could have protected her from. Because my dad and I worked from sunup to sundown most days, I was only ever in the kitchen to help with dishes. I thanked Mom and my sisters daily for making the food, but I couldn't imagine having to do it on my own when I was just a little kid. I'd have to thank them again.

Other than letting us carry the groceries in for her, she wouldn't let us help put them away and immediately started on cooking dinner for the three of us. I lay down on the couch just watching her move around the kitchen while Tyler played his game again. At one point it looked like she started dancing for a few seconds before she stopped herself, and God, if that wasn't the cutest thing I'd ever seen. When Ty was fully engrossed in the game, I got up and wandered into the kitchen, stepping right up behind her.

"Do you need help with anything?"

Her body tensed for a moment, and once it relaxed she turned her head up to look at me. "No, I'm fine. Thanks though."

"Could I help anyway?"

She continued to watch me with that same hurt and confused look from that morning. "Yeah, sure. You can make the salad." She grabbed a few things out of the fridge and brought them over to me before grabbing a couple more items that she'd bought at the store out of a bowl on the counter. "Dice these, and—wait, do you even like avocados?"

"I'll eat anything, darlin'."

Her mouth tilted up at the corners and her cheeks got red; I smiled to myself and made a mental note to call her that more often. "Well, if you don't like them, I can just put them in my bowl."

I grabbed the avocado from her and looked at it, a little confused. "Like I said, I'll eat anything. But how do you cut this thing?"

She laughed lightly and took it from my hand, sliding the cucumber and tomato in front of me. "Dice these first, then I'll show you how to cut the avocado." She handed me a knife and turned back to the stove.

I was flat-out awful at dicing those vegetables, but being in the kitchen with her had me smiling the entire time, and whatever she was cooking smelled damn good. "I think I did it right."

"There's really no way to mess up dicing veggies for a salad." She turned and looked. "You did it just fine. Haven't you ever diced something before?" I shook my head and she grinned at me. "Really? Well you did great. Let me show you how to do these."

She grabbed both avocados and handed me one of them before picking up her own knife. I'm not gonna lie, I purposefully kept messing up getting the seed out so that she finally had to reach over and grab my hands to show me what to do. I heard her intake of breath as soon as our hands touched, and I had to look away so she wouldn't see how wide I was smiling.

Hell. Yeah.

She finished showing me how to cut up the avocado and had me grab bowls and plates while she finished up whatever was on the stove. Every time I looked at it, she'd turn me away and say I wasn't allowed to see her secrets. I didn't know what was going on all day, but she was now acting just like she had that morning. Every smile and every touch had me falling for her that much more.

I touched her arm so she'd look up at me and I almost forgot what I was gonna ask as soon as her eyes met mine. "Uh, did I upset you this morning? I swear I didn't mean to. I had no idea about your dad."

She looked down, then back at the stove. "I didn't expect you to know about him. And what were you thinking upset me?"

"When I told you I'd teach you how to ride."

Cassidy huffed and shook her head once. "No, Gage, that didn't upset me. I would really like to learn how to ride, if you ever want to show me."

Did she think I would offer if I didn't want to? And would it be bad if I asked what those two things had to do with each other? "Of course I will. I mean, I heard what Tyler said, but I do think you'd like the ranch. I can't wait to take you there." Ah, too much. Too much.

"Sounds great." She picked up a spoon, then set it right back down and put both her hands on the counter before looking back at me. Her mouth opened and her eyebrows pulled together, then she looked into the living room at

Tyler and back at me. "Dinner is about ready," she said softly. "Would you mind putting the salad on the table?"

When I turned around with the bowls, I saw Tyler staring at us and held back a sigh. I was gonna get crap for this later.

Cassidy had made crispy chicken fettuccine Alfredo, and all I could say was damn. I had to agree with Tyler that it was better than Aunt Steph's, and it rivaled Mama's cooking.

I stood up to help when she started clearing the dishes, but Tyler stepped in front of me before I got far. "I'm serious, man, she's mine."

"I heard you the first time."

"You sure about that?"

I glanced back at Cassidy. "Yeah, I'm sure. But you're the one who brought her here; you can't expect me to never talk to her, or offer my help when she's making us food. If we're all gonna live together, you need to get over the fact that I'm gonna be friends with her."

He remained quiet and smiled, waiting for Cassidy to return to the kitchen. "I couldn't care less if you're friends with her. Just don't forget that I'm the one who's been there for her every day for the last eleven years. Not you. I still see how you're looking at her, I'm not fucking blind, Gage."

Cassidy

"I'M KIND OF TIRED, I'm going to bed. Thanks for showing us around today, Gage."

Tyler stood and walked over to me. "Want me to come with you?"

I shot a quick glance behind Ty to Gage, who was openly glaring at his cousin. "No, you guys need to catch up, I'll see you later."

"Sleep well, Cassidy," Gage said.

I smiled and waved like an idiot. "Night."

Tyler hugged me and Gage winked when I looked over Ty's shoulder at him. Seriously, this guy was so confusing! I walked to the bathroom I shared with Tyler to wash my face and brush my teeth before slipping into some pajamas and crawling into bed. I could hear the boys talking and Gage started laughing, warming my entire body. I sighed and flipped onto my side. I didn't understand him at all. First, he had a girlfriend, then he'd almost kissed me last night, and this morning I could have sworn he was flirting with me. Then he got upset when we wanted to go out this morning and Tyler told me that when he went to talk to him about it, Gage said he didn't want me living here, but tonight in the kitchen he kept finding a reason to touch me and wouldn't stop smiling at me. What the heck? I didn't know how to even act around him.

I must have fallen asleep, because I felt a little groggy when Tyler slipped into the bed later that night.

"Sorry, I didn't mean to wake you," he said softly.

"It's fine, I meant to wait up for you. I guess I was more tired than I realized."

He pulled me close to his body and wrapped his arms around me. "You've had a long last three days, you needed to sleep."

"True. Did you guys have fun talking?"

"Yeah, it's good to see him again. It's been a long time since we hung out."

"I'm sorry I'm ruining that; you really shouldn't have brought me, Ty."

He leaned back a little so he could see my face. "Cassi, I'll take you with me everywhere I go. And don't worry about Gage, he'll get over it eventually. I'm sure it's not you that he doesn't like, he just said it's going to mess up his relationship with Brynn having a girl live with him."

"I don't want to do that." *Yes, yes, I do.* I'd never experienced jealousy until I met Gage last night, and it was one ugly feeling. "When I turn eighteen, I'll get my own place, Ty."

"No, you won't. He'll get over it, and I want you with me, okay?"

I curled into his chest and nodded. "Love you."

Tyler leaned back again and tilted my face up to his. "I love you too, Cassi." His lips fell onto mine and I scrambled back, pushing against his chest as hard as I could.

"What the hell, Tyler?!" We slept in bed with each other, but we'd never actually kissed before.

"I'm sorry! I thought you wanted me to."

"What? Why would I want you to?" *Oh my God, seriously, what the hell just happened?!*

He sighed and relaxed his hold on me. "I don't—I don't know what got into me. I'm sorry, that was really stupid."

"Is that why you brought me to Texas with you?"

"No, it's not, I swear. You're my best friend, I would have never left you there. I'm sorry, like I said, that was really stupid."

I crawled off the bed and grabbed my pillow. "Maybe I should sleep on the couch tonight."

"No! Cassi, come on, don't do that. I'm sorry."

"It's fine, it hasn't just been a long three days for me. It's been even longer for you. I think we're both too tired and we aren't thinking clearly."

"Cass." He sighed and got out of the bed as well. "I'm sorry, I don't know what I was thinking doing that." He hugged me loosely and stepped back. "Please get back in bed."

"It's all right, I promise. I'm just going to sleep out there tonight—I think it would be best for us. I'll be back in here tomorrow, okay?"

"I'll go out there, you can stay in the bed."

I put my hand on his chest and pushed him onto the bed. "I'm way shorter than you; that couch was practically made for me. Good night, Ty, see you in the morning."

About the Author

MOLLY McADAMS grew up in California but now lives in the oh-so-amazing state of Texas with her husband and furry daughter. Her hobbies include hiking, snowboarding, traveling, and long walks on the beach . . . which roughly translates to being a homebody with her hubby and dishing out movie quotes. When she's not at work, she can be found hiding out in her bedroom, surrounded by her laptop, cell, and Kindle, and fighting over the TV remote. She has a weakness for crude-humored movies and fried pickles and loves curling up in a fluffy comforter during a thunderstorm . . . or under one in a bathtub if there are tornadoes. That way she can pretend they aren't really happening.

Visit www.AuthorTracker.com for exclusive information on your favorite HarperCollins authors.